MIDNIGHT . . .

The door was open and Lord Barkham was pouring two brandies which he set by a small loveseat at the fireplace. He rose to offer one to me, and then instead pulled me to him so swiftly that my glass fell to the floor.

"Leave it," he ordered.

Suddenly everything in the room seemed to be spinning and I could focus only on the flames which continued to leap in the fireplace.

"Please don't," I moaned. "Please, not this."

"Serena, my love, don't fight me. Trust me, I won't harm you."

Strong arms stretched around me as I tried desperately to clear my head enough to govern my body, but Lord Barkham seemed to know things about it that were far greater than I had ever guessed.

Was this, too, to befall me here at Camberleigh? . . .

CAMBERLEIGH

EVELYN GREY

BERKLEY BOOKS, NEW YORK

CAMBERLEIGH

A Berkley Book / published by arrangement with
the author

PRINTING HISTORY
Berkley edition / March 1985

ISBN: 0-425-07643-1

In memorium
William T. Leslie
A gentleman and a gentle man.

CAMBERLEIGH

Chapter One

I THOUGHT the rain would never stop as the coach sped its way to Camberleigh Hall.

I longed to get out and stretch and find some refreshment for myself and for Jaspar but the driver said we must press on if we were to arrive by dusk.

As if sensing my thoughts, Jaspar jumped down from the seat where he had huddled with me for most of the ride to poke his nose into the small picnic basket that Mrs. Thurston had prepared for our travels.

"Oh, Jaspar I'd love to let you have some of those delicious cakes but there is nary a crumb left. Come back up and let my cloak warm you."

I don't know how I should have endured this trip, not to mention these last weeks, had it not been for my spaniel, Jaspar. He had come to me three years before as a puppy, hungry and obviously abandoned by some local farmer, and we had loved each other from the first.

Those were happy days, and now it all seemed so long ago.

I opened my reticule and took out the letter that I must have reread one hundred times during the past fortnight.

Somehow just touching the tissue and seeing the flowing script brought tears to my eyes.

It had been only weeks before that my dear mother had pressed this—and another, as yet unopened—letter into my hand, bidding me to read it upon her death.

1

I had been quick to assure her that both letters would remain sealed for years to come, but in my heart I think we both knew that life was slipping quickly from her frail body.

It had been several days before I could actually bring myself to open her letter which, I was soon to find, was my only legacy. The Thurstons had helped me with the funeral arrangements, and we buried my mother in the small courtyard cemetery beside my father, who had died so suddenly two years earlier.

Money had been scarce since his death, but my mother—even as she became ill—had struggled to keep this burden from intruding on my young life. Thus it was that I found myself alone and destitute other than the bit of money I was able to garner from the sale of our small farm.

The letter, although much of what it told me was new and confusing, did prove of some solace as it held the last words of my beloved mother. I can hear her lilting voice even as I reread it now.

My dearest daughter Serena,

By the time you read this I shall be gone. I had often prayed that I could live to see you grown to adulthood with a home and family of your very own.

I smile at what I have just written, for I can imagine you resenting the implication that you are but still a child. I recognize that at seventeen you have in fact become a woman, a woman whose fairness of face is matched only by a fairness of heart.

How proud I am of you. But it is that very fairness, gentleness, and innocence that causes me to think of you as my little girl. Perhaps I have been too protective, too quick to shield you from the harshness of life. If I have done so I beg your forgiveness, for my acts spring only from love. I can only trust that in time you will come to understand.

Where shall I begin?

Not at the beginning, I think, for without my being there to answer your questions, the words would seem cold and meaningless. If I know Cam and Richard, they will explain things far better than I ever could.

You know that your father and I settled in Seven Oaks

shortly before you were born, as you know that ours was a marriage of equals in heart and mind, although we were not from equal stations in life. Your father was of titled noble birth; my family were of modest means. But I had love and protection in my adolescent years, which gave me the strength to carry on. My only brother, Samuel, emigrated to the New World to seek his fortune a year before your birth and it has always been a great sadness that he disappeared from my life forever.

How strong and proud Samuel was. Like you, Serena, he shared a passion for adventure and a love for animals—and he had a tempestuousness that you shall always have to guard against in your nature. I always regretted that you did not have the benefit of a sibling relationship. Your dear father never shared my sympathies in this matter, and I have oft-times wondered if not for just cause.

But I am straying. You knew that your father was born of high standing, and we led you to believe that he had left his ancestral farms and estates of his own volition—and in the care of his brother—to pursue his own ambitions. I must reveal now that was but a half-truth. To deceive you in this matter was always painful, but we believed it was for your own good and always trusted that someday you would come to understand.

Your father's brother Richard did assume control of the family land and houses after your father left. A friend has provided some small news over the years, and I know that Richard still presides over Camberleigh. He resides there with his wife Maura and their two children; a girl about your age and a younger boy. And your grandmother, the widow of the Earl of Camberleigh, your father's father, also resides there.

Yes, my Serena, your grandmother is alive—and your full name is not Serena Miles but Serena Miles Camberleigh.

I realize that this must come as shocking news, however I must also tell you the rest of my story. Your father and I did not leave Camberleigh of our own choice. We were banished from there for the remainder of our lives.

I fear that I have neither the strength nor the will to

describe all the terrible events that put us in that appalling situation. I can only assure you that we were victims of an evil that even today I do not fully understand and that your father was innocent of any of the heinous acts of which he was accused.

Your father was the most honest, decent man I have ever known, beloved by all who knew him. Hold this knowledge close to you. It will not completely shield you from the events and people who would do you ill, but it will give you strength and, I hope, peace.

Your father always provided a modest but secure existence for us. After his passing we lived off the meager funds that we were able to save over the years. Had my health not begun to fail I could have resumed teaching of letters to the local children, but this was not our destiny.

My final request will undoubtedly come as a further jolt. Upon my death I want you to go to Camberleigh. You will find yourself with only the farm and our possessions—including your father's books—and no means of maintaining them. As difficult as it may be, I ask that you sell them; the Thurstons will ensure that you realize as much as possible.

With the money you can purchase a ticket on the coach to Camberleigh, and whatever is left put aside for warm clothing, lodging and food along the route. It is a long journey to make on your own, but you will of course have Jaspar. I realize it would be useless to try to convince you not to have him accompany you. You two share a special love, and you will need a good friend in these months to come.

The other letter I gave to you is to be presented to your grandmother at Camberleigh. I must warn you that even your existence may be a shock to her—to the entire family, in fact—but I pray that time has healed wounds inflicted long before you were born.

I deeply wish that I could suggest another plan, for there is terror in my heart that I am offering up my only daughter to those who betrayed her father. But there is no other choice—and you are, after all, a Camberleigh and have a God-given right to the security that comes with the inheritance of the name.

My dearest daughter, may God speed and watch over you both now and in years to come. May you find the strength to endure, the insight to forgive and the love to protect. Be watchful, Serena. All is not always as it seems.

Your loving mother,
Samantha

I replaced the letter as Jaspar licked away the salt from tears that had flowed far too frequently in the past weeks.

"Not much longer, miss, we be nearin' Camberleigh." It was the driver, Mr. Bottoms. He had been one consolation. A jolly old man, he had somehow sensed my sadness and uncertainty and had tried to buoy my spirits through what had indeed proved an arduous journey.

"Oh, Jaspar," I whispered, "what would Mr. Bottoms think if he knew I thought him a jolly old man? Why I quite think he would boot us out of this buggy, baggage and all."

My traveling companions—a couple making the journey to visit their daughter and her newborn son in Yorkshire—had disembarked long before, which had been much to my relief for they were given to incessant senseless banter. In truth they had been a pleasant enough couple, and another time I might have joined in their gaiety, but I was unable to clear my head of the events of the past fortnight.

The rain appeared to be lessening as I turned my eyes north toward Camberleigh. Although usually eager to experience new sights, I realized that I had paid little attention to the changing landscape during this, my first venture from the small seaside town where I spent my childhood.

There was a different texture to this land—a lushness and a richness of harvest to which my eyes were unaccustomed. Prosperity: that was the difference. I had never thought in terms of whether our farm was bountiful, but now as I gazed upon a never-ending panorama of plentiful fields and farmlands, I realized why the sale of our home had brought but a paltry sum.

Jaspar's whimpering brought me momentarily out of my reverie.

"You smell the difference too, don't you, little one." One

doesn't think about places smelling differently, but then, I had known no other country than that by the sea, and it was the sea that I now missed most. How often Jaspar and I had walked along the green serpentine cliffs looking down on waters that seemed translucent, drinking in the fresh salt air.

On the last walk we had taken—to gather foxglove and primroses to rest on my parents' grave—a ship was just setting sail from our harbor. It had seemed an omen of sorts, for I too was setting out for a new port of call.

The coach had suddenly slowed its pace, and I prayed that it had not become disabled on this the last leg of our journey.

"This is it, miss," called down Mr. Bottoms. "You see them big stone pillars up ahead? That's the entrance to your Camberleigh."

As we passed through the entrance, with its massive iron gates flung open as if in welcome, I had a sudden impression that somehow my life would never be quite the same again.

The grasslands were lush, dappled with shadows of late summer clouds and crowned with islands of beech and maple trees. The lawns were undulating carpets of green, rolling on as far as the eye could see. The hedgerows and privets were massive, rising like battlements from their pastoral foundation.

There are certain events in life one never forgets. My first sight of Camberleigh Hall was one of those events.

It stood at the end of a long tree-lined drive, a spectacular creation of towers and turrets and crenellations. The effect was overwhelming, a castle that indeed must be the most majestic in all England.

Being of greater than average stature, I had never, even in childhood, felt small. But as I gazed at this massive creation I was dwarfed not only by its size, but by its sense of superiority.

Jaspar, who had fallen asleep with his head on my lap, now awoke with a start as the coach pulled to an abrupt halt. I wondered if he was as mystified as I about the turn of events over the past weeks.

"Let me be getting you down first, miss, and then I'll tend to your baggage."

"Thank you, Mr. Bottoms. I must admit that my legs feel as though they would never stand on ground again."

"Aye, it was a long trip, lass, but you and your friend there are good little travelers. I never heard a cross word pass your lips. It was a pleasure bein' of service to you."

"Thank you for your kindness, Mr. Bottoms. I can only say that I hope that on any other journeys I must make I shall have the benefit of a driver as thoughtful and courteous as yourself."

I wrapped my cloak tighter about me. I was pleased now that I had left it on, for although by no means grand of style or cloth, it was warm. Mrs. Thurston had been right about it being that much cooler here in the north and although still late summer, I noticed a chill settle in the air as dusk approached.

"There, that's the last one off, miss. Would you be wantin' me to take 'em on in for you?"

"That's not necessary, Mr. Bottoms. I'm sure there is someone who will see to them."

"If you don't mind me askin', what brings you to Camberleigh? I was wonderin' whether you was the new governess, knowin' what trouble folk around here say they have on that score."

I couldn't help laughing at Mr. Bottoms's jolly curiosity. Yes, I suppose I did look like a governess. I had chosen my simplest dress for the journey, a gray muslin frock with a high collar and small pearl buttons along the bodice. A far cry from the attire I was certain of most visitors who called at Camberleigh Hall.

"No, Mr. Bottoms, I am not the new governess. It will probably come as much of a shock to you as it did to me to learn that I am a Camberleigh."

"Oh, I didn't mean to say nothin' that would offend you, miss. I just didn't think."

As I began to reassure Mr. Bottoms, Jaspar broke off and bounded up the steps to the imposing doors of the house and I, of course, gave chase.

I had just reached the top step, corraled Jaspar, and was chastising him for spoiling the dignity of our arrival when the doors before me were flung open and out sprang a figure that loomed before me like a mythical apparition.

"Pray tell what do we have here?"

"I do apologize, sir, but you see my spaniel broke off and I was running to fetch him before he created any further commotion," I replied.

"Hello, fellow," the apparition said to Jaspar, "do you always cause your mistress such distress? Or is it actually she who gets you into predicaments?"

"I beg to pardon, but neither Jaspar nor I wish to cause anything untoward. We are both simply tired from our long journey," I replied curtly.

Just then another man, far older than the first, appeared at the doorway. "Master Justin, is there a problem here?" he queried.

"No, Giles. I think not; just a damselle and her dog in distress."

"Excuse me, but we are not in distress. And now I should like to see her ladyship."

"Her ladyship?"

"Yes. The Earl of Camberleigh's widow."

My strange apparition bent down from a towering height and began scratching Jaspar behind the ear, which immediately set the dog's tail to wagging. "Ah, Jaspar," the man said, "I suppose you would like to see her ladyship too?"

My eyes flew to the face of this man who seemed to be mocking me and I found myself staring into eyes that were the darkest I had ever seen. The eyes were solemn but the face that framed them was strong. The dark skin gave evidence of few hours spent indoors. The mouth was taut except at the corners, where a small but definite smile played.

"Perhaps I should handle this, sire," broke in the older man stepping forward.

"Yes, I rather think you should. The lady seems quite determined. And would you see to it that my mare is brought round. I shall be heading back to Mayfair presently. I bid you good day, miss. Does my fair damselle have a name?"

"She does, and it's Serena. Serena Miles."

"Justin Barkham at your service," he replied with a sweeping bow. "Take good care of your mistress, Jaspar. Giles, I'll return the week next." And with that my stranger, who now had a name and an inordinate amount of assurance, bounded down the steps past poor Mr. Bottoms, who was looking a mite perplexed over our little parley. And small wonder; I had no sooner announced to Mr. Bottoms that I was a Camberleigh than I presented myself as Serena Miles. It would take time for me to accustom myself to using the name—not to mention feeling—that I was truly a Camberleigh.

"Is her ladyship expecting you, miss?"

"No, she isn't. But I have something here for her ladyship which I believe should explain." I searched in my reticule for the sealed letter from my mother. "Ah, here it is."

"I will see that her ladyship receives it," replied the man I now knew to be called Giles.

"Well, I don't know. I was admonished to present it personally."

"I assure you that I will deliver it promptly. If you will allow me to show you into the library, you can rest there until her ladyship gives me further instruction."

"Thank you. That would be very kind. Let me say a word to my driver and perhaps you could have someone see to my baggage."

"Well it is a little out of the ordinary. As you said yourself her ladyship is not expecting you, and it is not my position to assure you of your reception. You do understand?"

I realized the rationality of this, but ever since first reading my mother's letter I had never once thought that my reception was other than guaranteed. I had braved everything up to now, but I didn't think there was enough left in me to face rejection. My feelings must have been clear on my face, for Giles said, "I didn't mean to upset you, miss. Follow me into the library. I'm sure this can all be settled quickly. I'll take your spaniel to the cook. She'll provide water and something to eat for the little fellow."

I could feel Jaspar pushing against my foot in resistance to this suggestion. Ordinarily the very mention of food would have set that brown and white body wriggling from front to hind quarters, but ever-protective, he would not take our separation lightly.

"Come along, Jaspar," I urged. "I'm sure they'll find something nice for you in the kitchen."

As we strode through the entrance I was stunned by the magnitude of the great hall that lay before me. The floors were of rich light-colored marble. Straight ahead an immensely wide staircase floated to the heavens. On the wall above the stairs were portraits—of my ancestors, I supposed—gazing down from their lofty pinnacles.

We passed into a long corridor and an endless succession of doors, all closed, which I found alien to the memories of my own home, which always had had a feeling of open airiness and welcome. Giles finally opened one of the portals, and we entered the library.

The room had a musty smell. Heavy dark green velvet covered the windows, adding to the room's oppressiveness. But, oh the books! Certainly this must be the largest collection in the world. How my father—who had possessed only enough volumes to fill one of these cases—would have loved this room. His books had meant so much to him. I suppose that was why, despite my mother's instructions, I couldn't bring myself to part with the small collection he cherished so dearly.

"Rest here, miss, whilst I take your spaniel to the kitchens and then deliver your letter," said Giles, tugging at Jaspar, whose aspect had now gone from perplexed to forlorn.

"Thank you. And could you see if the driver, Mr. Bottoms, could be offered refreshment? We've had a long journey and I requested that we not stop, as I wanted to arrive before nightfall. I'm sure he would greatly welcome some small repast."

"Yes indeed." And with that the doors to the library closed again and I was alone.

As I settled on a soft high-backed couch, my thoughts turned to my parents. How often had they stood in this library so many years before? Had my mother come to tease my father away from poring over his books, as she had so often at Seven Oaks? Had he laughingly responded that he could never resist her charms? How much in love they were. Until father's death I never understood how one could die of a broken heart, but I think from that moment I saw life ebb slowly from my mother's being.

What, I wondered, was in the letter to my grandmother? And why was it sealed? My mother had never kept things from me before. Why now, when I am unable to question them? More than once it had crossed my mind to open the letter, but each time I had started to break the seal I would see my mother's face admonishing me.

I was startled out of my reflections by the sound of the door opening. There in the entry stood a boy about seven years of age. His face was almost translucently pale, and the saucerlike eyes that peered from it were framed with fringes of gold lashes.

"Hello," I said. "And what pray tell is your name?"

"I'm Master Oliver," a small voice responded.

"How do you do, Master Oliver. I'm Serena. Serena Miles."

"Are you my new governess?" As he approached I noticed that he appeared to drag one leg, but it was difficult to tell for certain, given his outlandish apparel. He was dressed in enough clothing for two boys, let alone a single one as frail as he.

I laughed. "No, I am not your new governess but you are not the first person today who has thought that to be my station. I expect you live here, Master Oliver, and am I to assume that you are a Camberleigh?"

"My father is the Earl of Camberleigh. Do you know him?"

"No, I have not had the pleasure," I said, adjusting the folds of my cloak.

"Are you awaiting someone?"

"In a way, Oliver. May I call you just Oliver?"

He nodded in assent. "I prefer it, actually, but father says it's not proper, my being the son of an earl and all."

"I see. Well, I shall call you Oliver and you may call me Serena. And in answer to your question, I am hoping to see your grandmother."

"Oh, Grandmama. She doesn't see many people, you know."

"Why is that, is she ill?"

"I don't know, really, but she stays in her rooms most of the time."

Suddenly the door opened again, this time to reveal Giles carrying a tray of tea and crumpets.

"Master Oliver!" Giles gasped, "what are you doing here?"

"I was just visiting with Ser—" He gulped. "—Miss Miles."

"Well, you daren't let Mrs. Scoapes find you here. There will be hard times to pay if she discovers you're missing. I would suggest you get back to the nursery this instant."

"Giles," I intruded, "Master Oliver can stay here with me while I wait. We were just becoming acquainted."

"That's very kind of you, miss, but he really must be getting back to the nursery. It's almost time for his dinner."

Oliver looked sorely disappointed and as he limped slowly back toward the door I called out, "I enjoyed our talk, Oliver.

Perhaps we will be able to visit again sometime soon."

He turned and smiled at me tentatively, then went out.

As Giles set the tray down before me I realized that it had been hours since I had last eaten.

"I presented your letter to her ladyship and she asked that I bring you some refreshment."

"Did she say . . . anything else?" I asked, trying not to show my anxiety.

"She said that she would receive you shortly."

I let out an inner sigh of relief. Mother's letter had at least gained me an audience. "And how is Jaspar?" I asked.

"Well, Cook was a bit put out, I fear, for she was just in the midst of preparing dinner for the staff but I think she was flattered, as your spaniel seemed to warm to the scraps he was presented and now the two are trotting about like old friends."

"And Mr. Bottoms?" I queried.

"Her ladyship ordered that the driver was to take his leave. He was given some food and drink, and before he departed he asked that I send his regards and hopes that you have a pleasant stay at Camberleigh."

"Thank you, Giles."

"I shall return when her ladyship calls to see you." And with that the library door was closed once again.

I poured myself a cup of tea, which was strong and warm. There were a few small cakes and scones and a delectable fruit nectar jam.

The nourishment seemed to renew my strength, but perhaps it was more from a sense of relief. My stay now seemed assured, since the driver had been released.

It was hardly the kind of reception I had envisioned. My romantic nature had led me to believe that my grandmother would sweep into the room, arms outstretched, enfolding me into the comfort of her bosom. Instead, I was sitting alone in a library—my only friend banished to the kitchens—awaiting to be summoned before a woman who until days previous I didn't know existed. A woman who now held my fate in her hands.

I must have drifted off, for I awakened to the sound of Giles's voice saying, "Her ladyship will see you now, miss."

I gathered the folds of my cloak about me and followed Giles out of the library and back to the great hall. As I slowly followed Giles up the monumental staircase, I was able to regard more closely the ancestral portraits of the Camberleighs.

They did not appear quite so intimidating as they had from below. Several were even quite amusing, captured in garbs or stances of some discomfort. The one element that seemed woven through all the portraits was the appearance of eyes—they were all a clear deep blue with a directness and a searching quality that I had so often seen in my own father's eyes.

As we progressed upward I realized that the portraits were hung chronologically, a parade of the Earls of Camberleigh over the years. I paused before one portrait, the second to the last at the top of the stairs. I would have known him anywhere. The eyes, aquiline nose, gently waving hair touched with gray at the temples. And that distinctive cleft of the chin which I now touched in my own chin. My father had always said it meant we were kissed by the angels.

This was my father's father, Charles. The late Earl of Camberleigh. As I moved to the final portrait, I knew that this must in fact be my father's brother, the present Earl of Camberleigh, my uncle.

The face that looked out from the final ornate gilt frame was somehow different from the rest. The features here were broader, less refined. Along the left cheek was a scar so pronounced that I was amazed that the artist had not softened it in oil. But again it was the eyes that drew me. These eyes held nothing familiar. Instead of the clear blue openness of the eyes of my father and his forebears, these eyes were dark, almond-shaped. There was a shrewdness, a piercing quality that made me feel that he was looking into my very soul.

"Follow me, miss."

Watching Giles move down the hallway before me I realized that he was even older than I had first assumed. His gait was slow, almost doddering as he led me along a hall graced with full suits of armor set off by elegant tapestries hanging from the ornate moldings.

The doors here were also all closed. The castle—for the house was indeed a castle—was very still, the only sounds emanating from the soles of my boots as they met the marble floor.

What lay beyond those doors? Was there happiness here? Who were these people—my ancestors, my relatives? Were they kind, would they welcome me into the fold or . . .

Giles had paused. "Her ladyship's quarters," he announced as he rapped lightly on a door. "Please enter."

I stepped into a room that was so dark I could scarcely make out the massive furnishings.

"Your ladyship?" I called out.

I pressed forward toward a large bed on which a figure lay. Candles burned at either side of the bed, casting strange shadows on the figured brocade canopy.

"Come over here and sit beside me." The voice was frail but I detected a softness, a gentleness in its manner.

I moved forward and took my seat on a chair at one side of the bed.

The woman who lay before me looked up from the letter she had been reading, the letter I had brought. She peered at me full in the face, seeming to search for something she had lost.

By the candlelight I could see that her hair was like spun silver, and coiled high on top of her head. Though lined by the ravages of time, her face still sported strong cheekbones and eyes the color of violets.

"I hold here in my hand a letter that says that you are the daughter of my son, William. Which would make you my granddaughter. There is much information here that is accurate and would seem to support the truth of this. On the other hand, Serena—if that is in fact your name—I am sure you are aware that we are a wealthy and powerful family. There are many who would invent a ruse such as this. If this is indeed the case, such a deception would be dealt with by the highest courts in our land.

"I must tell you that this turn of events has come as the utmost shock to me. This is the first I have heard of the fate of your father and mother for almost eighteen years. Nor have I known of your existence, assuming you are who this letter says you are. I have not had the time to take this in—or to think it through properly. Your arrival brings back many memories, most too painful on which to dwell, and their disclosure would be of no benefit to you. I am an old woman, and if nothing else I have learned that haste in judgment or action is often unwise.

"I am certain you are tired from your long journey, and I think it best for us both to face these things tomorrow. Perhaps the clarity of the day will enlighten the paths we should take. Now I must rest. Giles has been instructed to show you to your room. A tray with your dinner will be brought to you later and we shall continue our discussions in the morning." As she lay back against the pillows her arm fluttered as if in tremor and her hand closed tightly over the letter that lay beneath.

I sat for a moment, stunned. It was clear that I had been dismissed without being permitted a word on my own behalf. I wanted to shout out, "I am your granddaughter, your flesh and blood, why can't you accept this," but I could see that the effort of the one speech she had made had been almost too great for the old woman, and I moved slowly away from the bed.

I had moved only a few paces when I stopped and turned around. "Your ladyship, there is one small favor I might ask."

"Yes?" came the reply.

"Might Jaspar be brought to my rooms?"

"Who is Jaspar?" she asked, her shoulders rising again from the pillows.

"My spaniel. He has traveled this long journey with me and I believe the cook was providing him some small sustenance, but he will be lost and confused without me."

"Well, it is most unusual but perhaps for this one night."

"Thank you, your ladyship." And with that I moved from the candlelit space near the bed, across the darkness of the room and back out into the hallway. Almost immediately, I saw Giles approaching, as if timed by some magical force.

"I am to show you to your room, and Charlotte will be bringing your tray up shortly. The footmen have already placed your bags."

"Thank you, Giles, that is very kind. Her ladyship also granted that my spaniel might stay the night with me."

Giles regarded me skeptically for a moment, then nodded and replied, "Yes of course. I'll attend to it." As we walked in silence I began to appreciate fully the immensity of Camberleigh. Room after room of closed doors lay wherever my eyes could see.

The corridor narrowed abruptly as we moved into another

wing of the house, which I gathered was less used. The ornate tapestries and paintings had now disappeared, and this corridor was lined with mirrors. I was somewhat taken aback by my reflection. I did indeed look tired and worn. My dress was stained and my cloak had been about me so long it seemed to cling to my very form.

Giles had now stopped and was opening yet another door. "This will be your room, miss," he said, ushering me into the room. "It will just take me a moment to light these candles."

As light suffused from the tapers I looked about. The furnishings here were spare. A few small chairs, a writing table, a bed and a dressing table. A fireplace stood in one corner. The effect was severe but not indifferent. In fact, I found the simplicity somehow peaceful.

"Your baggage is here. Charlotte will help you unpack when she brings your tray."

"That won't be necessary. I have only a few things to unpack. Most of what is there are books, and they needn't be touched at present. If you could just see that Jaspar is brought to me I would be most appreciative."

"I'll be bidding you good evening, then."

Closed now in the sanctuary of my own room, I sank onto the bed in sheer exhaustion. My limbs ached and there was a dull pain in the small of my neck. I felt my eyes welling with tears. My journey had brought me these many miles and to what end? To have been received in such a fashion was hardly occasion for great celebration.

I could not fathom my grandmother's response. Did she indeed take me for some impostor who would gain access to the household on such a pretext? Did she really believe I possessed the guile to have invented such a scheme?

I could empathize with her surprise and shock over the revelation that I was her granddaughter, for the news had dealt a stunning blow to me only a short time before. But to have suggested that I was an adventuress seeking the fortunes of others was beyond my wildest comprehension.

I arose from my bed in response to a knock at the door. I opened it to Jaspar running full tilt into me.

"Oh, Jaspar," I cried, falling to my knees and throwing my arms about him as he licked my face and squirmed in delight.

"It's easy to see this be where he belongs, miss." I looked up to see a lad of about ten peering down at me with a big toothy grin.

I laughed.

"He caused quite a ruckus he did in the kitchen. I thought Cook would have 'is hide but then before ye knew it she was talkin' to him like he belongs."

"Well, my Jaspar does have an ingratiating way when he wants to."

"Beggin' your pardon, miss, but are ye the new governess?"

Before I had a chance to answer a woman appeared at the door carrying a tray from which wafted enticing aromas.

"Now be off with ye, Robbie, there's plenty of work down in the kitchens," the woman said as she bustled into the room, Jaspar right on her heels.

"I'll be bidding good night, then," said the lad, closing the door behind him.

I now turned to the woman, who seemed to have taken everything instantly in hand.

"Now then, there's venison and corn meal and some nice currants," she said, laying out the dishes and linen and silver on the writing table.

"You settle down and eat and I'll get the fire goin' so you won't have to keep your cloak about you like that. And then I'll tend to your dresses and things."

"I would indeed appreciate the fire, but you needn't bother with the baggage. There really is very little to unpack."

"It's up to you, miss," she replied as she began setting the logs off the hearth. I had just sat down to my meal when she sprang up and scurried over to my side, curtseying so deeply that her aprons spread wide over Jaspar.

"Oh, forgive me for losing me manners and not presentin' myself proper. But I lost me thoughts when I saw me Robbie dawdlin'. He's a good lad, but sometimes he gets to dreamin' and forgets his chores. My name is Charlotte, miss, and I'm here to assist if you be needin' me."

I looked at my new acquaintance, who seemed to be like Jaspar, in perpetual motion. She had a full rounded figure, obviously aided by the cook's good works. From her crisp white cap escaped a mass of black ringlets and when she smiled

I saw the same toothy grin I had seen on Robbie just moments before.

"It's a pleasure to meet you, Charlotte," I replied. "And you have no cause for worry about Robbie, he had only just come to deliver Jaspar here when you arrived. And I fear that I forget my own manners. My name is Serena."

"'Tis a pleasure to meet you, miss. Now you eat what Cook has prepared. Pardon me for saying so, but you look like you could be usin' a little sustenance." Her dark eyes twinkled in the candlelight.

"Thank you, Charlotte. It smells delicious but I don't feel very hungry."

"Well I'll just get the fire goin' and then I'll leave you to rest."

I watched as she diligently lit the logs, thinking that she was the one note of cheer I'd had since my arrival at Camberleigh. I wondered if that was an omen of what was to come.

"There, that should help take the chill off." Charlotte moved back from the fire, its warmth now spreading through the room. "And now I'll be biddin' you goodnight. I'll be here in the morning to tend you—so don't go worryin' now."

I nodded as the woman bustled out. Jaspar and I were now left with just each other for comfort.

As if sensing my need, Jaspar moved closer, pushing against my leg. The food before me had grown cold and I indeed had little care for food. I rose to remove my cloak, and Jaspar sat up, staring at me expectantly.

"No, Jaspar," I said, "we aren't going anyplace—at least for now. I am weary of this day and I am most certain that you are too."

I opened one of my bags and withdrew my nightdress. It felt good to get out of my gray muslin and my boots, which I now saw had been badly stained by the rains. I had worn my hair braided tightly coiled at the back of my head, thinking it a practical style for the journey. As I now removed the pins and let it fall about my shoulders and back I felt more myself. My mother had once told me that in London it was not stylish to wear one's hair loose and flowing, but my father had said that his two ladies had hair like amber fire and it should be left free to flame by the light of the sun.

As I crawled into the soft goosedown bed, Jaspar settled himself at the foot. "Sweet dreams, Jaspar," I whispered, snuffing out the candle by my bed. I lay quietly staring up at the ceiling, where images played by the light of the now dying embers. Tears welled again in my eyes as my reverie turned once more to my former home by the sea—now so far away and gone forever.

Chapter Two

I AWOKE to the sensation of Jaspar licking my nose, which was his wont each morning. I enjoyed lazing about in the hours when the day was just coming to life but Jaspar never wanted to lose a second of the daylight hours.

"How does life look to you today?" I asked, propping myself up.

The room took on another dimension by day. Sunlight streamed in through the leaded-glass windows, giving new color to the wood of the furnishings. A bookcase which I had not noticed the night before lay against the wall behind the fireplace. It would be a good place for my father's books.

I threw the covers back and climbed down from the bed. Moving to the windows I was entranced at what lay before me. To the left, turrets sprang up stretching toward the sky. To the right was a rose garden displaying a profusion of colors from the palest creams to richest burgundies. And in the distance as far as the eye could see lay rolling green fields spotted by small woodlands and lakes.

As I stood gazing out over the lands of Camberleigh there came a knock at the door. Jaspar scurried over in welcome as I called out to enter.

"Good mornin'." Charlotte bubbled carrying in a basin of steaming water. "I was thinkin' you might want to wash up before your mornin' meal. And ye shouldn't be standin' on this cold floor without boots or you'll catch your death. I see you didn't touch your dinner. Well, I'll make sure Cook gives you a little somethin' extra this mornin'."

In spite of myself I laughed. Charlotte was determined to take charge of my existence at Camberleigh. "Good morning, Charlotte," I replied. "Yes, thank you, I would like to tend to my toilette. I still feel the effects of my journey and I would like to face the day to my best advantage."

"I'll be back in just a bit."

"Well, Jaspar," I said when Charlotte had left. "That woman is going to make sure that we do not perish here. I don't have the heart to ask her to leave us to our own devices, and I don't know that she would pay much heed anyway."

I bathed quickly and then turned to the task of unpacking. The dress I chose for the day was a blue muslin with a softly draped bodice and cording at the waist. I rubbed my boots clean and was just sitting down to attend my hair when Charlotte reappeared.

"I've brought you your tray, Miss Serena. There's porridge and some nice fruits and freshly baked bread." Putting down the tray she moved to stand behind me. "Such beautiful hair—the color bein' so unusual and all."

"I was just wondering how to fix it. Have you any suggestions?" I asked.

She took my hair in her gentle and cool hands and in only minutes she had dressed it so that it fell softly at each side. From the crown on top she let curls cascade down my back. I stared at my reflection, pleased with the effect.

"Charlotte, you are a woman of many talents."

"Oh, don't go joshing me."

"No, I assure you I am being sincere."

"Well I enjoy it, miss. And with me 'avin just Robbie I don't get much chance to dress a lady's hair."

"What do you think, Jaspar?" I asked my friend, who had been watching these ministrations in silence. Tail wagging, he moved to where Charlotte had set the tray.

"It appears that Jaspar is more interested in Cook's offerings than my appearance."

"Well, he's a smart one. Take a lesson from 'im and eat that good food yourself. Now I'll be removin' your basin an' then I'll be back for your tray."

The breakfast was delicious and both Jaspar and I gained strength from it. When I had finished, I went back to the window and spied someone working down in the rose garden. I thought it strange that with all these beautiful flowers I had not yet seen a single blossom inside the house.

Jaspar's whimpering at the door reminded me that he had not been out, and I knew that he would not be patient much longer. I pulled a shawl from my baggage and joined Jaspar at the door. Once in the hall I realized that I was uncertain how to find the staircase. But Jaspar trotted ahead with assurance and I thought it wise to follow.

The spaniel had led me down several corridors when I finally realized that this was not the way I had followed Giles last evening, but just then I saw Jaspar poised on what I assumed must be the back stairs.

I made my way down cautiously and found myself in front of a glass door leading outside.

Just then I heard Charlotte's voice coming from somewhere down a passageway to my right.

"It's not right to be talkin' like that, Molly. You an' your skuttlebutt is always causin' trouble in this house."

"Who're you, defendin' her," said a younger voice. "You know the likes of the last ones and you also be knowin' how they are. An' with you saying she so pretty and all, what am I gonna think."

"I just be tellin' you to keep your mouth shut if you know what's good for it," Charlotte retorted.

I gathered that it was me about whom they were arguing, though I could not imagine why. I didn't want to hear more, nor did I wish to be caught eavesdropping, so I quietly opened the door and stepped into the courtyard beyond.

Jaspar bounded ahead and I followed him along a long path that led to an old arbor. A small stone bench stood at the entrance to it, and I paused there. It was clear that someone loved these gardens and took great care with their upkeep. The evergreens were pruned into a dozen different shapes, each with its own distinct personality. Hedges of late summer rhododendrons spread their flowering limbs gracefully over the dewy grasses.

Camberleigh rose out of this encircling of green like some

mythical monster rising from the sea.

Oh Jaspar, I thought, where shall we turn if we are indeed turned out. There was scarcely enough money left even to return to the Thurstons. And having six mouths to feed already, I could not expect that they would give me shelter for long.

As I stared up toward one of the towers in the north wing I thought I saw a figure staring down at me from a high window. I blinked, for the sun had been bright, but when I opened my eyes, the figure—if there had been one—was gone.

"Come, Jaspar," I called. "I think we've had enough of the outdoors for this morning." We moved back along the path and into the house.

Once back into my room I noticed that my bed had been made and my morning tray removed.

Suddenly I heard voices from the hall.

"I told ye she was here but a half hour ago, and then when I came back up for the dishes she was gone."

I peered back out to find Charlotte with Giles in tow.

"Oh," she exclaimed, "thank heavens. We've been lookin' high an' low for you."

"I'm sorry to have concerned you, Charlotte," I replied. "But Jaspar here wanted to take his morning constitutional and I thought the air would do me good as well."

Giles, who had remained silent up to now, stepped forward and announced, "Her ladyship wishes to see you in her quarters miss."

So the time had come to learn my destiny. Well, delaying the matter would be fruitless and I sensed that one didn't dally once her ladyship had called.

I knelt down to Jaspar. "Jaspar, you must stay here for a spell, but I shall return shortly."

"Don't worry about the little fellow. I'll keep an eye out for 'im."

"Thank you," I said, and turned to follow Giles.

My grandmother's quarters appeared larger by daylight and I thought that the views from her windows must be the castle's most spectacular.

She was not in bed now, but seated on a chair beside it. She wore a dress of pale mauve with rueshing about the collar and cuffs; the color seemed to enhance the violet of her eyes.

Her legs were covered by a small throw and one hand was poised on the head of a wooden cane. She motioned me to come sit beside her.

"Did you sleep well?"

"Yes I did, your ladyship. Frankly I thought I would not be able to quiet my thoughts long enough, but I was more tired from the journey than I had imagined."

"And what were those thoughts?" she asked, studying me more closely.

"Well, when I set out for Camberleigh it never occurred to me that I should not be received as your granddaughter," I replied honestly. "I sold our house and the few possessions that were left and paid what was due the local merchants. With the money left over I purchased my passage and had a few coins left for lodging and food along the way. If you were not to permit me to remain I shouldn't know where to turn. I know not the contents of the letter I brought you, but I swear on the graves of my parents that it is not a forgery." I dropped my head so that she would not see the tears forming about my lashes.

"My dear, for reasons you may never know, I want to believe you," she replied. "But I have little proof. Only this letter, which you say is penned by your own mother's hand. Perhaps, but as I never saw the handwriting of the wife of my son, William, I can have no certainty."

"There are things in the letter of a personal nature, it is true," she continued. "But it would be—unfortunately—not too great a task for a clever person to spin this tale from gossip of servants—or even from those who masquerade as friends. I have given great thought to this matter and I believe I have a solution. The letter mentions that you are quite adept with letters and have spent a fair time teaching them to local children. Is that true?"

I nodded in assent.

"I am not now willing to accept you into this household as a Camberleigh—as my granddaughter—for the very reasons I have outlined. However, were I to turn you out now and later find that I had indeed made a ghastly mistake I should not rest for the remainder of my life—and perhaps full well beyond that. My son, Richard, has a child, a boy of seven—"

"I met Master Oliver yesterday in the library," I interrupted.

"He is a frail child who needs constant attention. We have had a succession of governesses who have apparently not been to my daughter-in-law's liking, and we are in need of a governess now. I am suggesting that you be that governess."

My eyes flew up and faced hers squarely, and I realized she was not speaking in jest.

"If you accept my offer I shall present you as the granddaughter of an old friend who was sent to us for employment when the family fell on hard times. You shall live here at Camberleigh, and you shall be expected to dine with us on occasion. But your sole duty will be to Master Oliver. You would, of course, be paid wages for your services."

I could only think how ironic it was that several times since my arrival I had been mistaken for the new governess and now I was in fact being offered the position.

I wondered whether I could endure to stay at Camberleigh in such a capacity when these were my only living relatives and this had been my father's home. On the other hand, if I did not accept this offer where was I to turn?

"One thing more before you give me your decision," said my grandmother. "I warn you that should you accept this position I must have your solemn oath that you will care for Master Oliver with your very life, as if he were in fact your real cousin. Should you violate this pledge you shall rue the day you ever set foot in this house."

I thought of the young boy I had met the evening before. He had appeared a sweet child, if somewhat shy. I had always liked children and had often been told that they responded well to me, which was in part perhaps because I missed having brothers and sisters of my own. I was not certain that I completely understood the responsibilities of a governess, but watching over Master Oliver was a task I felt certain I could undertake. Apart from that, I had no alternative; it was clear that there really was no decision to be made.

"I shall accept your offer, your ladyship," I replied, pulling myself up to my full height in the chair. "But I am curious about one thing. If you suspect that I came to Camberleigh as a fortune hunter, why would you trust your only grandson's care to me?"

She withdrew the hand from the cane and moved it to her brow and covered her eyes.

"Too often in my life, Serena, I have not followed my own instincts and have allowed myself to follow the judgment of others. My instincts tell me that you will be a good companion to Oliver. And the child needs one who will watch over him well."

"And now we must make plans," she continued, having not completely answered my question, I felt. "Your timing was propitious, for my son Richard has been in London on business and is not expected to return until tomorrow. In the past he has always hired the governesses. But since he was away and since I shall present you as the granddaughter of an old friend — Lady Jane Carfield, who resides outside of Cornwall I shall tell him — it will seem perfectly natural that I should have stepped into this role for the moment. And because of the personal association it will not appear improper if you are to enjoy a few privileges that would normally be above your station. Your present room is not far from the nursery, so if you are comfortable there then there you shall remain."

Hearing no resistance she continued. "The boy Oliver has a tutor. Mr. Masters seems capable enough, but of course since you have some experience with letters it will be a good supplement to his regular teachings. Your principal charge will be to see that he is well looked after and that he mind his manners well. You will also be expected to provide some diversion from his studies. Richard, I fear, has not been able to spend a great deal of time with the boy. And his mother has never gotten over the shock of his malformation at birth, though I sometimes wonder if it is as serious as we all make it out to be. My granddaughter Clarissa is about your age, but I fear her mind is more occupied with the social season than the needs of her younger brother — and perhaps that's as it should be."

Sighing, she looked at me and said, "I think I have covered it all, unless you have something more to ask."

"The only other question I have," I replied, "is what is to become of Jaspar?"

"Oh yes, Jaspar, your spaniel, is it not?"

I nodded.

"You seem to have quite an attachment to that animal. Well,

26

I see no harm in allowing him to remain with you as long as he stays out of Cook's way and is not aggressive with Oliver."

I smiled at that, for the idea of Jaspar displaying aggression to anyone, much less a small boy, was inconceivable.

"When should you like me to begin?"

"I should think as soon as you have unpacked and settled in."

"That has already been taken care of."

"Then you can commence this afternoon. Serena, what we have discussed here is in confidence. I suggest that you do not have much conversation with the servants. They are prone to gossip and it would be most unseemly if the details of our arrangement were to reach their ears."

"Of course, your ladyship," I replied.

"Then it's settled."

As I rose to leave I saw the exhaustion in her face and I realized that this business had taken a greater toll in her than it had in myself.

As I reached the door she called out to me, "How did your father die, Serena?"

"There was a fire," I replied, "at one of the small farms near us. Two of the children were trapped in the back. He braved his way through the flames and was able to pull them out alive but he was burned very badly. He died a day later in my mother's arms."

I thought I heard a small cry as I closed the door behind me.

I made my way back to my room posthaste, to find Jaspar sitting expectantly inside the door.

"Well, Jaspar," I said, "since we appear to be in this together I suppose I had best tell you the decision I have made," and I began to recount the discussion of the past hour.

A knock at the door interrupted me. "Come in," I called.

Charlotte entered, peering around as if in search of something. "Oh 'tis only you, miss. I could'a sworn I heard voices."

"It was me Charlotte, talking to Jaspar."

Shaking her head, she replied, "You two are really a pair. While you was gone he made nary a move from that door."

I smiled, roughing the gold-brown locks about Jaspar's ears.

"I've finished me rooms, miss, and this bein' me afternoon

free I'm goin' to visit me mum who lives in one of the cottages down yonder, but if I can get you something I'll be pleased."

"You go along and enjoy your day. I have everything I need."

Once Charlotte had gone I found myself wishing I was not going to begin my duties as governess that very afternoon. I was curious to explore Camberleigh and discover what lay beyond its closed doors. But I supposed there would be time enough for that.

I wondered about my cousin Clarissa, what she looked like and whether we shared the same love for nature and books. But it made little matter, for in my status as the governess I was certain that she would not receive me in sisterly fashion.

Apparently my uncle spent a fair lot of time away, which could make it difficult for a small boy growing up, particularly if his mother was not able to cope with his physical limitations. I remembered a woman in our small village who had a child whose arms were misshapen by a chance of birth. I had once said to my mother that the woman appeared not to notice that the boy was different from the rest of her brood and didn't she think that odd. My mother had replied, "Not unless you think love to be odd." But then I was certain that my aunt must love Master Oliver.

A knock at the door brought me to my feet.

"Who is it?" I called out.

The door opened and I found myself looking at a woman with the most dour face I had ever seen.

"I am Mrs. Scoapes, the housekeeper," she said, entering the room and placing a tray on my writing table. "Her ladyship has instructed me to bring you your midday meal and inform you that I shall take you to the nursery after you have eaten."

Jaspar, who had been lingering behind one of the chairs, now bounded out to make his greeting.

Startled, Mrs. Scoapes drew back exclaiming, "What is that animal doing here?" I explained that his presence had been approved by her ladyship.

The woman's eyes narrowed and she replied, "I'm certain matters will take a different course when the Earl returns. I suggest, miss, that you eat promptly for I have no time to spend escorting you about. And that may be the customary fashion for your hair, but I suggest that you bind it back; it is most unsuitable for your role as governess."

Turning, she left the room quickly, giving me no chance for a response.

Her presence left a sudden chill in the room. Jaspar lumbered over by the fireplace and lay down as if chastised.

It was apparent that I could expect indifference not only from the Camberleighs, but from the servants as well. It was strange that she should refer to my "role" as governess, which implied that she knew of the arrangement between her ladyship and me. But that seemed to fly in the face of logic, for it was her ladyship who had been concerned that our alliance be a secret. I put the subject aside and prepared to enjoy my luncheon.

Sitting before my dressing table, I returned my hair to a severe coil and hoped that one day Charlotte might again fix it in the style I found so pleasing. As I was completing my task, Mrs. Scoapes entered and stood silently, indicating that I had had more than sufficient time to prepare myself.

Jaspar did not move from his station at the fireplace. I bade him to remain, and rose and followed Mrs. Scoapes into the corridor. We walked along side by side, giving me opportunity to study her at close hand. She was a large woman who moved quickly but with a heaviness of foot. She wore a dress of solid black. The only prominent feature on her face was her nose, which bore a dark blemish or mole at its tip.

"Mrs. Scoapes," I said. "I have noticed that all the doors I have seen in this house are closed. Is there some reason?"

"All the doors at Camberleigh are closed," she answered enigmatically. "And one doesn't take well to those who try to open them. I should remember that, if I were you."

As we entered the nursery I was amazed at its starkness. There were adequate furnishings, but few of the amusements one would expect for a boy, particularly the next Earl of Camberleigh.

"Master Oliver is apparently still in the schoolroom," said the housekeeper. "Follow me."

We passed through double doors into a small sitting room and then into a narrow back corridor. From the other side of a door I heard a man's voice.

"Master Oliver, you must pay more attention. We have three more lessons before nightfall."

"But I am truly weary, Mr. Masters," the small voice responded.

"I cannot be responsible for the consequences should you not complete these," retorted the adult voice.

With that Mrs. Scoapes opened the door.

"Master Oliver, I have brought your new governess."

Oliver turned slowly from his desk. His eyes met mine and opened increduously.

"But Serena—Miss Miles—last evening you said you were *not* my new governess," he blurted out.

"Yes, I know, Master Oliver," I replied with all the earnestness I could muster. "I had not then been formally hired, and did not think it proper to suggest it."

I turned to see Mrs. Scoapes already departing. I was left with Oliver and the man called Masters, although there had been no introductions. He was of average height with chestnut hair dappled with gray, even though he was no more than ten years older than myself. There was a ruddiness to his skin and an openness in his gaze.

"So you are the new governess," he said, eyes roaming from the top of my head to the tip of my boots. "Then I should present myself. I am Thomas Masters."

"How do you do, Mr. Masters." I moved forward, hand extended. "I am Serena. Serena Miles."

"Well, that's a new name," he replied. "We've had Juliettes, Margarites, Annes. All pretty. But none quite so statuesque as yourself."

I blushed at this quite forward remark.

"I understand that there have been a number of governesses recently," I replied. "Perhaps the Earl did not find them suitable."

The teacher regarded me quizzically and then said slowly, "It would be more correct to say that it was his wife who found them unsuitable."

"I shall only hope that Lady Camberleigh and I shall be of like minds when it comes to Master Oliver."

"Where, may I ask, was your last employ, Miss Miles?" the tutor asked.

"I'm afraid we must. Come, Jaspar," I called.

We had less trouble with the rusting gate this time and were soon making our way up the path toward the hall, as the residents of Camberleigh referred to the castle.

As we entered the front doorway, a female voice called out. "There you are, Oliver. Mrs. Scoapes is very upset. It is past the hour for your medication."

I turned to face a girl about my age; my cousin Clarissa, I instantly assumed. She was the prettiest girl I had ever seen. Everything about her was petite and as exquisitely carved as fine crystal. Her hair fell in waves from its crown and was so fair it was almost white. Under long dark lashes swam deep brown eyes flecked with light. Her mouth arched in a bow so perfect it might have been placed there by the delicate strokes of a brush.

She thrust the folds of the tissue skirt of her pale yellow dress toward us as if insisting that we make note of its finery.

"Who are you?" she asked haughtily, turning her attention to my presence.

"I am Serena Miles," I replied. "Master Oliver's new governess."

"So they found someone," she said curtly. "Well, your stay may be short-lived after Mrs. Scoapes finds out about this. They've been looking high and low for Oliver. It's well past time for his medication."

I colored under the chastisement. "I am indeed sorry, miss, I was not aware that Master Oliver received medication. Mr. Masters made no mention of it."

"Clarissa, it's not Miss Serena's fault," Oliver said, coming to my aid. "I forgot to tell her."

"Well, that's foolish," she replied. "You know what the doctors said. Anyway, it's not my affair. I must go down to the drawing room. Mama is receiving Lady Bellmore for tea. I suppose that means I shall have to be pleasant to her cross-eyed oaf of a daughter. What a bore."

As she flounced off, I took Oliver in hand and we wound our way back upstairs to the nursery.

Oliver paused before the door and looked up at me with sad eyes. "Don't mind Clarissa," he said. "She sometimes says things she doesn't mean."

The nursery was empty, but I could hear Mrs. Scoapes and Mr. Masters arguing in the schoolroom beyond as we approached.

"It is your responsibility, Thomas, though you seem to refuse to accept it," the woman was saying. "Master Oliver must be brought under greater discipline and you certainly don't think it's going to be coming from that chit who just arrived."

"I am employed as a tutor, not as nursemaid," Mr. Masters replied. "The girl said she would return him shortly and I believed her."

"And well you should, Mr. Masters," I said, ushering Oliver into the schoolroom with me. "Apparently there has been some misunderstanding and for that I do apologize. I was told nothing about any medication, and if we were absent too long I do apologize. I will indeed take greater notice in the future."

Mrs. Scoapes, who I was certain had been waiting to pounce on me for any misstep, seemed thwarted by my readiness to accept the blame. Mr. Masters regarded me thoughtfully and I could sense relief from little Oliver.

Producing a bottle from a pocket of her dress, Mrs. Scoapes proceeded to administer to the boy the vilest-looking liquid I has ever seen. He grimaced but drank it silently; it was a routine he had learned to tolerate without complaint.

Replacing the medicine in her pocket, she turned to me. "Master Oliver must return to his studies now. I suggest you return to your room." And with that, her heavy chain of keys clanking, she departed. It went through my mind that the Camberleigh household had a true propensity for dismissal.

My face must have reflected my annoyance, for I heard Mr. Masters laughingly say, "You'll have to get used to old Scoapes if you are to survive in this house. Her bark is worse than her bite, but then I would never want to corner an old dog."

"Dog!" I shrieked. "Where is Jaspar?"

He had been with us when we had encountered Clarissa, but that was the last I remembered seeing him. "You'll have to excuse me," I said quickly. "I must find my spaniel." I flew into the outer corridor calling his name.

I ran to my room thinking he might have gone there, but no. I would have to retrace my steps.

To my great alarm, as I reached the top of the main staircase

I heard barking and high-pitched screeches from the floor below. With dread I flew down the stairs and rushed to a door that was ajar and from behind which the commotion had been emanating. There in the middle of the room sat Jaspar nibbling from a tray of sweet cakes that had obviously fallen to the floor. Clarissa was wiping the front of her dress while three other women stood looking on in horror.

"Oh, Jaspar," I cried. "What have you done?" Hearing my voice, he sprang quickly to my side, leaving the mess of sticky confections strewn about the floor.

"Where did that animal come from?" asked one of the women as they all turned to regard me. "He frightened us half to death, bounding in here and creating all this confusion."

"I fear he is mine," I confessed. "I had thought he had followed me to the nursery but he must have been diverted." I moved to where the debris lay and began to pick up the remains.

"The nursery?" the woman asked.

"She's the new governess, Mama, and she did not give Oliver his medication and so now he shall probably have to lay abed again for several days."

I shot an incredulous look at Clarissa, who stood smiling smugly.

"A maid will see to that mess. Is it true, what my daughter says?" the woman asked.

"It is correct that I am the new governess, your ladyship," I replied, rising from the floor. "And it is true that Master Oliver was delayed in receiving his medication, but when I left him a few minutes ago he was resuming his studies with Mr. Masters. I doubt he will need to be abed except to sleep peacefully this evening." I caught Clarissa's eyes, which were almost afire with anger.

"Well, please remove yourself and that animal immediately," requested Lady Camberleigh.

As I moved toward the door I heard Clarissa's voice. "Mama, this dress is ruined. I shall have to have another and perhaps it should be exacted from Miss Miles's wages."

I slowly ascended the staircase. Even before I could receive any money it seemed it was to be garnished for the replacement of some silly dress.

Despite Mrs. Scoapes's admonition to return to my room, I realized that in my hasty departure I had not bade good day to Oliver and Mr. Masters. Ordering Jaspar to sit in a corner of the nursery, I crossed to the schoolroom. Peeking in quietly I found the two deep in study; Mr. Masters asking questions to which Oliver was to give the answers. I was struck by the harshness of the tutor's tone whenever the boy missed a response. I had always found in my own teachings that most of the children did not answer questions they did not understand. And so we would make a game of it to see how they might better perceive the subject. But what I was watching here was no game. This was a battle.

I closed the door softly and returned to my room. The scene I had witnessed had disturbed me and I needed to be alone with my thoughts.

I was just about to go out for a late afternoon stroll when a maid appeared at my door.

"Excuse me, miss, but Lady Camberleigh wishes to see you in 'er quarters. And if you'll take my advice you'll be goin' in a hurry. She's in one of 'er moods and I'll be tellin' you there's hell to pay when she gets like this." The girl's tone was conspiratorial.

I followed the maid's directions to the quarters in the west wing with dread. After the ruckus in the drawing room I was certain I was not going to be received graciously.

I knocked and was bidden to enter. The sitting room revealed a style of furnishing I had not yet encountered in the house. Everywhere I looked there was gilt—on the chandelier, on the sconces, the tables, the console, the sofa, and even the chairs. And the furniture was carved with heavy and grotesque contorted human faces on the brackets and legs.

Lady Camberleigh was seated in front of a large gilt mirror, her back to me. I thought how pretty she must once have been. But time or events had not been kind to her, and what must once have been was now hollow and dissipated.

"Well it's Miss Miles, our new governess," she said, looking up at my image in the mirror.

"Yes, your ladyship," I replied quietly. "The maid said you wished to see me."

"Wished to see you?" she screamed, whirling in her chair

to face me. "I won't tolerate the sight of you. How dare you insult me in front of Lady Bellmore and her daughter. Believe me, you'll pay for this. He's gone too far this time."

I was stunned by her tone and her accusations. "Lady Camberleigh, please listen," I pleaded. "I deeply regret any embarrassment caused by my spaniel and I should be happy to send my apologies to Lady Bellmore if you would find that suitable."

"You will do nothing—unless I tell you to. Do you understand?"

"Yes, ma'am."

She looked at me as if now seeing me for the first time. "Well," she said bitterly but a bit more calmly. "I see his tastes are changing. Where did you come from? Oh, don't bother to answer. I'm certain your credentials are impeccable. They always are."

"I'm afraid I must correct a false impression. I assume you are inferring that the earl hired me for this position, when in fact that is not the case. It was her ladyship the Earl's mother who gave me employment."

"Oh, so now those two are collaborating," she spat. "Well, that's a new twist. He's always managed some discretion in these matters before but apparently he no longer cares who knows of his philanderings. Well, Miss Miles, I would be careful if I were you. If you have any designs on building your fortunes here you should pack your baggage and return to wherever you came from this instant. That's what the last one did and I can't say that I blame her."

My head was throbbing. I had never had anyone speak to me in such a fashion. I was distressed, but more than that I was angry. How dare she imply that my presence here was some conspiracy between her ladyship, the Earl and myself.

"Lady Camberleigh, I must beg your leave, for I truly feel unwell," I said a bit icily. "I can only assure you that my apology for the day's mishap is sincere and that on other counts I have spoken the truth."

As I turned to leave she called out. "Don't think this is the end of this. Your hiring may have been out of my control but not your dismissal. Remember that."

* * *

A tray was brought to my room, but I could not touch it. Neither Jaspar nor I was hungry. He was undoubtedly sick from the cakes. I was sick at heart.

Chapter Three

IT WAS raining when I awoke the next morning and Jaspar and I still lay abed when Charlotte arrived.

"Morning miss. Oh, what am I goin' to do with you—not eaten your supper again. Cook is going to start thinking it's her cookin'."

"Charlotte, you're a bright light in what appears to be a gray day," I said, getting up and going over to the basin she had just brought.

"Seem a bit off this morning, miss. Not feelin' poorly I hope."

"No, I just slept fretfully. Yesterday was an upsetting day, I fear, Charlotte."

"So I heard. I don't take to no gossipin' but I couldn't help hearin' that the little feller there caused quite a to-do in the drawing room."

"That he did, Charlotte," I replied, describing the scene as I had witnessed it.

"Oooh, I wished I could of been there. Must've been a real sight." Charlotte laughed heartily. "It must have got Miss Clarissa good."

"It's no laughing matter, for I think they intend to dock my wages to pay for a new dress."

"Oh, she has so many gowns you could not count. T'would be a mean thing to do, that would. You be wantin' me to do your hair again this morning?"

"No thank you, I shall simply braid it today."

"Seems a shame to be pullin' it back," Charlotte replied, obviously disappointed.

"Perhaps another time."

"Mrs. Scoapes says you was to go to the nursery and that you'll be 'avin your meals there from now on."

Well, I thought, apparently I was not to be dismissed—at least immediately.

"Charlotte, could you do me one favor?"

"Anything that's in me power."

"I shan't have time to take Jaspar out. Could you see that he is walked a bit this morning. I think the rain will probably let up in a short while."

"I'll be 'avin Robbie do it. He loves the animals, he does, and he'll take right good care of the little fellow."

The nursery was dark when I entered and it was not until I had drawn back the heavy velvet draperies that I realized that Oliver was still asleep.

I went over to him and gently ruffled his blond locks. His forehead felt warm to my touch as he stirred awake.

"Good morning, Oliver."

"Good morning, miss—" and then he remembered our pact "—Serena."

"You feel a bit feverish. Are you feeling out of sorts?"

"I am all right," he said.

But his eyes looked even paler than usual and his skin was definitely too warm.

"I think it would be wise if you were to remain in bed today. I will speak to Mr. Masters and I'm certain that he will agree. Perhaps if your fever lowers I can read to you later. Would you like that?"

"Yes, Serena," he said without much conviction.

"But first let us see what Cook has prepared," I said, picking up the two trays that had been brought in before my arrival.

I propped Oliver up in bed and placed a tray before him.

"I'm not very hungry," he said softly.

"Please just eat a little. It'll do you good. And then you can rest."

"But you don't understand. My father returned last evening and he shall expect me to review my lessons with him this morning."

"Well I am certain he will postpone it once he knows that you are feeling a little under the weather." A cloud seemed to settle over Oliver's eyes as he pushed his tray aside. "Let us not discuss this now. You rest and I shall go find Mr. Masters."

I removed the tray, pulled the covers up about Oliver's shoulders, and made my way to the schoolroom where I found the tutor seated making notations at his writing table.

"Good morning, Miss Miles. Where may I ask is our small charge?"

"I have left him abed," I replied. "He seems a bit feverish, and I don't think he should be up and about today."

"Miss Miles, I fear he shall have to rise. The Earl has returned and will want Oliver to recite his lessons. I will have to review them with the boy before such time."

"Mr. Masters, perhaps I have not made myself clear. Oliver is ill, and as his governess I cannot permit something that may be harmful to him."

"Miss Miles, you will soon learn that there are certain things here at Camberleigh that are out of your control. You may not agree with them, but you will have to learn to accept them if you are to remain here. Whatever you may know about the Earl, you obviously do not realize that he is a stern disciplinarian."

"Well that is all well and good, but he must love the boy and care for his welfare."

Mr. Masters rose from his desk. "Yes, I do believe that he cares about the boy's interests, but I wouldn't say that love was quite the appropriate word."

"Whatever the case may be, for the present I have concluded that Oliver is best off exactly where he is—in bed."

"It appears that our new governess has a determined spirit," Masters said with a smile. "My suggestion is that we put our differences on this matter aside. As we will be spending a fair amount of time together with Oliver, it would be far more agreeable if we were friends."

I studied the face of this man who could be so stern one moment and then warm and quite human the next. He had offered his friendship, a commodity that did not seem to abound here at Camberleigh, and something that I sensed I would need.

"Shall we form a pact, Mr. Masters? I shall not intrude in your teachings if you will not intrude concerning my decisions about Oliver. In cases such as the present one, where one affects the other, let us agree to discuss the matter openly and freely."

"It's settled then," he said, extending his hand. "But only if you shall promise to call me Thomas."

"Thomas, it is," I replied, noticing that his hand held mine a moment longer than necessary to confirm an agreement. "And now if you will excuse me I shall return to the nursery."

I looked in and found that Oliver was sleeping peacefully. It was a good opportunity for me to collect some embroidery I had begun that would provide diversion while I watched over the boy.

Halfway back to my room I encountered Mrs. Scoapes. "There you are. The Earl would like to see Master Oliver in the library. See that he is properly attired and you may bring him there yourself."

"Mrs. Scoapes," I began, "Oliver appears to be out of sorts this morning and I have left him resting. Would you be so kind as to inform the Earl. Perhaps if the boy is better by this afternoon his father might see him then."

The housekeeper narrowed her eyes at me. "I wouldn't be correcting the Earl's orders if I were you, miss. You may be able to turn his head on some matters, but not where Master Oliver is concerned."

"Mrs. Scoapes, the boy has a fever. I don't think we need send for the doctor but I must recommend that to roust him from his bed at present would be untoward. Please communicate this to the Earl. If he should wish to discuss the matter with me I shall of course be pleased to do so." I moved past the woman's stolid figure and continued on to my room.

Jaspar was not in the room, but I expected that he was in Robbie's good hands. And sure enough, for no sooner had I found the embroidery than the door burst open and in raced Jaspar followed by Robbie.

"Oh pardon me, miss. I didn't think ye was here." Robbie's toothy grin gleamed brightly.

"No bother, Robbie. I have just returned for a moment. Jaspar, you look as though you enjoyed your morning romp."

"He were a perfect gentleman. I see how you be fond of 'im. He's a regular."

"Well, I'm glad you two have become such fast friends and

I do appreciate your taking care of him this morning."

Robbie pushed his unruly locks from his forehead. "I could tend to him most every mornin'. I works into the night so I don't start me chores 'til later than most."

"That's very kind, but I wouldn't want to intrude on the small time you have to yourself, and besides, I wouldn't be prepared to pay you anything—at least right away."

"Oh, miss," he said, flushing, "I couldn't be takin' your money. T'would be a treat for me."

I now turned to Jaspar, who had listened intently to this dialogue. "Well, Jaspar, would you like to spend your mornings with Robbie?" The dog's brown and white body wriggled in assent. It appeared that Jaspar and I each had a newfound friend.

"I'd better be takin' me leave, but I'll be here then again tomorrow mornin'. Take good care your mistress, Jaspar." The jolly lad headed for the door, and as he opened it another face appeared.

"Well, if it isn't Molly," he said.

I looked up and saw a maid I'd never seen before. "Miss," she announced, "his lordship wishes you to meet 'im in the library."

"Thank you . . . Molly, is it?"

"Yes, and good day to you," Molly said.

The two closed the door behind them, leaving me to pull myself together. As I smoothed my hair back, catching some loose strands in the braided coil, I looked at my reflection in the mirror. I had never truly thought a great deal about my looks. Not that I possessed no vanity, it was just that in the last few years I had been occupied by so many other matters. Sometime before his death my father had looked up at me one day and said, "Serena, you are growing into a great beauty." I had kissed him, loving him for his flattery but not thinking further about his comment. The face that I saw now I could not call beautiful. My brows were too strong, cheekbones too high, and hair an uncommon color. My full lips, which always appeared to be slightly rouged, were awkward when compared to Clarissa's diminutive heart-shaped mouth. My mother had said once that my passionate nature was reflecting in my face as I grew into womanhood. I hoped that the trepidation I felt at present was now not also reflected there.

Evelyn Grey

As I descended the master staircase I glanced up at the portrait of the man I was about to meet and I prayed that the harshness in the artist's rendering would not be realized in person. But then I took some solace in thinking that he was, in fact, my uncle; how different could he be from my own father?

I poised at the library door, took a deep breath, and knocked.

"Enter," returned a deep resonant voice.

The man stood facing a roaring fire, his back to me as I stepped into the room.

"Excuse me, sir, but I was told you wished to see me."

He turned slowly and I stifled a gasp, for here was a living embodiment of the portrait above the stairs.

"So this is our new governess. Miss Miles, isn't it?"

"Yes sir, I am Serena Miles."

Moving over to a butler's tray he picked up a decanter and refilled a glass he held in his hand.

"Would you join me in a spot of brandy, Miss Miles?"

"No thank you sir. I do not partake," I replied.

"Oh but you should. It has an interesting effect on the senses."

I felt myself shrinking under his regard. His eyes seemed to look through me, not at me.

"Why don't you come over here so that we can get acquainted." He motioned toward a chair near where he stood. "It appears my mother has better taste than I sometimes give her credit for, but then of course she is doing a favor for an old friend."

Was he testing me? Had something been said that he mistrusted my presence here?

"Yes," I said slowly, "her ladyship was extremely kind to offer me this position. I feared that without credentials from past employ it would be difficult to secure a position."

"What was the nature of your family's financial problems?"

"Land investments," I responded quickly, hoping that my grandmother had not been too detailed in her version of this story.

"Ah yes, land. One must always be cautious of overinvesting. Actually, much of the Camberleigh estates have been acquired in just such a manner from barons who have had to

44

divest at any price to survive. But I'm sure that is of no interest to you."

"I fear that it is not something that I have a great knowledge of," I replied honestly.

"Well, as my son's governess you need not trouble yourself with such matters as these. There are some things, however, that you do have to know in order properly to care for my son." He swirled the dark liquid in his glass. "First of all, I am certain you will agree that I, as Oliver's father, am the one who has the boy's best interests at heart." His tone was not unpleasant, but firm.

I nodded in assent.

"Then why, may I ask, did you counter my request to send Oliver to me?"

"As I explained to Mrs. Scoapes, sir, Oliver is unwell. It does not seem serious, but he was feverish and I thought it wise to keep him abed."

He downed the brandy and refilled his glass.

"I am quite certain that you have observed that Oliver is a sickly child in general. Were we to react every time he is weak or out of sorts he would never rise from his bed. The boy has to come to know discipline. Someday he shall be the Earl of Camberleigh and he will need all his faculties for that role."

"I understand that, sir, but at present he is but a small boy," I said.

"I want a man to be made of him, Miss Miles, and as his governess it is your responsibility to carry out my wishes. Mr. Masters is a fine tutor. I suggest you not interfere where you are not needed."

I remained silent. He reached up to his face and ran an index finger along the reddish scar on his cheek. Try as I did I could not help but stare.

"Does my scar intrigue you or repulse you?" he asked, causing me to quickly avert my eyes.

"Neither, sir," I replied. "I rather think that my only reaction is curiosity, wondering how you came to receive it."

He laughed. "I suppose you would like to hear that it was in some gallant duel to save the honor of my family. I fear that the truth is far less romantic. No, I received this mark of distinction when I was but a small child." I looked at him questioningly. He hesitated a moment, then said quickly, "It was from a horse whip wielded at the hand of my mother."

I felt as though someone had struck a blow at the back of my neck. The room seemed hot and stifling, and a million twinkling lights played before me. I could hear the Earl's voice calling my name but I was unable to respond.

"Here, Miss Miles, drink this." He put a glass to my mouth and forced a burning liquid down my throat.

"Now another sip," he said, once more pouring the brandy against my lips.

I felt myself regaining my sensibilities and pushed his hand away, assuring him that I could drink no more.

"I do indeed apologize if I shocked you, Miss Miles. I was about to explain that of course it was an accident but I fear you gave me no opportunity to finish my story."

"I do apologize sir," I answered, feeling foolish at my little performance. "It was simply inconceivable to me that . . ."

"I understand. Now let us move on to other topics. I'm afraid you and I have spent more time talking than I had intended, and thus I shall not be able to meet with Oliver and review his lessons. But I shall expect that meeting to take place tomorrow morning, no matter how you judge him to feel. Please plan to bring him here to the library after his morning meal."

"Yes sir," I agreed.

"My mother has suggested that she would like you to dine with us on occasion. It is somewhat inappropriate, but seeing that you are related to an old friend of hers I am willing to make allowances. We dine promptly at eight. I shall expect you to join us this evening."

"That is very kind," I began, suddenly flustered. "But I am quite unprepared. You see, when I came here it was with the hope that I should take a position and have not brought suitable gowns."

"Well, suitability can be attended to in the future. For the present, what you have with you must suffice. I might add that even in the simplest dress you display the most charming aspects of young womanhood."

I thought his remark most forward, but then perhaps I was not sophisticated in the ways of flattery.

His eyes held mine for a moment and I noticed that they

CAMBERLEIGH

had become slightly glazed. It caused them to appear less penetrating, but there was something else there as well, something I could not identify.

"So it is settled," he said, rising. "We shall see you this evening at eight."

"It will be an honor," I replied, moving toward the door.

"Just one more thing. Don't forget what I have said about Oliver. I am a man of my convictions and I do not allow their being defied. By anyone."

I returned forthwith to the nursery where Oliver was still sleeping peacefully. Taking out the embroidery I had carried in my pocket I settled into a small chair beside the bed, feeling just a bit heavy-headed from the spirits I had drunk.

As I looked upon his delicate, almost ethereal face I could not help but think how different it was from the Earl's hard, angular features. Oliver in fact looked more like what I envisioned my father had looked like as a child—less robust, perhaps, but sharing the same gentleness of feature and aspect.

My uncle puzzled me. On the one hand, I found him cold and insensitive, certainly where Oliver was concerned. On the other, I could not deny that he had been hospitable. I had no doubt that some would even find his stern determination to be disarming.

A maid came in with our midday trays and I motioned for her to place them on a table beside the door. Oliver stirred and as his eyes opened to meet mine, a smile spread over his face.

"Well, how are you feeling after your rest?" I asked, placing my hand on his brow. "I do believe that the fever has gone."

Sitting up, he said, "Yes, I do too." And then he suddenly remembered his lessons. "But my father must be very angry."

"I met with your father a little while ago, and he has agreed that we postpone the recitation of your lessons until tomorrow morning." The look of relief in Oliver's face was remarkable. I did not tell him that only the press of other matters on his father had given us this reprieve.

"How is Jaspar, miss?" he asked, only too happy to change the subject.

"Oliver, remember our agreement—you are to call me Serena," I said, returning his smile. "Jaspar appears to be in fine fettle. Robbie McKee, the son of Charlotte the maid, who has

47

been assisting me since my arrival, has agreed to care for him in the mornings when I am here with you. They seem quite taken with each other."

"Can he still come with us on walks, Serena?"

"Of course," I replied, realizing that he was fearful he might lose his newfound friendship with Jaspar.

"Do you have any other friends here at Camberleigh who could come on walks with us?"

"No," he replied, pulling at the covers. "Father says that it is important for me to tend to my studies. That there is time enough for other things."

"Well, your father is a wise man. Knowledge is a powerful thing, and when someday you become the earl you will need great wisdom to manage the estates and tend to all the people Camberleigh holds in its employ."

"I know."

"But that's not all. My own father was a man of letters. I don't think I shall ever know anyone who loved books as he did. But he was also a man who understood that we must all have balance in our lives. And pleasure and companionship and sharing is all a big part of life. So you and I shall try to make certain that along with your studies you experience other things as well. And I think the best way for us to start is by you and I becoming good friends."

"I'd like that," he replied brightly. "But you know I *do* have another friend."

"Pray tell, who is that, Oliver?"

"Uncle Justin."

Where had I heard that name? Oh, not that arrogant Justin Barkham I had encountered upon my arrival at Camberleigh.

"That wouldn't be Justin Barkham, would it?"

"Do you know him, Serena?"

"Not really. We met only by chance on my arrival here two days ago."

"Did you like him?"

Like him, I thought, I had found him to be a swaggering boor. "Well," I said slowly, "our meeting was so brief that I have no real judgment."

"Oh, I know you will like him. He's not my real uncle, of

course, but almost. We do lots of things together. Well, not so much of late because of Clarissa, but we used to."

"Does he reside here?" I asked, hoping that this man was not living under the same roof.

"No, his home is at Mayfair. But he comes here often to do business with my father. Might I have something to eat now?" he asked, spying the trays against the far wall. "I really do feel better."

"Of course," I replied. What an odd alliance that must be, I thought as I went to fetch the trays. Two strong men—each, I was certain, used to being in command—in business together.

"Let's see what tempting things Cook has prepared today."

Oliver and I ate in silence, both of us hungrier than we had realized.

"Well Oliver," I said, seeing his clean plate, "if you continue to eat like that we might be able to put some weight on those bones."

"The doctor told Mama that I shall never be truly strong— because of my leg, you know."

"I don't pretend to be a physician, but I shouldn't think your leg should have a great effect on your strength."

"Sometimes I get weak though, like this morning."

"I don't see any great harm to that. Your fever appears to have gone and your color is much improved. I shall send a maid to help you bathe and dress and then Jaspar and I shall fetch you for our afternoon adventure."

It was heartwarming to see Oliver smile. I sensed it was not something he had done often in his young life.

The rain had stopped and the sun had drunk most of the moisture from the leaves and grass as we made our way along the walkway once again toward our secret garden. Jaspar trotted ahead as if certain of our direction.

"What is off that way, Oliver?" I asked, motioning to a small path that veered off through a grove of trees to our left.

"That is the back way to the stables," he replied slowly.

"Oh, why don't we go down there today."

Oliver made no reply.

"Oliver, did you hear me?"

"Yes, Serena." His voice was soft.

The boy's mood had become so diffident that I asked, "Is there some reason you don't want to visit the horses?"

"Not really," he answered vaguely.

I would not have insisted, given Oliver's reluctance, but I thought it would be a new, more interesting destination than the garden.

Jaspar seemed momentarily confused by our change of direction but soon joined us willingly. As we made our way along the footpath, I could not help but notice how fidgety Oliver had become. "Oliver, you're not feeling poorly again, are you? Do you want to return home?" I queried.

"No, miss. I'm all right," he insisted. But I wondered at the source of his agitation and worry.

Jaspar's bark told me that we were close to our destination and soon the stable buildings hove into view. As we approached, a stable hand led several horses out into the yard. Though not having an experienced eye in these matters, I could tell that these were fine examples of horseflesh. But I would have expected nothing less; they did, after all, belong to Camberleigh.

I put my hand out to Oliver, who grasped it willingly.

"Well it's Master Oliver," called out a bronzed gray-haired man who had been shoeing a mare. "You're obviously not wantin' a horse today, bein dressed as you are. What can I do for you?"

"Oliver is just showing me the stables," I said with a smile. "I am his new governess, Serena Miles."

"My pleasure, miss. My name is Carroll an' I manage the stables hereabouts. This is a surprise. Master Oliver doesn't often pay us a visit—unless he's with the Earl, of course."

Jaspar suddenly began to put up a terrible fuss over near some water troughs that a young man was filling from heavy pails.

"Jaspar, stop that barking and come over here." Just then the lad straightened up and I saw that it was Robbie. "Well no wonder he's barking, it's Robbie."

Robbie placed the pails aside and came over to us. "Good day to ye, miss," he said with a broad grin.

"So this is where you spend your days, Robbie. I might

have known, you loving animals as you do. Oliver, this is Robbie McKee, the boy I told you about who is caring for Jaspar in the mornings."

"How do you do," Oliver said, shyly extending his hand.

Robbie looked down and, catching my nod, grasped Oliver's hand firmly. "I be doin' fine, thank ye . . . Master Oliver."

"You be gettin' back to your chores now, Robbie," said the man I now knew as Carroll. "He's a good worker, our Robbie, and he's got a special way with horses. I seen 'im contain the meanest o' the lot."

Oliver watched as Robbie untethered one of the horses and led it away from the trough, and I knew not whether his intent look was one of envy or admiration—or both.

"Well Oliver, it's a fair pace back and we don't want to overdue our outing. What do you say that we head back?"

"All right, Serena," he said, reaching once again for my hand.

"T'was a pleasure meetin' you, miss. I hope you'll be stayin for a spell, though it don't seem to be the habit with the governesses at Camberleigh."

"Thank you Carroll," I replied. "I expect we shall see more of each other, for I am not intending to leave—at least in the foreseeable future. Come along, Jaspar."

As the stable path neared the fork with the main walkway, whom did I spy moving toward us but Mr. Masters.

"Well, I see our young charge seems to have quite recovered," he said as we drew near. "It wouldn't be that all this was really a ruse you two concocted to get out of your day's lesson?"

"Really Mr. Masters—Thomas—I resent your implication. Master Oliver was indeed unwell, and you should simply be pleased that he is so rapidly recovered."

"I am, Serena," he replied, and catching the look in his eyes I realized that he had been teasing. "May I walk back to the hall with you?"

"Of course. It would be pleasant to have your company."

Oliver, having no interest in adult conversation, moved ahead with Jaspar.

"You seem to have befriended the boy in a very short time."

"I hope so. He is a sensitive child and could use close

companionship. Thomas, may I ask you something."

"You may *ask* anything. Whether I can answer it I don't know."

"Why have there been so many governesses here? And why did the last one leave without notice or anyone knowing her present whereabouts?"

Thomas's step slowed beside me. "What makes you ask?"

"I don't know." I replied looking off toward Oliver. "It just seems a bit odd. And everyone is always bringing up the subject."

"I shouldn't trouble myself about it if I were you. The important thing is that you have arrived and seem to want to stay."

That was true, but the constant allusions from every quarter about past governesses was disturbing.

"Serena?"

"Yes, Thomas."

"Would you dine with me this evening? I have a small cottage just a stone's throw from the hall and I should be delighted if you would join me. It would give us a chance to become better acquainted and although I can by no means rival the cook in terms of lavish presentation, I am certain you would find the meal suitable."

"How kind of you, Thomas," I said, feeling that he was indeed endeavoring to be friends, "but I am dining this evening with the family."

The cheer that had been in his face gave way to a scowl.

"I see. But of course that would be your preference."

"Preference is not the issue," I replied. "Her ladyship is simply being polite, given the circumstances."

"Her ladyship?"

"The Earl's mother."

"Ah. Your grandmother is an old friend of hers," he said, looking as if for a response.

"That is right," I replied shortly. "But I believe we covered that when we first met."

Oliver and Jaspar had moved a fair way ahead of us and now paused, waiting for us to catch up.

"Is there a back entrance to the hall, Thomas?" I asked.

"There are two, in fact. One on the far side leads from near the kitchens out to an old arbor. That one is closest to your room. The other is just ahead, and it takes you near the chambers of the Earl and Lady Camberleigh."

"I see," I replied, spotting the entranceway of which he spoke.

"I must leave you here," Thomas announced. "Oliver, I shall see you bright and early to begin our numbers again." Then, reaching up and pulling back a strand of my hair which had fallen over my brow, he said, "We'll have our meal another evening then." And with that he was off.

As Oliver, Jaspar, and I made our way up the stairs from the rear entry we had used, there suddenly came the loud crashing of glass from behind the closed door of a room above.

"Don't you give me orders," a woman's voice said.

"Maura, you are in no condition to be receiving Lady Bellmore." This was the Earl. "You know what a gossip she is."

"'My condition', as you call it, is a result of my being shut off here like this all day."

"That is of your own doing, Maura," replied the Earl.

"My *doing*. Oh yes, Richard, you love to remind me that I am a faded matron with nothing but a cripple for a son."

My eyes flew to Oliver, who like myself had stood transfixed. Tears now sprang to his eyes as they did to my own. I snapped my fingers for Jaspar and put a hand on Oliver's shoulder and we slowly crept back down the stairs and found another route to his room.

Oliver did not utter a word, but stood simply staring out of the window at the rolling hills beyond that were darkening with the approach of evening. Not even Jaspar could distract him. I wanted to give him some word of comfort, some reassurance, but I could not find the words and I doubted that he would accept what would probably have seemed false reassurances anyway.

His evening tray had already been placed in the room.

"See what Cook has prepared," I said, lifting a lid to reveal the delicacies beneath.

"I am not hungry Serena," he replied, still at the window.

"Well, then let us get ready for bed," I said, realizing that to insist on the food would be futile. "Perhaps you shall want a little nibble later."

As I readied him for bed I thought how vulnerable this small frail body was that was now my charge. I pulled the covers up around him and instinctively bent down and kissed the moisture from his cheek.

"Good night Oliver."

"Good night Serena." He shut his eyes tightly in what I knew was not sleep.

When I might have normally dressed for the evening with anticipation I did so now with dread. I could not imagine sitting through the evening with those two people. How could they be so cruel to each other? I realized that they had not been aware that their tete-a-tete had been overheard, but that was besides the point. They had exhibited an insensitivity not only to themselves but obviously to their relationship with Oliver.

I chose an emerald green gown for the occasion. It had been my most frivolous purchase before leaving Seven Oaks, but as I scrutinized it now I was certain that it would appear plain in contrast to the finery that would undoubtedly be displayed in the dining room. I wished now that I had thought to have Charlotte dress my hair. It remained in the severe coil-at-the-back style I had adopted.

I possessed no jewelry other than a small cameo my mother had left me, but it did not seem suitable for the dress, which, although cut low in the front, needed something sparkling across my neck.

A distant gong told me that it was exactly eight o'clock as I gathered the folds of my dress and made my way down the great staircase.

I knew not the direction of the dining hall, so I paused to listen for voices. Moving back past the drawing room, the scene of my misfortunes of yesterday, I paused in front of massive double doors carved of oak.

Feeling it unnecessary—indeed inappropriate—to knock, I entered the dining hall without announcement. I was forced to hold back a gasp. The room before me was massive, with ceilings that seemed to soar to the heavens. Ornate candelabras hung from the ceiling, their candles casting a warm glow around the cavernous room.

About a mahogany table—which I was certain could seat

fifty when need permitted—sat my dining partners. My grandmother appeared frail but elegant in a gown of amber lace; a footman stood rigidly behind her. My aunt had obviously taken great care with her toilette, for in a red-gold faille with diamonds at her ears and throat she appeared almost regal. Clarissa could not have looked more beautiful. She wore a gown of pale pink gossamer, which gave her a look of being touched by angels.

My scrutiny was abruptly halted by an unexpected sight. There sat Justin Barkham, looking at me with an amused look on his far too handsome face.

"Ah. Miss Miles," my uncle said, rising. "Please join us." He indicated a vacant high-backed chair to his left, opposite Lord Barkham. I moved silently to the seat as it was withdrawn for me by a footman. "I must say you look charming tonight Miss Miles," my uncle continued.

"Indeed she does," offered Justin Barkham, regarding me with a wry look.

"I do apologize," said the Earl. "You have not been introduced.

"Justin, this is Miss Serena Miles, Oliver's new governess."

"I have already had the pleasure, Richard, but it is a pleasure to have a proper introduction," he replied, dabbing a napkin to his smiling lips.

Clarissa intruded cattily, "How do you know Miss Miles, Justin? Were you acquainted with her previous employers?"

"I fear not, Clarissa my dear. Actually, Miss Miles was somewhat in distress when we first met—it was just at the moment of her arrival, I believe—but I am pleased to see that she has regained her composure enough to join us here this evening."

How dare he, I thought. Clarissa looked from one of us to the other, bewildered.

"Well, Miss Miles—Serena," interjected my uncle, "it appears that you are not as firm of management as you . . . appear."

"I have many faults, sir, but determination and resolve are not among them."

"Ah, a woman of conviction," said Justin Barkham. "I salute you," he said, raising his glass in toast.

I flushed as the members of the table turned to me their arms extended in air.

"I fear I do not know what we're toasting, Justin," Clarissa intruded demurely.

I thought him about to answer when the food was mercifully brought to the table.

I was not prepared for the sumptuousness of the meal. There was first trout, then squab, accompanied by an array of vegetables that tasted as though they had been plucked direct from the garden.

The conversation turned to business. As I had gathered earlier in the day, Justin and my uncle obviously had dealings that were closely allied.

"What have you done about the tenants Justin?" my uncle queried.

"Very little actually, Richard," responded Justin Barkham. "I know you say that the crops are down this year. And certainly the books you showed me yesterday reflect a drop in profits, but I haven't been able to pinpoint the cause. Lord Kelston's man told me that their harvest was up this year and there is no reason why we should be down. The properties between here and Mayfair are far richer—indeed the richest in the country."

"Perhaps," retorted my uncle, "but the fact is that we are not seeing the yield. The only answer is to tax the farmers. Heavily, I might add. Then they will produce."

"You may be right Richard, but if they are already producing to capacity and not realizing the margins, if we were to inflict additional burden through taxation I don't know that they could survive."

"I appreciate your egalitarianism Justin, but you know as well as I that one must take a firm hand in these matters. My father and your grandfather did not build what lies before us from charitable deeds but instead from skillful manipulation of goods and services. It is our heritage to continue that, and I suggest you take heed should you want your sons and their sons thereafter to enjoy the benefits of what our forebears hath wrought."

The rest of the table had been silent throughout this exchange. My aunt appeared preoccupied with the wine and Clarissa toyed incessantly with a flaxen tendril next to her ear.

Only my grandmother appeared to share any interest in the dialogue between the two men. She now put down her fork and turned her attention to them both.

"You know, Richard," she began slowly, but in a strength of voice that surprised me, "your father was a man of extraordinary business acumen. He was also a fair and decent man who had great belief in the common man. Camberleigh—and Mayfair I might add—were built not on greed, but on the principle that if you permit a man to develop something for his own he will not only realize his own commitment and obligation but finally pass the merits of his labors on to others. Our family has been here for generations, and so have many of these farmers. I cannot believe that they do not possess the same ethics and sense of pride in hard work that their ancestors displayed. I do not approve of this taxation. I think it is foolhardy, and I will not have the Camberleigh name tarnished by this kind of avarice."

"Well, that's quite a speech, Mother," Richard retorted, "but since the managing of the estates falls under my ken, I shall continue to follow a course that seems most prudent at present."

My grandmother's eyes found Justin Barkham's and I thought for a moment that she was going to plead for his aid, but Clarissa abruptly diverted further discussion.

"You know, Mama, if I am going to have my season I shall have to have proper gowns. Why, I do not possess one dress that would be elegant enough for the parties and balls."

Justin laughed. "My dear Clarissa, I can hardly imagine that from the finery I see you display about the hall that there are not a few that would be suitable."

Clarissa smiled demurely, her eyes hidden behind her dark lashes. "Why Justin, I do believe you don't want to see me have my new dresses for fear I should prove too devastating to my potential admirers."

"Clarissa, my love," he responded, "you should be devastating were you wearing but an old flour sack."

Having received the compliment for which she had been searching, Clarissa relaxed and returned to play with her tendril of hair, keeping her eyes on Justin Barkham. "Well, we all know that the only reason I'm having a season is to please

Grandma. Otherwise we could have announced our betrothal in its stead."

"Maura," said my uncle, off on another track, "may I say you are looking lovely tonight, though a bit tired. Perhaps it was receiving your guests yesterday—Lady Bellmore, was it not?"

Lady Camberleigh appeared not to have heard her husband's question which I well knew stemmed from an unveiled anger only hours earlier. She lifted her face and regarded him I thought almost benignly and then drained her wineglass, which had just been refilled moments before.

"Well, Miss Miles, how is Oliver?" asked my uncle, turning to me. "Much recovered, I trust."

"If you are referring to the fever sire, yes I am pleased to say that it had disappeared so completely that by the afternoon we were able to take a pleasant stroll—"

"Richard," interrupted my grandmother, "you did not inform me that Oliver was ill."

"There was no need, Mother. There was nothing wrong with the boy. He was simply unprepared for his recitations with me today and chose to play on the sympathies of Miss Miles here."

I was about to protest when I sensed that no matter what I said it would be turned to the Earl's advantage, so I remained silent.

"How is that little spaniel of yours, Miss Miles? Is he still getting you into compromising positions?" Justin Barkham asked, an annoying glint in his eye.

"He is well, thank you, Lord Barkham. Her ladyship has graciously permitted me to keep him with me in my room and Charlotte's boy, Robbie, has agreed to care for him during his off-hours."

"Robbie," Justin Barkham said as if trying to recall the name. "Isn't he the toothy-grinned lad who works down at the stables?"

"Yes," I responded quickly, surprised that he knew of him.

"Knows his horses that boy does. Other than Richard, he's the only one who can get within twenty paces of that stallion."

"He does appear to have an extra sense when it comes to

animals," I replied. "Even Carroll the stable manager commented on it."

"When, may I ask, did you meet the stable manager, Miss Miles?" asked the Earl.

"Oliver took me there today."

"Oliver?" he asked incredulously.

"Well, we had not walked in that direction and I asked him to take me there."

"I see," responded the Earl thoughtfully.

My uncle seemed about to continue but the servants began clearing our plates and serving dessert—a parfait of strawberries, meringue, and cream—and his attention swung back to business.

"Justin, I don't want to go on about this, but I do intend to resolve these financial matters as soon as possible. I think it would be wise if you were to plan to remain at Mayfair for the next several weeks so that we might conclude this taxation issue."

"I am as eager to reach an agreeable conclusion as you but I want some time. I shall be making a trip to London soon on some other matters, but I will put aside as much time as is needed."

"Well that at least sounds a bit more reasonable," interjected my grandmother.

I had relaxed somewhat now that the conversation had shifted away from the subject of myself when Justin Barkham turned to me again. "Your father, I understand, was an important landowner, Miss Miles. How did he feel about tenancy?"

I caught a quick warning glance from my grandmother as I began to speak. "I am afraid, Lord Barkham, that I paid little attention to my family's financial affairs. I would like to be able to provide an answer, but if I did it would not be an intelligent one and had better be left unsaid."

"Well said Miss Miles, but I do insist that you call me Justin."

"Justin," Clarissa put in, dark lashes sweeping over limpid eyes, "is that really necessary? After all, Miss Miles is just the governess here, even though she is related to a friend of grandmama's."

Evelyn Grey

This uncalled-for remark was met with a pained silence all around. The Earl's wife, who had been silent through most of the meal, then spoke up. "Richard, I do believe that I shall have a brandy."

I realized that I had paid little attention to her during the meal but now as I regarded her I saw a return of the woman I had seen the day before.

"Richard," she repeated, "I will have a brandy."

My grandmother had quietly signaled to the footman. Moving from her chair, cane in hand, I watched her rise and start toward the door.

"You will excuse me," she said, "but I fear that I have grown weary of the evening."

The Earl rose in acknowledgment. "Good night, Mother. Rest peacefully."

As if taking my cue, I found myself saying, "I must be retiring also. Master Oliver will be rising early, and I wish to be there to greet him." The men bid my leave. "Good evening, Mr. Barkham. Good night, sir," I said, addressing the Earl. "Rest assured that I shall have Oliver prepared to meet with you in the morning."

As I walked to the door I felt as though all eyes were upon me. Particularly those of Justin Barkham.

I returned to my room to find Jaspar sleeping peacefully by the fireplace. He raised his head for a moment, blinked and then went back to sleep. Charlotte had obviously come in during my absence to stoke the evening embers. Changing into the nightdress which had been carefully laid out on the bed my mind wandered back over the day's events.

This was not a simple household, I thought, drawing the comforter about my neck. There were so many different undercurrents that it was difficult to draw one impression, one conclusion about Camberleigh and those who inhabited it. I did realize that I could not permit myself to think of them as my relatives. For until my grandmother was willing to accept me and present me as her granddaughter, I would have to continue my role as governess. If only there were some clue, some evidence beyond my mother's letter that would allow me to gain my rightful status, but I knew not where to search.

I had to admit that I felt a twinge of envy upon learning

that Clarissa was to have her season. I could imagine myself gowned in exquisite taffetas and lace, being presented at his majesty's court with dapper gentlemen vying for my attentions. But then, Clarissa was betrothed to the odious Justin Barkham and of that I could feel no jealousy. If anything, I felt sympathy. The man seemed determined to annoy me, and I thought the wisest thing was to put as much distance as possible between Mr. Justin Barkham and myself.

I fell to sleep, my hand on Jaspar's warm body—and Justin Barkham's eyes looking down on me.

Chapter Four

CHARLOTTE was drawing the draperies back as I awoke.

"Well miss, I see ye be sleepin hard this mornin'."

"Oh, I must have been more tired than I realized." I said, looking around for Jaspar.

"Robbie's got the little feller. You was sleepin' when he came up an' didn't want to disturb you."

"He's a fine boy, Charlotte. And his way with animals appears not to have gone unnoticed. Both the stable manager and Lord Barkham commented on it."

Charlotte broke into a broad grin. "Oh, that does the cockles of me heart good, miss. That Mr. Barkham's a fine gentlemen, and if he noticed me Robbie that makes me right humble."

I was about to differ with her opinion of Mr. Barkham, but seeing the look of pride on her face, I didn't have the heart to assault her illusions.

"I cleaned up the gray dress you wore fer travelin'. Seein' as you don't have all that many I thought you might be wantin' it today."

"Thank you, that was very thoughtful."

I dressed quickly and made my way to the nursery where I found Oliver already eating his breakfast.

"Hello, Serena."

"Why Oliver, you are up already. May I join you? That looks delicious." I had feared I would find him in poor spirits this morning, but a night's rest appeared to have softened the pain of the afternoon before.

"What would you like to do today Oliver? After your lessons, of course."

"Could we go for another walk? With Jaspar?"

"I can't think of anything that would please him more. Or me."

"Good morning Master Oliver." The voice came from behind me. "It's time for your medicine."

I turned to see the square form of Mrs. Scoapes framed in the doorway.

"Good morning Mrs. Scoapes," I said.

She moved past me without uttering a word and proceeded to administer the amber liquid to Oliver.

"Mrs. Scoapes," I ventured, "what is that medicine?"

"I don't see that it's any of your concern, miss," she replied coolly. I drew the housekeeper across the room out of Oliver's earshot. We kept our voices low.

"On the contrary, Mrs. Scoapes, I think it is most definitely my concern. As long as Oliver is my charge I think it is important that I know everything I can about him."

"I think we can assume that the time that Oliver is in your charge will be brief, Miss Miles," she replied, eyeing me critically.

"Mrs. Scoapes," I replied. "I feel I am safe in saying that you are not overly enthusiastic about my presence here. I don't know why, but if I have offended you, I beg your forgiveness. Whether you accept it or not, my interest here is in Master Oliver's well-being. I only asked you about the medicine so that if you were at some time preoccupied or indisposed I might be certain that he would receive his proper dosage."

"I have seen the likes of you here before, miss, and I am certain I will see them again." She replaced the bottle of medicine in her pocket. "The medicine is in my control. If you doubt what I say, I suggest you discuss it with the Earl himself."

"I shall do that," I replied, feeling my temper flare. "And now if you will excuse me I must take Master Oliver to the library for his recitations."

As I assisted Oliver in dressing I made a note to speak to the Earl not only about my confrontation with Mrs. Scoapes but also about the boy's wardrobe. There was not an item of clothing appropriate for a small boy. The shirts, breeches and vests were suitable for a gentleman but could not be very comfortable for a child.

Oliver's hand was in mine as we paused to knock at the library door. "Come in," the Earl called out. "Ah, Miss Miles and Oliver, my boy. You seem to be looking fit this fine morning."

I found it strange that as we entered the room Oliver made no move to go to embrace his father; rather he lingered by me, his hand tightening on my own. I gave him a small prod and Oliver moved forward to address his father, who stood with his arm resting on the fireplace.

"Good morning sir."

"Well, tell me all the things that you have learned in my absence. Do be seated, Miss Miles. It will prove interesting for you to learn of Oliver's progress."

I smiled, pleased that I would be allowed to remain feeling that I might prove of some moral support to the boy.

What followed was an exhaustive recitation covering a wide range of subject matter—everything from Latin to world history. As I sat listening I could not help but be impressed by the sophistication of knowledge possessed by a child so young.

Once—and it was only once—Oliver faltered, and I was startled that the Earl made no move to assist the boy but remained at the mantel, his eyes cast down at the boy in the same regard that the artist had captured in the portrait.

Oliver looked over at me, his eyes imploring.

"Take your time Master Oliver," I said. "Often a thought that seems to escape one can be recaptured by simply putting your mind to rest."

The Earl obviously did not approve of my intervention, but whatever rebuke he was about to make was thwarted as Oliver came forth with the information.

"Well Oliver," the Earl said, "it appears that Mr. Masters is making good headway. I am pleased. But I know that we can see even more improvement if you pay greater attention to your work. And feigning small illnesses is not going to deter our efforts any further, is it now, Oliver?"

I saw the boy's lip tremble as he shook his head.

"If you have concluded, sire," I said, trying to keep my anger in check, "then may I ask a moment of your time whilst Oliver returns to the schoolroom?"

"But of course. An unexpected pleasure."

Left alone with him, I scarcely knew where to begin.

"I would offer you a drink Miss Miles, but you indicated yesterday that you do not imbibe—other than perhaps a glass of wine, which I noticed you sipped at dinner."

"That is correct sire."

"Well I must say I find that refreshing. I am certain that you have noticed that my wife unfortunately does not share your reserve. In fact she is often inebriated."

I coughed, feeling uneasy at the unexpected opening of our conversation.

"I am not telling you this to embarrass you, but rather to help you to understand some of the affairs of this household. My wife was very beautiful when I married her," he said, pressing on. "You can still see the resemblance, if somewhat faded, to Clarissa. Ours was a relatively happy marriage until the boy was born. I shall never forget the scream that escaped her lips when she first saw him. He was premature as well as being deformed, and the shock was simply too great for her. She withdrew from us all—particularly the child—and we finally decided that it would be best if she were spared the pain of being around him. It was not, in fact, until a year ago that she laid eyes on him again."

I sat incredulous as he moved over to the butler's tray and poured himself a brandy.

"By then," he continued, "she had become a recluse of sorts. Her only consolation, it seemed, was whatever wine or spirits she could inveigle from the servants. What few friends we had I of course could not permit her to see. The managing of the estates had by then become a full-time occupation for me, and one that frequently took me away from Camberleigh—perhaps for too-long periods of time. In any event, my wife now insists that she is much stronger and that she would like to resume her proper role in this house. I am certain that you can see that that is quite impossible, although I am permitting a few small dinner parties with close acquaintances whose silence I can trust.

"As for Oliver," he pursued, pulling up his chair closer to mine, "I know what that boy needs and I shall not be persuaded differently. He seems to have developed an affinity for you in a short time, which pleases me, but I repeat that I shall be the one to direct the course of his development."

"I do not want to countermand you sire," I replied. "Indeed, in just a brief spell I have grown very fond of Master Oliver. I would hope that we would both have his best interests at heart."

"Good, Serena—you wouldn't think me improper if I called you that?"

"No, sire, not if that is more comfortable," I replied.

"Very well then Serena, what did you wish to speak to me about?"

"There are two matters, sire. First of all I thought you should know that I had a rather unpleasant encounter with Mrs. Scoapes this morning."

He laughed. "I realize that the woman is quite humorless but not someone to be unsettled over."

"Perhaps. But the disagreement was over Master Oliver's medicine. I simply suggested that she acquaint me with its nature and dosage so that I might administer it if ever she should be indisposed."

"And she absolutely refused?"

"Yes," I replied, surprised that he knew what had transpired.

"You see, when my wife became ill, it was Mrs. Scoapes who tended to Oliver a great deal of the time. As he grew, we of course employed governesses and she became the house-keeper. I think in some sense she still feels responsible for Oliver and is perhaps a bit resentful that her role is no longer critical. The handling of the medicine is in some small way her lingering connection with him. As to your giving the boy his medication in the event of her illness, I must say that I have never known the woman to be ill in all her years of employment here, but I shall speak to her about it anyway."

"Thank you, sire," I replied, feeling suddenly almost sorry for the woman.

"You said there was another matter, Miss Miles."

I nodded. "It's about Master Oliver's wardrobe."

"His wardrobe? Good Lord, you are not going to tell me

that the boy has nothing to wear," he exclaimed.

"It's not that sire. It's just that he has nothing that is befitting a small boy. He does not appear comfortable and, if I might suggest it, I think his awkwardness of gait might be less pronounced with looser-fitting britches."

The Earl sat regarding me and I tried not to appear nervous, but I feared that my recommendation had offended him.

"Very well Miss Miles. A tailor and seamstresses are to arrive next week, as it appears Clarissa must be outfitted for her season. I will ask them to speak with you about what you recommend for the boy. And at the same time you may ask them to prepare some gowns for yourself. Call it an appreciation for the help you are providing me."

"That is very kind of you sire, and I will tend to matters for Oliver, but I fear I could not accept so generous an offer on the part of myself."

"Nonsense, Serena, you must learn to accept a gift offered in gratitude in like kind."

I was suddenly startled by the sound of the door slamming behind me. I whirled about to see Lady Camberleigh, her hair disheveled and wearing a flowing nightdress of red satin and lace, weaving toward us across the room.

"Well isn't this a cozy fireside chat," she slurred.

I stared, not knowing quite whether to respond or flee the room.

"Maura," said the Earl, rising and taking her by the arm, "go to your room this minute. You are not yourself and I won't be responsible for what you might force me to do while you are in this condition."

"Oh yes," she spat back, tearing her arm from his grasp. "Let us talk again of my condition. You think that you can fool everyone, Richard. But not me, do you hear? Yes, your poor, stupid, sodden wife has a tongue. And I am going to use it to let everyone know what a charlatan you really are. You and your *principles*. Ha—that's a laugh. You who have paraded yourself before every trollop. from here to London and back again."

"Miss Miles," said the Earl. "I think it best if you were to leave."

I nodded, rising swiftly and moving toward the door.

Lady Camberleigh called out, "Be careful my dear Miss Miles. Things are not always as they seem."

As I climbed the stairs to return to the schoolroom I was struck by the familiarity of that parting comment. I remembered that it was also the closing line of my mother's letter to me— and it had now been delivered by Lady Camberleigh.

I scurried down the corridor and ran full tilt into Charlotte carrying a load of bedclothes.

"Oh Charlotte, I do apologize," I said, stooping to retrieve the items she had dropped.

"There, miss, I'll git those. My gracious, you was comin' along here as though somethin' was chasin' you," she said, looking up at me. "Now's I see you I'm thinkin maybe it were. You're as pale as one of these sheets."

"I'm fine Charlotte," I retorted. "I was just in a hurry to return to Master Oliver and I must have been daydreaming."

"Well I won't be keepin you then, miss. Good day now," she said, trundling off with her bedclothes back in hand.

I entered the schoolroom quietly, not wishing to disturb Mr. Masters and Oliver, who were deep in study. Mr. Masters looked up and smiled at me as though pleased to have me there, but I put my finger to my lips, indicating that we should not interrupt the lesson. And thus the two continued while I took a chair at the side of the room.

My mind was confused about the morning's events. I had gone to the library quite prepared to do battle if need be with my uncle over Oliver. I had thought him to be cold and unsympathetic where the boy was concerned. But what had happened did not seem to support that appraisal. The story about his wife had been a shock to me and I realized how protected my life had been until now. What did I feel for Lady Camberleigh? Was it sympathy? No, I think my sympathy was more with Oliver, the innocent product of this union. While I had not truly warmed to my uncle, for I sensed this was not a man one would ever be close to, I did fancy that I had perhaps now a better understanding of his aloofness. His wife's actions would indeed be a great embarrassment. On the other hand her venom seemed targeted most directly at the Earl himself, and I wondered if there had not been something to provoke it beyond the heartbreak of Oliver's condition. It seemed inconceivable that any mother could be so coldhearted unless there were extenuating circumstances the Earl had not described. My ruminations broke off as I heard my name being called.

"Ah, Miss Miles, what thoughts have taken you so far away from us today?" said Mr. Masters, moving toward me.

"I am sorry, Mister Masters—Thomas. Nothing of great consequence."

"If I were hearing Miss Clarissa say that I could well believe it, but somehow I think all your thoughts have consequence."

"You flatter me, but then you do not know me very well."

"That is true but I hope to change that," he replied, smiling down at me. "Which is why I am again going to invite you to be my guest for dinner this evening. And before you say no, let me apprise you that Mrs. Scoapes informed you that the family would not be dining together this evening and thus a tray would be sent to your room. Now, although my offerings are humble, they might be more agreeable than sitting off by yourself plucking away at a lonely meal. Please say yes, it would give me great pleasure."

I was indeed about to object for it did not seem proper etiquette to be dining alone with the tutor unchaperoned in his chambers, but his gaze was so beseeching that it seemed equally improper to decline.

"When put that way I can scarcely refuse. But I hope you shall not regret it, deluded as you are about all my thoughts having great import."

"Let me be the judge of that, Serena."

Oliver, who had looked up to listen to our conversation, appeared embarrassed by its conclusion. He now returned his eyes to his book, but I'm sure he was less absorbed in it than he would have liked us to believe.

"Master Oliver and I have considerably more work to do here, so you have a chance for some time on your own. Why don't you return this afternoon and then you can take Oliver on a jaunt. I shall then give you a paper with directions to my enchanted cottage."

I agreed, pleased actually to have some time to myself.

"I will be back later, then, Oliver," I said, getting to my

feet. "And I shall bring Jaspar along."

"Oh yes," he responded, face lighting up at the sound of Jaspar's name.

Jaspar bounded to greet me as I entered my room and I knelt down to hug him and assure him I had missed him greatly. We were not accustomed to even short separations and although I recognized that under the circumstances he could not be with me at all times, it was an adjustment for us both—more difficult for me, perhaps, for he at least did have Robbie.

As I began to examine my wardrobe to see what I might wear that evening, my eyes fell to the cartons of still unpacked books. Thinking that this would be a good time to arrange them I dragged the boxes over to the bookshelves behind the fireplace.

Breaking the seal and removing a number of handsome leather-bound volumes, I felt a sudden tightening in my throat. I swallowed, trying to stem the tears. These books brought back so many memories to me. I could see my father poring over them, my mother humming in the kitchen. I remember once that he had closed the book he had been reading and suddenly put his head in his hands, a low moan escaping his lips. I had sprung to him fearing him to be ill and he had held me so tightly that I thought my lungs would burst. "Papa, what is it?" I had asked and he had replied, "Only a memory of long ago." I wondered now if he had been thinking of this house and his family.

I began arranging the thick volumes of Chaucer, Voltaire, Shakespeare and other authors whose names I did not recognize. I had read many of them, of course, and some—the ones my father had read to me as a child—I knew almost by heart. But one day I should like to read them all—discovering old friends and meeting new ones.

I had become so absorbed with the books and my memories that I had scarcely noticed the time that had passed or that my luncheon tray had been slipped inside the door. I hastily ate, giving some of it to Jaspar, then quickly washed my face and tightened my braid into its coil.

"Master Oliver has completed his studies," Mr. Masters announced as Jaspar and I entered the schoolroom, "and if his looking round every five minutes is any indication, I would say that he has been anxiously anticipating the arrival of you two."

"Good," I said, "then we shall be off."

Oliver sprang from his seat, joining Jaspar, who was already out the door.

"Let me give you this," Mr. Masters said, drawing a piece of paper from his pocket. "This will tell you how to get to my cottage. It is only a short distance. Come at eight; it will still be light so you shouldn't have any trouble."

"Thank you, Thomas," I replied, tucking the directions into the folds of my dress. "I shall see you at eight then."

Oliver was in good spirits, and the warmth of the sun and smell of freshly cut grasses buoyed my own senses as well.

We discussed our destination and Oliver suggested that we go once again to our "secret garden" that we visited on our first outing. We headed down the now familiar walkway. As we approached the heavy iron gate, which we had found so difficult to move only days before, I was startled to see that it was swung full open. Oliver was also puzzled.

"Well, it looks as though we are not the only visitors to this garden," I said. "But perhaps my strength is simply greater than I had thought and my pulling on it the other day was enough to allow it to swing freely."

"Perhaps someday I shall be that strong," Oliver responded.

"I'm certain you shall, but for the moment I think we should rest. It is a longer walk than it appears." I motioned to the bench.

We sat in silence for a while, Oliver entranced by Jaspar's nuzzlings and I simply enjoying the tranquillity of the setting. I thought again what a pity it was that the pool was so overgrown; I, who had grown up near the sea, longed to see the magic of reflections and light as it played on the water.

"Serena," said Oliver, breaking the reverie finally. "Do you like Mr. Masters?"

"Of course I do. Thomas is a very pleasant man."

"But do you like him . . . specially?" He continued looking down at the pool "Like Clarissa likes Uncle Justin?"

I laughed, realizing what he was implying.

"Heavens no. But he has been very kind since my arrival and I value his friendship."

"But you are my friend too, aren't you?"

"Of course, Oliver," I replied, putting my arm about him. "You and I are great friends."

Relieved, he now looked about for Jaspar. "I don't see him, Serena."

"Oh where has that dog got to now." I peered around the garden and my eyes fell on a break in the boundary privet hedge that I hadn't seen before. "Oliver, what is beyond that opening over there?"

"Just fields."

"Well, he might be out there investigating new territory. Let's go see if we can find him."

We moved through the privet to the meadows beyond, which were filled with late summer wheat dotted here and there by invading wild flowers.

"There he is Serena," Oliver said, loping forward and dropping to the ground next to Jaspar, whose total attention was riveted on a small hole into which he had undoubtedly chased a field mouse or some other small creature.

I too fell to my knees and rolled over onto my back, gazing up at the sky.

"Oh Oliver," I said, "lie back here next to me and look up at the sky. Have you ever seen any more beautiful clouds? You know, my mother and I used to play a game—we would find clouds that looked like objects we knew. Now that one there, that is definitely a teapot. It's small and softly rounded and it has a delicate little spout. Do you see it?"

"Yes Serena," he said with a laugh. "And there's one that looks like Cook's hat."

So absorbed were we by searching for new images among the frothy puffs soaring above us that I did not hear the horse's hoofs until it was too late. I sat up and saw a man atop an enormous horse riding full gallop straight for us. I put my hand up and screamed for him to stop.

"Get down," the rider called out, and I threw myself on top of Oliver, who had risen to a sitting position. A chill shot up my spine as the pounding hoofs shook the earth only inches from us, and then I felt the rush of air as the horse soared over our heads.

Jaspar wriggled out from under my weight and began barking at our phantom rider. I struggled to my feet and pulled Oliver up, brushing off his jacket.

"Are you all right Oliver?" I asked, holding him to me.

"I'm fine Serena."

"I swear I shall thrash whoever that is," I said, turning. The rider had swung his horse around and was cantering back to us.

"Are you all right?" he called.

"Uncle Justin!" Oliver cried out, breaking from my grasp.

I thought it couldn't be, but as he drew closer I saw that it was indeed Justin Barkham.

"Lord Barkham," I shouted at him, "do you realize you could have killed us? You were headed directly for us. Didn't you see me wave or hear me scream to you to stop?"

"Well, if it isn't Miss Miles," he said, ignoring my question and dismounting. "I should have known. And I might ask you what *you* were doing here."

"We were playing games with the clouds," Oliver piped up.

"Well that sounds an interesting pastime. Perhaps I could join you sometime."

The arrogance of this man! How could he stand here calmly and invite himself into our games when he had just almost caused us serious bodily harm.

"You still haven't answered my question," I pursued. "Why didn't you stop or veer away from us?"

"You obviously know very little about horses, Miss Miles. Galloping at the pace I was and with the height of this wheat there was no way that I could have stopped or changed direction before reaching you. The only thing for it was to jump. You should actually be thanking me. A less experienced rider might not have had the foresight to go over you."

The ego of this man was impossible. He was managing to take a nearly disastrous incident for which he was completely at fault and turn it into an act of heroism.

"Oh come now, Serena. The deep frown does nothing for your pretty forehead. I'm sorry if I frightened you but you are, it would appear, unbruised—except for your pride."

"I'm fine Uncle Justin," Oliver said, smiling up at him.

"I know you are Oliver," Barkham replied, swinging the boy up into the saddle.

"Get him down from there this instant," I cried. As I took a step forward toward the horse I felt the heel of my boot catch on something on the ground and before I could stop myself I had fallen head first into the wheat.

Justin Barkham was laughing as he bent over me, an animal-like scent about him which came I knew from hard riding. I had rolled over and was attempting to get to my feet when his hands reached out and held my shoulders for a moment, solemn eyes exploring mine.

"Unhand me, Lord Barkham," I said.

"Not until we reach a truce. For whatever reason, you choose to spar with me. I would find it far more pleasant if we could be friends."

"I am simply concerned with Oliver's safety—and my own, I might add. So if you promise to try not to threaten us, then I shall no longer spar with you, as you put it."

"I do so promise. I have a feeling it would be extremely pleasant to seal this pact with a kiss, but my instincts tell me that I would simply be asking for trouble so I shall simply offer you a ride back to the stables."

"Might I ride with you too, Uncle Justin," asked Oliver, who had been quietly sitting atop the mare watching this little scene.

"Of course, Oliver. That is, if Miss Miles approves."

I nodded, brushing pieces of wheat off my dress.

"Ah, what is this?" Justin Barkham asked, picking up a piece of paper from the ground. "You must have dropped it when you fell." His eyes scanned it for the moment and then he held it out to me.

I could feel myself blushing as I took the paper I knew to be the directions to Thomas's cottage. I thought if anyone had to see this paper, why did it have to be Justin Barkham. I awaited a comment.

He said nothing, but turned to the mare and mounted with great agility. Taking Oliver's arms and placing them about his waist he tugged at the reins and started back toward the stables. Realizing that I was going to be left to follow on my own, I called to Jaspar, who came running.

I was always a few steps behind, not able to quite keep pace with the mare. Great conversation and laughter sprang between

Oliver and Justin Barkham and I found myself straining to hear what it was that seemed to be amusing Oliver so. For the life of me I could not fathom what the boy found so engaging about Lord Barkham, but I had to admit that the man displayed a genuine fondness toward Oliver, and I again cautioned myself to keep my disdain to myself as I had with Charlotte earlier in the day.

"Not weary are you, Serena?" called down Lord Barkham from his seat.

I was in fact hot and sticky and my feet hurt but I was not about to give him the satisfaction of knowing how uncomfortable I was. "Not at all, Lord Barkham. I am quite used to these long jaunts."

He turned back just in time to catch me rubbing my ankle. "I can see that," he said with a wink.

This man has not a mannerly bone in his body. It will serve Clarissa right to be shackled to him for the rest of her life.

As we finally reached the stables, Robbie came forward to lead the mare. If he was surprised at the sight of me hobbling along after, he did not appear to show it.

Lord Barkham dismounted and swung Oliver down by my side.

"Well, this is where we part company, Serena. I have some work that I must tend to. I must say it has been a charming afternoon. Totally unexpected, but then the unforeseen is at times most pleasurable. Perhaps the next time we meet it shall not be such a distressful encounter, although I am beginning to think, Oliver, that our fair damselle is often in distress." He smiled at me.

"Good day Lord Barkham," I replied tersely, taking Oliver in hand.

We made our way back to the hall in silence. We were both tired, and I was too annoyed with Justin Barkham to trust what I might say. We returned to the nursery where Oliver's evening tray awaited him, and after seeing to it that he had bathed off the dust and grime of the afternoon and changing him to his nightclothes, I sat and watched him eat.

When he had finished eating I tucked him in and kissed him gently on the brow.

"Serena?" the small voice asked.

"Yes, Oliver?"

"Are you going to have dinner with Mr. Masters tonight?"

I paused. "Yes, I am. Why do you ask?"

"No reason, really." He yawned.

"Well, good night then. Sweet dreams."

As Jaspar and I trudged back to our room I found myself wishing that I had not, in fact, made the engagement with Thomas for I was indeed weary. But it was too late now to cancel my visit to his enchanted cottage, as he had referred to it.

I was appalled by the sight of myself in the mirror. No wonder Justin Barkham had laughed at me. I was a sight, my hair hanging in strands from the braided coil with broken stalks of wheat dangling about. There were smudges under my eyes where I had tried to rub away the perspiration, and my dress looked worse than it had upon my arrival at Camberleigh after the long journey.

I sat wondering where to begin trying to pull such disarray together when there was a knock at the door.

Charlotte entered carrying a tray.

"Charlotte," I cried as if receiving a long lost friend, "what am I going to do? I am supposed to join Mr. Masters for dinner this evening and look at me."

Charlotte's eyebrows raised, doubtless wondering what I could have gotten into to look like this. "Pardon me sayin' so, miss, but ye look as if you'd had a roll in the hay, if'n you know what I mean," she said, laughing. I must have looked shocked. "Oh, I'm not sayin' that was what you was doin' but a far sight you are from when you went off for your governessin'."

I laughed also, appreciating that she had shown me the humor in a situation I had seen only as almost hopeless.

"I'll be back in no time with some hot water. Meanwhile, get out of those clothes an' get your hair unbraided and brushed good."

I had completed my assignment by the time Charlotte returned with a basin. It was amazing what a little hot water could do to revive one's spirits, I thought, fastening my petticoat and pulling over my head the brown merino I had chosen for the occasion.

"Seein' as how you're meetin' Mr. Masters an' all, would you want me to be fixin' yer hair like I did the other day?"

"Oh, would you? I'm so tired of this braid and I don't seem able to do anything with it myself."

Pleased that I had enlisted her aid, Charlotte took my heavy hair in her hands and with what seemed magical dexterity had soon returned it to the style I had found so appealing.

"There, you be lookin' like a princess, miss."

I studied my reflection. "Well hardly that, but it is certainly an improvement."

"You're a real beauty, Miss Serena," Charlotte said, "but ye don't even know it. 'Course, some would say that's part of ye charm."

I rose and picked up the paper bearing the directions to Mr. Masters' and placed it in my reticule. Sensing he was to be left alone again, Jaspar moved over by the fire, which Charlotte was now tending. I was wont to take him with me, but Thomas had not included him in the invitation and it would have been rude to foist on him an uninvited guest.

"Now you be having a pleasant evenin'," Charlotte admonished. "And don't you let Mr. Masters be lettin' you come back to the hall alone. T'will be dark by then and you don't know the walks around here all that well."

"I won't, Charlotte," I said, amused at the role of mother she seemed to have assumed with me.

I left by the back stairs down past the kitchens and the servants' quarters. I took the walkway, as the note instructed, past the rose garden that my room overlooked, and down to the old arbor that Jaspar and I had discovered that first day. I paused to look back at the house, which I thought could never be more majestic than from this vantage point. My eyes traveled up to the towers of the north wing and there framed in a window again was a figure. I had thought it perhaps to be a trick of the light the previous time, but now there was no bright sun to distort my gaze. My eyes strained, but I could not determine if it was a man or a woman. As if realizing that I was aware of its existence, the shape suddenly disappeared. I found it a bit disconcerting to think that I was being watched, but then perhaps I was flattering myself that someone was indeed interested in my comings and goings.

The directions led me to a small path behind the arbor. The area was wooded here, but obviously well traveled so I had no problem underfoot. When I spied the cottage in the clearing in the trees at the end of the path, I understood immediately why Thomas called it enchanted.

It was a squat little house, crafted of stone with a steeply pitched slate roof. Ivy and wisteria clung to the walls all around, giving way only to the mullioned windows. The door opened as I approached and Thomas appeared, moving his arm down in a low sweeping bow. "Ah, fair princess who cometh from yon castle, enter my humble home and partake of bread and wine with this man who would be your slave."

"I am but a lonely maid, sire," I retorted, joining in the game, "who seeks only simple fare and the company of one so noble as yourself."

"Then enter, fair damselle, and let me warm you by the fire."

"Oh Thomas, I truly do understand why you call it enchanted," I said as I crossed the threshold. The furnishings were simple but had a look of great comfort. Savory smells wafted temptingly about the room from black kettles hanging in the fireplace. A jug of wine and two glasses had been placed on a table nearby.

"Let me take your shawl, Serena, and then let us drink the fruits of the gods." Thomas motioned me to a chair by the fire, then poured the wine. "A toast to you, Serena, the loveliest ever to have graced this abode."

"Your flattery could turn one's head Thomas," I replied.

"It is a faint praise. You really do look lovely this evening. You should always wear your hair like that. It makes you look far more a woman and yet almost vulnerable."

"It was very kind of you to invite me here Thomas," I said, looking into his warm, open face. "I must admit that I felt it slightly improper to come here unchaperoned but now that I am here I feel very comfortable."

"I'm pleased, Serena. Camberleigh can be a lonely place and I hope you will seek refuge here often."

"How long have you been here, Thomas?" I asked, resting my glass on the table beside my chair.

"It will be two years this winter."

"Did your family come from this region?"

"No. My family—as it were—came from London. In actuality there was just my father and myself. My mother left me in his care when I was very young. She was an actress, and it seems that the life of the stage suited her far better than her role as a wife and mother."

"That must have been very difficult on both you and your father," I replied, noting the solemnity of his tone.

"Not really. He ran a pub and was often not home till the early morning hours. It gave me a chance to read, and that opened new horizons for me. I read of men setting forth for new worlds and finding gold and other treasures greater than the mind could fathom, and I dreamed that I too would one day sail the high seas of adventure."

"And did you?"

"I fear not," he laughed. "Not unless you call taking a coach to a small manor outside London on the prospect of teaching three overly indulged young ladies an adventure."

"I would agree it doesn't have the same romance and excitement," I replied.

"And what of your dreams, Serena?" he asked.

My dreams. When Jaspar and I used to sit on the cliffs watching the sea below I used to dream that one day a beautiful ship would arrive and its captain would spy me from its bow and send his first mate to fetch me. He would declare undying love and we would marry and set sail into the sunset. But that was long ago, and I knew not what my dreams were today.

"I suppose it sounds foolish, but I don't know if I even have any dreams."

"It must be difficult," he said, regarding me thoughtfully, "for you to be forced to assume a position here at Camberleigh when you might have assumed a far different role."

His comment startled me so that my hand knocked over the wineglass on which it was resting. "Oh Thomas," I cried, jumping up in dismay, "how could I have been so clumsy. I do hope you will forgive me."

"There is nothing to forgive, Serena," he said, rising to fetch a cloth and mop up the spreading pool on the floor.

"There, you see. No harm done."

He righted my glass and refilled it, then sat down again opposite me.

"Perhaps you should not have refilled my glass," I said. "I must have drunk more than I thought."

"You have scarcely touched it. Now relax that worried look from your face."

"Thomas," I ventured. "What did you mean when you said that I might have assumed a different role here?"

"Only that had your family not fallen on hard times you would have come here as a guest and not a..." His voice trailed off.

"Not a servant, is what you were about to say."

"Yes, I suppose I was, but that truly is not the right appellation for either you or myself. As tutor and governess we may not enjoy the privileges of the nobility, but we are a station above the chambermaids and cooks. Actually I find it not disagreeable. We have many of the benefits with none of the responsibility. I would say that is having the best of the lot."

"Well, I guess you do have a point," I said, relieved that there had been no more then that in his remark.

"Now," he said, rising, "you will think me an inelegant host if I do not serve you the meal I promised."

We sat at a small oak table on which had been placed a small basket of field flowers. The stew and freshly baked bread he had prepared was delicious and I marveled at his resourcefulness.

"There is plenty more," he said, noting that my plate had been eaten clean.

"I couldn't," I demurred. "But you can see for yourself that I enjoyed it thoroughly."

"I thought myself that it tasted particularly good tonight, but I think that is less my cooking than the company. May I get you a small brandy?"

"No, thank you, Thomas," I replied. "I fear it is late and I must be getting back to the hall."

"So soon? I feel you have only just arrived. My intention was to get to know you better, and I fear all that we did was to talk about me. I hope I didn't bore you."

"Quite the contrary. I've enjoyed the evening immensely."

"Good. Then perhaps I can look forward to your returning some evening in the near future."

"I should like that. But now I really must be going."

"Then I shall get your shawl and escort you back," he said, picking up a candle. "Not the best thing to light our way, but it is all I have at the moment."

Offering me his arm, for which I was glad since I realized it would be very dark on the path through the wood, we wound our way slowly back to the hall. As we passed the arbor I looked up to the north wing of the house. The tower was dark and there was nothing visible in any of the windows.

We reached the door that led through to the back staircase. "It will be dark inside," Thomas said, handing me the candle. "Take this."

"But won't you need it for your return?"

"Don't worry about me. I know the way well. After all I travel that path several times a day. I would see you in, but I fear if someone found me escorting you about at this hour that they would get the wrong impression, so I shall bid you good night before I make any advances that would have you think other than kindly thoughts about me."

I climbed the staircase cautiously, as the light of the candle was barely enough for me to see clearly. I had just reached the top when a sudden draft snuffed out its light. What a predicament. Well at least I had reached the top of the stairs and I knew the way to my room. I pulled my shawl about me and began to grope my way along the wall of the corridor. I had just reached the corner when suddenly I felt a strong hand clasp mine. Before I had a chance to scream, another hand closed over my mouth. I was aware of an enormous male arm encircling me and pulling me to a chest that was barely covered by an open shirt.

"Well," said the voice in a ragged whisper, "what do we have here?"

As I struggled to free myself from this awful grasp, the hand that held my mouth flew off. Again before I had a chance to scream, moist lips were pressed hard against mine, and a warm tongue found my own, coating it with a strong taste of brandy. Hands tore at me, exploring my breasts through my thin wool dress. I felt as though I were drowning and that someone was forcing me down deeper and deeper into a turbulent sea. I kept trying to swim back to the surface, but a hand pushed me down further into an oblivion from which there was no return.

The water churned about me, licking my body with soft wet lips, then tossing me up and over, and finally swallowing me whole. I was carried farther and farther out to sea until suddenly I was picked up by a great wave and thrown ashore where I lay still as the surf rolled gently up and over, caressing every fiber of my body.

I awoke with a start.

"Jaspar?" I called out, sitting up in the massive poster bed.

But this was not my room! And where were my clothes? My head felt heavy and there was a dull pain in my stomach. I reached down and my fingers recoiled at the dampness beneath me.

I swayed in horror as I suddenly realized what had happened. Bile rose in my throat as I struggled to regain my senses. Who had done this to me? Was my attacker still lurking close by, waiting to violate me again? I swung my legs over the side of the bed and my feet landed on my dress, which lay in a crumpled mass on the floor.

I put on my clothes mechanically, unable to move quickly even though I had an urgency to escape. The hallway was dark as I gingerly pushed the door open, but I could tell I was not far from where I had been attacked. I moved cautiously down to my room.

I closed the door, locked it behind me, dropped into a chair. Even Jaspar seemed subdued, and I scratched him behind the ears absently.

Light was filtering in through the windows as I climbed into my bed. I lay staring at the ceiling, seeing nothing. What had happened to me was like the worst nightmare I'd ever had, yet I knew it had been real—hideously and terrifyingly real. I had never felt so alone or so helpless. The same questions kept nagging at my brain. Who? Why? If I only knew the identity of my attacker I could expose him for the madman he was. But who would believe my story without some sort of proof? And even if I knew who my assailant was, what assurance would I have that anyone would take the word of a governess over this man's? No, it would be of no gain to speak up. But how could I remain in this house, knowing that the maniac might be living under the same roof. Would I ever again be able to trust those about me? I thought not. But what other option did I have? I had no money, no prospects. My only relatives were here at Camberleigh, although with each passing day I doubted more that that should ever be made clear. I must remain here. And I must remain silent. But staring hard at the ceiling there in the dim light of that awful dawn, I vowed that one day I would have my revenge.

I had slept only an hour or so when I heard a knock at the door.

"I can't get in, miss. The door is locked." It was Charlotte.

"Just a moment," I called out, pulling myself from the bed and drawing my robe about me.

I opened the door and she bustled in with a basin of steaming water.

"Well, how's my lass this mornin'? Not too good by the looks of ye."

"Good morning Charlotte," I replied in what I hoped was a normal voice.

"So how was your evenin'?"

"My evening?" I said, shuddering at the very thought.

"Yer dinner with Mr. Masters?"

"Oh," I said, realizing that I had not even given a thought to that in the past hours. "It was very pleasant."

"Pleasant, eh? Well that doesn't sound too promisin'. And here I was thinkin' there was some romance brewin' under our very noses. Shows you what a matchmaker I am. He didn't do nothing improper, now did he miss?"

Thomas? I thought. No, it couldn't have been. He had left me at the door. And besides, the man who had attacked me seemed larger. Thomas was too gentle to have ever committed such a crime.

"Well?" Charlotte prodded.

"He was a perfect gentleman. And I didn't mean to imply that I did not enjoy his company. It was a lovely evening. I'm just a bit tired today."

"Well you wash up while I take the little feller down to Robbie. He's waitin' for him."

I rubbed my skin almost sore trying to wash away the violations that had been visited on me the night before.

Several deep purple marks had appeared on my shoulders and about my breasts, vivid reminders that I had struggled in vain. I put on my high-necked blue muslin, which I knew would cover all evidence but a small scratch by my left ear. As I brushed my hair I looked to see if my face would give any hint to the invasion that had been made on my body. I was paler, perhaps, but only one who knew me as well as my own mother would guess the cause.

I had just completed my braided coil when Charlotte returned.

"Well now, are you feeling a mite better?"

"Yes, thank you."

"If you be wantin' anything for the rest of the day, better be tellin' me now. There's a party that arrived last night, an' all the maids is doin' double."

"People arrived at Camberleigh last night?"

"T'were two gentlemen, business associates of the Earl. Cook is fit to be tied, arrivin' unexpected like they did then wantin' a fancy meal. I don't reckon they'll be underfoot too early this mornin' though, since they was up half the night drinkin' brandy in the library."

Brandy? It couldn't be. Not my uncle's friends. But Charlotte had said they were business associates, not friends. Even if it was one of them would there be a clue, some sign that would reveal itself to me?

"You go along Charlotte. I will be with Master Oliver, and I can't think of anything I might need."

Oliver was already up and about when I reached the nursery.

"I was waiting for you Serena, and I'm hungry," he said, looking at the breakfast on the table near the door.

"Well, I'm pleased to hear it," I said, going to fetch the trays. "What shall we do after your lessons today?"

"I don't have lessons today. Mr. Masters never teaches on Sunday."

Odd, I thought, that Thomas hadn't mentioned it the night before, but then he most likely assumed that I would know.

"Well then, you and I have the day to ourselves," I said.

His eyes darkened.

"Is my company all that bad?"

"Oh no, Serena."

"What, then?"

"Father says you are to take me down to the stables as soon as we have breakfasted."

"Ah, so that's why you have riding breeches on. Well then, eat your eggs and sausage so you'll have all your strength."

I ate not from hunger but simply to maintain a semblance of normalcy. Noticing that he was tugging at the high collar of his stiffly ruffled shirt, I said, "You know, I had a discussion with your father the other day about your wardrobe and he has agreed that we shall have some new things made for you when the tailor arrives later this week."

"But I have a lot of clothes."

"I know you do, but I thought that you might be more comfortable in some things that are a bit less formal and perhaps a bit looser fitting. It might even help your walk a bit."

"My father said it would be all right?"

"Indeed he did," I responded heartily. "Well you and I had best walk off that morning meal or Cook will be rolling us down the path to the stables."

As we neared the stables I saw Robbie leading the most beautiful stallion I had ever seen. He stood at least seventeen hands high. He was pure black with the exception of a white star-figured shape on his head. Sinuous muscles rippled as Robbie threw a saddle up over his back.

"Oliver, what a beautiful horse."

"That's Medallion. He belongs to my father."

"Hello, Robbie." I waved. "Well, look who is here," I exclaimed as Jaspar came bounding to our side.

"Hello, Miss Serena, Master Oliver. You'd best stay back. Medallion here got a lot of anger in 'im."

My uncle appeared from behind the stables, a large crop in hand.

"Good morning, Miss Miles. Oliver."

"Good morning, sire. I was just commenting on what a beautiful horse you have."

"Excellent taste, Miss Miles. Would you care to join Oliver and myself on a ride?"

"As you can see sire, I am far from dressed properly for

such an outing. In fact, I do not own proper riding attire."

"Well, we shall have to correct that when the seamstress arrives." Turning to Robbie, he said, "Saddle up King's Ransom for Master Oliver."

I saw Robbie open his mouth as if wanting to say something, but handing Medallion's reins over to the earl, he wordlessly turned on his heels and started back to the stables.

The Earl climbed atop the stallion and I was struck by the sight. The two powerful forces united as one in this way was a majestic sight, but at the same time almost frightening.

Oliver's hand grasped mine as Robbie led a chestnut stallion toward us. Medallion pawed at the dirt and began to back up as the other horse was brought alongside. My first thought was that the horse was much too big for Oliver, but I was not acquainted with his riding skills so I remained silent.

Oliver moved forward, and Robbie helped him up to his seat. I think I shall never forget the look on Oliver's face as the two horses moved off. It was one of pure unbridled terror.

"I don't be likin' that, Miss Serena," said Robbie, wiping his brow.

"What do you mean, Robbie?"

"Putting them two horses together is jest askin' for trouble. That Medallion's a mean one but King's Ransom's a fighter. If 'e ever cornered i'im it'd be like two cocks fightin' to the death."

I felt my blood run cold.

"But the Earl must know that, Robbie."

"Sure he does."

"Then why would he allow Master Oliver to ride him? I heard him specifically ask for King's Ransom."

"I wish I knew, miss. He's a funny one, the Earl is. But it's not me place to be figurin' what goes on inside his head."

I was at a complete loss to know what to do. The two had disappeared from sight and I prayed that I would not have long to wait until their safe return.

I seated myself on a bench near the main stable building. I felt weak, and my body ached. I knew full well the cause, but I could not permit self-pity or the heartache that swelled within me to preoccupy my thoughts while there was any threat to Oliver.

I looked up at the sound of a rider's approach but saw that it was only Justin Barkham. The last person that I wanted to see at this moment.

"Well, Miss Miles. You look as though you've lost your best friend."

"I pray I have not, Lord Barkham."

"Oh, come. Whatever it is cannot be that dire."

"Perhaps not. But I shall not be myself until I see Oliver return safely through those gates."

"Ah, so Master Oliver is off for a ride. Well, you needn't worry. He may not yet be the most proficient horseman, but his mare is a gentle creature and she will not lead him too far afield."

"He is not on the mare, Lord Barkham. The Earl is with him on Medallion and Oliver is on a horse called King's Ransom."

His eyes narrowed as he looked down on me.

"King's Ransom? Are you quite sure?"

"If you doubt me, ask Robbie."

"Which way did they go?"

"Down the trail over yonder. But that was some time ago," I replied.

"Damn fool," he muttered, turning his horse and galloping off in the direction I had indicated.

Now what had I done? If all was well, my uncle would be furious if he discovered that I had sent Justin Barkham in pursuit.

It seemed an interminable length of time before I saw riders appear down the bridlepath. As they approached, I realized with horror that one horse was riderless. I started to run toward them, Jaspar following close at my heels. As they drew closer, I saw that Oliver was atop Lord Barkham's horse, the latter's arm about his waist.

The Earl rode by me as if I were invisible.

I heard Lord Barkham say, "There has been an accident." I looked at Oliver and gasped as I saw a gash near his right temple from which poured a thin trickle of blood. "I don't think it is serious, but I think he should be put to bed without delay. I shall have someone fetch the doctor, simply as a precaution." Robbie held the horse as Lord Barkham climbed down cradling

Oliver in his arms. Tears welled in my eyes as I looked down on the small, pale frame.

"He'll be all right, Serena. Just a nasty shock. I don't think there is anything broken. I will carry him up to the hall."

I nodded, too distressed to respond.

Once back at the hall, Lord Barkham carried Oliver up to the nursery, with me following in close pursuit.

He was conscious, but disoriented, which I guess was natural given the accident. I undressed him and put him to bed, placing extra covers about him for warmth. As I bathed the cut on his head, Oliver looked up at me.

"Is my father very angry with me?"

"Of course not," I replied, shocked at his question.

"The horse was going so fast and I just couldn't stop him."

"I know Oliver. But that is over, and now you should just rest."

He was asleep when the doctor arrived. The man was older than I had expected, a small man with a considerable paunch which I sensed came as much from overindulgence as it did from age. Bushy whiskers lined his full cheeks and he was constantly pushing his spectacles back up to the bridge of his nose.

"You must be Miss Miles," he said, opening a small black bag. "I am Dr. Carruthers."

"How do you do, doctor," I replied, leading him over to Oliver's bed.

"Hello, Master Oliver." The boy's eyes fluttered open. "Seems you had a bit of a spill, eh? Well, let's just see that nothing is broken."

Oliver winced only once as the doctor prodded and probed his young patient. "I don't think it's anything serious," Dr. Carruthers said. "He's going to be very stiff for a few days and I would like you to keep him in bed until that gash quiets down a bit, but before week's end he should be in fine fettle."

Now turning to regard me more closely he said, "You know, Miss Miles, I think you could do with a bit of bed rest yourself. You look all done in."

"I'm fine really, doctor. Much relieved in fact, now that I know Oliver will be all right."

I tried to persuade Oliver to eat a bit from the trays that had been brought to the nursery, but neither of us was very hungry. Settling down in a chair by the bed, my hand placed in his.

Startled suddenly by a knock at the door, I realized that I must have fallen asleep. It was Lord Barkham. I motioned to him that Oliver was sleeping.

"The doctor has said that he will be fine," he whispered.

"Yes. But he will need bed rest for the next few days."

"You look as though you could use the same thing."

"I wish everyone would stop telling me what I need or don't need," I retorted edgily. "Master Oliver is my charge, and I shall be well as long as he improves."

"Well, he is fortunate. We would be all be well served with you as our guardian angel."

I looked up into his dark solemn eyes and for once saw none of the usual taunting impudence that he had displayed toward me since my arrival. I thought he was about to say something further, but he simply turned and moved to the door and left without further comment.

Chapter Five

THE NEXT few days passed slowly. Oliver gained strength, but as the doctor had predicted he was stiff from his fall and his head ached, giving me rise to believe that he had sustained a slight concussion.

I spent my time between the nursery and my own room, not venturing out of the house except for short necessary walks with Jaspar. I rarely saw Charlotte, for the Earl's business associates were still ensconced and the household staff was kept busy, for they were apparently demanding guests. Since my itinerary about the house was so circumscribed, happy to say I never ran into these men or even heard their voices.

I had not seen Thomas since dining with him and thought it strange that he had not come to visit Oliver. I was certain that the tutor had been informed of the accident and—despite the fact that Oliver was not fit for his lessons—I did wonder of Thomas's absence. I also realized that his presence did much to buoy my spirits.

The Earl came to visit Oliver only once. The boy had been asleep and the Earl had motioned me not to disturb him. He looked down at him for a few moments and without a word left as quickly as he had come.

On the second day of Oliver's confinement my grandmother entered the nursery.

"Grandmama," Oliver called out, his face brightening as he saw her.

She returned his smile as she moved slowly over to his bed, leaning her full weight on her cane.

She eased herself into a chair by the bed and took Oliver's small hand, covering it with her bony fingers. "And how is my grandson feeling today?" she asked.

"Oh, much better, Grandmama. I even told Serena that I thought I could be up and about soon."

"And what did . . . Miss Miles say?"

Oliver, suddenly realizing that he had used my given name, became flustered.

"I think we might venture forth for a small walk in a day or so, your ladyship," I interjected. "That is, of course, assuming that Oliver continues to improve."

My grandmother was silent for a moment.

"Miss Miles can you tell me whatever possessed that stable hand to put Oliver on such a spirited horse?"

"Oh, but it was not the fault of the stable hand," I blurted out before thinking.

"Then who, pray tell?" Her pale violet eyes were searching mine. I looked down, biting my lip, for I knew not what to respond. "Miss Miles, I asked you a question."

"It was the Earl's request," I replied softly.

My grandmother sat back in her chair. I was about to move over to her for she had remained so still that I had grown concerned when she rose, kissed Oliver on the forehead, and moved slowly and, it appeared, painfully to the door.

Turning back to me she said, "That I have gained a granddaughter through your arrival here, Miss Miles, is less than probable. But Oliver it appears has gained a valued governess. For that I am thankful."

The next day I rose early, for Charlotte had told me that the seamstresses and tailor had arrived the evening before on a late coach, and I wanted to meet with them as soon as possible so that they might start on a new wardrobe for Oliver. We had scheduled an appointment in the nursery, as the room was large enough for measurements and examination of the large variety of bolts and cloths they had brought with them.

They were a cheerful lot, bustling about industriously. They had obviously frequently been employed by the family many times previously, and I was pleased that they appeared to approve when I informed them that we would be adopting a more relaxed mode of dress for Master Oliver; nor did they object when I suggested I make some suggestions of my own for designs.

Luncheon was provided on trays so that the sketching and selecting might go uninterrupted. Oliver appeared to enter into it all happily—as much to please me as anything, I thought.

The camaraderie that we had formed seemed so pleasant that we all looked up startled at the sudden loud shrieks we heard from the hallway.

"I will not have it." I recognized Clarissa's voice. "I haven't a thing to wear and you have allowed that Miss Whatever-her-name-is to steal my seamstresses so that Oliver might have new clothes. Well, it is simply preposterous. Oliver never goes anyplace, and it is my season and you are determined to make me a laughingstock."

"Clarissa, that is not true." It was the Earl. "I had no idea that Miss Miles had them working in the nursery. She had some foolhardy notion about Oliver and I permitted her to have a few things made, but had I known that it would take time away from making my lovely daughter even more beautiful, then I should never have allowed it."

With that the door opened and in flounced Clarissa, a confection in a gown of pale cream muslin with dozens of pale blue ribbons tied about its bodice and sleeves.

"What is the meaning of this," she cried, looking about the room, her eyes finally resting on me.

"Miss Miles," said the Earl, "you were under no authority to enlist the services of these people until my daughter had made full use of them."

"I regret the misunderstanding, sire. It was just that you had given your permission, and with Master Oliver being confined of late I thought it would provide some diversion."

"It seems to me that Master Oliver should be up and about by now. He certainly looks well enough to resume his studies, and since my daughter shall be requiring the services of these good people I would suggest that you focus your duties more properly." Clarissa looked at me smugly as if she were enjoying every moment of my rebuke. "Now," continued the Earl, addressing the embarrassed onlookers, "I should finish up here and join Miss Clarissa in her quarters. And I shall expect you to outdo yourselves when it comes to her new wardrobe."

"Oh, Father," cried Clarissa, smiling sweetly, "couldn't we wait until morning? Justin has promised to take me out in his new coach. He would be unconsolable, I fear, if I were not to join him."

If the Earl was even slightly embarrassed at having created this commotion for naught, he did not show it.

"Very well. Miss Miles, you may continue here today. But that is all the time you shall have, so make haste with it."

Clarissa left, beaming, on the arm of her father.

I tried to carry on with our project as though nothing had happened, but the intrusion had dampened everyone's spirits. Not the least of all Oliver's.

As I sat reviewing the sketches and making the final selections I found myself becoming angrier and angrier. Never once had the Earl displayed any love or affection for the boy. In fact he seemed almost unaware of his existence, except when it came to some matters of discipline. I of course did not look for Lady Camberleigh to visit her son; it appeared that were they to encounter each other it would be purely by chance. He was such a gentle boy, but any spirit he had was further broken with each new encounter. My grandmother seemed to believe that I had some value as a governess, but at times like these I wondered whether Oliver's destiny was not already beyond my grasp.

As I entered the nursery the next morning I was surprised not to find Oliver propped up in bed awaiting my arrival. Hearing voices close at hand I crossed to the schoolroom, where I found Oliver deeply engrossed in his lessons.

"Good morning, Serena," Thomas said, rising to greet me.

I smiled, brightening at the sight of my friend. "Thomas, I had become concerned about you when I had not seen you all this week."

"I am pleased by your concern, Serena, but there was no need. When I was informed of Master Oliver's mishap, and learning that it was not serious, I took the opportunity to go down to London for a few days to attend to some business. I returned late last evening and received a note from the Earl bidding me to commence Oliver's lessons this morning."

"I see," I replied, thinking that the Earl had lost no time in getting Oliver out of his sickbed.

"I would appreciate it, Thomas, if you could finish his lessons by early afternoon. He is still weak from his accident and I would like to get him out into the fresh air for a spell."

"I doubt the Earl would approve, but I will not deny you this request. I shall have him ready when you return."

I went back to my room and seeing that Robbie had already taken Jaspar in tow, I laid down for a brief spell. Some time had passed when I awoke. I had not realized how tired I had been, but I knew that since Oliver's accident—and my ghastly experience—I had slept fitfully. I rose and went to the window. My eyes were drawn to two figures below. I recognized the pale yellow-and-white gown Clarissa had worn when I had first met her. The man could only be Justin Barkham. As I watched, she put her arms up, encircling his broad upper back. As he bent down, I moved away from the window, embarrassed at intruding upon this intimate scene.

I quickly changed my boots and returned to the schoolroom. Thomas was just folding up his books. "We've had a good lesson today, considering it was our first day back. Wouldn't you agree, Master Oliver?"

Oliver nodded, but I could see his full attention had now turned to me. "Could we go out now?" he pleaded.

"I think that could be arranged," I replied.

As we sauntered down now familiar footpaths toward our secret garden, I noticed that Oliver's limp was more pronounced than usual. Perhaps the fall had indeed done more damage than the doctor had assumed. But he appeared not to be in pain, so I thought it best not to make mention of it.

As we approached the fork that led down to the stables, I turned to Oliver and asked if he would mind if we went down there for a moment as I wanted to check on Jaspar. He said not and we wound our way down. When we got there I spotted Robbie with my beloved spaniel in tow. The dog's ears pricked up at the sound of my voice and he came bounding toward us, barking his welcome.

"Well Robbie, it appears that you and Jaspar have become almost inseparable," I said.

"Aye, miss. I'm hopin' ye don't mind, but seein' as you're so busy up at the hall, I thought t'would be better to keep him with me when I can. An' he's a fine little helper, he is."

I turned and saw Justin Barkham striding toward us.

"Serena—Miss Miles—wanted to see Jaspar," Oliver said to Lord Barkham. "It's my first day out since I fell."

"Well, then, that is cause for celebration. I'm taking my new buggy over to Mayfair to pick up some papers your father needs. Would you like to join me?"

"Oh, could I, Serena?" Oliver asked, looking at me imploringly.

"I would think that could be permitted, as long as you will have him back in time for his evening meal, Lord Barkham."

"Then it is arranged."

"Uncle Justin, could Miss Miles come with us?" Oliver asked.

"No Oliver, that would not be proper," I replied quickly, embarrassed at the suggestion.

"I don't know if it's proper or not, but I was about to suggest that very thing myself. Serena, won't you please join us, if for no other reason than to see that I don't let Oliver bounce out of the buggy."

"Oh please, Serena," Oliver pleaded, taking my hand.

"Well . . . put that way, I suppose I shall have to accept. I don't think I could endure watching Oliver recuperate from another accident."

"And I'll be keepin' an eye on the little feller, miss," piped up Robbie, who had been taking this all in. "He'll be safe and sound when ye return . . ."

I thought the buggy to be the smartest I had ever seen. Pitch black, with red and gold trim on the doors and wheels. The horses that drew it were dapple grays, so identical I wondered if they had been born twins.

Oliver and Lord Barkham bantered happily as we rode along down past the landscape I had seen when I had first arrived at Camberleigh. I now marveled more than ever at the richness of the land and the endless stretches of verdant lawns and trees. We had only gone perhaps a mile when I noticed that the green changed to fields of wheat and maize-colored crops. Near the hedgerows were occasional clusters of small houses that appeared in need of attention. I wondered if some were occupied at all, since many of the windows had been boarded up by wood or in some cases burlap.

"Excuse me, Lord Barkham," I said, "but might I ask who owns these dwellings?"

"These are tenant farms," he replied. "My grandfather and Richard's father were great friends. When my grandfather moved up north here with his new bride, he bought a large amount of acreage that had originally been part of Camberleigh. On this land he built Mayfair. The two agreed that as long as their ancestors continued to reside at these contiguous properties the expenses of running the farms and the profits reaped therein would be divided equally."

"But many of these farms look to be terribly neglected," I replied.

"They are," he answered dispassionately.

I wanted to inquire further, but realized given the conversation I had heard in the dining room that I would be treading on dangerous ground, given Lord Barkham's and the Earl's conflicting ideas.

Mayfair was so different from Camberleigh! The house was far less imposing and grand, but perfect in its symmetry and architectural design. Eagles soared above great Cotswold stone pillars at the entrance to the drive. And all around it spread gardens with flowers of every description. Whereas the gardens at Camberleigh were all formal and at the rear of the castle, here there were blossoms everywhere lending their color and warmth. There was even a certain welcoming quality to the well-proportioned elegant stone facade.

"Well what do you think of it?" Justin Barkham asked.

"It's truly lovely," I replied sincerely.

"Not as impressive, perhaps, as Camberleigh," he said, "but I have always preferred it. I've always thought Camberleigh to have a foreboding quality. My grandfather said it was a house that had a furrow in its brow. He wanted Mayfair to have smile lines."

He pulled the buggy up before the massive oak doors and swung Oliver to the ground. I gathered my skirts and eased down the step, brushing off the dust that had collected on our brief jaunt.

"I see you insist on faring for yourself," said Lord Barkham. "More's the pity, for although I doubt you to be as light as young Oliver, I fancy that you are indeed softer."

I was reminded again that this man could be so bold, and I was furious with myself for becoming flustered at this forthrightness—and more than a bit angry that I had come here at all.

The reception hall at Mayfair appeared to run the full length of the house, with massive paned glass doors at the rear that opened onto gardens beyond. The light that streamed in was caught by the prisms of an enormous chandelier hanging directly in the center of the room.

"Justin, is that you?" a woman's voice called out.

"Aunt Anne," shouted Oliver as he hobbled quickly into a room to our left.

"Come this way, Miss Miles," Lord Barkham said, motioning me into the room Oliver had just entered.

He moved swiftly past me and embraced a woman who sat with her back to me on a sofa. Enormous sprays of flowers were strewn about a table before her.

"You naughty reprobate. I don't see you for days and then you show up unexpectedly. I should have had a lovely tea prepared with Oliver's favorite biscuits, had I known."

"I have been over working with Richard on this taxation business. Actually I am just back now, as there are some papers that I need."

"How is he, Justin?" she asked.

"Who?"

"You know perfectly well *who.*"

"Oh, Richard."

"Well?"

"He's as arrogant, egotistical, selfish, and cruel as he has always been. But I don't think our guest wants to hear about that."

"Guest?" she said, turning. "Oh, Justin, and here I am, a

complete mess from these flowers."

"Nonsense. Miss Miles, I would like you to meet my sister, Lady Ormsby."

The woman rose and, placing the basket that had rested on her lap on the table, approached me, hand extended in welcome. My first reaction was surprise, for I had rarely encountered a woman of my same stature. I judged her to be eight or nine years my senior. One could not call her pretty, for although she possessed similar features to Lord Barkham, on a female countenance they were too strong to be beautiful in the classic sense. But there was a handsome, totally self-possessed quality about her, and I was drawn to her immediately.

"Miss Miles," she said, "I am being a bore. You will think me a discourteous hostess, but that dreadful brother of mine seems to take pleasure in putting me in compromising situations. Now come over here and tell me all about yourself."

"Serena is my governess," Oliver piped up.

"Ah well, then aren't you fortunate, Oliver," Lady Ormsby replied. "Justin, don't just stand there. Ask James to arrange for some tea. And be sure he tells the cook that Oliver is here so that we might have some of those nice biscuits."

I hoped that I had covered my surprise at Lady Ormsby's warm hospitality even after she had learned that I was but a servant in the Camberleigh household. Placing her arm in mine, she guided me over to the sofa and we sat down side by side.

"Well now," she said, studying me, "when did you come to Camberleigh?"

"I have only been in residence for these few weeks past," I replied, "although it seems much longer, somehow."

"Where did Richard find you? If you pardon my saying so, you look far too regal to be a governess, even to our own dear Oliver."

"I was not acquainted with the Earl. You see my—"

"Miss Miles's grandmother," broke in Justin Barkham, now reentering the room, "is an old acquaintance of Juliette's. Miss Miles's family suffered financial reversals and she was sent to Camberleigh."

Ordinarily I resented someone speaking on my behalf, but I loathed being forced to recount this lie and was almost grateful for Lord Barkham's interruption.

"Ah, that explains it. It must be a difficult adjustment for you, but I for one am pleased that you are here. 'Tis about time that Oliver had someone of breeding to watch over him. And selfishly I must admit that it is dreadfully lonely here at times with the men off on their business excursions. I welcome the company of a woman acquaintance."

"That is very kind of you, Lady Ormsby."

"Nonsense. I shall most likely drive you crazy with my incessant banter, so it will be you who shall be being kind to me. And if we are to know each other better I must insist you call me Anne—and I shall call you Serena."

"Well, Oliver, it looks as though the ladies are going to be thick as thieves. We had best beware that they do not plot our demise."

"Aunt Anne and Serena wouldn't do anything to hurt us, Uncle Justin," Oliver replied, moving over to where we sat on the couch.

"I knew you would champion our cause," Anne replied, enfolding Oliver in her arms.

A butler brought in a large silver tray with the tea things on it and placed it on the table.

"Serena, would you pour the tea and allow me to finish with these flowers before they wilt and my reputation as an expert flower arranger is ruined?"

I smiled. "Of course."

"I trust we are not using our best china, for Miss Miles has a propensity for minor mishaps," said Lord Barkham.

"Really, Lord Barkham," I replied, placing a cup back on the tray, "I hardly think there is reason for you to think that I will break your china."

"Yes, Justin," Anne put in, "you are an impossible tease. Serena, don't listen to a word of it. He used to do the same thing to me as a child. I was almost your age before I realized that I was not a moronic female and that I simply had an impossible brother."

I warmed even more to Anne with this latest vote of confidence. It was odd that a brother and sister could be so different. Anne appeared such a genuine and giving person, whereas her brother seemed to derive pleasure from making others uncomfortable. I thought of how direct and comforting Thomas

Masters was by contrast, but then he was a simple man, unencumbered by the obligations of power and money attached to the management of Mayfair or Camberleigh.

"Just what do you know about this invitation I received?" asked Anne, handing him a manila envelope bearing the Camberleigh crest.

"Oh, that must be for this Saturday evening?"

"I know that," she responded exasperatedly, "but what is it for?"

"Several of our business associates have been at Camberleigh for the past days and I suppose Richard feels obligated to host a dinner in their honor. And you, my dear sister, are probably being enlisted to provide female non sequiturs at the dining table."

"Hmm," she mused, putting the flowers down on the table. "That must mean that Maura is feeling better."

"I wouldn't count on that."

"I'm not counting on anything, Justin. You of all people should know that. In any event I don't think this is an appropriate conversation given the givens," she said, nodding discreetly in Oliver's direction. "You will of course be there, Serena?" turning to me.

"I fear not. I have not been invited—at least to date."

"Well, I will take care of that. Just leave everything to me."

"Please don't, Anne," I replied, embarrassed that she would intercede on my behalf in such a matter.

"Don't be silly. My motives are totally selfish. If I am to spend an entire evening smiling at a bunch of boorish associates of my brother's, I want to know that I have a friend there who can enjoy my performance."

"And performance it usually is with my dear sister."

"Justin, this is of no consequence to you," Anne reproached. "Well, Serena, will you be there if I can arrange it?"

"Anne, even if you could," I replied, "I have nothing appropriate to wear."

"Stand up."

"I beg your pardon," I said, startled by the suddenness of her demand.

"You heard me. Stand up. Let me take a look at you."

I rose and stood as all in the room stared at me.

"Just as I thought," said Anne, looking pleased with herself. "You and I are about the same height. I don't have your delicate bone structure, but that's easily fixed. With a rip here and a tuck there it will be perfect." I must have looked completely bewildered, for she added, "I have just the dress for you."

"Oh, I couldn't." I felt that I was being swept along by something totally out of my control.

"Of course you can—and you will. I know exactly the gown. I've never worn it. My poor seamstress thought it would be perfect, but I fear it is far too feminine for me."

"There is no sense in arguing," Lord Barkham said, sensing that I was about to protest again. "My sister is a very determined woman and when she makes her mind up there is no stopping her."

"Come with me," Anne said, taking me by the hand. "Let me at least show you the dress I have in mind."

Recognizing that there was truth in what Lord Barkham said, I followed Anne from the drawing room up the staircase to her quarters. There was something about this house that made me feel lighthearted and more carefree than I had felt in months. Whoever had selected the fabrics, wall coverings, rugs, and other furnishings had exquisite taste and a real feel for color and design. There was a vitality here that I had never once felt at Camberleigh. Moreover, here most of the doors were open, as if in welcome.

My breath was quite taken away when we entered Anne's bedroom. It was as though one had planted a garden inside instead of out, for everywhere I looked there were baskets and urns filled with the most glorious arrays of flowers my eyes had ever beheld.

"What a beautiful room," I said, inhaling the heady scent that filled the air.

"I am glad you like it. I feel that I do go quite overboard at times, but flowers are truly in my blood. When my father built Mayfair he wanted to be able to shower bouquets on my mother every day of the year. Needless to say our winters often make that impossible, but for the most part he achieved his dream."

"Does your husband share your love for flowers?" I ventured.

"Anthony? . . . Yes he quite did, actually."

"Did I hear you say 'did,' Anne?"

"Yes, Anthony has been dead almost seven years now."

"Oh, I am terribly sorry," I replied. "It must have been dreadful to have lost him so young."

"Yes, it was dreadful," she said, tucking a rose deeper into its vase. "But not for the reasons you think. I was very young and very much in love—I thought. He was kind and gentle and quite attractive, really. And he was devoted to me in his own quiet way, bringing me small trinkets and always telling me how attractive I was. I was flattered and I welcomed the attention. You see, my mother had been ill for a long time and had really not been able to provide much love or consolation to me. I married Anthony shortly after my mother died. I now recognize that it was more from need than love. He was a dutiful husband, but none of it was what I had imagined. I longed to travel and entertain and do things—I wanted to discover all of life that I had not known theretofore. But Anthony was a reticent person. He seemed content with just passing each day quietly and with no intrusions. It is ironic that on the one trip that he made after we were married he met his end."

"How *awful*," I said with a gasp.

"He was traveling by coach to London. There was a bad storm and the horses, frightened by a bolt of lightning, broke away. The coach overturned. The driver, who survived, told me that Anthony was killed instantly. We had been married only eight months."

"You must have mourned him for a long time," I said quietly, thinking of my father's death that in a way had been as sudden.

"I hope it won't shock you if I say no, I did not. Of course I felt a sense of loss, but as time passed I realized that it was more like the loss of a distant cousin than of a husband. It took me almost a year until I understood that I had not truly been in love—rather, I had been in love with love."

I could not fully comprehend what Anne had told me. I was a romantic and had always believed that marriage was born of love and that it was the greatest bond two people could share. But I had little experience in these matters, with really only my own parents' relationship—which had seemed to me born in heaven—to draw on.

"And now I fear I've depressed you, Serena, when I only meant to explain. At times I think Justin is right. I do carry on too much. Let me go and fetch that dress."

She stepped into another room and returned carrying an enormous box, which she laid directly on my lap.

"Go on, open it."

I gently took out from its layers of tissue a gown that I thought the most breathtaking I had ever laid eyes on. It was off-white organza, and the shoulders and back, I realized, would be completely bare. The sleeves were puffy, and heavily gathered. The skirt was done in voluminous folds, each caught by a single seed pearl.

"Oh, it's beautiful!" I exclaimed.

"I knew you would like it. Now hold it up and let us see about the fit."

As I held it up and caught my reflection in a mirror I couldn't help smiling.

"Hmm," Anne said, pressing the gown to my waist. "T'will need several inches taken in at the waist, and a nip or two around the shoulders. Is there a maid over there who can sew?"

"That won't be necessary," I replied. "I am fairly adept with a needle."

"Are you? Well I can't sew a stitch. Good, then that's settled. Put it back into the box and you can take it with you."

"And I must be getting back. This is Oliver's first day out of bed, and I am certain that he will be tired."

"Well, if I know Oliver, he will have eaten every biscuit and even convinced Justin that he should take a few extra for the trip home."

Returning to the drawing room, my dress box in hand, I found that Anne had been right. But I could also see that Oliver had indeed grown weary and I bade Lord Barkham that if he had fetched all the papers he needed we should return promptly to Camberleigh. Anne fetched her basket, mumbling that she had far too few flowers to complete her arrangement, and saw us out into the center courtyard.

"You have been so gracious, Anne," I said, "I wish there

were some way that I could repay your hospitality and your generosity."

"There is," she replied, her eyes twinkling. "Just be there on Saturday evening."

The trip back to Camberleigh was relatively quiet. Oliver, ensconced between Lord Barkham and myself, began to doze off. I placed an arm about him, resting his head against my breast and humming a folk tune that my mother had often sung to me as a child. Lord Barkham appeared deep in thought, and I was relieved that I would not have to listen to any of his sarcastic quips about my character. Even though Anne had tried to assure me that it was simply his nature, I was not convinced that he did not find me in some way annoying.

The house was very still when we arrived. Oliver was sound asleep and Lord Barkham lifted him gently down from the buggy and carried him ahead of me up the stairs to the nursery. I lay the dress box on a chair and turned back the covers of Oliver's bed. It had grown quite dim in the room and I lit a candle so that I might undress him.

"I shall take my leave now. I see Oliver is in quite capable hands," Justin Barkham whispered.

"Thank you Lord Barkham," I replied softly. "And may I say I enjoyed the outing immensely. Your sister is charming, and I can see why you have great pride in Mayfair."

I felt his eyes upon me as I turned to ready Oliver for bed, but he made no reply and I soon heard the door close. I thought of awakening Oliver for his evening tray, but decided that it had not been long since he had devoured all those biscuits and what he needed more now was a good night's rest.

Dress box in hand, I made my way back to my room, where Jaspar greeted me, whimpering with pleasure. I knelt down and embraced him, realizing how much I had missed the pure unadulterated affection that he gave so willingly.

A tray had been left in my room and I ate the delicious roast of lamb hurriedly, for I was aching to try on my new gown. I doubted that I would indeed receive an invitation to the dinner party, but it didn't hurt to pretend, and no one would see me in the confines of my room.

I slipped out of my gray muslin and pulled the layers of organza over my head. Anne had been right. The waist was too large and the sleeves needed tightening so that they would fit below my shoulders, but otherwise the gown looked as though it had been designed for me. There was nary a trace of the bruises left by my attacker—no outward evidence of the sorrow that would remain forever in my heart.

Jaspar perked up his ears as I began to waltz about the room to the imaginary sound of violins. I dreamed of entering a grand ballroom. All eyes turned to me, and as I moved into the crowded room I could hear whispers all about me. "Isn't she lovely" . . . "Who is she, I wonder."

I twirled to a stop in front of the mirror. Wouldn't they laugh when they found I was but a lowly governess. Even the most beautiful gown in the world could not transform my status.

I removed some pins from my sewing box and began making the necessary adjustments. I decided to merely pin the alterations in place, realizing that if I did not receive the invitation I would not be too greatly disappointed. I hung the gown carefully at the back of my closet and, donning my nightdress, went to the bookcase and withdrew one of my father's books. I moved to the window and felt the chill of approaching autumn that was in the air; the moonlight played strange shadows on the garden below, and I wondered what lovers were caught by its spell as I drew the window closed. I got into bed, pulled the coverlet about me, and opened the book. I had not read many pages before my eyelids became heavy, so I put out the candle and fell into deep slumber.

I awoke early, feeling refreshed by a good night's sleep, and was pleased to see Charlotte enter bearing my basin.

"'Morning, miss. Looks as if Camberleigh's startin' to agree with you. Got some roses bloomin' on those cheeks finally."

"Good morning. Yes, I do believe I feel stronger."

"Robbie tol' me you went on an outin' yesterday to Mayfair. I only saw it the once, but I remember thinkin' it must be the prettiest place on this earth."

"It is indeed very beautiful."

"Did you be meetin' Lord Barkham's sister?"

"Yes, she was very gracious."

"A real lady she is. She don't go puttin' on airs like some people, I won't mention any names. She's a real regular."

I smiled, wondering what Anne would think of being called

"a real regular." But in a strange and simple way it suited her.

"I'll be takin' the little feller down to Robbie now an' I'll bring your tray to the nursery seein' as how you're up and about so early. Today's me afternoon to go an' see me mum, but Molly will see that you gets your supper and all."

"Thank you Charlotte. Don't worry about me, I'll be fine."

I dressed quickly and went along to the nursery. Oliver had obviously rested as well as I, and we ate with relish the porridge and fruits that Cook had concocted for our morning meal.

I had to admit that I was eager to see Thomas, and I scurried Oliver into the schoolroom so quickly that even he found it bewildering.

"Good morning Master Oliver," Thomas said, rising from his desk. Taking my hand, he kissed it lightly. "Serena, you look lovely today."

I blushed and withdrew my hand quickly, embarrassed by what Oliver might think of any display of affection between us.

"May I speak with you privately for a moment?" Thomas asked.

I couldn't imagine what he had to say that could not be said in front of Oliver, but I nodded and followed him into the passageway that separated the nursery and the schoolroom.

"Would this fair princess deign to dine this evening with this lowly tutor who is besotted by her? 'Tis simple fare, but his humble abode has not been the same since she last graced its presence."

I laughed. "When put like that, how could I refuse? I would be delighted to join you. I only regret that I have no way to reciprocate your kind invitation."

"Your acceptance is the only reciprocation I need. You know the way. I shall expect you at eight."

We moved back into the schoolroom, and I assured Oliver that I would return for him early in the afternoon.

I had just left the nursery when I saw Mrs. Scoapes approach. I could not explain it, but every time I saw this woman I felt a sense of dread; it was as though she were an omen of ill fortunes to come.

"Miss Miles, the Earl asked me to give you this," she said in her usual monotone, handing me a cream-colored envelope.

"And Lady Camberleigh would like to see you in her chambers directly."

"Thank you Mrs. Scoapes." I turned the envelope over in my hand. The housekeeper stood there a moment, boldly waiting to see if I was going to open it, but I did not want her to have the satisfaction of seeing me upset if in fact it bore bad news, so I simply tucked it in my pocket and headed in the direction of Lady Camberleigh's quarters.

Once out of Mrs. Scoapes's sight I paused and quickly withdrew the envelope. Opening it, I read:

> The Earl and Lady Camberleigh
> request pleasure of your company
> at a dinner
> in honor of their daughter, Clarissa,
> at nine in the evening
> on the seventh day of September,
> in the year one thousand eight hundred and twelve

So I had received the invitation after all. I could not help but admit that I was thrilled at the prospect. The only damper on my enthusiasm was the discovery that the party was being given in honor of Clarissa, not as I had thought for the business associates. But perhaps this was just a small party to prepare her for her season.

I knocked at Lady Camberleigh's door.

"Come in."

She was seated before her dressing table wearing a robe of rose-colored velvet. She turned to face me and I was shocked at how ill she looked.

"You don't think I look pretty, Miss Miles? Oh, don't say anything. I see that look on my husband's face every day. You notice I didn't say every night, but then you know that, don't you."

Her words were slurred, as though she were on some medication that prevented her from thinking or speaking clearly. I wondered if I should go for assistance, as she really looked as though she should be in bed, but knew I would be blamed for interfering.

"I see he gave you the invitation," she said, pointing to the envelope I held in my hand.

"It was very kind of you and the Earl to invite me."

"I did not invite you, Miss Miles. My name may appear on that card but your name did not appear on my guest list. No, this was my husband's idea—but again, that shouldn't surprise you. Let's see . . . what reason was it he gave? Oh yes, so that you might help entertain his business associates. Well that's a new twist. He's never shared his bounty before."

"Lady Camberleigh," I said, clutching the invitation tighter in my hand. "I would not dream of attending if you do not want me there. Now that you have made your feelings known, I think we had best forget that I ever even received this. Excuse me, please."

I turned on my heel and started toward the door.

"Miss Miles, stay where you are."

"Lady Camberleigh, I beg your leave," I replied, trying to keep my voice from breaking.

"You can't expect that I would be pleased about your attending this dinner, but I am not such a fool as to countermand my husband. No, you shall attend. But I will not be embarrassed in your showing up in a gown that is totally unsuitable for the affair. The seamstresses are still here, and though I really don't want to take time away from Clarissa's wardrobe, I suppose there is no other solution. We will have you fitted this morning, and that should provide sufficient time for the gown to be completed."

"Lady Camberleigh, that will not be necessary," I replied without further explanation, thinking it ill advised to tell her about the gown that Anne had lent me.

"Return to your room, Miss Miles. I will see that one of the seamstresses is sent there straightaway."

I went to my room feeling heavy of heart. Any joy I had felt over receiving the invitation had been dashed by my audience with Lady Camberleigh. Well, I simply would not attend the dinner. I would go through with having this dress made, but I would become very ill just before the dinner. I would be disappointing Anne, but it couldn't be helped. The wildest horses would not be able to drag me out of bed.

Soon the seamstress arrived.

"Hello miss. I'm Fiona."

"Yes Fiona, I remember you from the other day."

"T'was embarrassing in front of the little boy an' all."

"Well, Fiona, what do you have in mind?" I asked, taking a bolt of cloth from her arms.

"I fear it is not what I have in mind, miss. Lady Camberleigh was very specific."

The cloth was of a gray velvet, and the rough sketch Fiona handed me showed a gown that was more appropriate for my grandmother than a girl of my age. It had a high neck and long sleeves; its only adornment was a rather interesting drape to the skirt. Well, I certainly couldn't have stolen the limelight from dear Clarissa in this, I thought. It would be surprising if anyone would even have looked at me. Well, no matter, I was not attending the dinner in any case.

The fitting took most of the morning. Fiona was a cheerful girl not much older than myself, and that managed to take the edge off my depression over everything surrounding the dinner party.

I scarcely touched the midday meal that Molly brought; I was anxious to take Oliver on a long walk outside the walls of Camberleigh. My mother had always said that one could walk their troubles off. That with each step one took the burden would seem lighter.

We retrieved Jaspar from the stables and wound our way back once again to our secret garden. I had missed seeing Thomas when I had gone to fetch Oliver, since the Earl had summoned him to the library. In any event, I would see him tonight.

The afternoon passed quickly. Oliver and Jaspar romped together, darting in and out of the hedges like playful puppies. I was content to merely watch them at play, happy that I had something to occupy my mind from its more somber thoughts.

On our way back to the hall I spied Clarissa and Lord Barkham strolling ahead of us. She appeared diminutive next to his tall broad frame. I wondered if they were the lovers I had seen in the rose garden below my window the night before.

"Uncle Justin," Oliver called out, running ahead with Jaspar at his heels. What happened next occurred so quickly I could scarcely believe my eyes. As Oliver reached the couple, Lord

Barkham caught him by the waist and swung him high into the air. At the same moment, as I watched in horror, Jaspar jumped full force against Clarissa, almost knocking her over. I called the dog's name and broke into a run, reaching them as Lord Barkham placed Oliver to the ground and was comforting Clarissa, whose dress was a mass of dirty paw marks.

"That *beast*," she screamed, "get him away."

"I am terribly sorry, Miss Clarissa," I said, drawing Jaspar aside. "I'm certain he meant you no harm."

"I shall have that animal destroyed."

I gasped as Oliver cried out, "No, Clarissa. Please, Uncle Justin, he is my friend."

Lord Barkham quickly sized up the situation and took Clarissa—who was by this time in tears—in his arms.

"You don't mean that. You are far too sweet to harm anything, much less a poor stupid dog." I was about to protest but his eyes told me to remain silent. "The dress can be cleaned and you undoubtedly will find it dreary anyway once you have your new wardrobe." He wiped the tears from her cheeks. "I think you had best take Oliver back to the nursery, Miss Miles."

I turned, taking Oliver in hand. Jaspar trotted along beside us as if nothing had happened.

From a distance I heard Clarissa say, "I swear, Justin, I shall tell Father and he will make her pay for this."

I wondered at how Lord Barkham could feel any affection toward her whatsoever. She was the most spoiled, cruel girl I had ever known. Was he so blind that he could not see how selfish and insipid she was? Well, it was not my bother. But it made me angry to see him protect her when she should have been whipped.

I took great care getting ready for my dinner with Thomas. I was disappointed that it was Charlotte's evening off, for I would indeed have liked her to fix my hair, but Thomas was used to the braided coil, so I doubted he would make comment. I had only one misgiving about the evening that lay ahead. I had certainly not forgotten that my previous visit to Thomas's house had been on the night that I had been so brutally attacked. But, I reminded myself, that had not been on the path to his cottage, but rather within the halls of Camberleigh itself. I shuddered at the remembrance of it all. If only I could put it out of my mind, I thought. But I knew that it was something I would never forget.

I followed the same route as before, past the rose garden and through the arbor to the woods beyond. Once I nearly shrieked as I heard the rustle of leaves behind me, but I swung about to see that it was only a small rabbit scampering by.

The door of the cottage stood open. I ventured in and looked about, but my host was nowhere in sight. I moved to the fireplace, which had several large pots hanging over it from which emanated gurgles and smells and the promise of a tasty dinner.

Suddenly arms gripped my shoulders.

I screamed and whirled about. It was Thomas.

"Serena, I didn't mean to startle you. I had just gone to fetch some flowers to shower on my fair princess as she arrived, but I see I was too late."

"Oh Thomas," I cried, "I thought . . ." I began to sob.

He pulled me to him and laid my head against his shoulder, holding me fast until my tears stopped. Taking my face in his hands, he kissed the lids of my eyes and then dried them gently with a handkerchief from his pocket.

"Serena, did you think I was someone else?"

"I . . . yes . . . I mean no. I was just frightened," I replied, regaining my composure.

"Come sit down here and let me get you a brandy. It will ease your nerves."

"Brandy? Why did you say brandy?" I asked nervously. I could feel my muscles becoming taut once again.

"Well, I just thought it would relax you. But if you prefer I shall offer you a glass of wine."

"Yes I would prefer wine, Thomas," I said, relaxing into a chair near the fire.

He poured glasses for us both. He handed me mine, then lifted his in the air.

"A toast to the fairest of them all, my princess Serena."

"Well, if I am to be your princess, then you must be my prince," I replied, "so I shall toast to the kindest of them all, my prince Thomas."

He settled into the chair opposite mine. "Did you and Master Oliver have a pleasant afternoon?"

"It was pleasant indeed—until our mishap." I proceeded to recount our run-in with Clarissa.

"Good for Jaspar," Thomas said, refilling his glass. "That girl could do with a little muddying."

"Were you ever her tutor?" I asked.

"No. Actually, that I not be was one of the conditions of my employ—*my* condition, that is. I had had quite enough of spoiled young ladies in my last position."

"I see." It seemed that Thomas shared my low opinion of Miss Clarissa, but I thought I had better change the subject. "You mentioned that you had gone to London last week. Did you visit your father?"

"Why do you ask that, Serena?" An odd look appeared on his face.

"Well, you told me that your father lived in London, and I just thought it natural that you might spend some time with him."

"Actually, Serena, my father died when I was there."

"Oh Thomas, no," I cried. "You didn't mention that he had been ill."

"He hadn't," he said, rising to stir one of the pots in the fire. "It was very sudden."

"How dreadful for you. But how fortunate that you were there. It must be a great comfort to you to know that he died seeing you."

"Yes, it was, Serena." I wanted to share with him that my understanding sprang from my own sense of recent loss, but that would have revealed far more than I was at liberty to do, so I remained silent. "Anyway, let us not talk of sadness. Life is for living, they say," Thomas said.

I nodded in agreement.

"I understand that there are to be great festivities at the hall tomorrow evening," he ventured.

"Yes," I replied. "The Earl and Lady Camberleigh are giving a party in honor of Clarissa. There have been a number of the Earl's business associates staying at the hall of late, and I imagine they feel it would be a good opportunity to launch their daughter into society."

"Yes, I had heard that this was to be her season—but for

what reason I don't know, since she is all but betrothed to that fellow Barkham."

I looked up, surprised that that was common knowledge.

"Wouldn't it be great fun to show up as uninvited guests?" Thomas said, a twinkle in his eyes. "Can you imagine Lady Camberleigh? *That* would send her running for that vial of hers."

"Actually, Thomas, I was invited," I said mildly.

"Oh, but of course. The Earl's mother would see to that. And I'm certain they feel it would not be improper for you to provide a bit of amusement, shall we say, for their guests."

"What do you mean?"

"Well, you can't believe that they have invited you just to sit there and be charming. Let me put it this way—I doubt that the Earl's business associates are gentlemen, Serena."

"How do you know that, Thomas?" I replied, indignant at what he was suggesting.

"Trust me. I know."

"Even if you were right, what could happen at a dinner party? Why, if I thought there was the slightest chance—"

"Perhaps we had best change the subject."

"Actually, I have no intention of attending anyway," I said half under my breath. I thought it best not to get into a description of my session with Lady Camberleigh.

Thomas rose and began setting the table.

I was disturbed that the two of us should be sparring, particularly over something that seemed so unpleasant—and inane. I could not help but be disconcerted by his comments about the guests at Camberleigh, but I did not understand why he would cast such a peculiar light on my role at the dinner party.

We managed during dinner—which was again a delicious stew—to divert our conversation to more mundane topics, but there was no question that our earlier conversation had put a damper on the evening.

"I suppose I should be getting you back, Serena, although I must say that I hate to part."

"It has been a lovely evening. But let us not allow Clarissa's silly dinner party to put distance between us. You have become a dear friend and I would hate to think of it causing a rift between us."

"Serena, forgive me. Perhaps I am just jealous thinking of the eyes of all those men on my fair princess. I must admit that I would like you to think of me as something more than a dear friend."

I gathered my shawl and we walked back to the hall arm in arm, again guided through the darkness by the light of a candle Thomas carried. As we reached the rose garden I looked up and again saw the figure in a dimly lighted window of the north wing tower.

"Thomas, look," I said, pointing up. But as I did so the light went out.

"What are you pointing at?"

"There in the north wing. There was someone in the window."

"I don't see anyone, Serena. Besides, that part of the castle has been closed for years."

"It's gone now. But I've seen it before. It's strange, but it's almost as though whoever it is, is watching me."

"I think my fair princess may have an overactive imagination."

"I really have seen someone," I insisted.

"I believe you, but I wouldn't be overly concerned. Perhaps they are opening some of the rooms again. I'm sure there is a very simple explanation."

"I suppose," I said, still looking up at the tower.

As we reached the door that lead to the back staircase, I was suddenly filled with dread.

"What is the trouble, Serena? You seem tense. You're not still worrying about your phantom in the window, are you?"

"No. I just loathe moving about in the house so late. It's very dark and . . ."

"Take this candle. It will guide you safely to your room."

Thomas took me in his arms and his lips found mine. His kiss was soft and gentle and I found myself responding to his touch.

"You are a very desirable woman, Serena. I would be less than truthful if I did not admit that you rouse my senses. But I know that you are young and inexperienced, and I would never want to do anything to hurt you. You know that, don't you?"

"Yes, Thomas," I replied honestly.

"Good. Then let me see you in before my senses overtake my best intentions."

As Thomas opened the door for me, he whispered, "Good night, my princess."

"Good night, my prince," I called back.

My heart was pounding like a hammer as I quietly stole up the staircase. I was careful to shield the candle with my hand, knowing that the light was my most important weapon. I was moving along the corridor and had almost reached my room when I saw another flickering candle moving toward me. I froze, spellbound. I could feel the blood rushing through my veins. The split second that I had to run or scream before this person reached me passed without my uttering a cry or making a move.

"Well, Miss Miles, isn't it a bit late to be wandering about unescorted, or have I chanced upon you returning from a tryst?"

"Lord . . . Barkham," I choked out, trying to find my voice, "you startled me."

"I see that. Or perhaps it was that you are unnerved at being discovered."

"I don't know what you are implying, but in any case my comings and goings are no business of yours."

"That is not necessarily true. Everything that goes on in this house is my business."

"I would say that that is perhaps a bit arrogant, Lord Barkham." I was becoming annoyed once again by his haughtiness. "At least until you and Miss Clarissa are wed."

He smiled that insidious smile that I had seen so often.

"That may be true. But as I am not even yet betrothed, that means that I am still available for the advances of one as lovely as yourself."

"Really, Lord Barkham," I snapped. "I find your impudence insulting. Now if you will let me pass, I should like to continue on to my room."

"By all means, but somehow I sense that you are not as innocent as you pretend."

I saw no reason to respond to this latest insult, and I brushed past him and marched swiftly to my room. I flung myself on my bed and sobbed I know not if from fear, anger, or pure sorrow. I had come to this house to be in the care and protection of my family, and what I had found instead was nothing but abuse—verbal and physical—of the vilest nature. I wished I had never left Seven Oaks. At least there I had a few friends. I might have been reduced to physical labor, but I would have had my pride. Camberleigh seemed determined to strip me of all I held dear in life.

Jaspar climbed up on the bed and lay with his head close to mine. I put my arm about him, thinking that here was the one thing that I knew I could trust.

Chapter Six

WHEN I awoke the next morning I realized—on top of all the other things on my mind—that tonight was Clarissa's dinner party. I also saw that I had fallen asleep without removing my clothes. I got out of bed and went to my dressing table. My eyes were red and puffy and my dress in a mass of wrinkles. My basin had not yet been changed, and I splashed cold water on my face to try to freshen my senses. I had changed into a robe and was braiding my hair when Charlotte arrived.

"Morning' miss."

"Good morning, Charlotte."

"'Tis a gray day—a mite of a chill in the air. Better be dressin' warm."

"Thank you, I will."

I continued working on my braid in silence. Charlotte removed the basin and took Jaspar down to Robbie.

When she returned I was still seated in front of the dressing table reworking my braid, which I did not seem to be able to get to perform properly.

"I don't mean to be intrudin', but you seem upset this mornin'. If I can be of 'elp I would be honored. Sometimes just talkin' can help you see somethin' more clear like."

"Thank you, Charlotte," I replied, touched by her concern. "There really isn't anything you can do. But just your offering is a great comfort."

"Pretty young thing like you should be out havin' a grand

time with lots of admirers showerin' you with sweet nothin's instead of being cooped up here cryin'."

"Well, that doesn't seem to be my destiny. My father always believed that our destinies were preordained."

"Sorry, but I don't know what that means."

"It means that what happens to us here on earth has all been marked out for us—that it is part of a set plan that you can't change no matter what you do."

"If that be true, I don't think I want to know me plan. It may be too late for me, but I'd like to think Robbie ain't always gonna have to tend at the stables and mop the kitchens. Not that that ain't respectable, but I know there's no future in it."

"Charlotte," I asked, turning to face her, suddenly stuck with an idea. "Do you think Robbie would like to learn his letters?"

"O' course miss. But I can't be makin' it on just me own wages what with me mum to take care of an' all."

"What if he could learn when he has some free time? Not every day, but a few times a week?"

"But where's he gonna do that, an' what's it gonna be costin'?"

"He'll do it right here in this room, and it won't cost anything."

Charlotte looked down at me, a puzzled frown on her brow.

"I will teach him, Charlotte. It's true that I'm not a tutor, but I have had experience teaching children their letters before. And Robbie is such a willing boy I would guess that he would learn quickly."

"T'would be a miracle, miss, but why would you be wantin' to give your time—and for nothing?"

"Robbie does me a great service by watching over Jaspar, and I can't afford to pay him. Don't you see, this could be my way of compensating him for his assistance?"

"He'd be thrilled, he would, and I would be ever so grateful. With some learnin' he might be able to work 'imself up to stable manager or e'en better someday."

"Then it's settled. You speak to him and let me know. Perhaps we could start with one or two meetings a week."

"You're an angel, miss," Charlotte said, coming over and

flinging her arms about me. "Maybe someday I can repay you for your kindness."

My own mood lifted as I saw the joy in Charlotte's face. She remained a few more minutes and then left, bursting to tell the news to Robbie. I had to admit that I looked far more refreshed than when I had first awakened, and it was even with some anticipation that I now looked forward to seeing Oliver and Thomas.

Oliver was a wreath of smiles as I entered his room.

"Well, look at you," I said, my eyes taking in the new shirt and loose-fitting breeches he was wearing.

"Fiona brought them. She said to tell you it was all she has had time to complete, but she thought you might like the surprise."

"Well she was right," I said. "They look wonderful. How do they feel?"

"They feel good and the breeches don't hurt my leg like my others, but . . ."

"But what, Oliver?"

"What do you think Father will say?"

"He may be taken aback at first," I said cautiously. "But I am certain he will come to see how well they suit you."

His eyes clouded, and I could see my assurance had not convinced him. I hoped that I would be able to say something to the Earl before the two met face to face.

We breakfasted on eggs and freshly smoked pork. Mrs. Scoapes arrived and gave Oliver his medicine. Her antipathy toward me seemed to have grown since delivering what she must have known was an invitation to this evening's party. Determined as I was not to attend, it now struck me that perhaps I should have lain abed all day so that there would be no question of my illness. But then that would have been unfair to Oliver—and selfishly I wanted to see Thomas.

Thomas was wearing a new black jacket, and I thought how smart he looked as he rose to greet us.

"Well, my princess and Master Oliver."

"Good morning, Thomas," I said, blushing slightly at this endearment, for this time it seemed not part of a game.

"Master Oliver, there appears to be a change in you today.

Let us see. Is it your hair? Yes, that must be it," he said, winking at me.

"No, Mr. Masters, 'tis my clothes," replied Oliver.

"Ah yes, now I see. Well, I would say it is a considerable improvement. Very stylish indeed."

Oliver looked pleased that his new attire had been favorably noticed.

"I shall leave you two to your studies, then."

"Why don't you stay for a while. It will give you an opportunity to see how well Master Oliver is progressing with his studies."

"Oliver, would you mind?"

"Of course not, Serena," he replied, his eyes smiling back at mine.

I took a seat at the rear of the schoolroom. Again I was genuinely impressed by how far advanced Oliver was in his lessons for his age. I thought of Robbie, who although a number of years Oliver's senior, would have to begin with the most rudimentary of lessons. He would never, I was certain, possess the knowledge that Oliver would in his lifetime, but if I could impart only a small thirst for wisdom I would feel that my efforts had been rewarded.

I only realized how much time had passed when a maid arrived with a luncheon tray. I had never before thought about what Thomas did when Oliver and I would break to take our trays in the nursery, but I realized now that he must dine alone most days.

"Well, Master Oliver, I suppose that is quite enough for this morning. We shall resume again for a brief spell this afternoon."

"Thomas," I ventured, "would you care to bring your tray to the nursery and have your midday meal with us?"

Oliver looked slightly aghast at my suggestion, and I quickly added, "On the provision, of course, that we not concern ourselves whatsoever with Oliver's lessons."

"I cannot think of more charming company. And if I mention geography or mathematics even once you may banish me from the room."

We were a happy group. Oliver and I regaled in laughter over Thomas's recounting of the antics of the three young ladies who had been his prior tutoring charges. I was sad that I could not share some thoughts and events of my own past, for I knew that Oliver would delight in hearing of the ships that took port in our small coastal town and of the seafaring tales that I had heard since childhood, but I realized it was too dangerous to pursue. I trusted Thomas, but I had given her ladyship my oath and I would hold fast to it.

I returned to my room after our luncheon, leaving Thomas and Oliver to resume their studies. As I passed the main stairs I heard great commotion from below, which I assumed were the preparations for this evening.

"Oh miss, ye startled me," Fiona said, entering the room. "I didn't think ye was here. I was just bringin' your dress."

She lay the yards of deep gray velvet across the bed.

I fingered the sleeves gently, noting the fine quality of her work. "You have great talent with a needle, Fiona," I said. I wished that I could hold the dress lovingly in my arms, but it had such a somber aura that I could not feign great enthusiasm.

"Thank you for your kind words, but I think I know how you are feelin'. It's not a very festive gown, certainly not for a young girl like yourself. But I was just following my orders."

"I know Fiona. I just regret that you were put to this task at all."

I had little to do before rejoining Oliver for our afternoon stroll, so I picked up the book I had begun the other evening. As much as I did not want to, my attention could not help straying to the evening's festivities. My only regret in not attending was that I would not see Anne, for I had warmed to her so quickly the other day. I could imagine Lady Camberleigh sitting smugly, watching me drown in the gray velvet she had so conveniently designed for me, while Clarissa—who would undoubtedly be gowned in something frothy and stylish—sat whimpering at the flattery of the honored guests. Well, I wouldn't give her the satisfaction.

Try as I did I could not put that infernal dinner party out of my mind even when Oliver and I went off to our secret garden. I would be glad when the day was over and any temptation I felt about attending had been resolved.

The dress lay where I had left it when I returned to my room with Jaspar in tow. The weather had cleared in the middle of the day, and as I went to the window and looked down on the rose garden I saw the sun would be setting in a golden sky. The air was crisp and I could not help thinking that Clarissa would have a beautiful evening to be launched into society.

I turned in response to a knock at the door.

"Come in, Charlotte," I called.

"Well, I don't know who Charlotte is, but I was longing to see you, Serena."

"Anne!" I exclaimed, moving to greet my unexpected guest. "What are you doing here?"

"Well, unless I am mistaken, Clarissa's big party is this evening."

"You know perfectly well what I mean, Anne. This is not the part of the house that . . ."

She laughed. "I arrived about an hour ago and I had to talk to three maids and one butler before I found out where they were keeping you."

"And now you've found me."

"Aren't you going to ask me to sit down?"

"I'm sorry, of course."

"What is this I see," she said, nodding to the dress lying on the bed. "I hope you don't mind my saying so, but it's a bit dreary. Certainly not you at all. I hope it is not new."

"It is the gown I was to wear were I to attend the dinner this evening."

"What are you talking about? Where is the dress I gave you? Wasn't it right? And what do you mean *were* you to attend. Of course you are attending. You received the invitation, didn't you?"

"I just prefer not to attend. Couldn't we just leave it at that?" I asked, sitting down by the writing table.

"No we can't. At least I can't, because I don't believe you."

"The invitation did come from the Earl," I began with a sigh. "But Lady Camberleigh made it quite clear that I had not been on *her* guest list—in fact she said as much. She insisted, however, that I attend. That dress on the bed is one she designed so that I would not disgrace her at the party."

"I see," Anne replied, getting to her feet and pacing back and forth. "Where is the dress I gave you?"

"There in the closet."

Moving over, she pulled it out. "Ouch," she said, putting her finger up to her mouth.

"Oh, I am so sorry. I forgot to tell you I had it just pinned."

"I will survive. Justin always says I have the constitution of a horse. How long will it take you to sew this?"

"What are you saying?"

"I'm saying that you *will* attend this dinner party and you will do it wearing this dress."

"Oh, I couldn't. Lady Camberleigh would be livid."

"You can and you will. Leave Maura to me."

"Anne, I just can't," I protested once more.

"Please, Serena—if only for me. You don't want to leave me to fend for myself with some pompous oaf they will undoubtedly seat next to me?" I shook my head. "Then start sewing. I shall come by just before I going downstairs and I shall expect to see you fully dressed." I did not reply. "Who is this, by the way, who keeps sniffing about my boots?"

"That is Jaspar."

"Well, Jaspar, watch over your mistress here and be sure she gets to work with her needle. I'm off, now that I see I have left you under capable eyes."

I gathered the folds of white organza on my lap, opening the sewing kit that I had left on the table. I had to smile at Anne's forcefulness. A short time before, I thought nothing could have convinced me to attend this dinner, and now here she had me sewing not the dress that was intended but the one she had lent me.

I started at a knock at the door, thinking Anne could not possibly have returned so quickly.

"'Tis only me," said Charlotte, bustling into the room with a tray. "What's that you be sewin'?"

I held the dress up carefully.

"Oooh, miss, I swear that's the most beautiful dress I ever saw. I don't remember it in your wardrobe."

"It's not mine. It was lent to me by Lady Ormsby for the dinner party this evening."

"Oh, miss, I didn't know ye was to attend or I wouldn't 'ave brought your tray. 'Tis going to be a grand affair. Molly's so excited she can barely keep from burstin', seein' as how she'll be helpin' to serve. Ye'll be the grandest lady there, in that dress. Would you be wantin' me to do your hair?"

Charlotte was so enthusiastic that I felt I couldn't barely dampen her spirits by telling her that I was attending only against my best instincts. She would not have understood my reluctance to accept what she saw as a great honor.

"That is very kind, Charlotte. If you have the time I would indeed be pleased if you would dress my hair."

"I'll come back later, when you've had a chance to bathe. I just freshened your basin, so there should still be some heat in it."

I finished stitching the dress and bathed leisurely. I opened the small scented vial that had been my mother's and touched the fragrant liquid lightly to my temples and neck. I brushed my hair vigorously, pleased that I had taken time to wash it the previous day, for it now shone by the candle lights in the room. I donned my best petticoat and drew my robe about me, awaiting Charlotte's return.

"Miss, you should see the fancy fixin's downstairs," bubbled Charlotte as she reentered carrying three pale roses. "I know you not be havin' jewels, so I thought a few flowers in your hair might be just the thing."

"I can step into the dress, so I thought it best to have you do my hair first. I don't want to muss your creation."

As her agile fingers worked quickly on my coiffure, Charlotte told me that Robbie had been delighted by my offer and that since he had a free hour in the middle of the day, perhaps he could meet with me just before I returned to Oliver in the nursery.

I agreed.

Charlotte not only had a real ability at dressing hair, but a strong aesthetic sense, and when she had tucked the three single roses into my hair even I had to murmur approval at my own reflection.

"An' now the dress."

As I stepped into it, I realized that the boots were not at all right, but the dress was a little long and would cover the worst of them. It buttoned in the back with the same seed pearl buttons which caught the folds of skirt. When Charlotte completed hooking the last, she turned me around to face her.

"Ye look like a fairy princess, miss," she said softly as I moved again to the mirror.

I hardly recognized the image that looked back at me. This was not the poor young girl who had arrived at Camberleigh only a few short weeks before. There was a regal quality to this reflection—and something else that I could not immediately put my finger on. Could it be that I had grown into a woman without even realizing it?

"I must be gettin' back down now, miss, there's a-plenty to do in the kitchens. Ye'll be the belle o' the ball, that's for sure."

I rose and kissed Charlotte on the cheek. "If I am, it will be in large part to you. Thank you so much."

It seemed an eternity before Anne arrived. Finally there came a knock at the door and she entered. When she saw me, she let out a loud gasp.

"What is wrong, Anne?"

"If I hadn't decided that we were to be fast friends, I think I would lock you in this room."

"What?" I said, perplexed.

"My dear Serena, I don't believe you have any idea how breathtaking you are. The other women at this dinner—myself included—don't stand a chance with you around. I cannot *wait* until Clarissa lays eyes on you. She'll be fuming."

"Anne, I don't think I had best go. It is easy for you. You are titled. You reside securely at one of the county's greatest estates. But I cannot afford to be embarrassed, much less to lose my position."

"Serena, do you trust me?"

"Well yes, but—"

"Then leave it to me. The guests will be gathering in the drawing room. Give me enough time to pay my respects before you come down."

Anne had left before I had had a chance to tell her how lovely she herself looked in a gown of peach-colored faille. She was a woman who knew instinctively what suited her best.

I waited until I thought if I remained in my room any longer Anne would come back up and fetch me. I patted Jaspar and bade him to be quiet until my return.

As I slowly descended the grand staircase, I felt the eyes of each ancestral earl watching me from their lofty heights. Giles stood in attention at the main entrance and had just opened the door as I reached the landing. I looked down and saw that there stood Lady Bellmore and her daughter. Any confidence I had been able to muster I felt quickly fade. They both glanced up at me, but whether from avoidance or lack of recognition, they made no acknowledgment. I continued my descent and then moved across the entrance hall to the doors of the drawing room.

Lady Camberleigh was speaking to an elegantly dressed gentleman with the blackest hair I had ever seen. He then made a small bow to her and headed in the direction of the Earl, who was deep in discussion with two other older gentlemen. I searched the room for Anne, but before my eyes could find her, Lady Camberleigh turned and we stood face to face.

She looked as though she had seen a ghost. She said nothing, her eyes exploring every inch of me.

"How dare you?" she finally spat. "This is an outrage. Where is the dress I designed for you? How dare you insult me this way?"

I reached up to my throat, searching for some response. Suddenly there was a hand on my elbow and a voice saying, "Serena dear, you look enchanting. I am so pleased that you favored me by wearing my dress. Now that it has found its rightful owner, I don't feel such a silly goose for letting my dressmaker convince me that it would be a divine addition to my wardrobe. Isn't it a charming dress, Maura? You must admit that it would make me look quite the dressed hen."

Lady Camberleigh's mouth opened, but before she could respond she was distracted by the return of the black-haired gentleman.

"You two ladies seem to be very proprietary over this mysterious vision of loveliness that has just entered our midst. Pray won't you introduce me?"

"Leave it to you, Robin, to be the first to attempt to corner the attention of this beauty who is throwing the rest of us lovelies into a jealous rage," Anne replied quickly. "Lord Robin Kelston, may I present Miss Serena Miles."

"Enchanted is hardly praise enough," he said, taking my

hand and brushing his lips lightly against it.

"Beware, Serena, Lord Kelston is considered quite the rogue in these parts. And if I hadn't seen him with his pants down many times I would scarce allow him to visit his attentions."

"Really, Anne," Lady Camberleigh said, obviously embarrassed by the turn of the conversation.

"Oh don't be silly, Maura. I only meant that we practically grew up together, and as a child Robin here had a naughty habit of going off to the bushes when he thought I wasn't looking."

Lord Kelston laughed. "I think, Miss Miles, that Lady Ormsby is going to be a lifelong reminder of my adolescent indiscretions, minor as they were. Won't you accompany me in search of a glass of sherry while I explain how I have reformed in adulthood?"

I smiled, excusing myself to Anne and Lady Camberleigh, and allowed—with great relief—Lord Kelston to lead me away. Unfortunately we were headed directly toward where Clarissa and Lord Barkham stood.

"Justin, old man, how have you been?" Lord Kelston asked. "Clarissa, you look devastating as always."

Wondering what barb Justin Barkham would throw this time to embarrass me with my new acquaintance, I looked up into his eyes. They held that solemn look that I knew so well, but there was nothing to betray his thoughts.

"Robin," he said, extending his hand. "It's good to see you. I understand that your estates are prospering. Miss Miles, I must say you have never looked more fetching."

"Oh, so you two know each other. Well, I should have known that I could not have been so fortunate as to have met Miss Miles before she was launched hereabouts."

"Launched?" blurted Clarissa, who up to now had stood silently gaping at me. "That's a laugh."

Lord Barkham put his hand to her arm. "Clarissa, don't you think we should go and speak with Lady Bellmore? Her daughter Priscilla has been looking this way."

"Surely," she said, smiling demurely. "Perhaps you would join us, Lord Kelston, for I am certain that Miss Miles will shortly be called away to the nursery." Without awaiting for a response, she turned and pulled Lord Barkham away. He leaned over and whispered something in her ear as they departed.

"What did she mean by that, Miss Miles?"

"She meant simply," I said, regarding him directly, "that my charge is in the nursery. I am the governess to Master Oliver."

He looked at me incredulously. And then suddenly he threw back his head and began to laugh.

"Lord Kelston, please," I implored, feeling my face grow hot as the entire room turned to see what he had found so amusing.

"Miss Miles—Serena—please forgive me," he said, his voice still filled with laughter. "But how it must gall Clarissa to have the governess as her great rival."

"I would hardly say *that,* Lord Kelston. That is kind, but Clarissa is a very pretty girl."

"Yes she is, but pale by comparison to you, my dear. And from the look in Justin's eyes I can see that he shares my sentiments."

"Lord Barkham is devoted to Miss Clarissa," I replied primly.

"If that is true, I am delighted since it means that there is one less to pursue your attentions."

I knew not how to respond. On the one hand I was greatly relieved and enormously flattered. On the other, I found it difficult to believe that Lord Kelston was being anything more than polite. Like it or not, he was a titled landowner and I was but a simple governess.

I noticed that Lord Barkham had moved over to speak to his sister. Anne, catching my eye, smiled in encouragement. Clarissa was holding court with Lady Bellmore and her painfully plain daughter. Clarissa was obviously carrying on about her attempt at embarrassing me, for they eyed me with haughty disdain.

Suddenly I realized that there was one face I missed here: my grandmother's. I hoped that she was not ill, for I had last seen her at Oliver's bedside well over a week before. Perhaps such gatherings as this were too taxing and she chose to remain in her quarters.

Giles announced that dinner was about to be served, and I saw that most of the guests were drifting toward the dining room. The Earl, who had been occupied in various conversa-

CAMBERLEIGH

tions since my arrival, now moved over to take the arm of Lady Camberleigh. She seemed to have grown bored with her conversation with the Bellmores.

"Won't you join me, Miss Miles. I can't think of a more charming dinner companion." It was Lord Kelston. I took his arm, relieved that I should not have to enter the dining hall on my own devices.

The room was resplendent with settings of crystal, china, and silver, all of which bore the Camberleigh crest. I thought that Anne must have had a part in the decorations as flowers of every hue and variety filled the vases and porcelain cachepots which were dotted about the room.

As we entered, Lady Camberleigh clutched Lord Kelston by the other arm and said, "Lord Kelston, I have chosen you to be in the honored position at my right. Miss Miles, you shall be seated along there next to the Granforths." She gestured to a place at the end of the table where sat a plain-looking couple. I had noticed them earlier, and I had assessed they had been invited out of propriety, not because of their great favor in the Camberleigh household.

"Oh Maura, I beseech you," Lord Kelston put in quickly, "your charms have long ago been captured by Richard and try as I would I am certain that I could never woo you away from one so powerful as he. But I am but a lost soul whose vices are still unknown to Miss Miles, and I might receive some small compliment from her were I to have good fortune. Won't you indulge me and let me sit near her while we dine. I shall be ever in your debt."

If Lady Camberleigh could have poured scalding grease over me at that moment, I believe she would have. But her sense of etiquette prevailed and giving a most alluring smile to Lord Kelston, she nodded replying, "Do ask Lord Granforth if I might not hear more about his trading plans with the New World."

As I was led down the long table I was happy to see that my grandmother had joined the festivities after all. She was at the center of the table on the opposite side. Her pale violet eyes searched my face and for a moment I thought I saw some small flicker of recognition. Could there be something about my present appearance that made her move closer to trusting what had been written in my mother's letter?

"Your ladyship," I nodded, acknowledging her regard.

Her eyes followed us until we had been seated, and I quite thought they would remain on me for the evening had not the Earl—seeing that all the guests were seated—risen to present a toast.

"As you all know, when Clarissa turns eighteen this autumn she shall enter her season. I should like to toast her now. To my daughter—who I know shall set London on its heels—the fairest of them all, Clarissa."

"Hear, hear," called out other voices, and the tinkling of crystal goblets as they kissed in air could be heard throughout the room. My eye caught the glance of Lord Barkham, who, I noticed, had raised his glass high but had not followed suit and drunk of it in celebration. I thought that quite odd, but then there was no predicting what that man would do or say next.

The meal commenced with a smoked fish that I did not recognize but found to be flaky and sweet.

"Tell me, Serena—if I may call you that—how did Richard, the Earl, manage to find you," inquired Lord Kelston. "And if you tell me that you were engaged in some other household I shan't believe you, for you are scarcely old enough not to be governed yourself."

I laughed. "I hoped it wouldn't show. Actually I had not met the Earl before my arrival here."

"That's unusual." I must have looked puzzled. "Well, it's quite well known in these parts that the Earl has always been the one to employ the governesses—and a fair lot he has had, I'll say. Her ladyship is gossiped to have a weakness, shall we say, where the child is concerned."

It was bad enough, I thought, that Oliver had to be ignored by his mother in this very household, but that this was open knowledge I found distasteful—and tragic.

"To answer your question, Lord Kelston, my grandmother is acquainted with her ladyship, the Earl's mother."

"But then how . . . ?"

"My family has recently suffered some financial reversals and I was forced to seek employment. Her ladyship generously offered me a position in this house."

"Ah. That explains it. You are far too elegant to have come naturally to the role of governess. If I may be personal, your bones, your skin, your hair—even the figure that is only vaguely disguised under that gown—are all traitors to your heritage."

I smiled, thinking how I only wished what he said were true, for then perhaps I might take my rightful place in this household.

My dinner partner now turned politely and engaged Lady Granforth in conversation. She had until now sat silently picking at her food. She was a pleasant but vacuous-appearing woman who was obviously only comfortable when her husband was at her side, for she continuously glanced down to where he sat, watching to see if he was enjoying his conversation with Lady Camberleigh.

I partook heartily of every course, savoring the tender meats and delectable sauces that I knew Cook had been preparing for days. The men, having engaged in idle banter too long, had turned the conversation to business.

"Gentlemen, the only answer is taxation," I heard the Earl say. "Kelston there is the only one of us whose profits are not down this year."

"I didn't say that, Richard," replied one of the older gentlemen. "It's true that my profits are down over last year, but we were light on rain this spring, which most assuredly had an effect on the crop."

"George's point is well taken," added the other older man I had seen in the drawing room. "Besides that I've made some investments—additional land and equipment, which I hadn't done last. All things considered, if I hadn't made those I might be even."

"Don't let Barkham hear you say that," the Earl replied. "I tell him that we must institute a tax and he comes back and tells me that we should invest. He claims that the reason we are off is that those farmers can't continue to use the equipment we've provided. Well, I say we won't get rid of the equipment, we'll get rid of the tenants. And we'll tax them right up front so they know where they stand."

"Richard, when was the last time you visited any of those

131

farms?" Lord Barkham put in angrily.

"I don't have to make house calls, Justin, to know what the return is on my investment."

"No, but it might give you some understanding about the condition that those people are living in. Some of them were so sick from the cold last winter from not having adequate wood or coal that they have not been able to work at full capacity since."

"You see, you are admitting that they are not producing in full. I do believe if you had your way you would have me riding about carrying a little black boy dispensing medications. My patience is wearing thin on this matter. When you understand the difference taxation will make, I'm certain you will come to your senses."

Lord Barkham had become more and more agitated during this conversation, and although far from completely understanding the issues, I had to admit that there was logic in some of what he said.

"Really, gentlemen," interjected Lady Camberleigh, "don't you think that you could refrain from this conversation at the dinner table. I am certain that the ladies are not at all interested."

"Perhaps we should ask them, Lady Camberleigh," responded Lord Barkham. "Miss Miles, what do you think of this matter?"

I was aghast that he should address me, of all people, for a response. He seemed to delight in making me uncomfortable, and I felt a blush of embarrassment as all eyes turned in my direction.

"As you know, Lord Barkham, these matters are hardly of my concern," I replied in as strong a voice as I could muster. "But since you have asked I can only give an opinion based on what I know." I gazed at him coolly. "Even the best farmer is only as good as his land and equipment. It seems to me that illness, inadequate supplies, a shortage of rain, all would take a toll on the crops and therefore the profits. Assuming all things were equal I suppose that there is a desperate need on the part of these farmers for training. The most modern equipment lies fallow in hands that do not know how to use it. I'm talking about education, not only for the farmers themselves but for their sons who shall one day be building and—hopefully—expanding on the groundwork that their ancestors have laid."

Were it not for the sound of someone clearing their throat, one could have heard a pin drop.

"Well, we must toast a very pretty speech from our little governess," said Lady Camberleigh, her eyes glazed as she stared daggers into mine. "But my husband shall be very cross with you, my dear, for not championing his cause. Perhaps you have not known his wrath before, but I can assure you that it will do nothing for that pretty skin of yours."

"Maura, that's quite enough." The Earl's scar seemed to stand full out from his face.

"Well, I for one say bravo," I heard Anne say. "It is far too often that we women are taken for having no better thought than what we are to wear or how to dress our hair, when we really often have important ideas to contribute. Don't you agree, Clarissa dear?"

Clarissa, who appeared more confused than anything, fingered a tendril of hair and replied, "Oh, yes, of course."

The arrival of dessert could not have been more timely. Lord Kelston appeared amused by it all and Lady Granforth continued to chat on as though nothing had happened. Only Lord Barkham continued to regard me with those unfathomable solemn eyes.

"Serena." Lord Kelston turned to me again. "Might I ask if you would go for a ride in the countryside with me one day soon? Knowing Lady Camberleigh, the men shall all retire to the library after dinner and I will not have an opportunity to see you again this evening. I would be most flattered if you would say yes."

"I would be delighted, Lord Kelston, but I fear t'would not be possible. My looking after Master Oliver leaves little time for recreation. Nor do I think Lady Camberleigh would approve."

"But you must have time off. A day—or an evening—perchance?"

"My days are dedicated to Master Oliver. Frankly, I have not inquired about time off. It simply has never occurred to me, since I have been here such a short period."

Evelyn Grey

"Well, we should rectify that, or I shall accuse Richard of treating you as a tenant farmer."

I laughed at the thought. "Considering this evening's conversation I would say that that would not fall on welcoming ears."

"Leave it to me."

I left the dining room in dread, for I could not imagine being incarcerated with Clarissa, Lady Camberleigh and the rest of the ladies for even a brief spell. My only salvation would be Anne.

"I shall leave you here, then, knowing that I shall see you soon." With that Lord Kelston turned to join the gentlemen in the library.

Happily, Anne found me just as we were to enter the drawing room. "Well, it seems that you have made quite a hit with Lord Kelston."

"He appears pleasant," I returned.

"Oh, he is a darling—and more. Robin could charm the petticoats off almost anyone. And that's the problem. He usually does."

"Has he ever been married?"

"No. He and my brother have always been too busy—but for different reasons. Mayfair is well maintained, but Justin works hard to keep it so. Robin, on the other hand, is so prosperous that he needn't ever dirty his hands. Which has left him an inordinate amount of time with which to break many a young girl's heart. Actually I always thought that Clarissa would be a good match for him. She's just innocuous enough not to care about his philanderings."

"But what of—?" I stopped myself, for Mrs. Granforth had joined us.

"Amelia, it is nice to see you looking so well."

"And you too, Anne. Although I have often thought how lonely it must be for you at Mayfair with your brother here or in London so often."

"It is at times, but I have my flowers—and now I've found a new friend. You two became acquainted at dinner, I believe."

"Yes. It's a pleasure my dear," Lady Granforth replied. "I must say that I admired what you said. I quite agree with you,

134

though I would never have the nerve to come out with it. And I do believe that if I did, my George would fall over in a faint."

Anne and I both laughed at the image of a swooning Lord Granforth.

"If you ladies will excuse me," I said, "I am a bit tired and must rise early with Master Oliver. Anne, thank you so much for everything, and I would love to chat further, but would you present my excuses to Lady Camberleigh?"

"Of course," she replied, knowing full well that I was desperate to avoid a scene in the confines of the drawing room. "We'll see each other very soon."

As I started up the master staircase I saw that my grandmother, with Giles's assistance, was also retiring early. We reached the landing simultaneously.

"Ah, Miss Miles," she said, looking up at me. "I would quite have expected you to be downstairs with the gentlemen, battling out the merits and demerits of this taxation issue."

I flushed. "I do apologize, your ladyship. I did not mean to cause any embarrassment."

"On the contrary, Miss Miles, I rather enjoyed it. Affairs of the mind can oft be as important as affairs of the heart. Do not abandon them."

She turned and moved away, Giles assisting her frail frame. I felt tears well in my eyes. If this woman never accepted me as her granddaughter, I might at least one day know that I had her respect for my mind, and that would mean more to me than anything in the world.

Jaspar was asleep when I entered my room, but he rose, stretched, and ambled over to greet me. I was more tired than I had realized as I took off the gown and placed it gently across a chair. It was the most beautiful dress that I would ever wear, I thought, and certainly the most beautiful of the evening. Clarissa had looked enchanting in an amber gown that matched the color of her eyes. And the emeralds worn by Lady Camberleigh must have cost a small fortune. But there was something about my dress that set it apart. It really was a dress befitting a princess. I wished that Thomas had been able to have seen me in it.

As I drifted off to sleep I shuddered a bit when I thought

of what gossip must be going on amongst the women in the drawing room. I took some solace that Anne was on hand to protect my good name.

I awakened once in the middle of the night, thinking that I heard something outside my door. I heard Jaspar stir also, but being an even greater coward than I, he simply snuggled closer to the bedstead. I arose, starting a bit as my feet touched the cold floor, and crept silently to the door. If someone was lurking on the other side, I did not really want to know; on the other hand, I knew that I must open it, for if it were my attacker we must come face to face. My hand turned the knob slowly, palms sweating. I looked out into the corridor, but saw no one. I listened a few moments for the sound of footsteps. But there was nothing but the distant voices of the men from the floor below. I closed and locked the door and returned to my bed, where I quickly fell back to sleep.

Chapter Seven

I AWAKENED to a steady knocking at the door. "It's me, miss," called out Charlotte. I rose and opened it.

"I didn't want to be disturbin' you, but you went and locked your door again."

"That's all right Charlotte. What time is it?"

"'Tis early miss an' I don't think much o' the household will be up before noon, so you can pretend I weren't here and go back to bed."

"I am certain that Oliver will be up and about, so it is time I rose anyway."

Charlotte placed the basin on the nightstand. "Well, tell me, was it grand? Did you be gettin' plenty to eat? I bet ye was the loveliest one there."

I laughed at Charlotte's boundless curiosity.

"It was a lovely party," I replied. "And you can tell Cook that the food was absolutely delicious."

"Oh, she'll be pleased to 'ere that. Seems a pity after all them fixin's that it's all over so quick, but then that's kinda like life, I guess."

I marveled that in Charlotte's own simple way she was often capable of drawing the most deft and unexpected analogies. If Robbie had inherited any of her reasoning ability I should find it pleasurable to teach him.

I put my hair back in its normal braided bun, donned my brown merino and headed for the nursery.

Oliver was in the nursery already having his breakfast when I arrived.

"Well, it almost looks as though you are actually anxious to get to your lessons this morning," I said.

"I don't have lessons today, Serena. Don't you remember it's Sunday?"

"So it is, and I must admit it slipped my mind." I was suddenly disappointed that I should not be seeing Thomas. "Well, then, what shall you and I do today?"

"I am to spend the day with Grandmama. Mrs. Scoapes said for me to tell you that your services would no longer be needed."

"What?" I gasped. Surely my appearance and my little speech at the dinner had not been such to merit my dismissal? It was beyond comprehension, yet my heart was beating fast and my breath was short. I didn't want Oliver to see my agitation, so I quickly excused myself and went in search of Mrs. Scoapes. I finally found the housekeeper just exiting Lady Camberleigh's quarters.

"Mrs. Scoapes," I said, "I have just had some disturbing news that perhaps you can clarify. Master Oliver said that you told him to say that my services were no longer needed, is that correct?"

"Yes, it is. Master Oliver will be spending the day with her ladyship."

"Ah. So you meant just for today?"

"Obviously you thought I had implied more," she retorted. "One doesn't usually draw conclusions unless those conclusions are there to be reached. Are we about to lose yet another governess, Miss Miles?"

You would love me to say yes, I thought. This woman was the most odious I have ever known. But I bit my lip and replied sweetly, "It only appears to be you who have reached the wrong conclusion, Mrs. Scoapes."

I turned on my heel and returned to the nursery and bade Oliver good day and then went back to my room, wondering what I should do with my newly found free time. I called for a tray and breakfasted leisurely, beginning again the book that I kept starting and stopping. In late morning there was a knock at the door. I opened it to see Anne.

"Surprised to see me?" she asked, gaily bustling into the room.

"Surprised but delighted! I thought you had returned to Mayfair last evening."

"Well, it was late and Justin was in no humor to see his little sister home, so I decided to stay the weekend."

"I can't tell you how much I appreciate your lending me that dress."

"I didn't lend it to you, dear. It's a gift. You don't think I could take it back after I've seen how devastating it was on you. Didn't you love the expression on Maura's face?"

"Frankly, it terrified me." I paused, gesturing for Anne to sit down. "Do you know Lady Camberleigh well?"

"Why do you ask?"

"Well, I find her to be very strange indeed. At times I have the sense that she is not well, but it's nothing specific."

"I see," said Anne thoughtfully. "You know of course that she suffered a complete breakdown when Oliver was born?" I nodded. "Well there is no question that she has not been the same since. But I often wonder whether that is the real source of her problems. Maura was, shall we say, a bit odd long before Oliver was born. Of course, I was a very young girl then, really a child myself, but I remember once being here with Justin and my father, and I found a dead sparrow out in the garden. I brought it to her to ask her if we might bury it, and she flung it from my hands and screaming fled the room. The incident obviously left quite an impression on me."

"Perhaps she is simply of faint heart. There are probably many who would not be able to deal with the sight of a small dead bird."

"You may be right, but there have been other things. I don't know," she said, shaking her head, "it's probably just my over-active imagination. As to her health, I simply do not know. I was surprised to see her looking so fit last evening, because Richard—the Earl—has told me that she has not been well for some time. She indulges quite heavily in brandy, but he is also convinced there is something more—some medication, perhaps, but he has no proof."

"Lady Camberleigh sometimes seems to be genuinely afraid

of the Earl," I noted. "And something happened with the past governesses. I don't know what, but there are all these inferences." Anne fingered the cup that sat now empty on my breakfast tray. "Listen to me, prattling away," I said, trying to make light of it. "I'm certain that you have better things to do than discuss this household."

"I did come here with another purpose in mind."

"What is that?" I asked.

"Well, I feel quite the conspirator. Lord Kelston has asked that I intercede on his behalf to see if you would join him on a coach ride this afternoon. I replied that I would be delighted, but only if I might accompany you. Needless to say that did not please him greatly, but what alternative did he have?"

"Since you have already arranged that, I trust that somehow you have already obtained permission from the Earl." I smiled at the almost brazen ingenuity of my new friend.

"Of course. And I know that since Oliver will be spending the day with his grandmother that you are perfectly free to join us. That is, if you care to."

"I do, but I fear that I shall prove quite a shock to Lord Kelston when he sees me stripped of all finery."

Anne regarded me closely, obviously seeing some truth in my statement.

"Might I look at your wardrobe?"

"Of course," I said, motioning to the closet. "But don't expect to find anything much there."

She came out of the closet carrying my pale blue muslin. "Put this on and I shall be back in a moment."

I changed into the dress wondering what great transformation Anne had in mind. In a few moments she was back, carrying several yards of silk ribbon and what I thought to be the most adorable bonnet I had ever seen.

"Now come over here," she said. She took the ribbon, which matched that on the bonnet, and deftly tied it about my waist, creating a large sash at the back. She told me to unbraid my hair. Once brushed, she let it fall softly at the sides and caught it at the back with another piece of ribbon.

"Now put on the bonnet."

I tied the bonnet in place and was quite taken aback at the effect that she had been able to achieve in a few moments.

"Anne, you are a genius," I said.

"Well not a genius perhaps, but I do think I have a good eye. More's the pity that I was born to wealth, for had I not been I might have some smart shop in London or Paris by now and be outfitting kings and queens."

"Would you like that?"

"I would enjoy the independence of it, though I certainly have that at Mayfair. And I do believe if one has a God-given talent that one should use it. But I am reasonably happy, at least for the time. And now that you have come, it shall take me away from my own problems."

It was strange. It was hard to think of Anne as someone with problems. She seemed so content, so assured. But then my mother had often said that we can never be sure about the private anguish of our fellow man and thus we must not judge too harshly.

"Let us not keep Lord Kelston waiting," Anne said, breaking my reverie, "or he shall think that I am retaliating for all those nasty tricks he used to play on me as a child."

I fetched my reticule and we hurried down the corridor and descended the main staircase to the forecourt, where Lord Kelston's coach awaited us. The coach was not as striking as Lord Barkham's brougham, but grander in scale and design, with hand-painted murals on the doors that were almost Venetian in flavor.

The driver who sat behind four beautifully groomed horses was an older man whose full whiskers glistened under a tall top hat.

"Miss Miles—Serena—might I say that you look charming, and I am delighted that Lady Ormsby has chosen to join us."

"Robin, don't be foolish. You know perfectly well that you would prefer it if I had taken to my bed suddenly with some indigestion. Unfortunately for you, my constitution is hearty, so let us make the best of it. I for one intend to have a most pleasant day, and I think it was most kind of you to invite me." Anne winked at me mischievously.

Lord Kelston positioned himself between us, leaning slightly to favor my side of the coach, I noticed, and we proceeded down the drive that had led me to my life at Camberleigh. At the bottom of the drive we turned off, and I was pleased to note that we were taking a route that I had not traveled before.

It was indeed a beautiful day. The air was brisk and clean. Flocks of geese sailed on the waters of the small lakes and ponds, and I noticed that the leaves were beginning to announce the arrival of autumn with faint turnings of red and gold at their tips.

Anne and Lord Kelston chatted happily, like the old friends they were. I smiled, for though they appeared on the surface to be constantly sparring or testing each other's wits, it was clear that the bond they had formed over the years was a strong one. I envied that, for I had had few friends of my own age at Seven Oaks. My parents always seemed uneasy when I would spend time with a new boy or girl in our town. I had not minded, though, for there was bountiful love within our small family and the families of the few farmer friends with whom my parents occasionally visited.

"Tell me all about London these days, Robin," I heard Anne ask.

"What I know about, you wouldn't be interested in hearing. If you are going to ask me about the latest style of the gowns, I fear I would be hard pressed to answer," Lord Kelston replied.

"I'm certain if I asked you what was in the gowns you could give me an answer. Or if I asked about the gaming tables. Are you still frequenting those?"

"Ah, but you said *if* you were to ask me, and of course you are not, for t'would be far too indelicate even for you, my dear Anne."

Realizing that she had been thoroughly rebuffed, Anne turned as if to admire the scenery.

"Serena, don't let Anne's insinuations frighten you," Lord Kelston said, taking my hand in his. "She just wishes that she had married me rather than that poor fellow Ormsby and is determined to attempt to thwart any sincere romantic interest I might have in the future."

"Robin Kelston you are a boor," said Anne indignantly. But I could not help wonder if at some time in the past romance had not indeed sprung between the two.

I noticed on the route that we were taking that the farms here too appeared sorely in need. The houses were dilapidated and I saw what Lord Barkham meant about the winters, for without proper fuel these people would scarce be able to survive in cruel weather.

"Whose farms are these?" I asked.

"These are more of the Camberleigh-and-Mayfair estates. It is an odd plotting of land, for by the eye it seems to have no symmetry, but were you to examine it on a map it would become clear. There is a small inn close by where I thought we might take luncheon. It is not grand, but in this case I think we should let convenience win out."

I smiled, pleased at the thought, for the fresh air had whetted my appetite and I longed to stretch a bit, unaccustomed as I was to riding for long periods.

The inn, which sported a sign that read "The Bird and Bottle, Patrons Welcome," was an ivy-covered cotswold, perhaps about three times the size of Thomas's enchanted cottage in the woods. Inside, the tables and chairs were all of heavily polished oak. A fire roared in a great fireplace which I thought odd, given the warmth of the day, but then realized that once out of the direct rays of the sun that it was cooler than I had thought.

We sat at a round table not far from the fire.

"Robin, this place looks deserted," said Anne, looking about.

"I'm certain they are just in the kitchens. It's owned by a couple called the Bartholemews. Very pleasant, but they are both hard of hearing."

Just then a young girl entered. She was about my own age, with a deep olive complexion. Her hair was almost as black as Lord Kelston's and her eyes were of an unusual almond shape. She wore a low-cut dress that was tightly laced at the bodice, which accentuated the swell of her full breasts.

"Lord Kelston, I didn't hear you come in. I hope I didn't keep you waiting." Her voice was lilting with a faint accent that I did not recognize.

"Not at all, Juanita. I was just telling my friends Lady Ormsby and Miss Miles here that the Bartholemews were undoubtedly in the kitchen."

"You haven't been in for quite a while, Lord Kelston. I hope you haven't been ill?" Juanita replied, a bit too forwardly, I thought.

"No. I've been about," Lord Kelston mused. "Just busy, I suppose."

"And what can I get you today?"

"Well, if I remember rightly, the best of the fare is whatever Mrs. Bartholemew prepares especially each day. Why don't you tell her that we would like that and some of her fresh bread."

As the girl called Juanita moved away, Anne, smoothing her hair, said, "Well, it looks as though you have made your presence felt about these parts, Robin. Too obvious, for my taste, but she's interesting, in a sultry sort of way. Where is she from?"

"Some island off the coast of Spain, I believe," Lord Kelston responded quickly. "But what are we talking about her for, when I am seated with you two visions of loveliness."

The meal, as promised, was simple but delicious and we all ate with great enthusiasm. I could not help but notice that Juanita managed somehow to brush her hand or leg against Lord Kelston each time she brought another dish to the table. I was embarrassed by her boldness, but at the same time I could not help but see that Lord Kelston was handsome, and even I was attracted to his charms. Anne bristled every time Juanita came by, but I wondered if it were not more to make Lord Kelston uncomfortable than because she actually found the girl's presence distasteful.

We ended the luncheon with a sumptuous berry pie. I saw that when Lord Kelston paid for it he buried some rather large notes at the bottom. Realizing that the meal, although substantial, could not have possibly cost such a large sum, I knew that these were obviously meant for Juanita's services—which I doubted had anything to do with today.

We settled ourselves once more in the coach, and I noticed that again Lord Kelston favored my side.

"'Tis a pity that we do not have the time to travel to my home," said Lord Kelston, "for I would truly enjoy welcoming you there, but I fear we could not make it there and back by nightfall, and I would be loath to be accused of absconding with you young ladies."

"Well, the thing I like best about that half-invitation is the reference to me as young," replied Anne. "How is your mother, by the way, Robin?"

CAMBERLEIGH

"As long as she has something to complain about she flourishes," he replied.

"Well, then, as long as she has you about, then she must
be thriving," barbed Anne. "Do give her my regards."

"I have a jolly good idea. Why don't you come and see her
yourself. We can plan an entire weekend—and of course you
will accompany Miss Miles."

"I fear that would be quite out of the question, Lord Kelston," I replied quickly. "As you are aware, Master Oliver is
my charge and I would not only not be permitted to leave his
side for such a time, but I would not feel right doing so."

"That does complicate matters. Anne, cannot you come up
with some solution?"

"Why is it left to me, Robin?"

"Because you have such a deliciously deceptive mind, my
dear."

"What about inviting the entire Camberleigh household? I
could at least suggest it to Maura. She is so worried about
Clarissa having a proper launch that she would undoubtedly
welcome the diversion. If you promised Richard a hunt, I'm
certain he would be tempted. I doubt that her ladyship would
make the journey, but that would not necessarily prevent it.
Leave Justin to me. Actually, he might be so relieved to get
Richard off this taxation topic that he might think very favorably
on it."

"That's very good, Anne," Lord Kelston replied, "as far as
you've gone. What about Oliver? You haven't forgotten that
that is the key to our having Serena with us."

"I think I can accomplish that," Anne replied with a thin
smile.

"How?" pressed Lord Kelston.

"You needn't know 'how' as long as I can do it. Relax,
Robin. All you need do is extend the invitation before you
leave this evening."

I felt slightly trapped by these plans of my two friends, but
I had to admit that the thought of a long weekend at Kelston
Manor was far more appealing than whiling away the hours at
Camberleigh with no one around.

"You know, I was surprised to see her ladyship looking so

145

well," said Lord Kelston. "My mother was quite certain that she should never recover from the old Earl's death. Some say, you know, that she died when he did."

I felt myself tense at this turn to the conversation, for this was the first time since my arrival at Camberleigh that there had been direct mention of my grandfather.

"How long ago did the Earl die?" I asked, hoping to keep the conversation alive long enough to learn something that might give me a clue to my own parents' departure from Camberleigh so many years before.

"Let's see," said Anne pensively. "I was but a child—"

"I know," interrupted Lord Kelston, "you were still in your cradle."

"Don't tease. Let me see, it must have been seventeen, almost eighteen years ago. I remember because Justin had just had his twelfth birthday party the week before and Father had given a large party at Mayfair. The Earl and her ladyship were there, Richard—oh, everyone was present."

Eighteen years, I thought. That was when my parents had left Camberleigh, according to my mother's letter. Had my father been so upset by *his* father's death that he felt he could not remain? Had the burden of running the estates seemed too great for him to assume? But that did not make sense, for his brother Richard, being the eldest, would naturally have been the successor, and my father needn't have involved himself in the everyday affairs of Camberleigh.

"You do really mean to say that everyone was present?" said Lord Kelston. "I would have thought that even then the plot was thickening."

"Yes, everyone was. But you know, it was odd. You certainly could never have guessed by the way those two treated each other that one would die at the hands of the other within days."

"What are you referring to, Anne," I said. I had not been able to follow the course of the conversation.

"Well, it's not very pleasant, Serena, but I suppose living there you have some right to know. You see the old Earl had two sons. Richard and his younger brother William."

My heart leapt at the mention of my father's name. At last

here, perhaps, was someone who would know the truth of it all.

"William was married," Anne continued, "to a woman who I realize now must have been just a girl at the time. I remember thinking she was very beautiful—and very kind. I also remember that I was jealous of Justin at his party, for he had received a score of presents. Sensing my mood, William's wife opened her reticule and gave me a lovely linen handkerchief with a small nosegay embroidered at its corner. I thought her to be my special friend."

"Yes, Anne, go on," I said impatient at her reverie—but at the same time touched that the girl of which she spoke must have been my mother.

"Well, one night—it could not have been more than a week after the party—news came that the old Earl was dead. I remember my father returning with the news, and he kept saying over and over 'I don't believe it.' Our families, as you know, were more than just great friends, and it was truly a shock to both him and my mother. For days I did not know what had happened. It was actually Justin who told me—leave it to him to have wanted to terrorize his little sister."

"What did happen, Anne?" I urged. I longed, even though she had warned me of its unpleasantness, to know the full details.

"The old Earl, it appears, had been murdered. By his own son, William."

My eyes flew to her face and I saw quickly that she was not jesting. But it must be, I thought, some sort of cruel joke being played out at my expense. My father was not capable of hurting anyone, much less his own father.

"There must be some mistake." I heard my voice mouthing my thoughts.

"Apparently not," Anne said. "For her ladyship, I suppose in a flight of anger, banished him and his bride from the estates. They were gone by morning, and to my knowledge, were never heard from again, which I suppose was acknowledgment enough of his guilt."

"But he couldn't have been guilty," I heedlessly cried, my head spinning, feeling as if my whole body was on fire. "They didn't prove anything," I said, jumping up from where I sat.

"Serena, what are you doing? Do sit down, or you'll hurt yourself," Anne screamed.

"Don't you see he couldn't have done it?" I replied, wiping the tears that now fell in torrents from my eyes.

"Good Lord, Serena," Lord Kelston said, his arm lunging out to grab me. I jumped aside to avert his grasp. There was a loud crack and then I felt as though I had been propelled into the air. I was floating and someone was screaming and I wanted to tell them to stop, but I couldn't. And then just as quickly as I was up I had the sensation of falling and there seemed to be another crack as something sharp dug into the back of my head. . . .

I was aware of motion and voices about me, but they were too far away to hear me. I wanted to tell them something. Something very important, but I could not remember what it was. And it did not seem that they would understand anyway.

"Serena, be very quiet, dear. We are almost back at Camberleigh."

Camberleigh . . . yes, I knew that name. But why were they not taking me to Seven Oaks? I wondered. My mother would be worried about me.

"Oh Lord, this is all my fault, Robin," I heard a woman's voice say. "Why did she stand up like that?"

"You can't blame yourself, Anne," said the male voice. "I can't imagine what came over her."

Anne. That was the name of someone I knew. She was concerned about me, and I must tell her that I was all right. But it seemed too hard. It was easier to stay where I was, drifting in what seemed a sea of nothingness.

"Serena, please talk to me." The voice was beseeching me again to respond.

I opened my eyes slowly and saw that it was dark. My head rested against a man's arm, and the woman who looked down upon me I recognized to be Anne.

"Thank goodness," she said. "You've given us such a fright."

I started to rise, but her arms held me down.

"Lord Kelston here was dying to think of some way to get you into his arms. And now that you've provided it, you don't think that he would ever let you go, do you?"

I smiled. I remembered now that I had been on an outing with Anne and Lord Kelston.

"You've had a serious fall, Serena. The coach hit a rut in the road and you were thrown clear. I thought for a moment that you had been killed, but Robin here kept assuring me that you had to live so that we might have our weekend."

Nothing she was saying made particular sense, but I realized that I must have taken a nasty bump on the head, for a pounding had commenced that I knew was far from normal.

"Good. We're here. I shall run in and find help. Robin, as soon as we have Serena out of here, go to the doctor and bring him back with you."

I lay not moving, it seemed, only moments before I heard Anne's voice: "She's in the coach, but be careful. She took a nasty fall, and I am not sure what but something might be broken."

I felt myself being lifted by arms that were so strong and powerful that they appeared to envelop me completely. I looked up and saw Justin Barkham's solemn eyes looking down on me. I wanted to protest, for he was the last person that I wanted to see me in this predicament, but I was not in any condition.

He carried me up the staircase and down the corridor.

"I should chastise my fair damselle for finding her in distress once again, but you look so fetching in that silly bonnet that I can scarcely do so."

"Put me down, Lord Barkham," I said weakly, trying to release my legs from his grasp.

"Not until I have you in bed, Serena," he replied.

"How dare you," I said, kicking at him again.

"Serena, I said that I was going to put you to bed. Not to bed you."

Despite my fragile state I felt a flush grow over me. That was not what he had said, but my mind was too blurred to think properly. All I wanted to do was lie down and be left alone. I thought it odd that he knew precisely where my room was, but then Anne had probably told him. Jaspar bounded forth as I was carried through the door and into the room.

"Hey, stop that!" Lord Barkham shouted and, realizing that Jaspar had taken it upon himself to come to my rescue, I called him away.

"I suppose I should be grateful, Miss Miles, for although your spaniel hardly looks able to gnaw through my boot, I think that where his mistress is involved he thinks himself a conqueror of all men."

"What are you doing," I said, trying to sit up but instantly realizing that I was far too dazed by the blow on my head to move quickly.

"You aren't going to lie here with your boots on, are you?"

"I shall tend to that."

"I don't think you'll be tending to anything for a while, by the looks of you. Now don't be so uppity—or do you think some dreadful fate will befall you if I should get a peek at your toes."

I remained silent at this last indignity, realizing that I had little choice.

"Nothing broken here," he said, rubbing my ankle. "T'would have been a pity to see something so elegantly turned to be swollen for weeks on end. Now let us see your head."

"Don't touch me," I said, grabbing the arm that reached up to untie the fastenings of my bonnet.

"If I promise to stop at the bonnet, will you let me proceed? Really, I have no idea why Anne didn't remove it immediately. Now it's caked with blood and I fear it will be painful when I remove it."

"Oh, Anne's poor bonnet. I've ruined it," I cried.

Just then the door flew open and Anne rushed in. "Oh, Serena I am so awfully sorry. How is she, Justin?"

"Ornery, if you want to know. At present, what she seems to care most for is your bonnet, which she is convinced she has ruined. Intelligence should tell her that she can replace a bonnet but 'tis a little hard to find a new head. Perhaps you can reassure her."

Anne took my hand and squeezed it. "What in heaven's name made you stand up that way, Serena? If I hadn't known better, I would have thought you had been shot."

The scene came back to me, but only in pieces. Something about my father and the earl, but I could not recall what had upset me so.

"Don't talk now, Serena," Lord Barkham ordered. "Removing this damnable thing is not going to be easy, but if I

150

know Dr. Carruthers, he will simply prescribe lobbing your head off. So although you scarce wish my attentions, I suggest that I am the lesser of two evils."

I felt as if my head were being torn open as he began to try to wedge the bonnet off.

"Anne, I am going to have to cut this away. See if you can find some scissors."

"But my hair!" I cried.

"Better a hack of hair, Miss Miles, than your head. Remember what I said about Dr. Carruthers."

Anne returned with the scissors, and I lay very still listening to their blades crunching their way through the fabric and bracings. I was aware of the massiveness of Justin Barkham's frame as he bent over me, and I thought how petite and delicate Clarissa must feel in his arms.

"There," he finally said. "Only one section left. But since this is where the lady is going to lose a few of her tresses, I would prefer to turn this over to my sister. That way when you recover you won't blame me for having marred you for life." He rose and began to take his leave. "I will send the doctor up as soon as he arrives."

"Well I have never done anything like this, but I suppose if I can cut flowers. . . . Just promise not to hate me if I make a mess of it."

"I couldn't hate you Anne," I replied, thinking that if anything I had grown to love this woman who had become my friend in such a short space of time.

I was begining to feel quite ill, but I did not have the heart to say anything to Anne, who was laboring feverishly at cutting away the last portion of the bonnet. The whole process was beginning to seem quite ludicrous to me, in my dazed state.

"There," she said, holding it up proudly as if completing a great accomplishment. "If I do say myself, t'will be hard to ever tell you've lost any hair at all, although I must admit that I am glad that I am not squeamish, for otherwise I should have fainted dead away, with the amount of blood you have lost."

The doctor arrived shortly, and I could tell from the pushing and prodding that I had had the best of the bargain with Lord Barkham.

"You've had a fairly serious concussion, miss, and that's a

nasty gash at the back of your head. You were lucky, all in all. One of the maids is bringing up some hot water, and the wound should be bathed and cleaned and then some of this ointment applied. I'm going to leave a bottle of medicated tonic, and I want you to drink a teaspoonful every four hours for the next three days. It may make you drowsy, but it's a good restorative and will keep you calm while you're healing. There's nothing broken, but you are going to have some nasty bruises on your backside. The important thing is rest." He gave me some of the medication and then left.

Anne stayed with me after Dr. Carruthers had gone. She closed the heavy draperies and got out my nightdress. I was grateful that the maid who appeared with the basin of hot water was dependable Charlotte, for I was not looking forward to being peered at by someone like Molly, who I knew would have the news of my infirmity spread about the entire household before morning.

"Oh, miss, when they told me to bring the basin quick I thought it were funny, you not normal askin' for one this time o'evening. But then I saw the doctor an' he tells me there's been an accident. I was prayin' it wasn't you that be hurtin'."

"You're Charlotte, aren't you," said Anne.

"Yes, yer ladyship."

"Well, Charlotte, do you think you could give me some assistance in washing the wound and applying this ointment the doctor left?"

The two worked on my head for what seemed an hour. I was vaguely aware of their chatting between themselves, but the medicine that Dr. Carruthers had given me must have been taking effect, I thought, for try as I would I could not keep my eyes open.

I seemed to be drifting again. I was walking down a long hallway to a chamber at the end. It was filled with people, but I could not see any of their faces, for they all wore shrouds of black. At the center one figure pointed to another and said, "I sentence you to banishment for murder." The accused figure dropped to its knees pleading, "I beseech you, I am innocent." The other figures in the room now called out: "Nay, he is guilty—banish him."

I awoke suddenly. The room was very dark, but I saw a

figure by my bed. "Who is there?"

"'Tis only me, Charlotte," she said, putting a cool cloth to my head.

"Charlotte, what are you doing here?"

"If you remember, you had a wee accident, miss. I came back to look in on you an' ye was tossin' and turnin' so I thought I should stay. Lady Ormsby said this would settle ye back a bit." She spooned some of the strong tasting liquid in my mouth.

"I remember now," I replied. "I was thrown from the carriage. How is Anne?"

"Lady Ormsby is fine, miss. When I came back to look in on ye, I found her sleepin' in this chair. Wasn't gonna leave ye, she wasn't, but I said I'd rest a spell with you. She looked all tuckered out."

"I am very appreciative, Charlotte, but you needn't stay. I'll be just fine." I felt a wave of drowsiness overtake me. . . .

Sun was streaming in the windows as I opened my eyes. My head felt as though little hammers were chipping away at it from all sides, and each movement I made seemed contrary to what my body wanted me to do. Jaspar was gone and I thought the hour must be late for him to be with Robbie. I sat up and lifted my legs gingerly to the floor. Everything seemed to spin, and I was afraid to try to stand, since my balance appeared to be affected. Oliver, I thought, must be frantic at not seeing me by now.

Just then the door opened and in bustled Charlotte with a tray.

"What are ye doin', miss?" she said, seeing me poised on the edge of the bed.

"I must be getting to Oliver, Charlotte. I can tell it is already late."

"Don't you be frettin' about Master Oliver, miss. He's been up an' havin' his lessons for hours now, an' he says to tell you that he will study his lessons proper if you be takin' good care and get well soon."

"But I don't understand. The Earl must be livid, not to mention Lady Camberleigh. She hardly cares about the boy, but having me shut up in this room and not tending to Oliver must not be setting well."

"I don' know about that, miss. But I know that the instructions came from her ladyship herself."

"The Earl's mother?" I asked incredulously.

"The very same. She tells Giles an' Giles tells Cook an' Cook tells Molly an' Molly tells me. She says you're not to return to the nursery 'til you're feelin' fit. An' I can tell it'll be many a day 'til you be up an' about like you were. So you might as well relax and have some of this hot broth that Cook made up special. An' you best be likin' it, 'cause Cook says the doctor left instructions that that was all you was to have 'til he said so. You should be havin' some more of your medicine now also."

I moved back up in bed, surprised but somewhat relieved at the turn of events. At least I was not to be turned out. It would have been a harsh action, of course, but I had assumed that Lady Camberleigh would seize any opportunity to have me removed from the household.

I ate the broth that Charlotte had brought, although not with great relish, and took another teaspoon of the medication. Try as I might I could not fight the heaviness in my eyes, and it was not long before I again drifted back to sleep.

A knock at the door brought me out of my slumber. This time it was Anne, with Jaspar in tow. The dog raced over to my bed, lapping at the hand that I put down to quiet his whimpering.

"Some boy was heading this way with him, and since I was coming to see you I thought that I would simply bring the animal along myself," she explained. "How are you feeling?"

"I could lie and say fine, but frankly I am not feeling all that well," I replied. "This weakness is infuriating. All I want to do is sleep."

"Well, the doctor said that that was the best thing for you. We are to keep you quiet and warm and allow you as much rest as possible."

I must have looked worried, for Anne came closer and, taking my hand, said, "You are not still worrying about that bonnet, are you?"

"No, it's just that I have made such a mess of things. I ruined your day. Lord Kelston must think me an idiot. And your brother must be smug about it all, as I seem to have solidly confirmed his theories about my always getting into trouble."

"Serena, I've never heard such ridiculous self-deprecation. You ruined nothing for me. Robin is so bewitched by you that it took several brandies and a great deal of coaxing to keep him from bursting through this door. As for Justin, he is not as harsh as all that."

"Is Lord Kelston still at Camberleigh?"

"No, he departed early this morning. But not without extending the invitation to Lady Camberleigh."

"What invitation?"

"Don't you remember my divine scheme to have us all be invited to Kelston Manor for the weekend?"

"Vaguely," I replied.

"Well, it worked. Sometimes I think Robin is right and I am truly calculating. I knew that she couldn't refuse if it were designed around Clarissa. He has arranged to have a ball in her honor, and we are all to attend. You, of course, shall be with Oliver during the day, but he managed to have you included in the evening affair by making it appear that he needed some pretty face to throw on the mercy of old Lord Lancaster."

"But, Anne, that is quite horrible."

"That's not what he intends, you silly goose, but it was the perfect bait for Maura. She was simply delighted by the thought of you being thrown to some old reprobate."

"When is this to take place?"

"Two weeks next, so you had best rest and be fully recovered by then. Speaking of which, I must leave you now if we are to keep our promise to the doctor and not overtire you. I am returning to Mayfair this afternoon. I wish that I could remain here with you, but I came quite unprepared and there are some things I must attend to at home."

She leaned forward and kissed my forehead.

"I shall miss you, Anne," I said.

"And I you. But it shan't be long."

Chapter Eight

THE NEXT three days passed uneventfully. Charlotte came regularly to give me my broth and medicine and dress my wound, but I saw none other save Jaspar, who seemed to resist leaving my bedside even for his necessary outings.

In my waking moments I kept trying to piece together the bits of information that were still scattered in my brain. Something about a party and my father and his father. My mother was there too, but I didn't know why. The party, I decided, was most likely the ball that we had been discussing at Lord Kelston's. But then what did my father have to do with it?

On the morning of the fourth day there came a knock at the door. I had awakened early to the sound of rain beating on the roofs below my room and had stirred little since Charlotte's brief morning ritual.

"Come in," I called.

The door opened and there stood my grandmother.

"Your ladyship," I gasped.

"May I come in, Miss Miles?"

"But of course." I struggled to put on my robe and rise to greet her.

"You stay abed where you belong," she said so commandingly that I sank quietly back against the pillows.

She moved over to a chair near my bed and looked down on me. Her pale violet eyes traveled over me as they had done before, as if in search of some small recognition.

"How are you feeling?"

"I am better, your ladyship. It was kind of you to permit me to remain in bed to recuperate. I fear I would not have been able to be of much service or company to Master Oliver."

"It was not kind, Miss Miles. As you have just expressed yourself, it was a necessity. I have come here today with some misgivings, for if this is some kind of ruse then I shall indeed have been played the fool."

"I don't understand, your ladyship."

"Oh, I know full well that you were indeed thrown from the carriage. No matter how great an actress you might be, I doubt that you would put your very life at risk."

I stared at her, trying to understand what she was saying. How—and why—could she think that I had feigned the accident?

"After hearing about the incident," she continued, "I summoned Lady Ormsby to my quarters, as I had learned that she had accompanied you on the ride. It seemed odd to me that if there had been a mishap that you were the only one hurt. She explained that for some reason you suddenly jumped up in the carriage and as they attempted to reason with you to sit down the carriage hit a pocket in the road and you were thrown out. Lady Ormsby also said that it was most likely her fault, for she had been going on at great length about my husband's death and the circumstances of it, and she was certain that she had alarmed you."

There was a throbbing in my temples as I searched once more to piece it all together. "There was a party," I said, beginning to recall. "A birthday party at Mayfair. And my mother was there and she gave a present to Anne. And then the Earl died. But he didn't just die, did he?"

"No, Serena, he didn't."

"He didn't just die, he was . . . murdered," I choked out. "And you said my father did it. It was you who banished him from this house."

I felt as though someone was lowering some heavy weight onto my body, making me totally inert. There had to be some mistake. This was all a bad dream. I was hallucinating from the medication. I would wake and see that it was just Charlotte bringing my tray.

"Serena, do you hear me? I want you to listen to me."

I closed my eyes and opened them, hoping to blot out the image before me. Now I understood the dream about the shrouded figures. I had wanted so desperately to see their faces. And now that I had, I thought that nothing would ever seem real again.

"Serena, you must understand that I think there remains the small chance that you are my real granddaughter. Thus I had to come to you, for your mother's letter revealed that you knew nothing of the events of eighteen years ago, and she feared what you might do with that knowledge. If you are an adventuress, you were simply playing your part well—so well that you could not predict the misfortune of your being thrown from the carriage. Perhaps I shall never know whether you are playing a game or not. But before God I must not risk losing again what I lost when I banished my son from this house."

I looked at my grandmother as she sat before me. Each time I saw her I realized what a great beauty she must have been in her time. How could she have been so confused, so insensitive, as to have done such a thing to her own son? How could she have believed my father capable of committing such a crime?

"Why?" I heard myself ask.

"Why what, Serena? Why did I expel your . . . my son from this house? I don't know, really. I was hurt and angry. I loved my husband very deeply. He had been my life. And when he was so cruelly taken from me, I was frightened and I lashed out. The evidence was there. I did not want to believe it, but it was irrefutable. And although you may not be able to conceive of this, I loved my son William. In many ways even more than my husband. You may think that exiling him was the cruelest thing I could have done. At the time, turning him over to the authorities seemed a far more severe and final action."

"But why did you assume that he was guilty?" I asked.

"Serena, I have told you. There was undeniable evidence."

"What was this evidence?"

"I don't want to go into that now. Suffice it to say that it appeared absolutely conclusive."

"What did my father say?"

"William, of course, denied it. But he too was in shock."

"My father was the most gentle, honest man I will ever know. If he denied it then he told the truth. You say that it would have been kinder to turn him over to the authorities. But then at least he might have had a fair trial. And I know he would have been vindicated. You gave him no chance. You judged him—your own son—and sentenced him in the face of his denials. Have you no trust, no compassion?" I could scarcely believe what I was saying. Had I not been in such a dazed state, I could never have spoken this way to my grandmother.

"I have lived these eighteen years in doubt, Serena. Perhaps my actions were harsh. But I have paid for them many times over, wondering if I was unjust. That is why your coming here—if indeed under pretext—would be more cruel than you could possibly imagine. For this has made the events of nearly two decades ago come alive again for me. I am now not only remembering them, I am reliving them."

"I do not want to cause you any pain, your ladyship," I replied. "I wish there were some way for me to prove that I am indeed your granddaughter. Particularly now since it appears I have something else to prove."

"What is that, Serena?"

"That my father did not in fact murder your husband . . . my grandfather."

"Serena, I must ask you to stay out of these affairs. There are times that I look at you and find myself wishing that the news that that letter brought was indeed true. Which is why I must steel myself sternly from believing it. I will tell you that I have taken some further action. I have enlisted the aid of my solicitor and requested that he conduct a small investigation. I should warn you that if you are indeed conducting a hoax—either alone or with outside accomplices—it shall be discovered and it would behoove you to leave as quickly as you came."

"Are you banishing me as you did my father?"

"I don't think we should continue this discussion any longer, Serena. We might both say something that we might regret. I think you understand the significance of what I have said. I trust that you will continue to keep our talks in confidence."

I watched my grandmother rise and move slowly and silently

to the door. On the one hand I wanted to lash out at her; on the other I wanted her to hold me in her arms. She closed the door quietly behind her.

This encounter, I suddenly realized, had taken its toll on me, for I felt totally spent. I longed to feel stronger so that I could think clearly about all my grandmother had said. Whatever the evidence, I knew that my father was innocent and somehow I must find a way to prove it, despite her admonition to stay out of the matter.

When Charlotte arrived later in the morning, she carried a small bowl with flowers, which she placed on my nightstand.

"Mr. Masters asked that I give ye these—oh an' this note, too. Real worried about you, he is. Said to say he hoped it wasn't his cookin', but I think he was just joshing me. Sweet on you I think he is, miss. 'Course, I can see why."

I smiled at Charlotte, who, like Anne, seemed ever my champion. I opened the envelope and pulled out the note inside.

My fair princess,
    Since Oliver told me of your accident I have not been myself. I have longed to see you to assure myself that, as rumor has it, you are in fact improving daily. However, I fear that propriety would not permit a visit to your room. I warned you that the Earl's business associates would be up to no good. Had I known it would take such a serious turn, I would have gone to greater lengths to caution you. But the important thing is that you recover quickly and fully so that I might entice you back to my enchanted cottage, where I might see your eyes by candlelight once more.

                                        Your servant,
                                        Thomas

"Looks like that note said somethin' you was wantin' to hear."

"Is it that obvious?" I asked.

"You sound like me Robbie. He's always sayin' that I can read what he's got on his mind."

"Then I guess I'll have to watch my thoughts in the future."

Charlotte laughed. "I've got some more news I think you'll be likin'. Cook says you can have somethin' solid tonight for supper, so that should whet your appetite."

I slept most of the afternoon, awakening only occasionally to the sound of thunder, which now accompanied the heavy rains. Charlotte came in with my evening tray, which bore far more than I could consume, much to Jaspar's pleasure. I was feeling stronger, and determined that the next day I should rise and dress no matter what protestations I was certain to receive.

I slept more soundly than I had since the accident and awoke for once without feeling that dreadful pounding in my head. I felt as though I had what my father used to refer to as sea legs as I made my way to the dressing table. I was shocked by my reflection. There were deep blue circles under my eyes and my skin was sallow. I brushed my hair back at the sides, careful not to disturb the wound at the back.

Charlotte arrived, reprimanding me, as I knew she would, for being up and about. I was loath to admit that even with all my resolve I still felt unprepared to tend to Oliver, and permitted her to escort me back to bed.

Two more days passed before I again attempted to rise. Although I had slept almost continuously, it seemed I had grown bored of my bed and longed to see Oliver and, of course, Thomas. I was by no means fully recovered, but the circles under my eyes were less prominent. I searched the closet for my blue muslin and thought it odd that it was not there. Perhaps the damage had been so great to it in my fall that it had been irreparable. I hoped not, for my wardrobe was meager enough as it was.

I was worried about what I should take in the way of clothes to Kelston Manor. Dear Anne had sent me a note via her brother telling me that she was readying for the weekend and would arrive at Camberleigh the day before our departure, since it was a far shorter journey from here to Lord Kelston's than it was from Mayfair.

I dressed slowly, wondering how long it would be before the ache in my joints would disappear. The house seemed very quiet as I made my way to the nursery.

"Oh, Serena," Oliver cried in delight, running toward me, arms outstretched. "I have missed you so. I wanted to come and see you, but they said I mustn't, that you were too sick. Are you still?"

I embraced him and kissed the top of his head.

Evelyn Grey

"I've missed you too, Oliver, and I'm much better, really. You know how you felt after your own accident. You become stronger and stronger each day. Well, what have you done with yourself since I've been ill?"

"My lessons, mostly. And then Mrs. Scoapes would make me read to her in the afternoons."

"But haven't you been out? Let me look at you," I said, pushing him back to examine him. "We'll have to get some sun on those cheeks. Where are your new clothes? Don't tell me you've outgrown them already?"

"Mrs. Scoapes said they weren't fitting to my station, whatever that means."

"I see, well now that I am back I believe you might wear them again, for I think that they are most becoming. Remind me to speak to Fiona if she is still about, to see how she is coming along with the rest of the items."

"Is that the seamstress?"

"Yes, Oliver. I'm surprised you remember her."

"She brought several more things, but she left a few days ago."

"I see. Well why don't you change now and then meet me in the schoolroom."

Thomas rose as soon as he saw me enter and rushed over, taking my hands in his.

"Let me look at you," he said, moving me over to the window. "My God, you really must have taken a nasty fall."

"That is not much reassurance for a lady," I replied, laughing.

"I didn't mean *that,* Serena, it's just that I have missed you so and seeing any harm come to my fair princess makes my blood boil. I'd like to wring that Kelston's neck."

"I missed you too, Thomas, but you mustn't be angry with Lord Kelston, for it was really not his fault."

"What are you protecting him for?"

"I'm not. It was my fault, Thomas. I stood up in the coach and he tried to grab me, but we hit a rut in the road and I was thrown out."

"The important thing is that you are alive and have come to me," Thomas said, taking me in his arms.

"Serena, I . . ." He broke off as Oliver entered the school-

162

room, a bit embarrassed, it seemed, at finding us in an embrace.

"Oliver, I shall return for you this afternoon and perhaps we might take a short walk," I said, quickly breaking away from Thomas.

"Will you bring Jaspar?"

"Of course," I replied. "I'm certain that he has missed seeing you too."

I returned to my room and rested until Molly appeared with my midday meal.

"'Tis Charlotte's afternoon off, miss, but if I can get you anythin' ye just let me know."

"Thank you, Molly, that is very kind."

"I just be wantin' you to know, miss, that you looked so grand the night o' Miss Clarissa's party. I was helpin' serve an' all at the other end o' the table but even I could see that the gentlemen couldn't be takin' their eyes off ye. An' we're happy that you is up an' about again."

"Bless you, Molly. I need a bit of flattery after seeing myself in the mirror these past few days."

I returned to schoolroom in midafternoon. Oliver looked at me as if I were an angel of mercy.

"I fear our lessons did not go very well today, Serena. Perhaps it would have been better if you had not tempted Oliver with thoughts of an outing," Thomas said reproachfully.

"I did not mean any harm, Thomas," I replied, somewhat startled by his tone.

"My duty is to teach the boy his lessons. If he cannot concentrate, he cannot learn. Hereafter, I would suggest that Master Oliver be allowed on these jaunts only when he has satisfactorily completed his studies. That way, perhaps he will concentrate on matters at hand."

I was shocked, for Thomas had never before been harsh with me. It was true that I had agreed to stay out of his lessons, and I thought that I had. I could hardly be blamed for Oliver's lack of attention for one single day. But I did not want to argue, particularly with Thomas.

"You are right, of course," I replied. "But the boy has been cooped up in this house ever since my mishap, and I am certain you will see a difference in days to come. Come along Oliver, let us see if we can find Jaspar."

Oliver and I wound our way down the stairs and out of the castle in silence.

"Let's head towards the stables," I said. "I wouldn't be surprised if our four-legged friend is there with Robbie."

"Serena," Oliver replied, taking me hand, "I didn't mean to make Mr. Masters get mad at you."

"I know you didn't," I said, squeezing his hand. "I think perhaps he was just jealous that you and I were to spend time together."

"Do you really think so?"

"I do," I replied. I didn't really think so, but I was not about to let the boy assume guilt for something that was clearly not of his doing.

We approached the stables, and sure enough there was Jaspar sitting dutifully behind Robbie, who was currying a horse.

"Look, there is Uncle Justin," Oliver called.

Of all people that I didn't want to see, looking like this, I thought.

Oliver ran to Lord Barkham and embraced him warmly. Whatever I thought of Justin Barkham, I had to admit that he seemed genuinely fond of the boy. And Oliver in turn absolutely idolized him. Under different circumstances I might have tried to temper their relationship, but then with the Earl being so distant with Oliver, the boy needed someone he could look up to as a father figure of sorts.

"Well, Miss Miles—Serena—it's good to see you up and about. Although not too soon, I hope."

"No, I may not *appear* totally recovered, but I am feeling much improved."

"I for one find you far prettier without those blue rings under your eyes, but I trust they will disappear, never to remind us again of your little escapade."

"I would hardly call it an escapade, Lord Barkham."

"Oliver, what would you do with someone who, no matter how often you insisted that they call you by your given name, continues to call you by your titled name."

Oliver looked confused.

"What I mean is that Serena refuses, it appears, to call me Justin."

"She calls me Oliver."

"So she does. Perhaps, Oliver, you can give me some point-
ers on how you accomplished that. I am about to go off on a
ride to one of the farms. Would you like to join me? On your
mare, of course."

"Oh, might I, Serena?"

"He will be quite safe, Miss Miles. His mare is nowhere
near the size of King's Ransom, and broad in the beam and
gentle to boot."

"Well, I suppose it would be all right, then," I replied. "But
don't be gone too very long."

I watched them ride off with no great trepidation, for once
I had seen Oliver's mare I knew what Lord Barkham had said
about her was true.

"Me mum told me what happened to ye, Miss Miles, an'
I'm glad t'was not worse. You coulda been killed, y'know,"
said Robbie as he approached with Jaspar.

"I know, Robbie. You know, I feel badly, for we were to
have started your lessons. Obviously, that was not possible,
but I haven't forgotten, and I think by next week we might
begin."

"I sure thank you, miss. I got plenty o' time, and when yer
feelin' fine again you can let me know."

"I think I'll take Jaspar off with me for a spell, Robbie. I
should be back by the time Lord Barkham and Oliver return."
I paused. "You do think it was all right for me to have permitted
Lord Barkham to take Oliver out, don't you?"

"Aw yes, miss. That mare's a sweet ol' thing an' Lord
Barkham's a man o' the saddle," he said admiringly. "He
wouldn't take no chances with Master Oliver."

It appeared that Lord Barkham had a certain appeal to young
men and old women, I thought as I moved back along the path
that would take me to the secret garden. Most likely because
they were not the constant recipients of his barbs.

I noticed that the gate was slightly ajar again and wondered
if someone else had visited here in our absence. Most likely,
Oliver or I had simply neglected to close it properly the last
time we were here.

I had come to love this garden, and I made note that some
day when I was feeling better I should try and find whoever
did such a beautiful job of maintaining the rose garden and see

if they might spend some time reclaiming this one.

I sat on the stone bench, relieved to rest my legs a spell. I was certain that the doctor would say that I was overdoing my first day out, but I had sorely needed the fresh air, unaccustomed as I was to be indoors for such a long period of time.

My thoughts went back to my conversation with Thomas in the schoolroom earlier. It had been so out of character to have him reproach me that I still didn't know quite what to think. He was the last person that I wanted to think ill of me, but on the other hand I could not permit him to be abusive. It was probably just a bad day. Heaven knows we all had them. Actually, I wasn't so certain that what I had said to Oliver about his being jealous did not border on the truth. He did seem terribly possessive—and for some reason that bothered me a little.

"Well, Serena," I said aloud, "are you perhaps a little frightened that this friendship is turning into a romance, and you aren't quite certain how to react?" It was true that what I felt toward Thomas was certainly that he was more than just a good friend. Thomas was sweet and gentle, and I felt warm and relaxed when he held me in his arms. I had had no experience in the ways of love, but perhaps this was what it felt like. I wished my mother were here, for she might advise me. Not that there was anything to advise, since Thomas had by no means made any declarations. I supposed time would tell. And in the interum I was flattered by Lord Kelston's attentions, though I believed Anne had blown them slightly out of proportion. Our upcoming weekend would tell me more.

"Jaspar, what is it?" I said, for I heard him suddenly growling deeply.

He was crouched on the other side of the pool, staring intently into the water. Suddenly he ran excitedly around the pool, barking. He repeated this three times, paying no attention whatsoever to my orders to stop.

"Jaspar, come over here. What are you doing, you silly dog. There is nothing in that pool."

But he stubbornly returned to his crouch and went on growling at the water. Resignedly I rose and went to the other side of the pool and peered down at the spot where he was focusing his distress.

"There's nothing there except some old lily pads. I doubt

that even fish could survive in it, it appears so unclean."

My assurances were obviously not making an impression, for Jaspar remained steadfast, growling unmercifully.

"Oh, all right then, I'll show you," I said, rolling up the sleeve of my dress. Kneeling, I placed my arm in the water and swirled it about the spot he seemed to have focused on. "You see, there is nothing there."

Jaspar quieted and moved closer to me as I conducted my little proof session. But the moment I removed my hand from the water, he resumed his crouched position growling.

"Well other than jumping in, which I have no intention of doing, I have no idea how to appease you."

I looked about for a stake or something that would be longer than my arm and that I could prod into the pool to show him there was nothing to fear. It seemed ridiculous to be going through all this but I knew him well enough to know that he would not relax until the fish or pond toad or whatever it was had been sighted.

I noticed that several pickets of the iron fence had rusted away, and I moved over to see if one might be lying in the weeds that had overgrown around it. I spied one at the far end and lugged it back to the pond.

I took the blunt end of the six-foot-long section and began easing it into the water around where Jaspar pointed. I had gone down perhaps four feet when I felt as though I had hit something. I moved the post in a circular motion around the solid object. There was definitely something there, but it could have been nothing more than a large rock, I thought. I had no way of judging how deep the pool was.

I pulled the pole out. "Well, Jaspar, do you think we have found sunken treasure?" I asked. I turned the pole around, for were I to try to draw something to the surface, I might have more luck with the pointed end, which was shaped more or less like a harpoon.

"This kind of fishing is not my sport, Jaspar, so don't be disappointed if I don't come up with anything."

Again I could feel something there, but try as I might I could not raise it. Whatever it was had considerable weight, and in my weakened condition I doubted that I had the strength to raise it on my own.

"Jaspar, this will just have to be left to another day. We

should be heading back to the stables now."

But he still did not move from this spot. I had never known him to be so determined, except for one time several years ago when he had been transfixed by a rabbit warren and it had taken me six hours to entice him away.

"All right. I will try once more. But you have to stop if I am not able to gain any leverage on it this time."

I gave one more tug and felt the weight lessen. Obviously I had freed the object from a rock or vegetation or whatever that was keeping it down. I drew up the post slowly. I could definitely feel something, and feared that if I pulled suddenly it might fall from the barb, which obviously had now hooked some part of it.

The thing floated to the surface like some massive fish that, knowing its end is near, rises to beach itself at a place most uncommon to it in life.

But the only thing this had in common with my imagined fish was death itself. For there floating before me was a human body so badly decomposed that I would not have been able to determine if it was a man or woman, except that the long strands of fabric which floated like ribbons from the distorted frame indicated the latter. The mouth was open wide, as if the victim even now tried to call out for help.

As if mimicking her own cries, I heard my own voice screaming. And then I was running. Running somehow for my own life. My hand felt something sharp as I flew through the gate and back onto the path. My body was wet. I stumbled once, but caught myself. If I fell, I knew I should not be able to get up again.

Suddenly someone was running toward me. I kept running, but I no longer knew if I was running away from something or toward it. I understood only that I must run.

Arms encircled me, stopping my motion. Don't they understand, I thought, that I have to run? I flailed against my captor, crying out I knew not what. I suddenly felt a harsh sting across my cheek and I no longer heard the screams.

"My God, Serena, what is it?"

I felt myself growing faint, and started to slip from the arms that held me tight. He picked me up and lay me gently on the grass at the side of the path. I rolled over, turning my face to the earth and allowed the fear to spew forth from my mouth.

When my body had spent itself of the venom that had attacked it, I rolled back and looked into the eyes of Lord Barkham.

"Lie quietly, Serena," he said, wiping my brow with a handkerchief he removed from his pocket.

Something warm and soft wriggled up next to my arm, and I relaxed at the familiar feel of Jaspar, whose barking—as my screams—had long since quieted.

"Serena, can you tell me what this is all about?"

"Behind the gate . . . in the pool . . . in the garden," I stammered.

"What about the pool and the garden?"

"Justin. . . . There is a body there."

"A what?"

"A body. I'm certain it's a woman."

"Serena, are you sure you're not having a relapse?"

"Please, Justin. I saw it there in the pool. It's horrible," I said, desperately trying to rid my mind of the image that was still vividly before me.

"Are you able to stay here for a few moments while I go to see what it is you think you've seen?"

I nodded. "Where is Oliver?"

"Oliver is fine. Robbie is showing him how to brush a horse down. I was just coming to look for you to let you know we had returned," he said, starting to rise.

I grabbed at his sleeve, "Justin, you won't let Oliver know."

"Of course not. Now promise me you won't move until I return. You've had a ghastly shock of some sort, and you must rest for a spell. Jaspar, you stay here and watch over your mistress. If she starts to rise, you start barking and I shall come running."

I lay where I was, too frightened or too exhausted to move. I found myself counting the minutes and then the seconds till Lord Barkham's return.

As I heard footsteps, I forced myself to sit up, my head spinning as I did.

Lord Barkham knelt down beside me. "You were right."

It was strange, but I almost felt relieved to have him confirm my horror, for otherwise I was certain that everyone would say the blow to my head had done more than temporary damage to my mind.

"Do you know who it is?" I asked.

"It's hard to tell, but I think I do."

"Who, then?"

"I think we best wait for the local magistrate to make proper identification."

I started to rise, and felt myself being gathered into Lord Barkham's arms.

"Put me down," I said.

"I will not. This has taken a far greater toll on you than you realize. Coupled with the trauma you suffered earlier this week, you are in no condition to allow that independent nature of yours to take hold. Besides, you don't think I am going to let an opportunity pass to hold you in my arms again, do you?"

"What?" I gasped.

"You mean you don't remember that it was I who carried you from Robin's carriage up to your room after your accident?"

"Oh," I said. "Yes, of course."

"If you would put your arm about my neck, it would make the carrying much easier."

I made not a move.

"For one who has midnight trysts, Serena, you are at times a bit of a prude."

"That comment does not even merit a response, Lord Barkham. It was you who insisted on carrying me back, not I. So I fear if you are uncomfortable that is no concern of mine."

"Oh, we are back to Lord Barkham again?"

"What do you mean?" I retorted.

"I mean that back there on the grass, when I came upon you in such terror, you called me Justin. Not once but several times."

"As you said yourself, Lord Barkham, I was in a state of terror. I was hardly responsible for my words—or my actions, for that matter."

We reached the front door and Lord Barkham kicked it open and walked through, Jaspar following at his heels. Just then I heard the sound of Clarissa's voice. "Justin, what on earth are you doing? Put that woman down."

"I intend to, my dear. Now would you please just open the door to the library?" he replied.

"The library," she said incredulously. "Justin, have you gone mad?"

"Clarissa, just do as I say," he barked back.

"Well you needn't shout," she said, opening the door wide so that he might pass, "but I don't understand what you are doing."

He laid me on the couch on which I had sat upon my arrival at Camberleigh.

Clarissa followed us into the room. "Miss Miles, I want an explanation for this. I am going to fetch my father immediately. He will deal with you."

"That is exactly what I want you to do, Clarissa," Lord Barkham replied.

Looking like the cat who had caught the mouse, Clarissa flounced from the room.

"I fear t'would have been better if you had simply taken me to my room, Lord Barkham," I said.

"Perhaps, but I am certain you realize that the Earl must be apprised of this immediately, and I thought you might be more comfortable if we had any necessary discussions right here."

I nodded.

He moved over to me, carrying a glass of amber liquid that I knew was brandy.

"Here, drink this."

"No," I said, repulsed at even the thought of brandy.

"Serena, don't be stubborn. A stimulant will do you good. As a matter of fact, I shall join you. Although you seem to find me most insensitive, what I saw there in the garden I found to be equally as unsteadying as did you, and I don't look forward to discussing it any more than you do."

The Earl entered at that moment, with Clarissa trotting along closely behind.

"Barkham, what is the meaning of this?" he stormed.

"Richard, may I speak with you privately for a few moments?" requested Lord Barkham, pulling the older man aside.

Clarissa stood watching me smugly as the two men spoke in whispers by the door.

"Clarissa, my dear, I shall have to ask that you leave us for a spell," said the Earl, coming over to where I lay.

"But father, I am not a child. I see no reason—"

"Clarissa, do as I say," he interrupted. "And tell Giles that we do not want to be disturbed."

Lord Barkham started to say something to her as she strutted by him but, determined to make an effective exit, she slammed the door behind her without paying him the slightest attention.

"Now Miss Miles," said the Earl, moving over to stand before the fire, "Lord Barkham has given me distressing news indeed. I realize that this is a strain on you, particularly since you are only just now up and about from your recent accident, but I must ask you to tell me everything that you know about this matter."

Contrary to my intentions, I had drunk the brandy Lord Barkham had handed me. As a result, everything now seemed rather distant, so instead of being a participant, I felt more as a voyeur on the scene.

"I don't know that there is much to tell. When Master Oliver and Lord Barkham went off for a short ride, I went to the small garden—the untended one with a pool—that one reaches by following the opposite path at the fork to the stables. There is a stone there on which I sat. I had not been there long when my spaniel Jaspar commenced running about the pool and growling at one particular spot in the pool. As he is not wont to do that without reason, I moved over to see if I could determine what it was. When I put my arm in the water and felt nothing, I retrieved one of the iron spokes from the fence that had rusted off and began probing into the pool."

"Yes, and then what?"

"I felt something, but it was too heavy for me to lift to the surface. And then some motion I made must have freed it, for I suddenly was able to lift it." A wave of nausea swept over me as the vision of that woman's face who seemed to be calling out to me even now flooded my memory.

"I don't think you need go on, Serena," Lord Barkham said. "I had come up to tell Miss Miles that Oliver and I had returned from our ride, as she had been concerned about our being gone too long. I met her in a quite hysterical state on the path, and when I went back to investigate the cause I quickly understood why."

"One thing I don't understand is how you gained entrance to that garden, Miss Miles."

"Through the gate," I replied.

"But that gate has been locked for years. No one goes there."

I did not want to reveal that Oliver and I had visited the

place often over the weeks, for I recalled that the boy had told me that he was not supposed to go there. "I happened upon it not long after I came to Camberleigh," I replied. "It is true that the gate was rusted and took some pushing and prodding to get it open, but it was not sealed. I thought it a particularly beautiful spot, and often wondered why it had not been as lovingly tended as the other gardens hereabouts."

"Do you have any idea who it is, Justin?" the Earl asked.

"I have a suspicion, but I think we should leave that to the local constabulary."

"No," the Earl shouted, pounding his fist on the mantel.

"What are you saying, Richard?" Lord Barkham asked.

"I don't want this reported, Justin. I will not have this family dragged through all kinds of sordid unpleasantness. Why in blazes did it have to be in that damned garden, of all places. You know what knowledge of this would do to my mother?"

"Richard, she is much stronger than you give her credit for. Besides, that was eighteen years ago."

"What was eighteen years ago?" I asked.

"Nothing," snapped the Earl.

"Richard, that's not fair. Since Miss Miles is already embroiled in this mess, you at least owe her an explanation."

"Well, what do you want to know then, Miss Miles? That my father was found murdered in that very spot and that it was my own brother who did it?"

"I don't know that I can take any more of this," I said, once again hearing myself speak my own thoughts. Tears welled in my eyes and began I to sob—not now from fear, but simply for pure heartbreak.

"There was no need for that, Richard," said Lord Barkham.

"You said yourself she should know the facts."

"Yes, but you didn't have to be so blunt about it. Miss Miles has had enough shocks in the past weeks."

"I'm all right, Lord Barkham, really," I replied, wondering why he had suddenly become so concerned about my welfare.

"Richard, let's not get all involved in the past. There is no way that we can avoid reporting this, particularly if there is any possibility of foul play. I know the magistrate, and I think I can get him to keep this quiet. Cam need not even know, unless of course there is need of a major investigation. I am certain, Miss Miles, that you will keep this in your confidence now that you understand how delicate an issue this could be."

"But what of Clarissa?" I asked.

"Let me handle that. I will simply say that a horse frightened you down by the stables and that in your weakened condition you collapsed and I brought you back up to the house. It's a bit farfetched, but I shall be able to distract her, I believe."

I could well believe that, I thought.

"May I have your word, then?"

I nodded. The Earl said nothing as he stood by the fire continuing to finger the scar, as I had seen him do so often. "Perhaps you are right, Justin," he said. "Maura has it in her mind that we are all going to Kelston's the week next, and that will take us away from all this for a while. Keep me informed of what that magistrate friend of yours finds."

"Might I help you up to your room, Miss Miles?" asked Lord Barkham.

"No, I shall be all right," I said.

"I would suggest that you spend a quiet evening."

"I had no intention of doing any other," I replied, resenting even this mild insinuation.

"Richard, I am returning to Mayfair this evening. I shall return tomorrow, after I have had a chance to tend to this matter."

"If there is nothing else, then I shall retire." I rose and moved toward the door, Jaspar at my heels, when it suddenly occurred to me that poor Oliver had been left down at the stables. "Oh. What of Master Oliver?"

"I will tend to that, Miss Miles," Lord Barkham replied.

I had never felt such total exhaustion. Someone had lit the fire in my room and I changed into my nightdress in front of it as I was chilled to the bone. Molly brought my tray and fortunately assumed that I was ready for bed so early due to the effects of my recent accident. Jaspar became the happy recipient of most of the good food that Cook had prepared, for although I knew that I should eat to help regain my strength, I had little appetite.

I brushed my hair again, careful not to disturb the wound, to which I applied some of my ointment. The moon was in full shadow as I moved over to draw the heavy draperies. I looked down upon the rose garden almost expectant of seeing the lovers arm in arm, but this night no figures appeared on the landscape.

Climbing into bed, I wondered if sleep would ever come to me this night. My life had been so simple and peaceful before I had come to Camberleigh. My days had been filled with long walks with Jaspar and cozy dinners with my family. It was true that after my father died our life had changed, but even when my mother became ill she had managed to communicate a strong sense of security and love. I felt none of that here at Camberleigh. Instead, there was an undercurrent of deceit and torment—and yes, even of evil.

I thought that I would never in my life forget the look on that face—that face which, in truth, had been little more than a skull. Who could she have been—and how did it happen? Had she, like me, been drawn to the garden and perhaps slipped on a rock or uneven edge and fallen into the pool, her screams silenced by the murky waters? Could it be that her fall had not been by chance? Could she have been so desperate over perhaps a broken love affair that she had seen no recourse but to end her life? There was still another possibility, but I could not permit my mind to dwell on it—for it would mean that someone who had been or was now at Camberleigh was a murderer.

It was an unsettling feeling to know that eighteen years ago my parents had left this house because of the purported murder of my grandfather. I wondered if the death of this woman whose name I did not know and whose face I had seen only in death would finally drive me from this house. With all these thoughts twisting and turning in my brain, I finally drifted off to a fitful sleep.

I awakened in the middle of the night. The bed was damp from my own perspiration, and I realized that I must have been reliving the horror of the day in my dreams. I changed my nightdress and went back to bed, where finally my body's fatigue overtook the energies of my mind.

When Charlotte arrived with my basin in the morning I did not stir, for I wanted time to myself to sort my thoughts a bit. I was just completing my braid when she returned with a tray.

"Molly told me ye was up and about yesterday. Someone should of tied ye to your bed, but you're a determined one. Those eyes look a mite better, but ye look plum done in."

"I'm really feeling much better, Charlotte. As a matter of fact, I was just going to the nursery to breakfast with Oliver before he begins his lessons."

"I don't think he has his lessons today, miss. 'Tis Sunday."

"Good gracious, I have lost all track of time. Well, I would still like to see him. If you just leave the tray, I will take it with me to the nursery."

"Don't be foolish. You shouldn't be luggin' things about. I'll drop it off 'fore I take the little feller down to Robbie."

I finished doing my hair and went along to the nursery. Upon opening the door, I was amazed to see Thomas there, talking with Oliver.

"Good morning."

"Thomas, I am surprised to see you here today. Isn't this your day off?"

"Yes, it is. But I wanted to speak with you. Might we step into the schoolroom for a moment?"

I could not imagine what could be urgent enough to have brought him here on his one free day.

"Oliver, I shall be but a moment," I said.

I followed Thomas through the passageway to the schoolroom.

"I hope there is nothing wrong, Thomas."

"The only thing that is wrong is the way I behaved yesterday."

"Whatever do you mean?"

"I mean that I snapped at you for no reason. It certainly was not your fault that the lessons had not gone well, and there was no reason for my taking my frustrations out on you. Can you forgive me?"

"I must admit that your sternness distressed me. But there is nothing to forgive, since it already seems long forgotten."

"You are such an understanding woman, Serena. I feel very fortunate that you have come here to Camberleigh. Your presence here seems to be having an effect on a number of lives, not the least my own."

"Well, if that is so, I hope that the effect is a positive one."

"I realize that it seems that my invitations are always on short notice, but would you dine with me this evening, fair princess, in the enchanted cottage?"

I paused, for although I could not imagine anything more pleasurable, the strain of the past days was still apparent, not only by how I looked but how I felt.

"Is it that you won't forgive me, or do you perhaps have another grand dinner to attend here this evening?" Thomas's voice was strained.

"Neither, Thomas. I am happy to accept your invitation. It will undoubtedly do me a world of good."

"Wonderful. Then I shall expect you at eight. I am glad, Serena, for I have missed you dreadfully these past days."

"I must get back to Oliver now."

"Till eight, then."

Oliver was toying with his food when I returned to the nursery.

"Well, how is my best friend?" I said, sitting down to join him.

"I'm not your best friend," he replied flatly, his eyes cast down on his plate.

"Oliver, whatever makes you say that?"

"I don't know."

"Oliver, what is it?" I replied, becoming concerned at his remoteness.

He looked up at me, and I saw that his pale blue eyes were swimming with tears.

"Oh, Oliver," I cried, stretching out my arms and pulling him to me. "What is it, please tell me."

"Am I really your best friend, Serena?"

"Of course you are. Why would you doubt that?"

"Because every time you see Mr. Masters, you look different. And you are always talking to him."

"Oh, I see," I replied. "And you would rather that I not talk to him?" Oliver shook his head. "Oliver, Mr. Masters has been very kind to me. And it is true that I consider him a friend. But that does not interfere with your and my relationship, and I mean what I have said—I consider you my very best friend here at Camberleigh."

"But you'll go away and then I won't see you."

"Now, why do you think that?"

"Clarissa said so. She said you were just like the others— that you soon would be gone and I would never see you again."

That girl was impossible I thought. Had she no sense? Didn't she realize that Oliver was fragile enough as it was without his hearing such things? He had so little that was stable or secure in his life, how could she torment him so?

"Well, Oliver, perhaps that is what Clarissa assumes, but it is certainly not what I intend. I should like to be close to you for as long as possible—and I hope that that is a very long time."

Oliver threw his arms about my neck. "I love you, Serena, and I don't ever want you to leave."

"I love you too, Oliver. If I could have picked a younger brother, I couldn't have picked a better one than you. Now, let's dry those eyes."

"I am going to see grandmama again this afternoon."

"How nice," I replied. "Well, then, perhaps we should take our walk this morning."

"Can we go to our secret garden, Serena?"

Good Lord, I thought, that was the last place I wanted even to hear about. "No, I think today we should pay a visit to the rose garden. We can sit in the shade of the arbor for a spell."

"Can Jaspar come too?"

"Not today Oliver. But tomorrow, I promise."

We spent the morning in the arbor. I told Oliver that I thought there might be a good chance that we would be taking a journey to Lord Kelston's the weekend next and that he and I might go along. He was thrilled at the prospect, and I found myself wondering that the boy was always so cloistered here at Camberleigh, but I supposed that his illness had something to do with that. I reproached myself quickly, for I could see that it would be easy to allow oneself to fall into the pattern of the rest of the household, all of whom treated Oliver as a sickly child. The only one who did not, I thought strangely, was Lord Barkham.

It was almost time for our luncheon when we returned to the hall. As we were about to enter, I saw Lord Barkham's carriage coming up the drive.

"Uncle Justin," Oliver called out as the vehicle stopped at the bottom of the steps.

"Hello Oliver," he said, climbing down and walking slowly up the steps. His eyes were more solemn than ever as he looked down on me.

"How are you feeling today?"

"Better, thank you. We must be getting in. Oliver is to visit with his grandmother this afternoon, and I shouldn't want him to be tardy," I replied, gathering up my skirts.

"Oh Miss Miles, I have something for you," he said, drawing an envelope from his pocket.

There was no writing on it and I wondered what it could be, but Oliver had already entered the house, so I turned to follow him.

Giles was just descending the stairs.

"Ah, there you are Master Oliver. Her ladyship says that you are to have luncheon with her in the dining room."

I told Oliver to run along, and then I returned to my room. I seated myself before the writing table and opened the envelope. The letter it contained was from Anne.

My dear friend,

Justin returned to Mayfair last evening. We dined rather late and I could see that something was troubling him deeply. He kept assuring me that it was my imagination, but I know him too well for him to deceive me. Thus it was under great duress that he disclosed the startling and horrifying events of yesterday.

You poor child. You had nary time to recover from that nasty accident when this awful episode should befall you. I can only imagine how terrifying it must have been. Justin has told me that the matter is to be kept silent at least until some investigation can be conducted. It is rather odd, but I suppose given the past and the delicacy of her ladyship's condition it is the wisest thing. I of course am sworn to secrecy, but at least I know that I can share it with you.

On a far brighter note, this incident has played beautifully into my scheme for the weekend, for Richard now has one more reason to take advantage of Robin's offer. Which means that I shall see you again five days hence.

Please try not to let this matter distress you too greatly. I am certain that it is a sadly common case of some young maid who had become burdened because of a small indiscretion and chose to end it the only way she knew how.

I urge you to rest well so that you are completely cured for our journey. Robin would never forgive me if you were not to accompany us.

> Lovingly,
> Anne

I closed the letter and placed it in my reticule, smiling at how she must have badgered her brother to extract the story from him. She had probably inveigled it all from him before he knew what had happened.

I spent the remainder of the day in my room taking Anne's advice, resting and returning to the embroidery that I had left idle lo these many weeks. Charlotte was wreathed in smiles when I told her that I would be dining with Mr. Masters that evening. And indeed my own spirits lifted considerably at the thought, and I dressed quickly, taking extra care that the wound on my head should not be visible. Charlotte asked if I wanted her to fix my coiffure, but I thought it better to wait for a few more days to have it fully dressed again.

There was a definite chill in the air as I made my way toward the cottage. I was pleased that I had worn my cloak.

Thomas stood in the doorway, his figure illuminated by the light from within.

"My fair princess looks quite as though she should be walking the moors keeping the hounds at bay, dressed as she is in that cloak," he said.

"I suppose I do appear a bit the woman of mystery floating in from the forest primeval," I retorted.

As I reached the door, Thomas suddenly knelt down and swept me full in the air, transporting me into the confines of the cottage.

"You sweep me off my feet, kind sir," I laughed.

"Not without intention, lovely lady," he replied, setting me down gently. The hood of my cloak fell back against my shoulders, and before I had had a chance to catch my breath Thomas's lips were on mine.

Startled, I pulled quickly back.

"What is the matter, Serena?"

"It was so sudden, Thomas. I wasn't expecting it."

"Sometimes that is when it is best."

"Perhaps that is true." I tried to gather my thoughts. "But I am not accustomed . . . what I mean is . . ."

"I understand, Serena. Which is one of the things that is so delightful about you."

I blushed.

"You're not frightened of me, are you, Serena?"

"No, why do you ask?"

"Perhaps it's nothing. You seem unusually tense. Has anything happened to cause you concern?"

"I suppose I'm just still shaken from my accident."

"Of course. How unthoughtful of me to have flung you in the air like that, when you must still be bruised. Come let us sit by the fire."

I removed my cloak. The fire was warm and the wine he offered began to relax me a bit.

"You know, it has occurred to me that we always seem to talk mostly about me. I know very little of your own family, except that you are here because your father suffered reversals on land investments. You must miss your parents very much."

I had wondered how long it would take before people started asking questions. I had been fortunate in that Charlotte was not a gossip, and the members of the household were scarcely interested in one whose family had fallen on hard times. But for Thomas it was only natural that he should be curious, after all I had queried him about his family.

"Yes, I do miss them. But I try not to think of it," I replied cautiously.

"Do you have any brothers or sisters?"

"No, there is just me."

"It must be particularly difficult on your family, then, being forced to part with their only child. Might you be able to rejoin them in the future?"

"I doubt it, but then one never knows." I realized my answers were vague and weak, but I was growing tense under his questioning. "Thomas, might we discuss something else? You see it is truly painful for me to recall my childhood. Those were far happier times, and I don't think that I shall ever see their like again. Perhaps some day I should be able to deal with it more openly, but for now the wounds are too fresh."

"I understand. I shall not raise it again unless you desire it.

Tell me, what is happening at the castle these days?" he asked as he refilled my glass.

"You certainly see and know as much as I," I replied.

"No, it is different when you actually live in a house. Sometimes the sounds of the night can tell you far more than those of the day. And you, after all, are occasionally included in the affairs of the household."

"I must not be terribly observant, then, for I can recount little of particular interest, unless you were to find the ball Lord Kelston is giving in Clarissa's honor to be worthy of discussion."

"Anything done in honor of that spoiled senseless girl I would find only amusing. When is it to take place?"

"Saturday next. We are to journey there the day before, I believe."

"We," he asked, obviously surprised that I had been included.

"Yes. Oliver has also been invited, and so I am to go as well."

"Ah, so you and he can be shuttered off somewhere while the nobility drones on about how they shall increase their estates."

"Actually, I believe I am to attend the ball."

"So that you can provide some small favors to the bilious old gentlemen who will be ogling you throughout dinner?"

"I think that to be harsh, Thomas. I shall simply be a guest— one who will hold little interest for any gentleman once Clarissa announces, as I am certain she will, that I am but the governess."

"You speak too lightly of your own charms, fair princess. Your last escapade cost you a wound to your head. Let us hope that this next does not cause you a wound that would be far deeper and take far longer to heal."

I flushed at his inference, and wondered what he might think if he knew that I had already suffered this greater pain.

The meal was simple but delectable as before, and as the conversation turned to Oliver and his studies, I relaxed and began to enjoy the evening. It was not late when Thomas suggested that he return me to the castle, and I was appreciative, for I was far more tired than I wanted to admit.

I donned my cloak and then reached for my reticule. As I picked it up, the handle caught on a chair, spilling its contents to the floor.

"Here, let me get that, Serena," Thomas said, bending over to retrieve the few items that had scattered about.

I had started toward the door but turned back, for it seemed to be taking an inordinate amount of time to gather up my small trinkets, and saw that Thomas was just replacing the note that I had received from Anne. I was momentarily worried that he might have seen its contents, but his face showed none of the shock or concern I would have expected if he had, given the nature of the letter.

When we reached the hall Thomas again took me in his arms and kissed me tenderly on the lips. I thought it odd that he did not enjoin me in the game of prince and princess that we had taken to playing, but then perhaps he did not know that I had come to expect it in some small way.

The candle burned strong this evening, and I returned to my room quickly—and, blessedly, undisturbed by any intruders.

The next few days passed uneventfully, with one exception. I had gone to the stables with Oliver one afternoon. Keeping him away from the garden had been quite easy, for he and Robbie were developing a fast friendship based on Robbie's instructing him on the care and handling of horses. We had remained a bit longer than usual, for it had seemed a good opportunity to embark on my lessons with Robbie. Oliver had entered into the enterprise enthusiastically, and I was surprised that Robbie was not intimidated by his presence; instead he appeared to welcome it. I conjectured that this was because he had been able to establish a superior knowledge in another area and therefore was not bashful about having his limitations in letters laid bare.

When we had returned to the hall and I deposited Oliver in the nursery, I headed back to my room, planning on spending the evening doing some mending on the few items that I should be taking with me for the weekend. As I approached my room I saw that the door was ajar, which was odd, for Robbie—who had returned Jaspar early that day—was always so careful to see that it was closed. The moment I flung the door fully open I knew something was amiss. Jaspar lay crouched in the corner by the bookcase. And there on the bed lay my beautiful white organza gown—or, I should say, there lay the remains of it, for someone, something had torn or cut it into shreds. Tears sprang to my eyes as the bits of fabric floated like large snowflakes through my hands. Who could have done such a vile thing? Someone, obviously, who hated me. But who? I knew that there were few here who I could regard as friends, but none that I considered an outright enemy.

I suddenly realized that Jaspar had made no move, and I darted over to where he lay. Whoever had done this had obviously frightened him badly. He whimpered at my touch, and I wondered whether this fiend had dared to lay a hand on him, but on examination it seemed that his meaning was more from relief at seeing me than from pain.

I had just completed gathering up the last fragments of the dress when Charlotte arrived with my tray.

"Good Lord, what happened here?" she cried out, seeing the shreds of white. "That's the beautiful gown what's Lady Ormsby gave you." I nodded. "It's been cut up in ribbons! Knowin' how you loved that dress, I know t'wasn't you that be doin' it, so I has to say there's been evil afoot here. Who could have done this?"

"I don't know, Charlotte. And if they were so angry with me about something, I can't imagine why they would ruin this dress. Except . . ."

"'Cept what, miss?"

"Except that whoever it was might have known that it was the only thing I had to wear to the ball at Lord Kelston's."

"You be goin' to a ball, miss?"

"I *was*. Now it's quite out of the question."

"Oh, miss, me heart breaks for you. First you have that terrible fall an' now this. It's not fair you should be sufferin' so."

"I'm certain there are far worse things, Charlotte. But I do wish I knew who had done this. My father always said it is better to know your enemies."

"I'll be takin' this away." Charlotte gathered the ruins of the gown in her arms. "No need for it to be remindin' you of this unpleasantness. Eat now, and be certain that if I hear anything about it, I'll let ye know. That Molly is a gossip, she is, and she seems to have ways of findin' things out."

"Thank you, Charlotte."

I had no appetite, but forced myself to eat, as I knew that more than ever I needed to keep up my strength. That night I lay awake in bed wondering how I would tell Anne about the dress and what it had done to our plans. I knew that she would not blame me, for the destruction had indeed been out of my control, but I also knew that she would be even more disappointed than I at the turn of events.

I rose the next morning and bathed and dressed quickly. I was anxious to see both Oliver and Thomas and get my mind off the evening before. Oliver was in good spirits, and as I looked at him I felt greatly pleased. For the first time I noticed that he had gained weight since my arrival and his skin had lost its gray pallor. And the clothes that Fiona had made suited him and truly did appear to provide greater freedom of movement.

We breakfasted and then went to the schoolroom, where I had decided to remain for his morning lesson, as it gave me an opportunity to be with Thomas. He was a fine teacher, and I was proud not only of his great wealth of knowledge but of his ability to impart it.

"That will be all for today, Master Oliver," I heard him say suddenly. "And as I am forced to be away for a few days, we will have no lessons tomorrow. Since you will be going to Kelston Manor for the weekend, you would miss our Saturday session anyway, so I'm taking this opportunity to make my small journey. Nonetheless I shall expect you to read some every day. I'm certain that I can count on Miss Miles to see that you do."

"Of course," I replied. I wondered what it was that had so suddenly created a need for this journey, for he had made no mention of it the evening before. Oliver rose and withdrew to the nursery, sensing that Thomas wanted a moment alone with me.

"I shall miss you, Serena," he said, placing a kiss on my brow.

"And I you, Thomas. When will you return?"

"I am not certain. I may be already back here by the time

you return from Kelston Manor."

"I trust that your journey is not caused by unpleasant news?"

"Just some things I must attend. I worry about you, though. I know you don't share my concerns for your safety, but I think that you are far too trusting when it comes to the attentions of someone like Kelston—or his friends, for that matter. You are simply being used and are too blind—or naïve, I know not which—to recognize it. I can only hope that you will come to your senses before it is too late. And now look, I've gone and troubled you. Just promise me that you will think of me while we are apart and that you will dine with me shortly after you return. There is something that I have been wanting to discuss with you. I had hoped we might do it sooner, but I cannot delay this journey. Will you do that for me?"

"Of course," I replied, wondering what it was that could not be said at that very moment. It was a simple promise, for I would indeed miss him, but my curiosity was certainly piqued at the thought of what he wished to share with me.

I was surprised to find Molly with Oliver when I returned to the nursery.

"Mrs. Scoapes left early this mornin' to be spendin' a few days with her sister up north, an' she left this for you. Said to give it to Oliver each mornin'," she explained, handing me the vial that I knew to be his medication. "He's had it this mornin' so you needn't be botherin' 'til the morrow."

"Very well, Molly," I replied, putting the medicine in my pocket and making a mental note that I must be certain to pack it in my valise when we went to Kelston Manor.

"Oh, an' Master Oliver is to 'ave his lunch with her ladyship. She says he'll most like be spendin' most of the afternoon with her."

"Thank you," I replied, somewhat disappointed that I should lose both Thomas and Oliver for the day.

I returned to my room and ate my meal quickly, as I wanted to do some work on my wardrobe. Although I would now not be attending the ball, I would still have to accompany Oliver, and I felt I should at least try to look presentable.

I wished that I still had my blue muslin, for it had been the most flattering of my gowns, but realized that it must have been discarded after my accident. The gray velvet that Lady

Camberleigh had designed for me still hung where I had placed it. I had a fleeting thought that I might be able to remake it slightly to take the edge off its dowdiness, but realized that would undoubtedly simply provoke Lady Camberleigh even further.

There was a knock at the door, and I opened it to see Anne. She stood in the doorway almost totally hidden by the immense pile of boxes she carried in her arms. "Help!" she cried with a laugh.

"Good Lord," I exclaimed, grabbing some of the boxes.

"You should have heard Justin accusing me of turning his new carriage into a gypsy caravan."

"What on earth have you brought? You must be intending to stay at Kelston Manor for weeks, by the look of things."

She smiled. "Well, I have been dying to show them to you. Oh, it is grand to see you again." She put down the rest of the boxes and embraced me warmly. "Thank goodness those blue circles have disappeared. You look quite recovered, but how do you feel? There's time and enough for that," she went on, not giving me a chance to respond. "Right now I want you to see these new gowns."

She opened all but one box. There must have been six dresses, each more spectacular than the one before.

"Oh, Anne, you are truly going to be the most beautiful lady at Kelston in these dresses," I said, fingering a dark green velvet traveling outfit that featured a lacy blouse, the collars and cuffs of which peeked out from the jacket, giving it just the spot of color it needed.

"I'm glad you like them," she replied, eyes dancing, "for they are yours."

"What?"

"Now don't be angry with me, but after your accident, when we had removed your dress and I went to hang it up, I realized that you really had naught to wear. So I took your blue muslin, which really was rather ruined anyway, back with me to Mayfair."

"I don't understand."

"Well, I needed it for the proper size! And since that wonderful Fiona was finished with Clarissa's wardrobe I inveigled her to come to Mayfair with me. She was delighted when I told her the reason, for she seemed to have felt badly, having had to have created that ghastly gray velvet for you."

"But Anne, I can't pay for these things. I am certain that I could scarce afford one, not to mention all these."

"They are not for sale anyway. Call them a gift. Now don't look at me that way, I know my not telling you was naughty, but you must indulge me this whim."

"Anne . . . I hardly know where to begin. Even with all these exquisite things I shall not be able to attend the ball anyway."

"Why not? You are not feeling too ill, are you? Oh dear. It doesn't have anything to do with finding that poor girl's body in the pool, does it?"

"No. I am feeling completely recovered, and although I wonder if I shall ever be able to forget my horrible discovery, it has nothing to do with either."

"Then what?"

"Well, I have dreaded telling you this, but yesterday afternoon I returned to my room to find the beautiful dress you gave me had been torn or cut into tatters."

"But that is mad! Who could have done such a thing?"

"I don't know. But it is obviously someone who does not want me to attend that ball."

"But who?" she pressed.

"I feel dreadful about it. I cried and cried when I saw it. Your lovely dress was almost unrecognizable."

"I understand you must feel terrible, but don't worry about the dress. It's a pity, for it did look wonderful on you, but we can always get another dress."

"Not for the ball, however."

"Aha!" she exclaimed, springing to her feet. "That is where you are wrong. Whoever did this dreadful thing is going to be quite taken aback when they see my pièce de résistance. Here, open this." And with that she handed me the one still unopened box.

I lifted the lid and withdrew a gown of azure blue. The fabric—which was a soft floating material I did not recognize—was shot through with threads of gold. The neckline was cut almost dangerously low and encircled by a gold ribbon. The puff sleeves stood up in an arc and were caught by the same gold ribbon that enhanced the bustline.

"Oh, Anne." I held it up to myself and ran to the mirror. "It is magnificent."

"It is unusual, but it is an idea that I have had for some time, and I then remembered that my father long ago had this and several other lengths of fabric shipped from India. When I pulled this out, I knew it would be perfect."

"It's more than perfect, if that is possible. Not quite befitting the governess, though." I laughed.

"Believe me, I wouldn't go wasting my designs on just anyone. You will do it justice and will be envy in the eye of every woman there. They will all be dying to know who designed it, but we shall keep it secret until they come begging. I shall have my shop yet, and by the time I open it I will have a ready-made entourage of customers."

"You have quite literally swept me off my feet with all this, you know."

"The person who is going to try to sweep you off your feet, my dear Serena, is Robin."

"Might I ask you something—something quite personal?"

"Of course."

"Were you ever in love with Lord Kelston?"

"Good gracious, no. Well . . . actually, I suppose I was infatuated with him for a while, but then I met Anthony, and I married him. The only reason that I regret things not having worked out with Robin is that it might have kept me from making the dreadful mistake with Anthony. But then all I would have been doing is trading one mistake for another."

"You are so much wiser than I am about these things."

"Not wiser, my dear, just more experienced. The only advice I can give you is that when you marry, do it for love. A life without passion is really no life at all," she said seriously.

I was not surprised at the earnestness of her tone, for I was certain that anything that Anne would enter into she would do passionately, giving herself freely to it all.

We chatted for another hour. She was anxious to have me tell her all the details about my finding the body in the pool and the incident with the dress. We both knew it would be impossible to discuss either event over the next few days, for we would have to keep both in confidence lest they fall on less than deaf ears.

Robbie brought Jaspar back in the late afternoon and Anne seemed pleased that the dog recognized her. She was taking dinner with the Earl and Lady Camberleigh in the dining room, and it was not long before she rose to leave.

"Darling, I would much rather stay here with you and prattle on into the evening, but I don't want to set Maura off before our weekend. She is so volatile that the slightest thing might cause her to cancel the whole affair, even though Clarissa is a priority at this time."

"I understand, of course," I replied. "In truth, I must see to getting both Oliver and myself organized for the journey, although you seem to have done everything for me but the packing."

"Just be sure you get some rest. Remember, I want to show off my creation to the best advantage."

We embraced, and Anne left me to wonder at this fortune of finery that lay scattered about the room. I hung each garment carefully in the closet and placed the boxes under the bed. I did not fear the marauder returning, for I felt that he or she had known that the white gown had been the only thing I had wear to the ball and once that was ruined so would be my chances.

When I reached the nursery I saw a maid had obviously been instructed to take care of Oliver's wardrobe for the weekend. Seeing that she had selected none of the things that Fiona had created, I made a few changes. Oliver had not returned by the time I completed my adjustments, and, assuming that he was still with our grandmother, I decided to return to my room.

It was peculiar to think of her as our grandmother. It had been well over a week since I had seen her last, and even though our meetings, few as they had been, had been tinged with suspicion and doubt, I longed to be in her company whenever possible and could not help but feel a little jealous at Oliver's time with her. I knew so little about this woman who was the matriarch of Camberleigh. Under the circumstances, I could not expect her to reveal much if anything about herself to me, and yet she was the one link to my past and my heritage. I longed to know of her own life, her childhood, of my grandfather and of my own father's days growing up in this house.

I didn't know if she had meant to frighten me or warn me

or both when she had alerted me of her letter to her solicitor. Whatever her intent, I had been delighted, for it gave me hope that some clue might turn up which would give validity to my mother's letter. I had no idea how long these things took, but postulated that it was a far longer process than I cared imagine.

Charlotte was tending the fire when I arrived back at my room.

"I was just about to give you up, miss. Ye better eat your supper, or I'll be tellin' Cook on you."

"Well, I wouldn't want that would I," I replied, thinking that Cook probably had a temper that one did not want to be acquainted with.

"You know, miss, I was thinkin'. With you goin' away for a few days, you will have to leave your spaniel here. But my Robbie can be lookin' after him for you. He won't have much to do, what with the whole household bein' gone, an' I know I can speak for him on this."

"I would appreciate it, Charlotte. Jaspar and I have never been separated for more than a few hours, and it is going to be difficult for us both, but he loves Robbie and I know that I would be leaving him in good hands."

"'Tis settled, then. I was thinkin' something else. In the morning I'll bring in an extra basin and we can wash your hair if you like."

"Oh, Charlotte, that would be wonderful," I replied, delighted at the thought. My wound had healed so completely that it now was but a memory, and my hair hadn't had a decent cleansing since my accident.

After eating I made a vain attempt at reading some in my book, but I was simply too excited at the prospect of the weekend. I changed into my nightdress and climbed into bed, hoping that sleep would soon overtake me. My last thoughts were of Thomas's warnings to me.

Chapter Nine

I AWOKE feeling totally refreshed to see Charlotte already in my room.

"'Tis a wee bit early, miss, but if we are to be doin' your hair an' all, I thought we should get a jump on the day."

She drew back the draperies, and I saw that it was an overcast morning.

"Don't worry. This'll burn off soon and it'll be a right nice day for travelin'."

Charlotte hummed pleasantly as she washed my hair, and I luxuriated at the attention. Suddenly it occurred to me that I was going to be left to my own devices in the matter of dressing my hair at Kelston Manor. "Charlotte, what am I going to do about my hair for the ball?" I asked. "I've watched you fix it but I don't have anything like your skill. Whatever will I do?"

"I thought you weren't going to the ball, miss, on account of yer dress was ruined."

"If I tell you a secret, will you promise not to tell?"

"I'm no gossip, miss," she replied conspiratorily.

I went to the closet and pulled out the azure and gold gown. Charlotte's mouth dropped open. "Oh, miss, it right takes my breath away. But where—?"

"It appears that Lady Ormsby has taken it upon herself to be my benefactor. She professes to have ulterior motives, but I think she is just naturally the kindest and most generous person I have ever known."

CAMBERLEIGH

"I can't wait 'til you come back so's I can hear all about it."

"But what of my hair, Charlotte?"

"I'll fix it now for travelin'. When ye gets to the manor they'll give you a girl to tend you. If you can, ask for Rowena. She's an old friend, and unless she's gone balmy in her progressin' years she'll still have a knack for workin' with hair. You just tell her her friend Charlotte says to do right by you."

I hugged her. Everything seemed to be falling into place, thanks to Charlotte and Anne. Perhaps all this was an omen of better fortune to come.

Charlotte coiled and twisted my hair and piled it on top of my head, then got ready to leave. I was loath to see her go, as it meant parting with Jaspar, who, sensing that something was about, had been at my heels the entire morning. I hugged him close to me, assuring him that I should return shortly and beseeching him to behave well for Robbie. As he trotted out the door with Charlotte, I felt as though I were sending my best friend to the gallows, but I knew that Robbie would care for him as if he were his own.

Packing was a joy, for I just couldn't get enough of my new dresses. There were too many for just a weekend, and choosing amongst them was a dilemma, for each was lovelier than the one before.

The dark green velvet I would wear for the journey. There was a cream-colored taffeta with bugle beads at the bodice which I selected for evening and a peach muslin with a matching bonnet for day. The gown for the ball I wrapped in extra tissue and placed carefully at the bottom of my valise.

I had just finished dressing when Anne arrived.

"Serena, you look ravishing. I'm so glad you're wearing the velvet, for it also has a bonnet. I forgot to give it to you last evening." She handed me a hat crafted of the same cloth. It had a broad brim and sported a jaunty feather that swept around the side.

"What is it Serena?" she said, noticing my frown. "Oh dear, you don't like it."

"Oh, no. I love it. It's just that this is all so much. I am concerned about Lady Camberleigh's reaction. I certainly don't want to do anything to distress her ladyship."

193

"Well, the same thing occurred to me, and I've taken care of that. I told Maura that I knew you had been included in the weekend, and I assumed that you had nothing appropriate to wear, so I had brought along a few of my cast-offs. I told her that I knew she wouldn't want you to be . . . well, an embarrassment."

"What was her reaction?"

"Exactly what I had assumed. Not being embarrassed takes precedence over almost everything with Maura. I believe she was quite relieved."

"You know, I hadn't thought of the arrangements for our travels," I replied.

"Robin was going to send a coach, but Justin wouldn't hear of it, proud as he is of his new carriage. Richard and Maura have gone on ahead with her ladyship and Clarissa. They left a short time ago. You and Oliver will come with Justin and me."

Although I wasn't looking forward to being in the company of Lord Barkham, I was glad that I should be with Anne and Oliver. I could not help but be irritated that Oliver had not been included in his family's coach, for I could never get used to the idea of his being ostracized by his mother.

Anne left me to finish gathering my things. I put on my bonnet and looked in the mirror. It was hard to recognize the image I saw there. I wished that inside I felt as glamorous and worldly as I appeared on the outside.

Oliver was dressed and waiting for me in the nursery.

"Serena is that you?" he said, looking at me in disbelief.

"What do you think?"

"You look beautiful."

"Coming from you that's the nicest compliment I could have."

Anne was already in the carriage when we emerged from the house, and Giles was seeing to it that the last of the baggage was properly loaded at the back.

A footman helped us up and we were well settled in by the time Lord Barkham arrived.

It was typical, I thought, that he should not make one mention of my appearance, for when he was not able to criticize he fell silent.

Charlotte had been right about the weather. The sun had burned off the low clouds, and the air was now fresh and warm. Oliver fell to talking with Lord Barkham about horses and the tricks that Robbie had shown him this past week.

Anne chatted on about who would be at the ball, rattling off names that were of course meaningless to me. I saw that Lord Barkham stole a few glances at me from time to time when he thought I wasn't noticing; I felt smug that my appearance obviously had made an impression after all.

We had ridden for well over two hours when Lord Barkham instructed the driver to pull over to the side of the road by an open field through which ran a small stream.

"Justin, what are you doing?" Anne asked, peering out of the carriage to see where we were.

"I thought we would rest here and take luncheon," he replied, opening the carriage door.

"Where, pray tell? There is no inn or tavern for miles unless my eyes and my memory deceive me."

"My dear sister, the earth will provide a strong seat, the birds will provide the music and what more charming company might I provide?"

"You haven't mentioned food."

"Ah yes, food. If Cook followed my instructions this basket is filled with squab, smoked fish, fresh bread and cheeses. And if Giles followed my instructions, there are several bottles of wine tucked on top."

"Are we going to eat out there, Uncle Justin?"

"We certainly are, Oliver," he replied, helping the boy down from the carriage.

"Justin, we can't sit out there dressed like this," Anne said indignantly, scrutinizing the meadows.

"Then you have two choices. You can remove your clothing and sit out there in your petticoats, or you can stay in here and starve."

"I swear, if you weren't my own brother I'd hit you with this parasol to try to beat some sense into you."

"But you secretly like the idea, now admit it," he retorted gaily.

"Serena, I do apologize for his actions," Anne said. "I'm certain that you know I was not a party to this."

"I really don't mind, Anne. Actually, this will not be the first time that I have dined in open air, and I must admit to being hungry."

"I cannot feign disappointment that you did not deem it necessary to remove your costume, Miss Miles, but I am pleased that you will join us," said Lord Barkham. "Let me help you down."

I ignored the impertinent remark. "Come, Anne. It's a beautiful day, and we can be very careful of our dresses. If only for Oliver's sake," I whispered to her.

Lord Barkham spread a large blanket on the ground and began ceremoniously unpacking the basket while Oliver inspected the banks of the stream nearby.

I decided Anne's protests had been mostly for effect, for she quickly joined in the spirit of things as we began to eat.

"Serena, might I go down there for a little while?" Oliver asked, pointing to a thicket a little way down the stream.

I nodded. "Don't remain too long, however." The stream was shallow and the water moved slowly, so there was no danger.

Lord Barkham poured himself another glass of wine. "Might I replenish yours, Miss Miles?"

"It is delicious, but I fear it should quite put me to sleep were I to have any more," I replied.

"Actually I am glad that Oliver has left us for the moment, for there is something I wish to discuss with you both," Lord Barkham said, lowering his voice slightly.

"I have spoken to the magistrate. It is still too early to tell, but it appears that the body you found was that of one Margarite Smythe."

"Margarite Smythe," Anne mused, "why does that name sound so familiar? I know, she was Oliver's last governess."

"That's correct. If you recall, she was there less than two months and then she simply disappeared. At the time I thought nothing of it, I must admit, since Oliver's governesses, until you, of course, Miss Miles, have seemed to have little stability."

"The real lack of stability—as you well know, Justin—is on Maura's part. I admit that there were none about whom one could become terribly enthusiastic, but Maura's tirades make it impossible for almost anyone to remain under that roof. Nevertheless, I can't imagine that she would have undone her so that the girl was driven to take her own life."

"It upsets me to have to say this, but it does not seem that that is what happened. There appears to be evidence that the girl was murdered."

I gasped so loudly that Lord Barkham sprang up in alarm.

"Here, drink this," he said, holding my wineglass toward me.

"No, I shall be all right. It's just that although I knew that foul play was a possibility, I could just not let myself even think on it. That poor girl. But why? If she had been there such a short time, she hardly had an opportunity to be acquainted with anyone."

"Serena, it is not necessarily someone she knew. The person might have been from one of the tenant farms or the stables. It could have been anyone—even me."

"Justin, don't say such a thing," Anne said, putting her hands to her ears.

"I said that merely to point out that this means there will be an investigation. The magistrate has promised to make it as discreet as possible, but until this thing is solved we are all suspects of sorts. Not you, of course, Miss Miles, but you will probably have to undergo some questioning."

"What did Richard say?" Anne asked.

"I haven't told him yet."

"Well then, you mustn't tell him—at least not this weekend."

"Anne, the man has to know. You can't try to protect him from everything."

Protect? What a strange choice of words, I thought, for I could not imagine the Earl needing protection from anything. I thought that others needed protection from him.

"I'm not protecting him, Justin," I heard Anne say. "I just don't want to spoil this weekend. Everything will come out soon enough, and if there was urgency in this matter I am certain that this journey would not have been permitted, so promise me that you won't say anything until we return to Camberleigh."

"Serena, look what I found," I heard Oliver call out. I turned and saw that he carried a small bird's nest, probably that of a wren or a swallow. "Might I keep it?"

"Well, I would replace it if I had found it, for in the spring some bird might be able to make use of it again."

"Then I shall leave it for them to find."

As Oliver went back to the thicket, I turned to Lord Barkham. "For quite different reasons, I also implore you to hold off saying anything on this matter. This is Oliver's first real holiday from Camberleigh, and I don't want him to remember it with whatever will unfold when the Earl learns of this."

"With such heart-rending appeals, how can I say no. All right, ladies. You have my word that I shall be silent until our return, but then Richard must and will be told."

"Thank you, Justin. There are times when I think it quite nice that you are my brother."

The driver had moved the horses back to the road from the stream where he had been watering them; and Anne and I now took to setting the remains of our picnic back in the basket. Oliver rejoined us, and it was not long before we were on our way again. Anne soon dozed off as did Oliver, which left Lord Barkham and I rather uncomfortably regarding each other face to face. He seemed to look right through me, and I felt myself shudder.

"Are you cold, Serena?"

"No, I am fine thank you, Lord Barkham," I replied, pulling the collar of my jacket closer about my neck.

"Would it be so difficult for you to call me Justin?"

"It would not be difficult at all, sire," I replied, picking at my skirt as if to brush something off. "I simply prefer to call you Lord Barkham."

"Why in blazes do you continue this game with me, Serena?"

"I don't know what you mean," I replied, gazing directly into his eyes.

"Don't you?"

I was just about to protest firmly that I truly did not understand when the carriage gave a small lurch and Oliver opened his eyes.

"Are we there yet?"

"Not yet, Oliver, but I think it's not far. Perhaps Lord Barkham knows," I said, stressing the words *Lord* and *Barkham*.

I then lapsed into silence and I turned to watch the passing scene. The landscape had changed slightly since our rest for luncheon. The farms here were larger and, by the looks of the tenant houses, they were far more prosperous. I recalled the argument at dinner when Lord Barkham had implied that the reason the Kelston estates flourished was that money had been reinvested in the form of equipment and improvements. I wondered if we were now on Kelston soil.

As if reading my mind, Lord Barkham said, "It won't be long now. You can tell by the look of the farms. With all Robin's indulgences, I've got to hand it to him. He's made a go of it since his father's death."

"Maybe so, Justin, but you also know perfectly well that it was his father who made the investments," Anne, awake again I now realized, said suddenly. "I think he knew that if he didn't his son would gamble it away in a matter of years, and he was probably right. Fortunately for Robin, he can now feel secure on his father's foresight."

"Did you have a nice nap, Anne?" I asked.

"Yes I did," she replied, stretching her arms. "I must have my beauty sleep, you know."

"I don't see any visible difference," Lord Barkham said. "Do you Oliver?"

"It's good that my ego does not rely on the flattery of my brother. Oh look, we are just entering the drive."

Several riders on horseback galloped by as if in announcement of our arrival. The approach to Kelston Manor was not as long as that to Camberleigh, though the stretches of greensward, the ponds and the small islands of woodlands were similar. The manor itself had neither the size of Camberleigh nor the perfect symmetry of Mayfair, but nevertheless held a grandeur all its own.

A number of other carriages had just arrived, and footmen scurried about the forecourt assisting men and women of all ages and sizes bedecked in their best attire.

"I had no idea that there would be so many people," I said, suddenly a bit frightened as I realized the enormous size of the affair.

"Robin is famous for show," replied Anne. "You can be certain that anyone who is in the proper register in this county will be here."

The door of the carriage opened, and I was helped to the ground by a young man whose eyes seemed to widen at the sight of me.

"Be careful, Oliver," I said, turning to my charge. "That is a long step down."

We had all disembarked when an older man approached us. "Lord Barkham, isn't it?"

"You have a memory, Henry," he replied familiarly. "I do believe you know my sister, Lady Ormsby. This is Miss Miles and Master Oliver of Camberleigh."

I saw that Anne did not extend her hand, so I too let mine remain at my side while the man bowed to us in acknowledgment.

"I believe that you are all to be in the south wing, but the housekeeper, Mrs. Mooreston, is better informed of that. She is just inside. Your baggage will follow momentarily."

I took Oliver's hand and followed Anne and Lord Barkham up the steps and into the center hall. A rosy-cheeked gray-haired woman who was rattling about with an ornately bound ledger in her arms greeted us. "I am Mrs. Mooreston, the housekeeper. We would be pleased if you signed the guest book, and then I shall see that you are escorted to your rooms."

We each signed the register as the woman explained that there would be a reception in the drawing room before dinner. Tea would be brought to our rooms in a little while, but if Lord Barkham wished anything stronger he should find it in the library.

"Now let me see," Mrs. Mooreston said, examining her register. "You shall all be in the south wing. Alfred here will show you to your rooms. Ladies, your maids will be along shortly."

I followed behind holding tight to Oliver's hand, as we were guided up the staircase and down a long corridor. Anne's room was the first.

"Come and see me after you've settled in," she said as she disappeared into the room.

"I will."

We followed the man called Alfred.

"Your rooms are here, miss," he said, flinging a door open.

"And Master Oliver will be right next door. The two rooms connect by an inside door."

My room was not large, but it was bright and cheerful, decorated totally in blue and white save for a colorful rug on the floor.

"Let us see your room Oliver," I said, opening the door to the adjoining room. "I'm so glad you'll be right next door. That way we can visit whenever we want."

"If we had rooms like this at Camberleigh, then I could see you and Jaspar all the time."

We moved back into my room, where a maid was placing a tray on a small table.

"Hello, miss. My name is Rowena, and Lady Kelston thought you might like some tea and scones after your journey."

"What did you say your name was?"

"Rowena, miss."

"Well, that is a coincidence, for I was given your name to look up."

"How is that, miss?"

"I believe Charlotte McKee is an old friend of yours?"

"You know Charlotte, miss?"

"Yes. She has become a good friend since I have been at Camberleigh."

"Oh, Charlotte's a good person. We be knowin' each other since we were just little ones."

"She tells me that you share her talent for doing hair."

"Ah, she's a great one for compliments. I don't have her knack, but it's true I've been known to turn a tress or two."

"Might I rely on your assistance, Rowena, during my stay?"

"T'would be an honor, particularly since you be knowin' Charlotte."

"Well, Oliver, shall we have a spot of this tea that Rowena has brought us?"

I removed my hat and we sat side by side and each ate hungrily of the jams and biscuits.

The baggage arrived soon, and I nodded appreciatively to Rowena, who offered to unpack it for me.

I responded to a knock at the door, thinking that it must be Anne come to see where we had settled in, but found instead that it was Lord Barkham.

"I don't mean to intrude, but I thought that I might take Oliver with me on a walk about the grounds. We have several hours until the reception, and I am certain you can use it to unpack or whatever."

"Well, that is up to Oliver," I replied.

"If you don't mind, Serena, I would like to go with Uncle Justin."

"Good. We won't be long then. By the way, Miss Miles, I thought you would like to know that my room is just there across the hall, so I shall be able to keep a good eye on your comings and goings."

"I really don't think that they are any concern of yours."

"Once more, that's where you are wrong, Miss Miles," he replied, turning on his heel and leading Oliver down the hallway.

Rowena had completed unpacking my things and removed the tea tray. I left the room and went to see how Anne was faring.

"I was just coming to see you," she said. "Have you had tea?"

"Yes, but I could do with another cup. Your brother has taken Oliver off for an inspection of the grounds."

"Good, then come join me," she replied, drawing me into the room. "Have you ever seen so many frills? Somehow this room doesn't seem very 'me'."

I laughed. "No, it doesn't. Clarissa, perhaps, but definitely not you."

"A stroke of decorating genius by Lady Kelston, no doubt."

"I assume you refer to Robin's mother."

"None other. Monique has a flamboyance all her own."

"Monique?"

"Yes. Oh, of course you don't know. She is French. Robin's father met her in Paris. No one ever knew quite what she was doing there or how they met, for her family was supposedly from the country, but he married her and brought her home as his bride. It created quite a scandal about these parts, let me tell you, for they returned with Robin already in a cradle. I don't really know all the details, but with the Kelston name being as prominent as it is, you can imagine that it set tongues to wagging."

"What is she like?" I asked, now growing curious about our hostess.

"She is quite a remarkable woman and I like her. Our families were close friends. You see, my mother was the first person to pay her a social call after their return from France. I don't think Monique ever forgot it. Eventually it all settled down, of course, as these things do. Monique is a magnificent hostess and before long she had the nobility absolutely clamoring to be included in her soirées."

"She sounds fascinating."

"Well, you've seen how charming Robin can be, and he definitely comes by it through his mother's side of the family."

"When did his father die?"

"Four years ago. He was considerably older than Monique. She was devastated by his death, and I often think how lonely it must be for her here, rambling about in this huge house alone."

"She has Robin."

"Robin? I doubt that he is about much. I think he still spends every free moment he can find at the tables."

"It can't be that bad."

"Oh, I suppose not. I do tend to go on some, don't I?"

"I wonder what Lady Kelston will think of me. I don't want to cause any embarrassment."

"You could embarrass no one, Serena. But if you'd feel more secure, I shall keep an eye out. I know, let us have a signal. If you need help, do something like opening your fan."

"I haven't a fan."

"Well then, take this one," she said, moving to the dresser and pulling out a small ivory fan. "I have several others, and this best suits your gowns."

"Let us hope that I won't need it."

"Don't worry about Lady Kelston. Even though I find her taste in furnishings somewhat overdone, she has a great eye for beauty. For that alone she will appreciate you."

I embraced Anne and returned to my room. Peeping into the adjoining chamber to see if Oliver had returned, I found him chatting with Rowena who had brought him his evening meal.

"It's a bit early for his supper, miss, but the kitchens being busy as they are, I thought it best to be sure that he was fed before I went forgettin'."

"Oh, Rowena. That makes me realize that I have not given Oliver his medication today. He was supposed to have it this morning, but I was so busy with packing and all, I forgot."

"'Twon't hurt him, I'm sure, miss," she replied, seeing Oliver grimace at the sound of medication.

I returned with the vial and gave him a spoonful, as I had seen Mrs. Scoapes do. Oliver followed it quickly with some fresh milk and I smiled, thinking back to my own childhood when I had done the same when my mother administered those concoctions that were supposed to give me strength after a prolonged fever.

"Well, what did you do on your walk?" I asked.

"We went down to the stables. You should see what a lot of horses they have. I wish Robbie could see too."

"Perhaps you can show them to me tomorrow," I replied.

"Uncle Justin says there is to be a hunt. Perhaps I might go?"

"I should think you are still a bit young for that, but we might go down to see them off. Would you like that?"

"Serena, are you going to the ball tonight?"

"That is not until tomorrow night. But there is a welcoming dinner this evening that I shall be attending."

"Will you come to see me before you go?"

"Of course. If you promise to be ready for bed, then I shall tuck you in before I leave."

"I put a fresh basin in your room, miss, and I'll return in just a spell to fix your hair, if you still be wantin' it?"

"Oh, yes, Rowena, I would be most grateful."

I bathed and had just finished putting on my petticoats when Rowena returned. As she gently unpinned my hair, letting it fall down my back, I described to her as best I could how Charlotte had styled it.

The effect she achieved was if anything more dramatic, starting higher at the crown and allowing the full length of it to fall from there. I added just a touch of rouge to my cheeks and lips which I thought still a bit pale. The cream taffeta gown had hung out nicely, and Rowena helped me into it, buttoning the same tiny seed pearls that matched the bugles on the bodice.

"I couldn't have done it without you, Rowena," I said, pleased at the overall effect.

"'Tis a magnificent gown, miss, but it's you that makes it so." With that, Rowena left me and I tiptoed through to the adjoining room, where Oliver was already in bed.

"Is that you, Serena?" he asked, sitting up.

"Yes, it's me, Oliver."

"You look beautiful. I bet you wish Mr. Masters could see you like this."

I warmed at that thought of Thomas. "Perhaps one day he shall," I replied, bending down to kiss his forehead. "You have sweet dreams, and I shall look in on you when I return. If you need anything in the night, just knock at the door."

"Serena?"

"Yes, Oliver."

"If you see Uncle Justin, will you tell him it's all right?"

"What is all right?"

"Just something. He'll know."

I kissed Oliver again and returned to my room, bewildered. It sounded almost as though they had had a disagreement. But bully others as he might, I didn't think Lord Barkham would browbeat this small boy, whom he treated much as his own son.

There was a knock at the door, and there stood Anne, looking elegant in a strikingly cut gown of moss-green taffeta.

"I knew it, Serena," she said, turning me around. "I shall have clientele for my shop after this very first evening. You look devastating—and your hair is perfect for the gown. Justin has already gone downstairs. You would have thought he would have waited, but he seemed preoccupied. I hope your discovery in the garden isn't going to make him a bore this whole weekend. But then, he did promise us his silence, didn't he, and I've never known him to rescind his word."

I paled at the thought again of that poor girl's body floating in the pond.

"Now I've gone and done it—reminding you again. I am sorry. Well, there is nothing like a little flattery to get one's mind off unpleasant subjects, so let us just wend our way down to the drawing room and accept the acclaim we both deserve."

I had closed the door when I realized that I'd forgotten

something and ran back into my room.

"What is it?" called in Anne after me.

"The fan," I replied, retrieving it from the bed. "I almost forgot our signal."

The drawing room was filled with people, none of whom I immediately recognized. We had gone no more than twenty paces when Lord Kelston appeared before us, beaming.

"My schemer," he said, addressing Anne. "Statuesque as always. And the reason for our scheme"—his eyes resting on mine—"more beautiful than I had dared remember. Come," he continued, taking Anne's hand, "there is someone who is dying to meet you." His other arm swung about my waist and we moved through the crowd toward a group on the other side of the room. As we grew nearer, I saw that it was none other than the Earl and Lady Camberleigh, Lord Barkham and Clarissa, and some woman I did not know.

"Mother, look who I have brought," Lord Kelston said, moving Anne to the middle of the group.

"Anne, how wonderful to see you. You look *trés* chic, but then you always do." The two women embraced.

Lady Kelston was of medium height. Her hair, which she wore parted in the middle and pulled into a full chignon at the back, was as black as that of her son. Long black lashes framed dark eyes, and her mouth, which was full and strongly rouged, flashed a smile that revealed perfect teeth.

"It has been too long, *cherie,*" she said to Anne in a deep voice that still bore traces of her French heritage. Our eyes met, and she pulled back from her embrace with Anne. "Ah, and who do we have here?"

"Mother, may I present Miss Miles—Serena Miles."

"Lady Kelston," I replied, curtsying slightly.

"*Ravissante,* mademoiselle."

"*Merci,* madame."

"Ah, and she speaks French as well, this magnificent creature. Well, then, we shall be good friends. You must call me Monique."

With that, Clarissa inserted herself into the conversation. "Lady Ormsby, my mother told me of your generosity to our governess Miss Miles in lending her a few of your things so that she might make the trip with Oliver," I heard Clarissa say.

While I had half-expected this, I had held out a thin hope that I might have gone through at least part of this weekend without everyone knowing who I really was. Any such ideas had now been dashed here at the very outset. I dropped my eyes and, gathering my skirts, forced out an apology and turned, looking for the nearest door so that I might quickly flee. A hand caught my arm and I turned to see that it was Lady Kelston who restrained me. "I am pleased that the boy created a way for you to join us, Miss Miles. I am certain that there is not a gentleman here who would not wish that it were they that was under your guidance. Lady Camberleigh, might I congratulate you. Although it would appear that it is your daughter and not your son who is in greatest need of governing."

Someone was laughing and I looked up to see that it was Lord Barkham. "Monique, for a French woman you always have had a way with words."

"Actually, my dear Justin, I think you know that I prefer actions to words, so perhaps you shall do me the favor of escorting our lovely Clarissa about—after all, the affair is largely in her honor," Lady Kelston replied. "If you will excuse me, Richard, Maura, I would like to present Miss Miles to some gentlemen over there who, unless looks deceive me, are already besotted with her from afar." Before I knew what was happening, she had linked her arm in mine and was moving me away through the crowd of milling guests. "Don't worry, my dear, I have no intention of throwing you to those wolves, but I thought it best to get you away from that group. Clarissa is just a senseless child who makes remarks at the expense of others which I swear half the time she does not understand herself. But her mother is a different matter, and I did not want to remain to hear or see what she might do. She was so lovely as a young girl. *Tragique*, that one."

"I am terribly sorry if I have caused you any embarrassment, Lady Kelston," I said.

"First off, you shall call me Monique and I shall call you Serena. Secondly, I am too old and I have seen far too much to be embarrassed by some petty display of jealousy. Come, let us have a glass of wine and let me learn more of you."

She ushered me over to a small alcove and I told her the

story that I had come to recount so well in the past weeks, loathing as I did that I could not be honest with this woman who had just moments before been my champion.

"How does it come that my son knows you?" she asked. "Not that I don't think he has an eye for beauty."

I told her about the dinner, the carriage ride the next day, and my accident. I also wanted to share the story of Anne's plotting this weekend, for I sensed that Monique might somehow appreciate it, but I felt that I should hold my tongue. That might have placed Anne in an awkward position with Monique.

"I see that you and Anne are well acquainted," she ventured.

"She has become a good friend," I replied.

"That eez good," she answered, her accent becoming more pronounced as the conversation became more intimate. "I like Anne. She is a strong woman. Oh, she has made mistakes, of course, like her marriage to that man, but then, we all do. The important thing is that she has learned from them." I made no response. "And what of the Earl, how has he treated you?"

"In truth I have not had many dealings with him," I replied, somewhat taken aback by her directness.

"I see. I am curious because from what you tell me he had no part in your being brought to Camberleigh, and Richard never likes things which are not his own decision."

"If he has had any objections," I retorted, "he has not expressed them to me."

As she took another sip of wine, I could not help but notice the ring she wore on her left hand. It was a large simply cut emerald surrounded by alternating diamonds and sapphires.

"You admire my ring?"

"It is truly beautiful."

"My late husband gave it to me on our wedding night. I have not taken it off since."

"He must have loved you very much."

"There are many who would say, Serena, that I married him for his fortunes. But to the day I die I shall know it was for love. And now, my dear," she said, rising, "I shall be called an inelegant hostess should I not mingle with my guests and allow these young men here the benefit of your company. But we shall talk again soon."

Anne must have been watching us the entire time, for Monique had taken no more than two steps before she was at my side.

"I have no idea what you two were talking about, but I knew I was right that she would like you," she gushed.

"She's fascinating," I replied. "Though not at all what I expected."

"That Clarissa. Some day I'm going to nail that mouth of hers shut. Here comes Robin. I shall have to make myself scarce, for he has already accused me of monopolizing your time. Remember the fan."

As I watched Lord Kelston approach, I noted that there could be no doubt that he was indeed his mother's son. The resemblance, now that I had met her, was uncanny.

"I trust that my mother did not bend your ear for too long, Serena," he said, leaning down to where I sat.

"Quite the contrary, Lord Kelston."

"Robin," he corrected.

"She is charming."

"That, my dear Serena, is what I was going to say about you. Will you join me for dinner?"

"I should be delighted, if you are certain that it will not take you from your guests."

"Do I have other guests?" he said with a smile. "I hadn't noticed."

Tucking his arm in mine, he led me through into the dining room, and I saw that many guests had already assembled there. The room was enormous. Three immense crystal chandeliers hung above the banquet table, their lights dancing off the crystal and silver on the table as well as from the lavish jewels worn by many of the ladies. The whole room seemed to shimmer.

I was surprised when Robin seated me to his right at the head of the table, for I had assumed that this would be reserved for Clarissa as the guest of honor, but then I saw that she was seated at the dead center of the table flanked by two rather foppish-looking young men who appeared entranced by her every move. But then where was Lord Barkham? I had not long to wonder, for his voice suddenly intruded as if from nowhere.

"I see, Robin, that you have an eye for more than cards these days."

"Ah, Justin," he replied. "Rarely does the eye have a chance to behold something so exquisite. If you weren't so embroiled in that taxation issue your eyes might have been opened too. Although I can't say with any certainty that they have not been."

"Might I join you?"

"Of course. But I should tell you, Barkham, that I should not be a good ear for your business conversations, given the present company."

"I am certain that Mrs. Robertson would be even less interested than you."

Robin rose to be introduced. There was a woman at Lord Barkham's other side, but I could not see anything of her save the bright crimson of her gown.

"Lord Kelston, may I present Mrs. Martin Robertson, most recently from the colonies in the New World."

"How fascinating," Robin replied. "Won't you join us. Might I present Miss Serena Miles."

Lord Barkham stepped aside. The woman who extended her hand was perhaps ten years my senior. Her cheeks and lips were heavily rouged, almost as if to match her dress. Her hair was shorn very short and brushed close to her face. There was a dark spot just to the left of her mouth and an identical one on her left bosom, which I decided had been artfully placed not by nature but by her own hand.

"How do you do, Miss Miles," she said in a throaty voice, the accent of which was not familiar to me.

I smiled and, as she took a seat opposite me, wondered if she were an actress, as my father had once told me that these people often had a certain flamboyance of style and character.

To my displeasure Lord Barkham moved to the seat next to mine, but since the chair next to Mrs. Robertson had already been taken by an older gentleman, I knew he had no other choice, since she was obviously the man's dinner partner.

"Well, what brings you to England, Mrs. Robertson?" Robin asked, his eyes lingering extra long on the mark on her breast.

"I have come back to settle some of my late husband's affairs."

"I'm sorry," he replied.

"It hasn't been an easy trip, I will admit, but it had to be made. You see, my husband was English and in the shipping business. He did a great deal of trade with his homeland, and there are many transactions that I must see completed before my return."

"Now. Lillian," said Lord Barkham, "you haven't completely made up your mind about going back. There is more here to keep you occupied than you think."

"Justin is an old friend—as you are, I believe, Lord Kelston—of Lady Caroline Ames and her husband, with whom I am staying during my visit. He has done nothing since my arrival but try to convince me to remain."

"And has he succeeded, Mrs. Robertson?"

"Not yet, but I must say I find him most persuasive," she replied. "Tell me, Miss Miles, do you have any relatives in the New World?"

"An uncle," I replied, realizing as I said it that it was a mistake.

"How interesting," she said, leaning forward. "What is his name?"

I felt my muscles tense. This was not part of the story that had been concocted, and I couldn't sort my thoughts quickly enough to know how to answer.

"Serena, Lillian asked you about your uncle," I heard Lord Barkham say.

"My uncle. Oh, yes. His name I believe was Samuel, Samuel Miles, but I am not certain. It was very long ago."

"It sounds vaguely familiar. Of course it is not an uncommon name, so even if I might recall, it might be the wrong Samuel Miles."

The service of the first course began, which fortunately diverted the focus of the conversation—at least for the moment—to talk of food and the differences between cooking methods and dishes in England and in Boston, where Mrs. Robertson was from.

Robin appeared to be enjoying himself enormously, and though I knew that he was only being a proper host, I found myself envious of the attention he was paying to Mrs. Robertson.

"You are very quiet tonight, Serena," Lord Barkham said suddenly. "You aren't fretting over that remark of Clarissa's, are you?"

"Quite the contrary, Lord Barkham," I returned. "Monique has made me see that your dear Clarissa really hurts only herself with her foolish tongue."

His eyes regarded me quizzically. "And what else did Monique tell you?"

"Nothing that could be of any interest to you."

I had thought to anger him by my comment, but to my frustration he appeared not miffed but relieved.

"I have just learned that Mrs. Robertson is a fine horsewoman as well as obviously accomplished in other ways," Robin said, suddenly clasping my hand as it lay on the table. "We must all go out for a ride tomorrow morning. What do you say Serena?"

I now regretted that I had at the last minute packed the riding suit that Anne had had made for me, for I did not relish the thought of going riding with Lord Barkham and Mrs. Robertson, but Robin seemed so genuinely eager that I join them that I could hardly refuse. Besides, I enjoyed his company, and whether meeting his mother had influenced me I wasn't certain, but I found him to be more appealing than I had before.

The rest of the dinner seemed to pass quickly. There was a round of toasts saluting Clarissa, who had given me a cold stare when she saw that Lord Barkham was seated beside me, but that vanished when he paid a flourishing tribute to her charm and beauty.

Anne, I noticed, looked strained, but I thought that probably due to the fact that she was seated next to the Earl and his wife and I could not imagine that they had proved cheerful company. The one person who was noticeable by her absence—at least to me—was my grandmother. Anne had said that she had come ahead with the Earl and Lady Camberleigh, but I had not seen her since my arrival.

After dinner, Monique announced that the guests who wished to might retire to the drawing room.

"Your mother is most refreshing, Lord Kelston," Mrs. Robertson said. "I have always thought it ludicrous to separate the men and the women after dinner, when in fact that is the time they most want to get together. And a spot of brandy never hurt to move that merger in the right direction."

Robin laughed—far too heartily, I thought.

Lord Barkham rose and assisted Mrs. Robertson from her chair. Robin took my arm, and we proceeded out to the drawing room.

"Ah, the evening is young, Serena, and I have you, the most beautiful woman in the room, on my arm. What more could I ask?"

"Robin, I know this sounds like I'm being a priss, but would you mind dreadfully if I excused myself? Even though you have made it easy to forget, we must remember that my real reason for being here is Oliver, and I really should look in on him."

"Fine," he replied. "And then come back down to the garden. I shall meet you there."

"I can't, Robin. If he should need me, I would feel dreadful if I were not there. Besides, it has been a long evening and I am a bit weary myself."

"Suit yourself," he replied, abruptly dropping his arm from mine.

"Don't be angry with me, please," I beseeched.

"I am not angry with you, Serena, just disappointed. Run along, if you must. But be certain to meet us here in the morning. You haven't forgotten our ride, have you?"

"No, I shall be here," I replied, pleased that he still wanted me to accompany him.

Robin moved off to catch up with Lord Barkham and Mrs. Robertson, who were now in conversation with Monique and some gentleman who I noticed had been seated near her at dinner.

As I moved up the stairs I thought that I should have let Anne know that I was retiring, but she would likely assume that I had gone to Oliver.

The sconces were all lit, making it easy for me to make my way to my room. I missed Jaspar's welcome that I was so accustomed to and wondered how he was faring back at Camberleigh.

Oliver was sound asleep as I entered his room and peered over his bed. I pulled the coverlet up slightly and noticed that his skin felt warm to the touch. My first instinct was to waken him, but on second thought I decided that the best remedy— if he was indeed feverish—was sleep.

I returned to my room and undressed, wishing that I had Rowena to assist me with the countless buttons at the back of my gown. The bed had been warmed, and not long after I snuffed out the candle I drifted off to sleep.

What seemed like hours later I awoke. I saw that it was still dark outside, for I had forgotten to close my draperies in my haste to get to bed. As I lay there I thought I heard the faint sound of voices in the hall. Climbing out of bed, I pulled my robe around me and, opening my door, looked out. Most of the candles in the sconces had fluttered out, making it difficult to see. Then I observed a small movement at the end of the corridor on the left and heard a click, and I realized it was a door closing. Not wishing to be found spying, I slowly closed my door. Making my way back to my bed, I suddenly realized that the door that I had seen was the one to Anne's room.

The floor was cold and I shivered as I got into bed again. It was odd, I thought, that Anne should be up and about at this hour, but then, I had no knowledge of the actual time and I realized that I had probably retired hours before the rest of the guests.

Early-morning sun streamed into the room as I opened my eyes to the new day. Rowena brought my basin early, which pleased me, for I was anxious to look in on Oliver. I bathed quickly, then donned my robe and went into the adjoining room.

"Good morning," I said, moving over and putting a hand on his forehead.

"Why are you doing that?" he asked.

"When I looked in on you last evening I thought you felt a bit feverish, but perhaps I was mistaken, for you seem perfectly normal this morning. Are you hungry?" He nodded. "Good, because I've told Rowena to bring our breakfasts up right away, though I scarce know how I can eat after last night."

"Was it a grand party?"

"Oh very," I said. "I could hardly believe the great number of people, and apparently even more are to attend the ball tonight. And many of the gentlemen toasted your sister throughout the dinner. The only people missing were you and your grandmother."

"I am to visit with her this morning."

"You are? I was going to suggest that you come riding with me."

"Oh."

"You wouldn't like to come riding with me, Oliver?"

"It's not that. It's just that I promised Grandmama, and I don't want to disappoint her. She gets very lonely."

"I'm sure she does," I said thoughtfully. "And I know that she loves you very much. I'm glad that you want to spend time with her. We can always go riding together back at Camberleigh."

Rowena arrived with the trays, and while we ate I told Oliver as much as I could recall about the party. When we had finished and he had dressed, I returned to my room, as Rowena had assured me that she would take him to our grandmother when she returned for the trays.

The riding suit was a deep royal blue, almost black, trimmed with a heavy ribbon of the same color. I braided my hair and wore it in a loop, which I caught with a tie at the back of my head. I had decided to try to convince Anne to join our party, since selfishly I knew her presence would not only be pleasurable for me but help put some distance between Lord Barkham, Mrs. Robertson and myself. Satisfied with my appearance, I went down the corridor and knocked at her door.

"Come in," a muffled voice replied.

She was still in bed and, realizing that I had disturbed her sleep, I began to close the door.

"Serena, is that you?"

"Yes, but go back to sleep."

"No, I am awake, come in."

As I approached, she sat up in bed. "Good gracious," she gasped, yawning. "You are all dressed. Don't tell me the hunt is on already."

"No," I replied. "But I promised Robin I would go riding with him this morning, and wondered if you might care to join us."

"That's very sweet, but I'm certain Robin doesn't want a chaperone. And besides that, it was quite late when I came to bed, and I must have drunk a great lot of wine, for there is now a small thud at the back of my neck to remind me."

"I know that you were late, for I awoke in the middle of the night and thought I heard voices in the hallway and came to check."

"And what did you see?" Anne asked cautiously.

215

"Just your door closing. I knew you must be tired, so I thought it best not to disturb you. But you really wouldn't be intruding, for we are to ride with your brother and Mrs. Robertson."

"Is that the American?"

"Yes, a widow," I replied.

"And not wearing widows weeds for long, I should say, by the look of that dress. Speaking of which, you were a sensation last evening. There wasn't a woman there who wasn't talking about your dress. I can't wait until they see what we have in store for them this evening."

"Well, if you are certain I can't convince you to join us, then I should be going along."

"You look very smart. Just run along and have a good time."

The party was gathered at the base of the stairs.

"Serena. Enchanting," Robin said, taking my hand.

"She looks so refreshed. I actually believe someone in this house slept last night," said Mrs. Robertson with a sly wink at Lord Barkham.

Really, I thought, if they were going to carry on in this manner, the least they could do would be to do it in private.

The stables at Kelston were built much closer to the manor than those at Camberleigh, and I quickly saw what Oliver had meant, for they appeared at least double in size. The mare I drew seemed docile enough, to my relief, since although familiar with horses I was nowhere the experienced rider Mrs. Robertson had proclaimed herself to be.

I had to admit that although in harsh daylight the woman seemed a bit more dissipated than the night before, there was still an air about her that could not help but draw attention.

We rode out together, Robin falling in alongside my mount. He rode well, although I had to admit that Lord Barkham, perhaps because of his size, had a more commanding look upon his chestnut stallion.

"You really shouldn't have abandoned us so early last evening," Robin said. "It turned quite amusing. Lillian was recounting tales of the colonies and the western expansion. Do you know that a number of years ago she traveled across the entire country in a covered wagon?"

"It must have been interesting," I replied. "But as you know,

I had to see to Oliver. He was slightly feverish, but appeared well recovered this morning."

"Well, tonight I shall not let you escape my clutches. If I know mother, we will see the sun rise before the ball comes to an end."

"Your mother is a most unusual woman."

"I'm certain that by now you must have heard about the scandal of my parents' marriage."

"Some," I admitted.

"Well, I must say to her credit she has managed to become one of the most sought-after hostesses in the county. Due in part I am certain to her insatiable appetite for, shall we say, the more expressive things in life. In that sense we are similar."

"Robin, may I ask you something?"

"Certainly."

"Why do you enjoy gambling so much?"

"I see that you believe what you hear," he said flatly.

"I didn't mean that. It's just that several people have . . . made references," I stammered. "I'm sorry. It is none of my business."

"Not necessarily," he replied, his eyes sweeping over me. "It's true that I do gamble. Why? I don't really know. The excitement of the game, perhaps the risk involved. Everyone has their excesses. I suppose mine is gambling."

"Have you ever tried to stop?"

"Good Lord," he laughed, "this isn't the little governess speaking, is it?"

It was as though my hand had been slapped, but then perhaps I deserved it.

"I'm sorry. I didn't mean to mock you. It's just that I don't like to have my motives examined too closely." We rode in silence for a while, and I noticed that Robin seemed restless. "Let's open these horses up. I feel like putting Lady Luck here to the wind."

"You go on, Robin. I don't feel adept enough to keep up with you."

He pulled his horse to a stop and turned back in his saddle.

"Lillian," he challenged, "here is your chance to show off some of that horsemanship." With that he gave his horse a kick and he was off.

Before I could even turn around I heard hooves pounding, and Mrs. Robertson galloped past in pursuit.

I felt a bit foolish for not having met his challenge, for now my very reason for coming out was rapidly disappearing over a rise in the distance.

"I gather we have been abandoned, Serena?" I heard Lord Barkham's voice say as he drew his horse up alongside mine.

"Perhaps you feel abandoned, Lord Barkham," I snapped. "I simply chose not to put my life at risk."

"Well, then, I would say you made a wise decision, for I really would not have relished following up the rear only to find you felled by some low-hanging limb."

"I don't know why you persist in thinking that your lot in life is to rescue me from disasters of my own creation."

"You're not telling me that the misadventures I have witnessed have taken place in my imagination, are you?" I looked up at him and saw that as usual he appeared to be enjoying making me feel uncomfortable, and I began to pull my horse away.

"Serena, don't go."

"Why, so you can continue to make me feel foolish?"

"No. As a matter of fact, I'm pleased we have this time alone. There are several things I wanted to discuss with you."

"All right, I'm listening."

He began to dismount. "We might as well rest for a spell. I doubt that our companions will return immediately."

This was against my better judgment, but looking around I saw that there was no sign of Robin or Mrs. Robertson on the landscape.

"Here let me help you down," he said, reaching up for me and swinging me down by his side.

"What is it you have to say?"

"Might we sit down first?"

I shrugged, and he laid out his jacket on the ground. "It's a pity we don't have another basket from Cook. I thought our picnic yesterday was pleasant."

"Oliver enjoyed it."

"Yes, I believe he did. Actually, one of the things I want to discuss with you is Oliver."

"What about him?"

"Have you noticed anything peculiar about the boy?"

"I'm not certain to what you are referring." I replied.

"I am referring to his health."

"You are going to have to be more explicit, Lord Barkham."

"Have you noticed that Oliver seems prone to spells of fatigue, occasionally accompanied by unexplained fevers?"

"Yes I have, but I assume that is part of his illness."

"There really is no illness, Serena. He as you know suffered a deformity at birth, but there is nothing in the nature of that that should provoke these other symptoms."

"It's strange that you should mention this just now, for when I checked on him last night before retiring, I thought he felt feverish. But then this morning he seemed to be fine."

"It is nothing consistent, and I certainly believe that he is stronger since you have been at Camberleigh—notwithstanding his accident, of course. But this occasional fatigue seems un-natural—and then, of course, there are the stomach pains."

"Stomach pains?" I queried. "He has never said anything about stomach pains to me."

"Oliver is a very stalwart little boy. Perhaps too much so, but that is Richard's doing."

I fell silent, for in my heart I could only agree. The Earl was still my employer, and I did not think it wise to speak against him.

"Well, perhaps it is my imagination," he continued, noting my silence. "But I would appreciate it if you would tell me when these symptoms arise. It might be enough to convince Richard to have Doctor Carruthers in for a thorough going over."

"You are very good to Oliver, Lord Barkham. And he loves you very deeply."

"That is the nicest thing you have ever said to me, Serena. Perhaps you are beginning to see that I am not the ogre you believe me to be after all."

"It is you have used the word ogre, Lord Barkham, not I."

I gathered my skirts and started to rise, but Lord Barkham's hand on my arm kept me where I was. "There is more I want to discuss with you."

I moved away from his grasp.

"I know that I promised not to discuss this matter this weekend, but I did not vow not to bring it up to you or Anne."

I paled, realizing that he was referring to the discovery of the body.

"It may be premature, for until I have had an opportunity to meet with the magistrate again, nothing is conclusive. But if it turns out that this was indeed a murder, then I fear we must also assume that your life is in jeopardy."

"What?" I shrieked.

"Serena, I know that this is upsetting, but you must listen to me."

"Upsetting isn't the word, Lord Barkham. But I tend to think it is more absurd than anything," I replied, trying to regain my composure.

"Please hear me out. The body you found in the pond has almost definitely been identified as that of Margarite Smythe."

"What has that to do with me?"

"Margarite Smythe was the last governess at Camberleigh."

"Oh, so you think some madman has a special penchant for governesses?" I said with a laugh.

"I wish you would not consider this a laughing matter. I am not saying that there is an association, but Margarite was not the first to have disappeared. Oh I know, Maura, it is true, sent a number of them packing, but which ones and why no one really knows. If there is even the slightest chance that Margarite was not the first to meet an untimely end, I think we have to be concerned."

"Lord Barkham, I appreciate your interest," I replied, "but I think it is precipitous at best. You yourself have agreed that it might be an accident or at worst the wrath of some . . . thwarted lover." I felt myself blushing at my own reference. "I think that I should inform you that I am far more capable of caring for myself than you seem to think."

His eyes had not left my face as I spoke, but now they averted at the sound of hoofbeats in the distance.

"That must be Robin and Mrs. Robertson," I said, gathering my skirts.

"The prodigal returns," Lord Barkham replied, rising and assisting me to my feet. "Please remember what I have said, Serena."

As I watched the twosome approach I thought how much

more interesting it would have been to have been off riding, free of all cares instead of listening to this diatribe for the last half hour.

"She is everything she said she was," Robin called out. "And more. She overtook me just after we climbed the hill."

The two brought their horses up near to where ours were now grazing. Mrs. Robertson looked flushed but radiant atop her mare, which seemed relatively dry given her hard ride. "Serena, my dear, you really should have taken the challenge," she said, "it was wonderful. But then, perhaps you have taken on a challenge of your own?"

I flushed as I looked down at my skirt, which was a bit rumpled and covered with pieces of grass. "I am certain that your ride was far more interesting than the things we discussed here," I snapped.

"I must apologize, Serena, for our delay," Robin said, dismounting. "I am afraid that I became quite carried away."

"There is no need to apologize Robin," I retorted. "But I must be getting back, for although Oliver was to be with her ladyship, he might be uncomfortable in unfamiliar surroundings."

"'Tis time to return anyway, if I am to be in any condition to lead the hunt this afternoon."

"That is the last thing I would worry about," interjected Mrs. Robertson.

Robin climbed down and assisted me back up on my mare. We led the way back to the stables with Lord Barkham and Mrs. Robertson close behind. My mind kept searching for some topic of conversation that would connect Robin and me in some way, but search as I could I was not able to revitalize the energy that we had earlier.

The stables were a beehive of activity, the grooms readying the horses for the afternoon's event. Robin was immediately preoccupied with the proceedings, and I decided it would be best to steal away quietly. Lord Barkham escorted Mrs. Robertson and me back to the manor, where the day had come alive with guests strolling about the sweeping lawns. One gentleman I recognized from the evening prior waved and called out to Mrs. Robertson. "You will excuse me, darlings, but Freddy is an old friend of my husband's, and he will think me terribly rude if I do not greet him. We will meet again this evening, of course. I am dying to see your gown, Serena, for if it is anything like the one you wore last night I should be furious. You looked far too young and virginal for my taste."

I must have shown my surprise, for Lord Barkham laughingly said, "Serena, if you don't close your mouth you're liable to catch something in it."

"The nerve of that woman," I replied.

"She was paying you a compliment."

"If that was a compliment, I hope never to hear her criticism."

"It's just her way. Actually, I find Americans most refreshing. They speak their minds, and they don't dither about as we English often do."

I wanted to say that she was simply as blunt as he, but the moment passed and he was already heading up the steps to the house.

Monique was descending the stairs when we entered and looked momentarily startled, I thought, at seeing Lord Barkham or myself, I knew not which. "Ah my *chéries,* you are out early this morning and in riding clothes! And here I have just managed to rouse myself. Will you not join me for some small refreshment before luncheon? I suppose that naughty son of mine is still sleeping off his indulgences, or I would suggest that he join us."

"As a matter of fact, Monique, Robin is down at the stables," I volunteered. "We all went for a ride this morning."

"You seem to have a very positive influence over him, Serena. Perhaps he is not as incorrigible as I once thought, eh, Justin?"

"Monique, you know that I think his only saving grace is having you for a mother, although in that gown you hardly look the part."

This last was certainly true. She looked more like Robin's sister than his mother. She wore a flowing emerald green robe with butterfly sleeves and mandarin collar. It appeared almost Oriental in origin.

"The work of your dear sister," she replied, turning so that we might receive the full effect. "She is very talented, you know. In Paris her designs would be a sensation. And if I am not mistaken, Serena knows of what I speak. *Alors*, now let us retire for a little pick-me-up."

"Monique," I intruded, "I hope that you will excuse me. I would love to join you, but I am anxious to see to Oliver."

"Ah yes, the little boy. For myself I prefer the company of grown men, but he is fortunate to have one who cares for him as you do. Of course, run along and I will see you later," she replied.

I turned to mount the stairs when Lord Barkham clasped my arm.

"Serena, I thought I might take Oliver on the hunt today."

"Oh, but he is far too young and inexperienced a rider for that, Lord Barkham," I replied, thinking that he must be mad to even suggest it.

"I didn't mean that we would actually go in full chase of the fox. We would simply go at our own pace. There is a certain pageantry to it all that I'm sure he would enjoy."

"I don't know. I would not want to risk another fall."

"I would not take any risks with the boy. But he can't be kept in a glass case forever."

"Are you implying that is what I am doing?"

"Lord, no. But I think some male companionship is good for him."

"Why not allow it, Serena," said Monique. "Justin is right. It would be a diversion for him."

"All right," I conceded, "but only on the condition that you will not overtax him."

"Good. I will stop by for him after lunch, then."

Anne's door was still closed as I made my way back to my room, and I decided that though I longed to see her, I would be a better friend if I let her sleep.

Oliver had not returned, and I felt some regret that I had not joined Monique, but with Lord Barkham present I would scarce have had a chance to speak to her on a personal basis. I removed the jacket of my riding suit and stretched out on the chaise, wishing that I had brought my embroidery to help while away the time....

The next thing I knew I was being jostled awake by Oliver.

"Well, I seem to have drifted off," I said drowsily. "When did you return?"

"Not long ago, Serena, but now they have brought the trays and I thought you might be hungry."

I laughed. "It couldn't be that you are the one who is hungry, now could it?" A sheepish grin spread over his face. "Well, now that my senses are alert to the smells, I don't think it will take much to convince me to join you."

"Did you ride all by yourself?"

"No, I was with Lord Kelston, Lord Barkham, and an American woman—Mrs. Robertson, by name."

"Did Uncle Justin ask about me?"

"He most certainly did. As a matter of fact, he has invited you to join him on the hunt this afternoon."

"He has?"

"Yes. And I have agreed, provided that some caution is taken."

"Oh, I shall be careful. I promise."

"Good. Then eat well so you have all your strength, but first take your medicine."

"Oh, must I?"

"For me, Oliver. It is for your own good."

I administered a spoonful of the liquid, and once his grimacing had subsided we set about delving into the variety of good things arranged on our trays.

"How did you find your grandmother, Oliver?"

"She was better today."

"Had she not been well?"

"She said that the journey in the coach was difficult. Maybe it's because she is so old."

More likely, I thought, because of the tension that must have existed in the carriage between the Earl and Lady Camberleigh.

"I told her that you looked like a princess last night."

"And what did she reply?"

"It was funny. She said I mustn't become too infatu . . . infactua—something like that—because then it would be much harder for me when you have to go away."

The solicitor, I thought, could scarcely have any information back by this time. But could she have already made up her mind?

"You're not going away, are you, Serena?"

"I hope not, Oliver. But somehow there are things that no

224

matter how hard we try we cannot control."

"I should go with you, then."

I looked into those translucent blue eyes that I had come to love so in such a short time, and realized that I would not miss Camberleigh at all by contrast, were I forced to leave.

I was grateful for the knock at the door, for Oliver had suddenly looked genuinely disturbed that I had not dismissed out of hand the possibility of my departure.

"Come in," I called.

"Uncle Justin," Oliver cried, running to greet Lord Barkham, whose frame filled the doorway.

"Might I come in?" he asked.

"I should not think that necessary," I replied. "If you have come for Oliver, it should take but a few moments before he is ready."

"Good. Then I shall just make myself at home," he responded, totally ignoring what I had said. "Oliver, dress in something more appropriate for riding. Don't rush, we have time. I shall be here watching Serena finish her meal."

Oliver moved off into the other room.

"I have finished my meal, Lord Barkham, so as there is nothing to watch, I suggest you return to your room, and I will send Oliver there when he is ready."

"Do I detect a note of hostility, Miss Miles, or perhaps you are concerned about the propriety of my being in your room. Or are you afraid?"

"Afraid? Of what, Lord Barkham?"

"I'm ready, Uncle Justin," Oliver said, returning to the room.

"And quickly, too, I see," Lord Barkham replied.

"Aren't you coming with us, Serena?"

"This is just for the men, Oliver," I replied evenly.

"Does that mean that I am a man now, Uncle Justin?"

"I should say that Serena might be the best judge of that, Oliver."

Oliver looked at me for an answer. "I suppose in a way it does. Although I must admit to having a special fondness for little boys."

"Much to the regret of some of us more mature fellows," answered Lord Barkham.

"I will see you later," Oliver piped up.

"Please leave the fox to someone else, Oliver," I said. "I doubt that Jaspar would want a companion in that form."

The two moved off, leaving me once again on my own. I thought of going to find Monique, but decided that she would undoubtedly be busy with last-minute preparations for the ball, so I decided to go to Anne's door and see if she had arisen as yet.

I knocked gently and was pleased when I heard her voice bid me to enter.

"Oh good, I was just coming to find you. You must have thought me a terrible bore this morning, but I was not in any condition to join you. How did it go?"

"It was pleasant enough," I replied, "though I can't say that Mrs. Robertson's presence added much."

"Do I detect a twinge of jealousy?"

"Of course not." I was disturbed at even the suggestion.

"Well, I have not spent much time with her, but I thought she seemed rather amusing."

"In that, you and your brother share the same opinion."

"Oh, really?"

"Well, she is an expert horsewoman, and I suppose that has impressed him."

"I doubt that is why he is impressed, but far be it from me to comment."

"I met Monique earlier when we returned from our ride. Something she said led me to believe that she knows that you are responsible for the gowns I am wearing this weekend."

"Monique is a very bright woman. Of course, I have come up with several things for her over the years, so her eye is somewhat attuned to my style of design. She has always tried to encourage me in this area, so I'm sure she is delighted."

"I saw very little of the Earl and Lady Camberleigh after our encounter early last evening. Did they join the group after dinner?" I asked.

"Maura went to bed—or I should say was put to bed. She was growing quite out of hand during dinner. It was most difficult for Richard. I swear were it not for Clarissa I don't think he would have come."

"I am surprised that you seem so sympathetic to the Earl," I replied.

"Do I seem so?" Anne said, rising and moving to the dressing table. "Perhaps it is because I have seen what that marriage has done to him over the years."

"You mean because your own was unhappy?"

"Partially. But the two cannot really be compared. I was bored and disappointed, but Anthony was not cruel. Weak, but not cruel."

"You imply that you think that Lady Camberleigh is?"

"I should prefer to use the word unbalanced."

"But you don't think she is dangerous?"

"If you mean physically, no, I don't think so. But sometimes the danger to one's emotions or psyche can be far greater." I thought of the effect that she had on Oliver and wondered if Anne were not correct.

"Well, let's get off this subject. Would you do me a great favor and come downstairs and assist me? I promised Monique that I would arrange the flowers in the ballroom for this evening, and I really could use another capable pair of hands."

"I would be delighted to help, but I doubt that I have your knack for floral arrangements."

"Nonsense. You have a natural affinity for flowers. You'll do splendidly."

The size of the ballroom was overwhelming. A gardener had brought in what seemed enough flowers to completely fill the manor and lain them just inside the doors that led out to another dance area, this one on a terrace open to the sky above.

I started slowly, carefully patterning my arrangement after those that Anne seemed to create so effortlessly, and soon found that I was experimenting on my own. There were twenty large urns in the room, and the sun was fading as we finished the last.

"If I do say so myself," said Anne, "we've created quite a splendid display. The fact that it is for that senseless girl makes me livid—on the other hand, it really was done to help Monique."

"When do you suppose everyone will return from the hunt?"

"Shortly, I would think."

"I should go upstairs, lest Oliver has returned already."

"I will join you. I want to rest for awhile, and I suggest that you do too if you intend to dance every dance."

"I doubt that I could rest, I'm too excited at the prospect."

Anne laughed. "I must say your enthusiasm is refreshing."

We returned to our rooms, I leaving Anne at her door after assuring her that I would come for her before going downstairs that evening.

Only moments later I heard Lord Barkham and Oliver's voices in the hall and I opened the door to see the two returning hand in hand.

"As you can see, I have brought him back as promised, safe and sound, though I am certainly a bit weary," Lord Barkham said.

"Serena, it was wonderful. I even saw the fox." Oliver's eyes were bright with excitement.

"Lord Barkham, you promised not to give chase with the others," I said, annoyed.

"We didn't," he replied. "Actually, the fox almost ran into us. We had hung quite far behind, and it must have escaped the hounds and doubled back. I think we were as surprised as it was."

"We had best get you out of those clothes Oliver, and get you bathed before your dinner arrives," I said, noticing that he had become somewhat disheveled from his ride.

"Perhaps I should let you strip me and bathe me, also, Serena, since I am most likely as odoriferous as Oliver," said Lord Barkham.

"Really," I gasped. "Your manners are at times atrocious."

Oliver's laughter did little to assuage my annoyance.

"Don't be angry, Serena," Oliver said, coming to take my hand.

"I'm not," I snapped. "Now go into your room."

I turned on my heel to follow him.

"Well, if you won't bathe me, will you at least promise to save a dance for me this evening, Serena?"

I did not look around, but simply followed Oliver into his room and closed the door. That man seemed to provoke me no matter what the situation.

I called for a basin for Oliver, and during his bath the boy chattered nonstop about his afternoon with his Uncle Justin. Even though I still seethed at the man's audacious remarks, I softened somewhat, realizing how happy he had made the boy.

Soon Rowena brought in our dinner trays.

I ate a small bit from mine, as Anne had cautioned that it would be wise, not knowing when the supper would be served. I had no coaxing to do to get Oliver in bed, for his eyelids had been closing even as we ate. He was asleep before I had even returned to my room.

A shiver of excitement ran through me as I took my gown out of the armoire and lay it gently on the bed. I called for another basin and gave myself a leisurely bath. I had at least an hour before Rowena would return to assist me with my hair, so I lay down on the chaise, closed my eyes, and transported myself to the moment of the ball. In my fantasy the ballroom was crowded with guests. There was a sudden hush in the room as my grandmother rose to make a toast. She walked over to where I stood and took my hand. "Ladies and gentlemen, I would like to present my granddaughter, Serena Miles Camberleigh."

A murmur went about the room and then came the applause, at first hesitant, then explosive. Everyone was embracing me, and then I was in a man's arms and we were dancing all about the room. I felt safe and loved, but try as I did I could not see the face of the man who was twirling me about the floor past the crowds of admiring guests.

I opened my eyes. The room had grown dark, and I rose to light the candles. Soon Rowena entered. "Sorry I'm late, miss, but Lady Ormsby asked if I could be helpin' her with her hair, too."

"I lost track of time anyway, Rowena. I fear I was daydreaming a bit."

"Lady Ormsby gave me this to fix in yer hair," she said, holding up a gold braid that matched the gold in the dress.

"Don't you think that it will be too much?" I asked.

"No, it'll be just right. You'll see. I'll weave it around so it will look like it's almost part of your hair."

As she worked, we chatted about Charlotte and I told her about Robbie, whom she had not seen for five years. When she had finished, she helped me step into my gown and fixed the back closing, which was a complicated cross-weaving of the ends of the gold band that encircled the bodice.

"Do you be havin' a beau, miss?" Rowena asked.

"Not really," I replied, thinking that although Thomas was a close friend, he could scarcely be called a beau.

"Well, you will after tonight, to be sure. There'll be gentlemen fightin' over you, looking as you do."

I laughed. "I certainly don't want to provoke any fights, but you are a dear to boost my confidence. I must admit I am terribly nervous."

"No need bein' nervous when you look like you do."

"I've never really danced before. Only with my father in our house when he would show me how he and my mother had danced when they were first married."

"Not that I be knowin' much about it, but if ye just follow the lead of the gentlemen, everything should be fine."

Now sounds of the orchestra began drifting up from below, and I could see from the window that the courtyard was filled with carriages of newly arriving guests.

"I suppose that I should go to Lady Ormsby," I said. "She will be wondering what is keeping me."

"Have a grand time, now."

"Thank you, Rowena."

Anne looked lovely in a gown of pale gray lace, the only adornment being sapphire earrings and a matching pendant at her throat.

"Serena, you look like a goddess," Anne said. "You actually appear to be shimmering under this light. I think this is my finest creation. Of course, I could not, even if I had searched, have found anyone more beautiful to wear it."

"Between Rowena and you, my head shall grow large if we are not careful. Oh, and I didn't forget this," I said, withdrawing my small fan.

"I doubt that you will need it, but don't hesitate if you are in distress."

As we made our way down the stairs, I saw with some concern that a receiving line had been formed in the center hall outside the drawing room. It had never occurred to me that I would have to go through this, but then I realized that I should have expected it, since Clarissa was undoubtedly known to many of the guests only as the daughter of the Earl and Lady Camberleigh.

Anne took my hand suddenly, as if sensing my distress.

"Stay right behind me. And don't look like that, or Maura will think she has willing prey."

We stepped forward as a large crowd that had just entered began moving along the line. Robin beamed when he saw us.

"Serena, you are dazzling," he said, taking my arm. "If I thought I could get away with it, I would demand that you dance only with me the night long, but some fellow would probably challenge me to a duel for your attentions, and since I've always been a terrible shot I would lose out totally. Promise me the first dance, however."

"By all means."

"I know she's quite overwhelming, Robin, but you could at least humor me by telling me I've never looked better." We both turned to Anne, who I saw quickly was feigning indignance.

"Lady Ormsby, I would never have thought that the little girl who chased me in the bushes would turn out this way," Robin replied, chucking her under the chin.

"I think I'd slap you if I didn't love you," she said.

"What's this about slapping?" It was Monique, who was next in line.

"It's just your son being naughty again, Monique," Anne said with a wink.

"Well, we shall have to forgive him, for when faced with you two looking like that I am certain that he quite lost his head."

The Earl of Camberleigh had just dismissed a rather robust woman who had been gushing effusively, and he now turned to Anne and me. His eyes rested on Anne for a moment, and then he focused on me.

"Miss Miles, I see that you wear no jewels."

"I have none, sire," I replied, my voice almost a whisper.

"You need none, for in that gown you appear a very jewel."

I thought I must have heard wrong, for I could not believe that he was complimenting me so.

"Well said, Richard," Monique added, then turning back to receive more guests.

Lady Camberleigh was next.

"Maura, you look splendid this evening," Anne said. "What a grand occasion it must be, your daughter's first ball."

231

She did look lovely, in a pale yellow gown, which, if a bit ingenuous in design, was most becoming in coloring.

"Good evening, Lady Camberleigh," I said, extending my hand.

If it were possible to look at someone without seeing them, then that is exactly what she did to me. I dropped my hand, realizing that she had no intention of taking it. We moved on— to Clarissa.

The girl stood at the end of the line next to a chair on which my grandmother was seated. Her eyes widened as they fell on my dress; then they narrowed.

"You never know who they will invite to these affairs, do you, grandmother. Of course, some people don't have the manners to know where they belong and where they don't."

My grandmother gazed up at me and studied me for a long moment. She then extended her hand. "It appears that my granddaughter is the one without manners, Miss Miles. But then, if I were a young girl I too would undoubtedly be jealous of one as beautiful as yourself."

Her hand was frail but warm in mine, and I clasped it strongly, wanting her to sense my appreciation for her remark. "That is very kind, your ladyship, but clearly your granddaughter has no cause for jealousy."

Clarissa looked genuinely embarrassed by this exchange, and I moved quickly off with Anne. Although I found Clarissa detestable at times, I also took no joy in causing her any anguish.

"I wouldn't be surprised if it was she who tore up your dress," Anne whispered. "That girl is just nasty and resentful enough to have done it."

I couldn't deny that the thought had crossed my mind once or twice, but never really seriously. She was vain and spoiled, but I couldn't imagine that she could be quite so vicious.

The drawing room was filled with men and women who had no doubt spent days, if not weeks, in preparation for this evening. I doubted that I would ever again see such a splendid display of gowns and jewels. Anne, it appeared, was a familiar presence in these circles, although I realized from some of the comments made by those who approached that she had not ventured out much since her husband's death.

"Don't look now, but here comes Baron Whittenfield."

"Who is he?" I asked, trying not to study the man who approached us.

"Quite the catch—or so they tell me. I'm not quite certain what he does, but whatever it is it must be highly profitable, for he is known to give the most lavish parties in all of London."

"Lady Ormsby, is it not?" he said, bowing to Anne.

"You have a good memory, Baron. It must be several years since I saw you last," she replied. "Might I present my friend, Miss Miles—Serena Miles."

He took my hand and kissed it lightly, and drops of perspiration remained on my hand as I withdrew it.

"Baron Gregory Whittenfield at your service. But how is it that we have never met? And don't tell me that we have, for I would not forget that face."

"No we have not, Baron. I am only recently arrived in this area."

"I see, and from whence did you come?"

"Near Cornwall," I replied.

"But that is where my family is from. Strange," he said, rubbing his chin, "I don't think I know of a Miles, assuming, of course, that that is your maiden name."

"It is, but there is no reason that you would know them," I replied, becoming anxious at the direction the conversation was taking.

"Now that I have met you, that is hardly true."

"Would you two excuse me for a moment," Anne said, "there is someone here that I have not seen for some time and I know once the ball commences that I should not have another opportunity."

"Of course, Lady Ormsby," the Baron said, moving aside for her to pass. "Now, where were we? Ah, yes, your family. Have you no other relatives in the area? Perhaps we have some mutual acquaintances."

I could see that he was not going to give up easily.

"Only my grandmother," I said, "Lady Jane Carfield," the last name sticking in my throat.

"Lady Jane is your grandmother?" he asked, a bit suspiciously, I thought.

I nodded.

"I see. A charming woman, charming indeed. Now I see that you come to it naturally."

I tried to smile, but the muscles in my face were too tense.

"How thoughtless of me," he said, taking my arm. "Let me offer you some refreshment."

As we walked through the crowd, I turned to study my new companion. He was tall and large of frame, but unlike Robin— or even Lord Barkham, for that matter—his size was more attributable to flesh than muscle. His skin was very fair, which suggested that most of his time must be spent indoors. His features were in no way unusual, and there was a puffiness to the skin between his nose and top lip that was made more noticeable due to the beads of perspiration that constantly formed there.

"Wait here and I shall fetch us some wine," he said, dropping my arm.

I stood looking about for Anne, but she was nowhere to be seen.

"Looking for me, Serena?" a voice whispered behind me.

I whirled about to find myself face to face with Lord Barkham.

"I most certainly am not," I snapped. "If you must know, I was looking for your sister."

"What, the Baron too much for you to handle?"

"First of all, I am not handling anyone, as you put it, least of all Baron Whittenfield, to whom I have just been introduced."

"Be careful of him. He is not a gentleman, and I wouldn't like to see you hurt."

"Not that it's any business of yours, but I am quite able to care for myself. And I trust my own judgment when it comes to who is suitable for me to talk to and who isn't."

"As long as it is just talk, I suppose you are right."

"Well, Justin, I should have known better than to leave Miss Miles for a moment with you around," the Baron said, returning and handing me a glass.

"Was he disturbing you?"

"I know that this will disappoint you, Gregory, but Serena and I are friends."

"I see. Well, then, I owe you an apology, Justin."

234

"None needed."

"I was just going to ask Miss Miles if she would join me for dinner," said the Baron.

"Well, I am superfluous to this conversation, then," Lord Barkham replied. "But remember, Serena, you promised me a dance."

He moved off before I had a chance to reply.

"It appears that Lord Barkham is quite taken with you, though I can't say that I blame him."

"I fear you are mistaken, Baron. For some reason, Lord Barkham simply enjoys goading me. He is, as you must have heard, almost betrothed to Clarissa Camberleigh."

"Ah, yes, the young lady we honor this evening. She's a pretty thing, but hardly seems Barkham's type. Although I suppose their marriage would indeed solidify the Camberleigh and Mayfair estates."

I looked up and was pleased to see Robin heading our way.

"Serena, I've been looking all over for you."

"What is it, Robin?"

"I just wanted you to know that I won't be able to dine with you. Mother has me chaperoning two elderly dowager aunts."

"I had no idea that you were promised to Lord Kelston for the evening, but I must say I am delighted to find that you can now join me, Miss Miles."

"For dinner only, Gregory," Robin replied. "She has promised the first dance to me, and after that I don't intend to let her go."

"We'll see about that, Robin," the Baron replied.

I was sorely disappointed that Robin would be occupied during dinner, for although I gave no credence to what Lord Barkham said about the Baron, there was an oppressiveness about him that I did not find attractive. But I had little choice, without being excessively rude, so I allowed the Baron to lead me to the dining room.

The dinner passed uneventfully. I was relieved that we were seated amongst a number of people who knew the Baron well and were anxious to talk to him about the upcoming social season, for it kept the conversation clear of any further queries about my family. My grandmother, I noticed, watched me closely during the meal. She was seated next to Clarissa, who had chattered away nonstop to Lord Barkham, who was on her other side.

I could scarcely see Robin at the end of the table, but I had gotten a glimpse of his dinner partners, and I could not imagine that he was overly thrilled with them. Anne was talking animatedly to some elegant foreign-looking gentleman, but she waved at me when she caught my eye.

Clarissa beamed as various of the guests toasted her success. I was surprised when her mother rose—somewhat unsteadily— her glass raised in air.

"This should be good," the Baron whispered to me.

"What do you mean?" I asked.

"Well, look at her," he said unsympathetically. "She can barely stand, she is so inebriated."

I looked and saw that she was in fact weaving before her chair. The room fell ominously silent.

The Earl, seated to her right, reached up and grasped her arm, apparently trying to force her back into her seat.

"No, I shall not be silent," she said in tones audible enough to be heard around the room.

"My husband—obviously—does not want me to make a speech," she slurred, "but after all, Clarissa here is my daughter. *My* lovely daughter. I know many of you find that hard to believe, but at one time Richard found me very appealing. Didn't you, darling?"

"Maura, please sit down."

"No!" she screamed. "To Clarissa, *my* daughter. Mine and only mine."

The Earl was on his feet, and began firmly to escort Lady Camberleigh from the table. Lord Barkham went over to assist him.

Monique had also risen, and was announcing that the ball was to commence. Robin had gone to attend Clarissa, who looked as though she had been slapped in the face. I didn't know whether to feel sorrier for her or my grandmother, who had grown suddenly very pale.

"Excuse me, Baron, but I must see if there is anything I can do for her ladyship."

"Serena, that would only draw attention. She will be properly tended to, and I suggest we follow the lead of the other guests."

I really did not want to spend any more time with the Baron, and looked frantically about the room for Anne. She spotted me and nodded as I opened the fan.

"Darling, there you are," Anne said, coming up to us. "There is someone here whom I've been longing to have you meet. You will excuse us for a moment, won't you, Baron?" She took my arm and propelled me through the crowd. "In here," she said, motioning to a door at the rear of the hall.

The room beyond was a small library, and I saw with relief that we were alone.

"I don't know about you, but I need something to settle my nerves," she said, going over to a decanter. Seeing my alarmed look, she added, "Don't worry. I don't intend a performance like Maura's, but I am not going to make it through this evening unless I calm down."

"I don't understand what happened," I said.

"I can't say that I do either, except that she appears to have lost total control of herself. I've seen it coming, but I had hoped for Richard's sake that he would be spared the embarrassment in public."

"But it's something more than that, Anne. What was that business about Clarissa being *her* daughter? It was as though she wanted him to have no part of her."

"I don't know. Perhaps it has something to do with Oliver and whatever trauma she still carries with her from his birth. Richard, of course, adores Clarissa, and perhaps she is jealous of the attention he gives her. Or it may simply be the ramblings of a mind that has ceased to be coherent."

"Do you think the Earl will return to the ball this evening?"

"I hope so," she replied. "It will cause a far greater stir if he does not. I suppose we had best return ourselves."

"I do thank you for responding to my signal. I just didn't think I could take one more moment with the Baron."

"He wasn't rude, was he?"

"Heavens, no. But he somehow makes me uncomfortable. I should think one would never really know what he is thinking."

The debacle in the dining room seemed long forgotten as I watched the smiling dancers twirl about the floor. I had missed the first dance, which had been promised to Robin, and as I saw him glide by with Mrs. Robertson in his arms I wondered if the opportunity would arise again. But as the music changed so did the partners, and it was now Lord Barkham who led the American back onto the floor.

"That is quite a costume Lillian is wearing," Anne said, following my gaze. "Provocative, but a bit too stark. It needs more fullness in the skirt." I smiled, wondering if whenever Anne looked at a woman she was redesigning her gown. "Ah, Robin has spotted us," she said. "And I see that my dinner companion is determined to carry out his threat of a dance with me. I scarcely understood a word he said, but perhaps he dances better than he speaks."

"Serena, I have waited all day for this," Robin said, taking my hand and leading me to the center of the floor. I hummed a bit to the music as he led me effortlessly about the room. My worries about my dancing had been for naught, as I found it easy to follow the steps. "It pleases me to have in my arms the most beautiful woman at the ball, but I fear that you shall make me lose my senses. I'm certain that you must know how desirable you are, Serena."

"I think, Lord Kelston, that you had best keep your mind on the music."

"I shall bend to your wishes, fair lady, but only because it is early. I am quite determined that by the end of the evening you shall do little to resist my advances—unless, of course, that would please you as part of our lovemaking."

"Robin, I think you are under a false impression."

"Why? You excite me, and I think you find me attractive as well. Would you deny our finding pleasure in each other?"

"I would if it were improper."

"What could be improper?" I flushed, and he held me tighter. "You don't think I regard you as someone like Juanita, do you?"

"Juanita?" I asked, thinking the name sounded familiar.

"She is the waitress at the inn."

"I don't know what there is about me that makes you think of Juanita."

"There isn't. I am simply trying to point out that whatever I might do with Juanita would have no relationship with how I feel about you. You are clearly not some servant girl with whom one simply has a roll in the hay, as it were."

"Well I should think not," I replied. "But I am not experienced in these matters, and have no intention of becoming so before I marry—if I ever do."

The music had stopped, and Robin continued to hold me to him. "Serena, I am very fond of you, of course. But we scarcely know each other. And frankly, I don't know if my family could afford another scandal—considering your position at Camberleigh, I mean."

"Do you think that I was suggesting that you marry me?" I replied, thunderstruck.

"Weren't you?"

"I certainly was *not,*" I replied adamantly. "I think you know very well what I meant."

"Come now, Serena, let us dance again. I love to be close to you."

I started to protest, but he had whirled me back onto the dance floor before I could resist.

"That was some spectacle at the table," he said, changing the subjects.

"Fortunately, Clarissa seems to have gotten over it," I replied, noticing her smiling at some young man who was obviously enchanted by her.

"The Camberleighs are an odd family. Richard takes things so seriously. His wife is addicted to something, everyone says. Even her ladyship is strange. Of course, one hears that she really hasn't been the same since her husband's death. But that was very long ago."

I saw an opportunity. "It must have been difficult for her to lose her younger son at the same time," I said as offhandedly as I could.

"I suppose. But she was a good mother to Richard as well."

"Why wouldn't she be?" I asked.

"I'm sorry. I forgot you probably don't know."

"Know what?" I asked, hopeful for some information that might prove helpful in establishing my identity.

"Richard is not her ladyship's real son."

"What are you saying?" I stopped dead in my tracks.

"Keep dancing, Serena, or everyone will think my charms are losing their powers. I said that Richard is not her ladyship's natural son. The old Earl was married before. His first wife died, and within a year he had married Juliette."

That explained a great deal, I thought. The lack of resemblance to my own father, perhaps even the source of the scar.

The music had stopped, and Robin was leading me over to a table filled with refreshments.

"I couldn't possibly eat anything after that dinner," I said.

"You don't mind if I have a brandy, do you?"

"Of course not," I replied.

A hand touched my shoulder, and I looked up to see the Baron smiling down at me.

"Might I have this dance, Miss Miles?"

"Go ahead, Serena. But I warn you, I shall reclaim you after this one dance."

The Baron held me to him so tightly that I felt my breath almost taken away. He did not dance as well as Robin, and his palms were hot and clammy against mine. "Do you travel to London often, Miss Miles?" he asked.

"I have never been there," I replied, realizing it was a dangerous answer.

"That is unusual, for your grandmother has a magnificent house in town, and for as long as I have known her she has spent the season there."

I felt myself grow tense, realizing of course that he was referring to Lady Jane Carfield. "Yes, that is true," I said, maintaining control, "but my family is in the country, and I have always been happy there."

"You fascinate me, Miss Miles."

"Why, pray tell? There is really very little unusual about me."

"Oh, I disagee," he said, pulling me tighter to him. "Your identity, for starters, fascinates me."

"Why?" I hoped my extreme anxiety was not apparent.

"Because you are not who you say you are."

"I don't understand what you mean," I said, trying to keep my voice as level as possible.

"Jane Carfield has been a family friend for years. If you were really her granddaughter you would know that she not only does not possess a house in London, but that she has not even journeyed there for over twenty years."

I fell silent. I wanted to stop dancing, for the room was now swimming before me and I felt at a complete loss of control. What was I to do? I had been caught in this ridiculous web of lies that my grandmother and I had woven. Once exposed, I could not even begin to imagine what would happen.

"Serena—if that is in fact your name—you have nothing to worry about from me," the Baron said calmly. "Come, let us get a breath of fresh air and outside we shall be able to discuss this matter more privately." Taking my hand, he led me from the floor and through the doors to the terrace. The air was cool and shocked me out of the numbness which had enveloped me since his accusation. "Perhaps we should stroll a bit in the gardens. That way we will simply be taken for lovers sharing a moment under the stars."

The thought sickened me, but I had no other recourse.

We were out of sight of the ballroom when I turned and asked, "What do you intend to do?"

Even in the darkness I could see his teeth flash in a wicked smile. "I am so glad that you have decided not to deny my allegations, for I should have found that very trying indeed. That was very wise of you." He began running his sweaty hands slowly up my arms.

"Whatever you believe you have discovered, Baron, does not give you the right to touch me," I said, reaching up to remove his hands.

"To the contrary, Serena, I think it will give me every right."

"What are you saying?"

"I sense that you would not be too happy should anyone at this ball learn that you are an impostor—particularly the Camberleighs, for whom I have been led to understand you are acting as governess. What you are doing in that house is really of little interest to me, though I must admit I would be fascinated to learn that you are in fact the Earl's mistress, particularly when his wife appears so out of sorts these days."

"How dare you," I spat out, gathering my skirts. "I will listen to no more of this."

"Ah, but you will, Serena," he said, grasping my arm. "To continue, what you are doing there interests me not, except that having discovered your ruse puts me at—shall we say—an interesting advantage."

"You are hurting my arm," I said, attempting to wrench away.

"Good, I like that. I like a woman to resist me. It makes the conquest far more satisfying. It dawns on me that we have something to trade, you and I. You should benefit greatly, I would think, if I were to remain silent. No one ever need know the truth. It could be our little secret."

"Why would you not reveal me?" I asked, wondering why this man who appeared so loathsome would be willing to protect me.

"Your naïvete is enchanting, Serena, but I do not for one second believe that you do not understand. However, if you would prefer to have it spelled out to you, then by all means I shall accommodate. You must know by this time that I find you very desirable. And although I find it amusing to talk to you and dance with you, I should find it far more entertaining to make love to you."

"You are a fiend," I said, pulling from his grasp and turning to find the footpath back to the manor.

"An unfortunate choice of words, but I shall not bother to contradict them. You can run, Serena, but who are you going to run to? The Earl? Even if he is in on this little game, how do you think Lady Camberleigh would react? Or Monique? Or your friend Lady Ormsby, for that matter?"

"I will tell them what you are doing," I said.

"And after I tell them what I know, do you think they will believe you? Besides, in truth, I have done nothing—yet."

What he said, I realized with sudden horror, was true. The only person I could go to was my grandmother. But I had promised to keep our pact in confidence. If this were to come out, it would place her in a totally compromising position, not to mention the humiliation. And without my being able to prove that I was really her granddaughter, what would happen to me? I had no money, no prospects. And once this came out I could certainly not hope ever to find another position anywhere in the county.

"I see that you are coming to your senses, Serena. And it is not such a distasteful proposition after all. You would not find me an inexperienced lover."

"You disgust me," I replied.

"Ah, but that tempts me even more, my pet. I've told you that I like a woman who resists me. The thought of taming you excites me. Tears don't, however, so I suggest you stop your sniveling."

"Baron, this is not what you think. You do not understand. I have done nothing wrong. Please," I begged, "do not do this to me."

"If you have done nothing wrong, my dear, then you have nothing to fear. Perhaps we should make the announcement to the guests together."

"No," I choked.

"Well, then it appears that I shall soon know the delights of that soft white skin."

"You are revolting," I answered.

"Now, now my dear, this really doesn't become you, and I am becoming impatient."

He withdrew something from his coat and, taking my hand, pressed the object into it. I fingered it, realizing instantly that it was a key.

"What is this?" I asked.

"That, my dear, is the key to my silence. Actually it is the key to my room, and I should use it tonight, if I were you. It is not difficult to find. You simply make a right at the top of the stairs. It is the fifth door on the right. The room has a large bed, so you should be very comfortable. If I am not mistaken, around midnight there will be a late supper in the dining room, after which the ball will resume. When supper is announced, you will excuse yourself, saying that you are going to check on your charge and freshen up. Instead, you will come to my room. I will join you there."

"What if I don't come?"

"That would be most unfortunate, for then I should have to make my announcement, wouldn't I?"

"Is there nothing I could say to dissuade you from this . . . this travesty?"

"I am a man of action, Serena. And now I think we should return before we arouse suspicions. I would suggest you act normally and dance or mingle as regularly you would with the guests. I shall not take up your time, so you may dance to your heart's content with Lord Kelston, who seems to have a particular appeal for you. But at midnight—or whenever supper is served—that shall be the end of your frivolity."

I followed the Baron back toward the ballroom. He tried to take my arm, but I protested and walked a short distance behind him. As we reached the terrace leading inside, he moved off. I climbed the steps and leaned against the stone balustrade at one end of the terrace, watching the figures whirling about the grand room before me.

I thought I was going to be ill and clung to the stone for support. The key felt as though it was burning an impression in my hand. I wanted to throw it out to the gardens below, but I restrained myself, hearing the Baron's words that it was the key to his silence. If I threw it away, I was throwing my life away.

After he was done with me, my life wouldn't be worth anything anyway, I thought. But at least I would not bring harm or embarrassment to my grandmother.

I tucked the key in the bodice of my gown.

"Well, there you are, Serena. Was the thought of dancing with me so unpleasant that you are hiding out here?"

I looked up to see Lord Barkham smiling down at me.

"Hardly," I said. "I just felt a bit faint."

"When you insist on dancing every dance, I should expect that it might be overwhelming. But then, Baron Whittenfield did not seem disposed to let you go."

"Don't let me keep you from the ball, Lord Barkham. I really feel quite recovered. Thank you."

"Then might I claim that dance?"

I shrugged. I couldn't, I supposed, remain out here all evening. "I suppose, if you insist."

"It is hardly flattering to make it sound as though I were leading you to the guillotine."

"I am sorry, Lord Barkham," I replied.

He led me onto the dance floor and took me in his arms. I was very aware of his size and strength as he guided me effortlessly about the room.

"Have you noticed how well you fit in my arms, Serena?"

"If you haven't noticed, Lord Barkham, I am exceedingly tall for my sex."

"Oh, I have noticed," he said, pulling me to him slightly.

I thought it ironic that here I was in the arms of the man that I continually tried to avoid and yet at this moment I never wanted him to let me go.

"Shall we get a glass of punch?" he asked. "I don't want you to go fainting on me."

I nodded. He fetched two glasses and, handing me one, led me back out to the terrace.

"Shall we stroll in the gardens for a moment?"

I nodded, relieved that he had not chosen the same path as the Baron.

As we walked I could suddenly feel tears flowing from my eyes. I tried to wipe them away, but as quickly as I did, more rolled down my cheeks. Lord Barkham stopped and turned my face up to his.

"Good Lord, Serena, what is the matter? Was my dancing that bad?"

I shook my head. "It's nothing."

"I don't believe you. You aren't the same. Far too contrite for the Serena Miles I know. Can you tell me?"

I shook my head, still unable to stop my tears.

"Give me that," he said, taking my glass and putting it as well as his own down on the grass. He took me in his arms. I was so distraught, so broken, that I did not resist.

He held me for some time without saying anything. His breathing was strong but, even against my ear, almost rhythmic, and I found it soothing.

"If you only knew how long I have longed to have you in my arms, Serena. When I think of it, I don't know that I didn't fall in love with you that very first day on the steps of Camberleigh. You looked so distressed and at the same time forlorn, but you were not going to have anyone say one word against your little Jaspar.

"I marveled at you during that dinner when you spoke your mind on the tenancy issue. I thought, now here is a woman who has a mind to match her beauty. When I first saw you after your accident, I actually felt weak all over. I was deathly afraid that I would lose you just as I was beginning to find you."

I felt his lips against my ear; then he was kissing my hair and then my neck. I felt as though I were in a dream. Whether it was shock or the effects of the punch I did not know, but I had no will of my own.

"Serena, there is so much I want to say to you, so much I want to explain."

His mouth closed over mine, parting my lips. His tongue tasted sweet as it thrust in and out, reaching—it seemed—to the depths of my throat. His body pressed closer to mine and his hand grasped my thigh and moved me full against him. The swell of his manliness pushed against my stomach, and I felt a slow spreading ache in the lower part of my groin.

I don't know what jostled me to my senses, but with a strong sudden push I moved us apart as quickly as we had come together.

"Serena, what is wrong?" he asked, grasping my shoulders.

"What is wrong, Lord Barkham, is that you have chosen to take advantage of my indisposition, sensing, I am sure, that I was so preoccupied that I would be a willing subject for you to trifle with."

"Serena, what nonsense is this?" he gasped, his hands shaking my shoulders.

"It is not nonsense, and I suggest that you should unhand me unless you want every guest in that ballroom running out to see what is happening."

His hands dropped to his sides.

"I don't know what game you are playing, Serena, but I don't find it amusing. The idea that I lured you out here to embarrass or defile you in any manner is absurd, and you know it."

"Is it, Lord Barkham?"

"If I have offended you, then I am truly sorry. But I cannot believe that is true, for unless I am totally deceived you want me as much as I want you."

"I trust that your pride will not be forever wounded if I tell you that you are utterly mistaken."

"Serena, I don't know what is going on. First you act very strange on the dance floor. Then we come out here and you start crying. And then when I try to comfort you and things take a course that can only be natural between us, you accuse me of trying to take advantage of you. Good Lord, if I didn't know better I would think that bump on the head you received weeks ago had addled your brain."

"I would appreciate your taking me back inside now."

"Not until we have settled this thing."

"There is nothing to settle. But if you fear what I might say to Clarissa or your sister, you can put your mind at rest. I am certain that they are most likely all too well acquainted with your indiscretions, and I should not like to add to them."

"I have no idea what Clarissa or Anne has to do with this, but I can assure you that I fear nothing that you might say to them."

"Then you are even more insensitive than I thought, for although I pity Clarissa her selection, I think she would be devastated to learn that her intended was even a greater rogue than she thought."

"Her intended?" he said, throwing his head back in laughter. "Is that what all this is about?" I made no reply. "Serena, the only intentions I have regarding Clarissa are that she not involve herself with some money-grubbing fop who is going to marry her only as an access to the Camberleigh estates, because my connection with Mayfair would mean that I would have to be involved with him."

"But I thought . . . I was led to believe . . ." I stuttered, confused.

"You should learn, my dear, not to believe everything you hear."

"It's not just what I have heard. I have seen the two of you together many times, even in the rose garden."

"Am I not permitted to be in the rose garden with Clarissa?"

"At night."

"I see," he replied. "And did that disturb you?"

"It did nothing of the sort," I snapped.

"Well, if you had ever been within hearing distance, you would know that I was simply counseling Clarissa."

"I can't imagine Clarissa being counseled on anything," I retorted.

"I grant you that on most matters she appears not to have a thought in her pretty head, but when it comes to her mother, that is a different matter."

"What of her mother?"

"She is sincerely worried about her, and from tonight's display I think you can see that there is some justification. I have always been around Camberleigh, and Clarissa knows that she can come to me for advice when she needs it."

"I can hardly believe that she thinks of you as an uncle as Oliver does."

"Clarissa is in love with the idea of being in love, Serena.

I am quite certain that she is in the ballroom at this very moment batting her eyes at some poor fool who is making the mistake that her attentions are being given exclusively to him. Now that her season has commenced, any delusions she was under about our relationship will soon be forgotten."

"Well, all this may be true, but it does not change anything," I replied. "Now, if you will take me back to the ballroom . . ."

"Not before I do this," he replied, crushing me to him with such an intensity that I felt my breath taken away. His mouth found mine again and his tongue entwined smoothly with mine. I wanted to push him off, but my body did not seem to follow my mind, for it made no resistance as his fingers ran gently over my neck and cupped my breast. "Serena," he whispered, "don't you see that we were made for each other? My God, I want you. I love you, Serena—and I want to spend hours, days, the rest of our lives showing you just how much." I shivered as he nibbled my ear, then traced its outline with his tongue. "Tell me that you love me in return, and you will have made me the happiest man on earth."

"No," I sobbed, "please don't do this. I just want to be left alone. Can't you see what this is doing to me? I beg of you, if you have any decency please let me go."

He held me a moment longer and then released me.

"Serena, I will let you go, but only because you are obviously distraught, and I don't think you are responsible for what you are doing or saying at this moment. I believe that I am not mistaken, that you care for me as much as I do you. I shall not abandon that."

I felt as though all energy, all fight, had been robbed from my system. I was limp with fear, exhaustion, and confusion as I stumbled along beside Lord Barkham back to the ballroom.

We had no sooner reached the entrance than Robin hailed us and came running over.

"Where have you two been? I've been searching high and low. The least you could do is dance with me once again, Serena, before the midnight supper."

I had no wish to dance with Robin, or anyone else, for that matter, but I did not seem to be able to make any move on my own behalf. As Robin took me in his arms, my eyes met Lord Barkham's. They had never looked more dark or solemn.

"You are so quiet, Serena," Robin said as he moved me expertly about the dance floor. "You aren't still angry with me for my earlier behavior, are you?" At that moment I couldn't even place why I had been annoyed. "Say you forgive me. I suppose I am a terrible boor at times, particularly when I don't get my own way. But you can't hate me for finding you so damnably appealing."

"I don't hate you, Robin," I replied. "I am just feeling a bit out of sorts."

"You do look awfully pale. Perhaps some refreshment will help. I would be honored if you would join me for supper, as it appears that my aunts have retired for the evening and my obligations are over."

Something bumped me from the rear, and I was knocked forward against Robin.

"Careful there, old man, you almost knocked the lady down," Robin said.

A voice which I immediately recognized as the Baron's retorted, "I do indeed apologize, Miss Miles. I trust that I did not harm you in any way."

This was no accident, I thought, attempting to regain my composure. More likely a reminder that it was time that I should be using the key, which lay like a dead weight against my chest.

Whatever I was to do, I knew that I could not continue dancing as I was.

"Robin, you really must excuse me," I said. "I am feeling less well than I thought."

"But the evening has only just begun, Serena."

"I know, but perhaps if I lie down for a spell I will be sufficiently recovered to return for the rest of the ball."

"If you must, but I shall be dreadfully lonely until you return."

I managed to laugh. "Robin, I could never think of you as being lonely."

"Can you find your way to your room on your own?"

"Oh, yes. And please don't make mention of this to anyone. I wouldn't want to cause a stir over something so insignificant."

I made my way out to the staircase as unobtrusively as possible. Fortunately, most of the guests were on the dance floor and only a few actually marked my exit.

I mounted the stairs feeling that I was climbing toward the gates of hell. I had just reached the top when I heard someone call my name.

"Serena." It was Anne.

I turned and saw her quickly coming up the stairs after me.

"Robin told me that you are ill. Why did you not look for me? You shouldn't be on your own if you are feeling poorly."

"It's nothing, really. I was just a bit faint. I shall be quite recovered in a few minutes."

"Of course you will," she replied. "Come to my room and I shall get a damp cloth for your head."

"No, I can't . . . I mean I really would prefer to go to my room alone. You go back downstairs. I shall rejoin you later."

"Nonsense," she replied, taking my arm and leading me down the hall.

I had no other choice but to follow her, but in doing so I was risking what the Baron might do or—worse yet—say. If I could only convince her that what I needed most was rest, perhaps she would leave me to sleep and I might make it to the Baron's room in time.

She insisted that I lie down on her bed, and I heard her wringing a cloth out in the basin. I felt tears come to my eyes and fought with all my strength to hold them back. Anne sat down on the bed next to me.

"Serena, what is this? Are those tears? My goodness, I didn't realize you were in pain."

"No," I choked. "I am fine, really."

"Serena, what is it? You're shivering."

She pulled me up toward her, her arms around my shoulders.

"Oh, Anne," I sputtered, "I can't bear this when you are being so kind."

"Bear what? Serena, I think you had best tell me what this is all about."

"I cannot," I sobbed, the tears now flowing uncontrollably.

She held me close to her, and I wept as I had done only twice before in my life. First when my father had died, and then my mother.

Only when it was obvious that my anguish was fully spent did Anne speak.

"Serena, I know that we have not really known each other all that long, but I feel in this short time that we have become fast friends. And friends should be able to confide in each other. I don't know what is troubling you, but let me assure you that there is nothing that you could say that would shock me, upset me, or make me think ill of you. I beseech you to tell me what is troubling you. Sometimes just discussing matters that seem grave lightens their severity immensely.

"I can't," I whispered.

"You can't or you won't?"

"I *can't.*"

"If it is a matter of confidence, I can absolutely assure you that I should never betray anything you tell me. I pledge that on the graves of my dear parents."

"You don't understand," I sobbed. "If I don't go now to Baron Whittenfield's room, I shall be exposed."

"Exposed for what?" she asked.

I shook my head.

"Now listen to me, Serena. I don't know what is going on here, but I think you had best tell me at once."

Before I knew it I was telling her that the Baron had discovered something in my past and threatened to expose me this very evening unless I went to his room.

"The monster," she gasped as I concluded.

She stood and began pacing about the room.

"Don't you see I must go, Anne? I cannot risk what he will say."

"Serena," she replied, returning to sit beside me on the bed. "I know that this will be painful for you, but if I am to do anything to help you I must know the entire truth. I must know what it is that the Baron believes he can blackmail you about."

"Do you swear to me that no matter what happens you will die having kept this story sacred?"

"You have my word."

She took my hand in hers and I began slowly.

"My name is not Serena Miles." I paused to see her reaction, but there was none. "It is Serena Miles Camberleigh."

"What?" she gasped. "But how?"

"My father was William Camberleigh. My mother was the

woman who gave you that handkerchief with the nosegays on it."

"I don't believe it," she whispered, her eyes not leaving my face.

"But it is the truth, and unfortunately that is the problem," I continued. I told her as succinctly as I could about my mother's death, the letters, my grandmother's reaction, the fabricated story of my past, the arrangement she had proposed, and her engaging the solicitor. "You see, without absolute proof I am lost should anyone betray this, for I would most certainly not be able to stay on as governess once it all came out."

"You must forgive me, Serena, if I appear somewhat at a loss for words, but this is all so fantastic that I think it will take me days to fully digest the impact of what you have told me."

"I understand," I replied.

"Does Richard know?" she asked.

"No. To my knowledge the only person who knows is my . . . her ladyship."

"I see," she said, rising and once more pacing the room. "How were you to get into the Baron's room?"

"He gave me this key," I said, withdrawing it from my bodice.

"Give me that," she replied, crossing over to me and holding out her hand.

"What for?"

"Never mind. Just give it to me. I think we shall have a little surprise for the Baron."

"Anne, you can't. Please don't get involved in this. It is my affair," I begged.

"Not any longer. Don't worry, I won't take any risks. I'm not that foolish, particularly where the Baron is concerned. No, I have a scheme which if it works the way I hope it will, Baron Whittenfield will very shortly be nothing more than a bad memory."

"But what can you do? Anne, he means what he says. I don't take this to be an idle threat."

"Nor do I, but don't worry. Just promise me that you will stay here until I return. Open the door for no one. I shall tap three times when it is safe and I can come back for you."

"This is madness."

"It would be *madness* if you allowed yourself to go there. I shudder to think of the consequences." We embraced. "While I am gone, fix your face a bit. We can't have anyone seeing you this way. There are rouges and powders all over my dressing table. Use whatever you wish. And lock the door when I leave."

She was gone before I had a chance to utter any further protestation. I felt sick at heart, for I should not have permitted her to become involved. If anything happened to her, I would never forgive myself.

I locked the door, then sat down at the dressing table. I was shocked by my reflection. I had little desire to redo my face, but began doing so automatically, trying not to let my mind dwell on what might be happening at this very moment elsewhere in the house.

I had no more than applied a bit of rouge to my cheeks than I was startled by a knock at the door. I rose quickly, relieved that Anne had returned so soon. Just as I reached for the lock, I realized that it had been two strong knocks, not the three light taps that Anne had indicated. I paused beside the door.

"Anne, is that you?" a male voice whispered. "Let me in."

I could not identify the voice, as it was muffled by the thickness of door. If it was a trick, I would be trapped. No, it was best to wait for Anne.

I sat down on the bed and waited. It seemed an eternity before there came three light taps at the door.

I flew to it, unlocking it and opening it immediately.

There stood Lord Barkham.

"I . . . thought," I stammered. "I mean . . . I was just lying down, and . . ."

"Serena, Anne sent me up to you." His face was serious.

"Oh, no," I moaned. He entered and closed the door behind him.

"You have nothing to fear. The Baron will be long gone by morning."

"But Anne promised me—she promised not to betray me."

"Serena, she hasn't. But you must see that she had to tell me. You couldn't expect her to deal with the likes of him alone, could you?"

"What did you do? What has happened? Where is Anne? Is she all right?"

"Anne is fine," he replied. "And I will tell you everything in due time. But we can't say here. Someone is likely to come in. I have told Anne to remain downstairs and just say that you were slightly indisposed. It is better if we make this appear as natural as possible."

"But I can't go back just yet," I said, looking up into Lord Barkham's eyes.

"Come down to my room. No one will disturb us there, and I can give you a spot of brandy while I explain what has happened."

"I hardly think that that would be wise, under the circumstances," I replied sternly.

"Serena, stop acting like a child. I shall not lay a hand on you, if that is what you are afraid of."

I realized that I was in no position to argue, though I loathed being compromised by Lord Barkham. What he had said, of course, was right. It would have been folly for Anne to try anything on her own, but I wished that she had enlisted the aid of Robin—or anyone other than Lord Barkham.

I followed him down to his room, which was just down the hall from mine.

"Let me just look in on Oliver for a moment," I whispered.

"Promise you will return?"

I nodded.

Oliver was sound asleep, and I tiptoed back out as carefully as I had entered.

The door to Lord Barkham's room was ajar, and he was pouring two brandies, which he set on a table by a small loveseat near the fireplace.

"How is Oliver?"

"Sleeping peacefully," I replied.

"Good. Now come over here and drink this. And don't tell me you don't want it. It's for your own good."

Before I could even take a sip, he downed his glass and brought the decanter over to the table. "First of all, let me say that I hope that the reason you reacted so oddly to me in the garden earlier this evening was that you were so upset by that bastard's threats that you could not think properly about anything."

"I regret to inform you, Lord Barkham, that one had nothing to do with the other," I replied.

"You don't sound very certain about that, but let us put that aside for the moment. What I want to know is how did you ever get involved with that man on a gambling debt? Anne said it was not large, but you should have known better." My mouth fell open. "I see you are shocked, but Anne had to tell me the reason behind this, why he had decided to collect. If I was going to do battle I had to be armed with information, at least."

"What exactly did Anne tell you?" I asked, regaining some of my composure.

"She told me that you had incurred this debt with the Baron over a year ago and that you chanced to meet him again tonight. When he demanded payment, you told him you were unable to pay it. He then decided to extract it another way."

"I see," I said, slowly understanding Anne's concocted story. While I certainly didn't like being portrayed as one who would be brazen or stupid enough to become involved in the tawdriness of playing for money, at least my secret was still intact—at least for the moment.

"I don't mean to chastise you, Serena, but I can't understand why you didn't come to me at once."

"It is my affair, and I deeply regret having involved you or your sister."

"Don't you think that now that I have paid the Baron off and cleared your debt for you that you might once and for all call me Justin. Particularly since I told him that you were to become my wife."

"You did what?" I shrieked.

"Keep your voice down, dear heart, or we shall have one hundred people swarming down upon us within moments."

"What do you mean you paid the Baron?" I hissed.

"Well, Serena, I always believe in paying one's debts or else they come back to haunt you."

"How much did you pay him?" I asked, dreading the answer.

"Two hundred pounds," he replied. "But you should know that better than I."

"Two hundred pounds," I gasped.

"I must say that bounder seemed surprised. I am certain that after learning that you were to become my wife—and what I threatened to reveal about his own peculiarities—the last thing he expected was that he would actually collect."

"Why, in the name of heaven, did you need tell him that I was to become your wife?"

"Because you would then be in a position where he would not dare to violate you."

"I see," I replied thoughtfully.

"Of course, I loathed making the first announcement of our betrothal to that monster, but then we can do it formally within the next few weeks—or days, if you prefer—and no one need ever know that the Baron had had first honors."

"You are mad," I replied, rising and commencing to pace the room.

"Quite. If being totally and passionately in love with you is madness, then I am a lunatic. Here, drink more of this. Perhaps it will stop your pacing up and down like a caged animal." He rose and handed me a glass he had just refilled.

I took the brandy automatically.

"That's better," he said as I moved back over by the fire.

"I suppose I should thank you," I said, finding some difficulty in realizing that it was indeed Lord Barkham who had saved me from a fate worse than death.

"Serena, you owe me no thanks. I would move mountains if I could if I knew that it was on your behalf. Surely you see that."

I did not know what I saw. My entire life was in confusion. No matter how I turned or who I turned to I seemed destined for some disaster. I took another sip of brandy and looked across at the man who regarded me so intently. The flame from the fire exaggerated the already strong planes of his face. He wasn't as handsome as Robin, I thought, but there was a strength that emanated from him. I could well imagine that he would prove an intimidating opponent to one like the Baron.

"You referred to peculiarities about the Baron," I said. "What did you mean?"

"Let us say it has to do with his sexual proclivities," he replied, watching for my response.

"You mean he has made similar threats to other women?"

"Very few, in fact."

"But what, then?"

"Very simply, his tastes are for young men—boys, to be exact."

I flushed deeply. I had once overheard my father make a similar charge about one of the sea captains who had come into port. I had not completely understood, for I could not imagine what bond might be shared and why it appeared to anger my father so.

"He has a habit, which by good fortune I know about, of paying off young hoodlums' debts to society by buying their way out of prison. He uses their indebtedness for a period of time, and then casts them back out on the streets."

"But that is criminal," I replied. "Can't it be stopped?"

"How? As long as he possesses the wealth and power that he does and as long as young boys wind up in the jails—even if only for some minor altercation—he is able to amuse himself whenever and however he wishes."

"I don't understand, then, what he intended with me?"

"You are young and very beautiful. Your body is that of a woman's, but in many ways your heart is still that of a child. It is a fascinating combination, one which he must have perceived as most alluring. The real tragedy, of course, is that he would have taken you in such a fashion as to complete his desires but has left you with nothing but emptiness and shame."

"And you suppose you would not do that?" I ventured.

"Why do you ask?"

"I don't know. It was a foolish question." I mustn't drink any more of the brandy, I thought, for I was obviously not in control of my senses.

"Serena, come here."

"Why?" I retorted, thinking it odd that he had the idea that he could order me about. "So that you can claim what you have bought and paid for?"

"Is that what you actually think? That I paid your debt so that I could have my way with you?"

"Isn't that more to the truth?"

"If that is what you think, then perhaps I should lay claim right now. You have never looked more lovely, you know."

He rose and came over to where I sat.

"You wouldn't," I retorted, sinking back into the chair.

"I would. But not for the reasons you think. I will make slow and passionate love to you—not because I paid the Baron two hundred pounds, but because I desire you as I have never desired another woman." He pulled me up to him so swiftly

257

that my glass fell to the floor. "Leave it."

He actually means to do this, I thought in panic. I hadn't really believed what I had been saying. I had no idea why I had even suggested it. I had wanted to hear him say that he found me attractive. I had toyed with him as he often did with me, but *this* was not my intention.

I stiffened as his groping hands began to untie the gold braid that closed my dress. If only I had not drunk so much brandy. Everything in the room seemed to be spinning, and I could not focus on anything except the few flames that continued to leap in the fireplace.

I suddenly felt myself swept up off the floor. The next thing I knew he was putting me down on the massive bed on the other side of the room.

"The brandy," I said. "Please."

"No, Serena, no more brandy."

"No, you don't understand," I said, trying to lift myself up.

"I understand very well."

I closed my arms over my breast, trying to shield myself from his advance.

"Don't hide yourself from me, Serena. I want to linger on every part of you."

He sat down on the bed next to me and removed his jacket. As I put my hand up to push him away I realized that his shirt was unbuttoned to the waist. His hand clasped over mine, pressing it against his collarbone and running it slowly over and down his chest.

He placed his other hand on my neck and moved it slowly down, his fingers tracing some imaginary line. It reached the bodice of my dress and then closed over my breast, which lay partly exposed due to the now loosened ties of my gown. I felt mesmerized by some force that was totally strange to me. He bent down over me and, now using his tongue, followed the same path his fingers had taken. His mouth closed over my breast and I felt my nipple grow taut, swelling in the warm moisture of his mouth.

Lifting me to him, his hands worked feverishly to undo the remaining fastenings to my gown.

"Damn these things," he muttered.

"Please don't," I moaned.

"Serena, my love, don't fight me. Trust me. I won't harm you."

I clutched frantically at my dress, then petticoats as he pulled them down, tearing fabric in his determination.

I rolled to the side, burying my face in the pillow to muffle the sound of tears.

He rose from the bed. I lay there wondering if perhaps he realized that I was too frightened or too inexperienced to satisfy his needs. I rolled over, hoping to see him readying to take his leave, but gasped as I saw that he had instead shed his breeches. I shut my eyes quickly, but not before I had seen the throbbing flesh which thrust forth from between his legs. I rolled back against the pillow and stiffened as I felt him lie down beside me, his masculinity wedging between my thighs.

"Although you seem to prefer not to look at me, Serena," he whispered, "I, on the other hand, could look at you forever. I must tell Anne that although her gowns become you she could never create anything to equal what nature herself has created."

"So you would admit this treachery to your own sister," I cried.

"A moment ago I don't think you thought it treachery, and in another I don't think you will either. And if you think that squeezing your thighs like that will hurt me, I can only assure that it is only giving me greater pleasure."

His arm stretched around me, his hand once again finding my breasts. I tried desperately to clear my head enough to let it govern my body so that it would not betray me once again, but it seemed that Lord Barkham knew things that were far greater than I had ever guessed.

His fingers played about my body, down along my stomach and my thighs, and I shivered as a slow ache built in my groin. He pulled himself up over me and lay atop me, his organ pressed full against me; his mouth closed over mine. Then he reached down and his hands cradled my buttocks, thrusting them up so that my legs were suspended in air. My legs tightened as he entered me with one sharp thrust. It seemed that he was probing to the very core of me.

His mouth closed again over my breast, his hands pushing my legs up farther and farther until I thought I could take no more of him. The ache was spreading, and I arched, urging him to release me from this tension. I felt as though I was climbing, floating upward, and I desperately needed to reach the top. The thrusts were quicker now, as if he too was climbing the same imaginary mountain.

When I thought that I could endure no more, I suddenly reached the top, floating there for a moment before drifting down and down until I came to rest on something soft and warm.

We lay in each other's arms for a long time without saying anything.

"Do you still feel that it was treachery that I intended, Serena?"

I remained silent. There was no doubt in my mind that there had been no deception in this act. But I had no words for this man whom I had fought against so long and who now seemed to have captured my very soul.

"Serena, tell me that it was as wonderful for you as it was for me. I don't think I can bear this silence."

"Justin, you have to understand that I am terribly confused," I replied.

"Then let me unconfuse you," he said, brushing his lips over mine.

"Please," I begged, "I must try to understand all this."

"What is there to understand? I love you. And I want to spend the rest of my life with you."

"That is not possible."

"What do you mean?" he replied, his eyes searching my face in the shadows. "If you are going to try to tell me that you do not share my feelings, I will not listen."

"I need time, Justin," I replied. "Just hours ago I thought that I would be defiled by Baron Whittenfield. And now you. I must have time to sort my thoughts."

"Surely you don't mean to suggest that I have simply traded places with the Baron?"

"No, I don't mean that. But these feelings that you have stirred in me are alien. I am not certain what they mean."

"My dear, Serena. You are a sensuous, passionate woman. These emotions are only natural. They simply have not been awakened in you before. There is nothing to think through. You will learn that love cannot be analyzed, much less rationalized. Just say that you will marry me."

"I cannot."

"Does this have anything to do with the night back at Camberleigh?" he asked.

"What night, Justin?"

"I think you know. Oh, I realize that you were barely conscious, but. . ." He broke off.

My eyes flew to his.

"It was you!" I cried. "It was you who did that to me," I choked out, my hands beating against his chest.

"Serena, stop," he moaned, grasping my wrists as they flew against him. "Serena, listen to me, please."

"Let go of me," I sobbed.

"Not until you have heard me out. Yes, it was me. And if there were anything I could do to erase the events of that night I would. I had been drinking heavily. Richard and I had had a row, and I was making no headway with him, so I turned to brandy. I have no idea what time it was when I saw you creeping down the corridor, but truly I meant at first only to frighten you. Don't ask me why. Perhaps I was jealous of whoever you had been with. I don't know. I remember taking you in my arms. Whatever intoxication the brandy had provided was nothing by contrast to what you did to me. When you fainted I took you to the closest room and put you on the bed. It is God's truth that I don't know what possessed me, but I took you then and there. I don't even remember going back to my room that night. In the morning I felt dreadful. But I was more sick at the pure baseness of my act than of anything else. Those next days were sheer torture for me."

"You must have been most relieved when you realized that I did not know the identity of my attacker. That made things very easy for you, didn't it," I spat, attempting to wrench my arms free.

"To the contrary. For if before I had desired you, after that night I was obsessed by you. Do you realize how difficult it has been not to touch or approach you since then? I have lain awake nights literally aching to have your body next to mine."

"And so you saw this as the perfect opportunity to violate me once again," I retorted. "Oh, you must have been delighted when Anne told you of my difficulties with the Baron. It played right into your hands. You would come to my rescue and I would be ever grateful. Well, it doesn't work that way."

"Serena, you must know that that is not true. I love you. I want you to be my wife."

"Your wife?" I gasped. "You have the audacity to even suggest such a thing after what you have done? I wouldn't marry you if you were the last man on earth."

"You don't mean that," he said, pulling me to him.

"You have violated me. And now you have humiliated me. I should have let the Baron have his way with me, for nothing could be worse than this."

"You don't know what you are saying, and I pray that you never do, for I think it would destroy you."

"You have done enough destruction. Now, if you will please hand me my gown, I shall return to my room."

"I cannot force you to remain. But I implore you to accept my forgiveness and to put this matter behind us. We can have a glorious future, Serena. Don't let that one mistake stand between us."

I rose and gathered my gown and petticoats.

"You have paid a high price for this evening's amusement, Lord Barkham. I hope that you consider it worthwhile, for the account is now paid in full. I warn you that if you ever even speak of this matter again I shall do everything in my power to see that you are revealed for what you are."

"My God, Serena," he whispered, trying to put his breeches back on, "have you no forgiveness? Are you so unblemished that you can have no compassion for one who admits to wrong?"

"There are some things that one can never forgive."

I fastened my gown as best I could in the darkness of the room. I prayed that I could get back to my room without being seen, for I knew that I must be a sight. I could not keep my hands from shaking, and my face was caked with the salt of my own tears. Any fight that I had left in me had been spent in these last moments.

"Serena, will you not talk to me?" He moved to where I stood. "After what we have shared here this night, you cannot shut out what is between us."

"There is nothing to say," I replied, turning toward the door.

"There you are wrong. I love you, Serena. And one day by

all that is in me I shall prove that to you."

The corridor was mercifully empty, and I stepped quickly to my room. As I closed the door I could hear the strains of the orchestra below and thought back to my fantasies of how this evening would end, with me twirling about the room to the last waltz of the evening. What a difference reality had turned out to be.

I changed into my nightdress and climbed into bed without even brushing my hair. I had known sorrow when my mother died, but the anguish that I now felt was accompanied by an emptiness that left me void of all emotion, all feeling. I sank into the limbo of sleep, thinking that life—which I had always held so dear—was not worth the living if these last weeks had set a pattern for things to come. . . .

Chapter Ten

I AWOKE to see Oliver peering down at me.

"Oliver, what time is it? Have I overslept?"

"No, it is early. Uncle Justin said I should let you sleep, but I thought I had better ask you if I might go out with him this morning. He is going to visit some of the farms hereabouts and has invited me to go along."

I bristled at the sound of his name, but realized that it would do no good to involve Oliver in this. Whatever I thought of Lord Barkham, the boy adored him and I knew that I would have to be careful not to damage that.

"Of course," I replied, "if you wish. But we shall be leaving in the late morning, I should think, so be certain that you are not gone too long."

"Oh, thank you, Serena," he said, flinging his arms about my neck.

He had long left the room when I remembered that I had forgotten to give him his medication, and I made a mental note to be certain to administer it before the journey back to Camberleigh.

Rowena arrived with my basin shortly thereafter and was surprised to find me up and about, for most of the guests would sleep at least until noon.

"Did ye have a grand time, miss?" she asked as she hung up the gown that I had let drop on the chair the night before.

"It was very beautiful," I replied, hoping that I sounded enthusiastic.

"Lady Kelston said I was to tell the ladies that the morning meal be served in the small dinin' room. But if you prefer, I can bring up a tray."

"No, I shall go down shortly," I replied.

"You may be findin' yourself on your own, for I haven't heard a peep out of anyone this mornin'."

"I don't mind, Rowena. Actually, it would be pleasant to have some time on my own."

"Would you be wantin' me to do your hair?"

"No, thank you. We shall be traveling later, and I shall braid it in a simple fashion. You run along. I'm certain you have more than enough to keep you occupied."

"It's going to take the whole lot of us to put things back in place. But I'll be back later and help with your packin'."

The water was hot and I washed with a fury that was reminiscent of what I had done the morning after my attack. I dressed in my traveling suit and braided my hair into a loose coil at the back of my head. It was certainly not the effect of the evening before, but I had little care for my appearance this morning.

When I reached the downstairs center hall, I was surprised to find Monique bustling about with the servants. "Serena, darling, it eez so early, could not you sleep?" she asked, her accent more pronounced than I remembered it.

"I am an early riser, Monique," I replied. "Besides, I was not up as late as I'm certain many of your guests were."

"Ah, yes, Anne told me that you were not feeling well. *C'est dommage*. You looked so ravishing, and I am certain that you broke many a gentleman's heart."

"It was a lovely party, Monique. I would have given anything to have remained, but the excitement must have simply been too much."

"Would you join me for breakfast? It will give us a chance to talk further."

"That would be very pleasant," I replied.

"Good. There is a small breakfast room at the back where we shan't be disturbed."

I followed her to a chamber that was decorated with gaily colored fabrics. The windows, which spanned the full length of one side, overlooked gardens and terraces beyond.

"What a charming room," I exclaimed.

"I am glad you like it. I had my husband add it on. I think he thought it frivolous, but I wanted a place that would be bright and cheerful. I always take my meals here when Robin is away."

The table was set with an endless array of fruits and breads and jams.

"I like a very strong coffee in the morning. But that is very French, I think. Will you join me?" I nodded. "So. Did you dance many dances with my son before you were taken ill?"

"Only a few," I replied.

"That eez too bad. You would be good for him. Of course, I cannot say that the same would be true in reverse. He is not strong enough for you."

I blushed at her directness.

"Now. Justin Barkham. That eez another story. There is a man who could arouse in you the passions and sense of adventure that I sense you and I share. *N'est-ce pas?*"

"I'm afraid I do not share your sentiments when it comes to Lord Barkham, Monique."

"Ah, but unless my eyes deceive me there is fire between you two. I see the way he looks at you, *cherie.*"

"The only fire that burns between us, Monique, is that of dislike. I find the man crude and unprincipled, and the less I have to see him the better."

"I see," she replied slowly, pouring another cup of the dark liquid.

"Perhaps, then, I am mistaken. But a former lover usually knows these things." I could not have been more stunned if someone had delivered a physical blow to my head. "I see that I have shocked you."

"It is . . . not that," I stammered.

"Well, in France we are perhaps a little less conventional about these matters. Or should I say more open about discussing them." She rose and moved to the windows. "After my husband died I was terribly alone. At times I thought there was no reason to go on. He had been my whole life, and when he was gone I just fell apart."

"I can scarcely imagine that of you. You seem so strong, so capable of handling anything," I said.

"I am better now, *cherie,* but much time has passed. Believe me, at first I was at a complete loss. It was Justin Barkham who helped me through that period. I needed a man. Oh, not just for the usual things—the business, the affairs of the estates. No. Even more for the needs of a woman, if you understand what I mean. I loved my husband, of course. But he was gone, and I must say that were I to have hand-picked a lover I could have chosen none better than Justin. He was passionate but tender, forceful but compliant. And the most important thing was that his lovemaking seemed to imbue me with a new strength." She moved back over to the table where I sat. "You have been very quiet, Serena. What are you thinking?"

"Are you . . . I mean, is he still . . ."

"Are we still lovers? *Mon Dieu,* no. It really was for only a short time. But we are good friends. And I think that I can see what is in his eye when he looks at you. Unless I am very much mistaken, Justin Barkham is in love with you, Serena."

I rose abruptly.

"Monique, please do not think me rude, but I really must return to my room."

"Cherie, don't go," she said, clasping my hand. "I have obviously disturbed you by my ramblings. I did not mean to. I just thought that it was important that you knew. Please forgive me."

"There is nothing to forgive. I simply must return and start preparing myself and Oliver for our departure, though I can scarce realize that our weekend has come to an end so quickly."

"But you must return here many times, Serena. I know that I am not as young as you, but I enjoy your company."

"And I yours, Monique," I replied sincerely.

"Perhaps you will come to London for Clarissa's season?"

"Oh, I should doubt that," I replied. "No, I think that Oliver and I will be firmly ensconced at Camberleigh throughout the winter."

"Are you happy there?"

"Why do you ask?"

"I don't know. I sense something. I cannot say what, but I think there is something that troubles you."

"I am really very happy there," I replied. "I love Oliver, and they have for the most part been kind to me. I consider myself fortunate to have the position."

"I want you to know, Serena, that if you ever are in need of anything, you must come to me. I know what it is like to feel alone. And to feel that one has nowhere to turn. My home is open to you, should you ever need it."

"You are very gracious, Monique. It is gratifying to know that I have a friend here."

As I passed Anne's door on the way to my room, I wondered if I should rouse her, but decided that she would prefer to rest as long as possible.

I packed my things slowly but deliberately. As I folded the ball gown, I spied a small tear under the bodice, and the events of the night before flooded into my mind. I would be able to repair the dress, but how could I ever repair the damage that had been done to my soul?

I still had not recovered from the shock of discovering that Lord Barkham had been my attacker. It was true that I had never liked the man from the very first. But I had never imagined that he was capable of such a violent act.

My conversation with Monique had only served to confuse me further. I did not understand why she had thought it necessary to share with me what she had. It had not been simply idle chatter on her part. I felt certain she had had a definite reason for wanting me to know of her relationship with Lord Barkham. What it was I could not fathom.

For me he was a violator, and yet the two of us women—whose lives and ages were so totally different—had lain with him. I wondered if she would be quite so much his champion if she knew what he had done to me. I kept thinking about the two of them as lovers. Had he touched her in the same way he had me? Had he lingered over her body as he had mine? Had he thrust himself as fully into her as he had me?

What did it matter what had transpired between them? It had nothing to do with me. It meant nothing to me.

An hour or so passed, and I was just becoming concerned about Oliver when he appeared at the door. "Serena," he cried, running to embrace me.

"What is this?" I asked, momentarily confused by his ebullience.

"Uncle Justin said I was to give you a big kiss."

How dare he, I thought. I tried to remain calm. "I think I have you all packed. Unless there is something you are hiding from me."

"Why would I hide anything, Serena?"

"I'm just teasing, Oliver."

"Uncle Justin says that he would like to be under way shortly. He has gone to awaken Aunt Anne. He says she should have been up hours ago."

"Well, we are readied," I replied, thinking that I wished there was some other way to return to Camberleigh than with Justin Barkham.

As if reading my thoughts, he said, "Mama and Papa have already left."

"So soon?" I asked.

"Yes. Grandmother wanted to return."

"I see. Well, we should not tarry, then."

"Do you think Jaspar will be there to greet us?"

"I'm sure he will be."

"Robbie is nice to me, Serena."

"And why wouldn't he be?"

"I just mean that he has shown me a lot about the horse and things."

"He is very good with animals," I replied. "I am certain that he can teach you a lot."

"I can help him with his lessons too," he replied.

"Yes, you can. Robbie does not have the benefit of Mr. Masters, so I am certain that he appreciates everything you share with him."

"Have you missed Mr. Masters?"

How strange, I thought. I had given Thomas little if any thought over the weekend.

"I have been very busy since being here, Oliver. But to answer your question, yes it will be nice to see Thomas again."

"Oh," he replied, avoiding my eyes.

"Is there some reason that you do not like Mr. Masters?"

"No," he snapped back, a bit too quickly, I thought.

"I suppose expecting you to be overly fond of your tutor is more than one should expect," I replied.

"I like Mr. Masters," he replied unenthusiastically.

"Well, the important thing is that you learn from him. He

is a good teacher, and that is valuable—as long as you are enjoying what you are learning."

"Uncle Justin says that practical knowledge is as important as book knowledge."

"What did the two of you do this morning, by the way?"

"We visited two farms. The people invited us in, and we talked and Uncle Justin asked about the machinery."

"I see," I replied. "He is very interested in what happens with the tenant farms—just as you will be someday."

"Uncle Justin says that if we had more equipment our farms would be able to be even more successful than those of Kelston Manor. What do you think, Serena?"

"Oliver, that is a very complicated dealing," I replied. "One needs years of experience to understand the intricacies of these things."

"Do you think that I shall ever be able to understand what is involved?"

"From what I have seen and heard in the schoolroom, I am convinced that you will be a superior Earl of Camberleigh. You have an enormous grasp of the academic studies that will enhance your abilities in later life, and even more importantly you have a sensibility that is unusual."

"What is a sensibility?"

"I suppose the best way to describe it is a caring. You care for people, for things, Oliver."

"Is that important?"

"It is the most important thing."

"That is what Uncle Justin says."

"Oliver," I snapped, "would you please not continually refer to your Uncle Justin?"

"Why?"

"Because . . . I just don't want you to."

"But why?"

As I looked at him I was suddenly struck by the openness of his regard.

"Oh, Oliver," I said, "I am so sorry. I am visiting things on you that are not fair."

"What do you mean?"

"Never mind, it is not important. The main thing is that you are thinking and feeling at so young an age. I admire that—"

We were interrupted by a knock at the door. I opened it, and there stood Anne, looking very tired and quite distraught.

"Might I speak with you a moment in private?" she asked.

"Certainly," I replied. "Come in. Oliver, would you do me a favor and double-check to see that we have collected everything from your room?"

He knew full well that it was only an excuse to get him out of the room, but he did not argue.

"What is it?" I asked. "I have never seen you so upset."

"We must be under way at once. There was an awful scene last night with Maura. Richard had taken her to her room and given her a draught, something to make her sleep. He left her, but apparently it wore off before he returned. She was in a state—ranting and babbling about I know not what. Richard was finally able to subdue her, but he obviously could not allow her to remain here under the circumstances. They have left already."

"Is her ladyship with them?"

"Yes. Justin wanted her to return with us, but she insisted on going with Richard. Actually it's a far better arrangement, for there would scarce be room in our carriage. Besides, someone is going to have to watch over Clarissa. I can't say I like the girl, but this whole thing with her mother is devastating her."

"But what is wrong with her, Anne? Doesn't anyone know?"

"No. I feel so helpless, I wish there were something I could do to help."

I thought about what I was going to tell Oliver. He would sooner or later hear about it. Even in a house as immense as Camberleigh Hall, one could not forever hide a matter as grave as this.

"I will come down immediately," I said. "But promise me that there shall be no discussion of this on our journey home. I would like to shield Oliver from it as long as possible."

"Of course. And I am sorry I had to visit all this on you, but I think you understand."

Anne left, and I fetched Oliver, trying to make it sound as though we wanted to get away before all the guests were up and about. Monique, who was obviously aware of the situation, saw to it that our baggage was taken care of. Anne had already taken her seat in the carriage, and the driver lifted Oliver up into his. I looked about for Robin, hopeful that I might see him once more, but he was nowhere in sight.

"Cherie," Monique said, kissing me on both cheeks, "Robin is off riding. I know that he will be devastated to have missed you, but I shall explain. Serena, remember what I have said. If you ever need anything, my home is yours."

"I cannot thank you enough. You have been most gracious. I hope that someday soon I might see you and Robin again at Camberleigh."

"One never knows," she replied, "but with matters as they are I doubt that there shall be guests there for some time."

We embraced, and I climbed into the carriage.

Monique just got to the top of the steps when Justin Barkham appeared at the door. I felt myself flush as he put his arm about her—and held her for a moment too long. I wondered what they were saying, annoyed with myself for such a thought.

We made the journey back to Camberleigh in relative silence. I was relieved that Oliver had had his outing that morning, for it had wearied him and he spent most of the trip dozing against me, my arm about him. Monique had arranged for the cook to prepare a basket of refreshments that we shared along the roadside midway through our journey. Lord Barkham and I managed to be civil to each other; actually, I was even somewhat surprised at his aloofness. Only once, when I had dozed off myself, did I feel that he was watching me, and I opened my eyes to meet his. If he's searching for some show of warmth, he will be sorely disappointed, I thought, turning to gaze at Anne, who sat quietly looking out the window.

Anne had worried me throughout our journey. She was tense, and appeared preoccupied. Surely not her usual breezy, ebullient self. I wondered what we would find upon our return. The matter of Lady Camberleigh worried me, but that was only one problem to be faced. The discovery of the body was also, I was sure, on all our minds. It certainly was on mine. The magistrate was bound to have some further news by now, and I hoped that his findings would prove that the poor girl had met her untimely death by some easily explained accident.

And then there was my own situation. My grandmother's solicitor would surely have some news soon. I did not know how one went about these things, but I supposed that he would travel to Seven Oaks. What he could find there I did not know, for I was certain that no one there had any knowledge of my parents' past life. Even the Thurstons, their closest friends, would have no knowledge of Camberleigh or my link to it. I had searched my mind over and over for something that would provide tangible evidence of my heritage, but could not come up with one solid clue. The solicitor therefore would also come up empty-handed. The only positive note was that he would also not find anything that would give evidence that I was but a charlatan or fortune hunter.

It was dusk when the carriage passed through the huge iron gates of Camberleigh. A light rain had started to fall, and its rhythmic sound on the roof of the carriage was almost in syncopation with the horses' hoofs as we advanced up the drive.

"You are not intending to return to Mayfair tonight, are you, Justin?" Anne asked suddenly, breaking the silence.

"No, I think we should remain," he replied. "There are several matters that must be tended to. Unfortunately, I must go to London tomorrow. I shall take the coach from here tomorrow. You won't mind if I send you back to Mayfair alone in the carriage, will you?"

"Of course not, though I should hate to leave you, Serena, what with everything being so unsettled."

"I will be fine, don't worry," I said, wondering if there was any truth to my statement.

"What is so unsettled, Aunt Anne?" Oliver asked, rubbing his sleep-filled eyes.

"Oh, nothing really, Oliver," she answered.

"I think what she means, Oliver, is that what with the opening of Clarissa's season, there will be a lot of activity about the hall," I said, hoping that he would find my explanation plausible.

"I think it's all silly anyway," he said. "That's all she talks about. It's boring."

"Spoken like a true younger brother, Oliver," put in Lord Barkham. "I think we men should stick together in these matters. If we let the ladies have their way, we would do nothing but plan our lives about what we are to wear to the next gala or ball."

"Don't listen to him," said Anne, pulling on her gloves. "Not all of us are as featherbrained as my brother would have you believe. And someday, when you are older, what you now find trifling you are likely to find enchanting."

"Unfortunately, she has a point," said Lord Barkham. "Though I am loath to admit it, we can be slaves to this frivolity—given, of course, that we find one who is worthy of our affections."

As the carriage pulled up before the house, Giles appeared with a large umbrella.

"Welcome back, Lord Barkham. I trust you had a safe journey."

"Yes, thank you, Giles. The Earl has returned, I assume."

"Yes. The coach arrived some time ago. He asked me to tell you that he should like to see you and Miss Miles in the library as soon as you arrived."

"I am coming too," Anne said, climbing down. "After all, there is nothing that can be discussed that I do not know about."

"Giles," I said, "would you please see to it that Master Oliver is taken to his room and that a tray is brought to him?"

"Of course, miss."

"You don't mind do you, Oliver? I shall be up as soon as I am through with your father."

"Could I see Jaspar?"

"He may be with Robbie. Perhaps you can have Giles find out. If you like, you are welcome to go to my room."

"I will take care of it, miss."

"Thank you, Giles."

I followed Lord Barkham and Anne into the library, where the Earl sat by the fire talking to a portly middle-aged man I did not recognize. Both men rose as we entered.

"Ah, Justin. I am glad that you are back. You know Constable Morrissey, I believe."

"Yes, of course," Lord Barkham replied, crossing over to take his hand. "This is my sister, Lady Ormsby, and Miss Miles—Serena Miles."

"Ah, yes, you are the governess, are you not, Miss Miles?" asked the constable.

"Yes, that is correct."

"I'm sorry, Anne," the earl said, "but would you mind

leaving us alone for a while. There is something of great delicacy that we must discuss in confidence."

"If it has anything to do with the accident in the garden, I know all about it."

"How did you find out about this, Lady Ormsby?" asked the constable as we all took seats.

"I fear she inveigled it out of me," Lord Barkham said. "But you can be certain that she will keep this in strict confidence. She fully understands the delicacy of the matter."

"I don't like this. The whole thing is getting out of hand," the Earl said, rubbing his finger along his scar.

"If you will permit me to say so, sire, I'm afraid this matter is going to become far more involved until the murder is solved," said the constable.

"Murder?" gasped Anne.

"Yes, there is no question that the young woman was murdered. Her neck was broken."

"Could that not have been from the fall into the pool?" asked Lord Barkham.

"I am afraid not. We believe that she was actually killed elsewhere and that her body was dragged or carried to the garden and placed in the pool. When you probed with that fence spoke, Miss Miles, you wedged the body free from the weight or whatever it was that was keeping it submerged."

"Constable, have you determined whether the body is definitely that of Margarite Smythe?"

"Yes, Lord Barkham. There is no question."

"Has the girl's family been notified?"

"It is our understanding that the girl had no living relatives, is that not correct, your Lordship?"

"To my knowledge," the Earl replied.

"But *who* could have done such a thing?" Anne asked.

"That is what we intend to find out, Lady Ormsby. I am afraid that we shall have to interrogate everyone who might have had any dealings whatsoever with the girl."

"Surely you don't mean that you will have to speak of this to Master Oliver?" I asked.

"Master Oliver is the son of the earl," Lord Barkham explained.

"I see," replied the constable. "I'm afraid that I shall have to talk to him briefly. He would naturally have spent a great deal of time with the victim, and he might, perhaps even without knowing it, be able to supply some clue to her demise."

"I am less concerned of the effect this affair will have on my son than on my wife and my mother," said the Earl. "Isn't there some way that you can keep this thing quiet?"

"A young girl has been murdered here, sire."

"The constable is right, Richard. If there is a murderer lurking about the premises, we can't take any chances."

"I know that you must be tired from your journey," said the constable. "But I felt that it was important to notify you of my findings as quickly as possible. I will return tomorrow, and I would appreciate your informing the other members of the family and the staff that I shall be talking to them over the next few days."

"I will see you to the door, constable," Lord Barkham said, rising.

"I return to Mayfair tomorrow, constable, so I suggest if you need to speak to me further that you do so in the morning," Anne said as the constable excused himself from the room.

When she was certain that the two had moved out into the hall, Anne turned to the Earl and asked in a hushed tone, "How is Maura?"

"She is quieter, but I've asked for the doctor to come. Frankly, I think this whole Smythe matter is going to undo her completely. I don't think she can withstand any interrogation, but the constable seems quite determined."

"What of Cam?"

"Mother was a godsend, and braver than I thought possible on our journey home. Maura was really quite hysterical, but Mother managed to quiet her—and more important, she kept Clarissa from breaking down."

"Richard," said Lord Barkham, reentering the room, "I suggest we all gather down here for dinner. The constable will be back the first thing in the morning, and I think everyone should be given the news."

"This ghastly mess couldn't have come at a worse time," said the Earl. "All this to-do over some stupid chit."

"Richard, *really*," Anne gasped.

"She meant nothing to you, Anne. I don't know why you are getting so upset."

"This conversation isn't getting us anyplace," broke in Lord Barkham, crossing over to the fireplace. "Serena, I think it would be wise if you joined us for dinner. I know you must be tired, but whether you like it or not you are involved in this."

"I told Oliver that I would look in on him," I said, getting to my feet. "I shall return for dinner."

As I mounted the stairs my feet felt like lead weights. I wanted to do nothing but go to my room, change out of my traveling clothes, and go to bed, but I instead headed for the nursery, where I found Jaspar looking on intently as Oliver ate his evening meal.

"Well, Jaspar, don't you have a welcome for your mistress?"

He cocked his head, disbelieving for a moment that it was really me, and then as recognition dawned he bounded to my side, wriggling his brown and white body frantically.

"I think he missed you," Oliver said, watching our reunion.

"It's the first time we've been apart since I found him," I said, pleased that he was as happy to see me as I was him.

"What did you and Uncle Justin have to meet with my father about?"

Now that he had asked, I supposed that this was as good a time as any to tell him. Better to come from me than the constable, I thought.

"Oliver, there is something that I must discuss with you after you finish your meal."

"I'm finished."

"Well, then, why don't we sit over here and have our little talk."

We moved over and sat by the fire, Jaspar positioning himself between us at our feet. I took Oliver's small hand in mind.

"What I have to tell you is not pleasant," I began cautiously.

"You aren't going away, are you? I don't want you to leave, ever. I would hate it here if you left."

"I'm flattered, Oliver. I'm not going anyplace—at least I am not planning to. But you realize that I won't be here forever. Some day you will no longer need a governess."

"What did you want to tell me, Serena?"

"Do you remember a young woman by the name of Margarite Smythe?"

"She was my governess—for a while."

"That's right. Well, it seems that Miss Smythe had an accident."

"But she left a long time ago. She didn't even say goodbye."

"She couldn't, apparently, Oliver. Because the accident she had was very serious—so serious . . . that she died."

"She's . . . *dead?*" he asked, his pale blue eyes wide and filled with anxiety.

"Yes, she is, Oliver. But there is no need for you to be frightened. Tomorrow the local constable will want to speak with you for a bit, and you must answer all his questions. He seemed like a very nice man, and he will make it as painless as possible."

"Why will he want to ask me questions?"

"Just to help him determine how she died."

"Will you be there?"

"I am certain that that can be arranged. Now, do you promise not to be worried?"

"I won't be if you are with me."

"Good," I said, embracing him. "And now I must get back to my room so that I might change for dinner."

I helped Oliver ready for bed and gave him the medicine I had once again forgotten to administer that morning. Then with Jaspar in tow, returned to my room, where I prepared to return downstairs.

I was amazed at the sight of Lady Camberleigh as I entered the dining room. I don't know exactly what I had expected, but I was quite taken aback by her appearance. She was dressed in a burgundy-colored gown set off by a handsome ruby and diamond necklace and earrings. But it was less her attire than her face that was so unexpected. Her eyes were bright, almost sparkling in the candlelight. Certainly not the eyes of a woman who had recently been given to fits of hysteria.

If my grandmother was surprised to see me, she gave no indication; her gaze was focused on her daughter-in-law. And Clarissa seemed so subdued that I wondered if the Earl had not already told her the news.

I was seated next to Lord Barkham. At least I would not have to feel his eyes on me during the dinner.

"I didn't know we would have the pleasure of your company

this evening, Miss Miles," Lady Camberleigh said, a bit too sweetly.

"I asked Miss Miles to join us, Maura," the Earl said.

"It appears that Miss Miles is becoming an integral member of our happy little family. Why, next you will be suggesting that she bring our dear little son to dine with us as well."

"Maura, please don't start," replied the Earl, his scar pulsing under the circles that lined his dark eyes.

"There is something that must be discussed, Maura," Anne put in, trying, I knew, to ease the tension.

"I wish that this could be avoided," Lord Barkham began, "but I fear there is no way out of it."

"What is it, Justin?" my grandmother asked, leaning forward in her chair.

"I will come right to the point. Cam, do you remember Margarite Smythe?"

"Let me see. Yes, of course. She was Oliver's governess for a brief spell."

"Why don't you ask Richard," Lady Camberleigh put in. "I'm certain that he remembers Miss Smythe—intimately."

"Maura, if you can't be civil I will see to it that you are returned to your chambers."

"Justin, why are you bringing up this name?" my grandmother asked, ignoring this exchange.

"You may remember that she disappeared rather suddenly in the spring."

"I certainly do," she replied. "But then, I wouldn't say that we have exactly had the best fortune in that department—until, of course, Serena arrived."

"Is that a slur on my ability to manage this household, Mother?" the Earl asked.

"I didn't say it was a fault of yours, Richard."

"It was clearly beyond everyone's control," Lord Barkham continued evenly.

"You see, the reason Miss Smythe disappeared suddenly was due to . . . a misfortune."

"Misfortune? What happened? Where is she now?"

"She's dead, mother," the Earl said bluntly.

Anne dropped her fork to her plate and said angrily, "Richard, that was cruel."

"Is this true, Justin?" my grandmother asked quietly.

"I'm afraid it is. But it is more complicated than that. Miss Smythe's death, you see, was not an accident."

"You mean she was *murdered?*" shrieked Clarissa.

"Clarissa, please be quiet," Lord Barkham said in an annoyed tone. "Hysterics will not help this at all."

"But I—"

"Clarissa, stop," the Earl said, pounding his fist on the table.

"Tell us what happened, Justin," my grandmother said calmly.

"We don't know, really, Cam. It was actually Serena who found the body, which is why she is with us this evening. At this point I don't think we need discuss the details of where or how this discovery was made. That will all come out soon enough. Suffice it to say that it was a grisly experience and one I am certain Serena would like to put out of her mind as quickly as possible."

"Don't you think murder was a bit drastic, Richard?" Lady Camberleigh said, looking straight at her husband and downing a glass of wine. "Or was she no longer your obedient servant? Perhaps she preferred another."

"Maura, that is quite enough." I was surprised to hear my grandmother's command. "I suggest that you get hold of yourself and cease drinking that wine as though it were water before you say something you will come to regret."

"My only regret is ever coming to this household or marrying your son, Juliette."

"Mama," Clarissa cried, "you don't mean that."

"Of course she doesn't," Anne said quickly. "We're all upset. Let us get back to the main issue."

"The constable will be here in the morning," Lord Barkham said. "And I'm afraid we will all have to submit to his interrogation. I am leaving for London late in the morning, and Anne shall be returning to Mayfair, so I think we should be the first to be questioned."

"Convenient, Justin," said Lady Camberleigh. "Perhaps I shall go with you, since it would appear that it will be most unpleasant here for the next few days."

"Mama, may I go too?"

"Your mother isn't going anyplace, Clarissa," the Earl said quickly.

"But Father, the balls begin in only a few weeks. I must be there for the commencement or I shall miss out on it all."

"I trust that this shall all be forgotten by then, my dear."

"I am very tired, Richard," my grandmother said suddenly. "Would you mind asking Giles to see me to my room."

"But you've scarcely touched your food, Mother."

"Please, Richard," she insisted.

"I would be happy to see you to your quarters, your ladyship," I said. "I should like to look in on Oliver before retiring."

"The perfect little governess," Lady Camberleigh said with a sneer. "I suppose that means that you shall retire also, Richard."

"No, my dear. There are a few things I want to discuss with Justin."

"So that he will corroborate whatever story you are planning to give the constable?"

"I think, perhaps, my dear, that you might better spend your time thinking of what *you* are going to tell the constable than continuing with these vicious insinuations."

I rose and moved to my grandmother, who had grown so pale that I wondered whether I should not ask for some assistance in getting her back to her room.

"Let me help you, Serena," Lord Barkham said, rising and coming over to take my grandmother's arm.

We assisted my grandmother out of the dining room and up the staircase. I was suddenly concerned at the toll that all this seemed to be taking on her. I prayed silently that she would be able to endure the troubling days ahead.

"As Lord Barkham is here, your ladyship, you will not need me any further," I said as we reached the upper floor.

"Please stay, Serena. I would like to talk with you both for a moment."

I looked up and saw Lord Barkham nod, bidding me to remain. I wanted to be as far away from him as possible, but I put my feelings aside for the moment.

We settled her into her room, and Lord Barkham poked life back into the fire.

"I know that this is unpleasant, Serena," my grandmother said quietly, "but there are certain things that I feel I should know about this whole thing."

"I'll be happy to tell you anything I can, your ladyship."

"One thing, Justin. Where did Serena find the body?"

"I don't think that is important, Cam."

"Justin, why are you avoiding this issue? Or must I ask Serena to tell me?"

"That won't be necessary, but frankly I'm afraid my answer will upset you. Juliette, it was where they found Charles."

"The pond," she gasped.

"I'm afraid so."

"But why? Why would someone do something so cruel?"

"I'm certain that it is only coincidence."

"But what if it is not? What if whoever did this knew that it would bring up the past?"

"I will do everything I can to see that that doesn't happen."

"Does the constable have any idea who might have committed this awful crime?"

"If he has any clues, he is not sharing them at this juncture."

"Serena, I shall expect you to stay very close to Oliver for the next few days."

"By all means, your ladyship," I replied. "I should tell you that I have already told Oliver about the death of Miss Smythe."

"You did *what?*" Lord Barkham barked.

"Perhaps I was wrong, but I thought it best to prepare him."

"How did he react?"

"He was upset, of course, but I assured him that I would remain with him during his interview with the constable."

"I think you did the wise thing, Serena," my grandmother said. "Now, I should appreciate it if you would leave Justin and me to talk. I think it would be wise if you got a good night's sleep."

"I will just look in on Oliver, your ladyship, before turning in," I replied. "I am fine, really. The shock of my discovery is well past. I simply hope for all concerned that all this can be cleared up quickly."

Oliver was in bed but still awake when I got to the nursery.

"I thought you would be long asleep by now," I said, sitting down next to him.

"I couldn't sleep," he said quietly.

"Are you worrying about what I told you earlier?"

He shook his head, but avoided my gaze.

I brushed his blond locks back on his forehead, and was

alarmed at how warm he felt.

"Oliver, you are feverish. You didn't tell me you were feeling unwell."

"I'm all right."

"You are not all right," I said, suddenly becoming concerned. "You're shaking. When did all this start?"

"I don't know—a little while ago."

I piled an additional blanket on the bed, wondering if I should alert the Earl.

"Can you describe how you feel? How do your legs feel?"

"They hurt, but mostly I feel very tired."

"I shall fetch you some warm milk. That should help you sleep."

The house was very quiet as I moved out into the corridor. As I knew the back stairs would be dark at this time of night, I took the main staircase. As I reached the bottom I heard angry voices coming from the drawing room.

"I tell you, Richard, I want you to stay away from her," I heard Lord Barkham say.

"You ought to pay more attention to your own linens, Barkham." It was the Earl.

"What is that supposed to mean?"

"You now perfectly well. You and Miss Smythe had become quite friendly, shall we say, during her brief time here."

"That's ridiculous, Richard, and you know it. It doesn't even deserve a response."

"Oh, you talk a good game, but you know as well as I do that you're a deader for a pretty face."

"I don't know where you are going with all this, Richard."

"Where I am going with it, my dear chap, is that I wouldn't be too quick to tell me where or on whom I should place my affections when you are probably sitting at the center of this mess. I should be very pleased to conveniently forget seeing you in those little tete-a-tetes if you simply steer clear of my own affairs."

"You know, sometimes I think Maura is right—that you are the one who is mad. Your insinuations, sir, are revolting. But your attempt to bribe me is even worse. If you don't stay away from her, I will not be responsible for my actions."

Thinking that I heard movement, I scurried away toward

the kitchens, trying to be as quiet as possible. I had just passed through the pantry when I heard someone call my name. I jumped back, startled.

"I didn't mean to be frightenin' you, miss. What you doin' down here so late?"

"Oh, it's you, Charlotte," I said, breathing a sigh of relief.

"I just be comin' back from me mum. She's been poorly of late, an' I wanted to be sure she was eatin' regular."

"I'm sorry to hear she's not well, Charlotte. Actually, I am down here to get some warm milk for Oliver. He is quite feverish, and I thought it might help him sleep through the night."

"'Tis a shame. I thought the lad was gettin' better of late. I guess the sickness just keeps comin' back."

"What sickness, Charlotte?"

"He gets the fever somethin' awful, and then the vomitin' starts. The little tyke was so weak there last spring I thought for a while we were gonna lose him."

"But I haven't seen any evidence of anything that bad, Charlotte. It's true he has had a few spells of fever, but it has seemed to pass quickly."

"You must be bringing him good luck. Here, let me get the milk for ye."

My mind was racing as Charlotte set about preparing the milk. I had not taken Lord Barkham's concern about Oliver terribly seriously, but apparently he was not the only one who was aware of this illness. And who was he telling the Earl to stay away from? He had definitely said "stay away from her," but who? Clarissa? Lady Camberleigh? I wished I could put out of my mind what the Earl had implied about Lord Barkham's relationship with Miss Smythe. After what he had done to me, I wasn't surprised, but it frightened me. I couldn't allow myself to think that he might be responsible in some way for her death. Perhaps she had also discovered him for what he was and threatened him in some way, and he had chosen to silence her rather than let her go. But why then was he warning me to be so cautious? Why did he seem so eager to have the constable pursue the investigation? Could it be that he was feigning concern to throw suspicion away from himself? He was capable of rape. But was he also capable of murder?

"Somethin' bothering you, miss? Looks to me like you've got your mind full," Charlotte said, handing me the milk.

"No, I was just thinking about Oliver."

"I don't mean to be nosey, but I have to tell you I'm longin' to hear about the ball. Was it grand?"

"It was most impressive. I could scarcely count all the people, and the gowns were beautiful."

"None more than yours, miss."

"Oh, I almost forgot. I met your friend Rowena soon after I arrived. She's a lovely woman, and she did masterful things with my hair."

"Would do me heart good to see 'er again. We was real close-like for years 'fore she took up at Kelston."

"She inquired after Robbie, too, and I told her that we had commenced with his lessons and how valued he was at the stables."

"He sure loves that little spaniel of yours. Wouldn't let him out o' his sight when you was gone."

"I better get this up to Oliver before it cools. Thank you for your help, Charlotte."

"T'was nothin'. I'll be in as usual in the mornin', miss."

I could hear nothing as I passed the drawing room, but I did not pause to listen closely. Oliver was so still when I entered that I thought he had fallen off to sleep, but as I got closer I realized that he was awake.

"I'm sorry it took me so long. Now sit up a bit to drink this."

"I can't, Serena," he whispered.

I sat on the bed and placed my arm under his back, raising him to me. His skin was burning and his nightshirt was soaked through. He drank the milk, with some difficulty, and I searched for another shirt, knowing that it was important to keep him dry.

"Would you stay with me, Serena?" Oliver asked quietly.

"Of course. I shall be here until you fall asleep," I said, taking his hand in mine.

I had closed my eyes, I thought, only briefly, but awoke suddenly, realizing that I had drifted off for I knew not how long. Oliver was still burning with fever, but now he slept. My wont was to stay the night with him, but I was so tired myself that I realized that I should get some sleep so that I might be prepared to nurse him tomorrow.

Jaspar was asleep as I crept into my room. The fire had burned down and the room was drafty and cold. I folded up a small blanket and laid it on the floor for Jaspar, then changed quickly into my nightclothes and climbed into bed. I had almost fallen off to sleep when I heard Jaspar emit a low growl.

"What is it, Jaspar?" I asked, pulling the covers tighter around my shoulders. I thought I heard the sound of footsteps moving along the corridor outside my room, but I did not trust my senses, for my nerves were so on edge from everything that had happened over the past weeks. I could not remember if I had locked the door, and I rose quickly to make certain. I had indeed forgotten, and I threw the lock quickly and returned to bed. Although I gave little credence to the warnings of Lord Barkham, I knew that I would be more at ease when the constable concluded his investigation.

Chapter Eleven

I THINK I would have slept till noon had it not been for Charlotte's early knock at my door. I dragged myself out of bed and unlocked the door.

"Mornin', Miss Serena."

"Good morning, Charlotte."

"Why, 'tis freezin' in here. The cold could go right to your bones. I'll get the fire goin' an bring you more blankets later on."

"Could you see that my breakfast is brought to Oliver's room," I asked, scurrying to get into some warm clothes. "I should like to see him as quickly as possible this morning."

"'Course, miss."

I splashed some hot water on my face and quickly braided and coiled my hair. With a pat to Jaspar and a quick peek in the mirror, I hurried to the nursery.

Oliver was awake, but I quickly saw that he was no better. His cheeks were flushed, and there were deep circles under his eyes, exaggerating their size.

I went to him and smoothed his hair from his brow.

"No better, eh?" I asked, concerned that the fever had persisted through the night.

He shook his head and winced as though in pain.

"Do your legs hurt?"

He nodded.

"Anywhere else?"

"My stomach."

"I think we had best call for Dr. Carruthers."

"Please don't, Serena," he beseeched.

"You want to get well, don't you?"

"Yes, but father will be very angry."

"Don't talk nonsense. He will see that you are sick. You just rest here, and I shall return momentarily. Charlotte is bringing my tray here, and we shall breakfast together. You may not be hungry, but you should try to eat something."

I had no idea where to find the Earl at this early hour, but decided to try the library and drawing room before intruding in his and Lady Camberleigh's quarters. He was in neither place, but Giles was just crossing the main entranceway as I moved back into the hallway.

"Excuse me, Giles, but do you have any idea where the Earl might be? Master Oliver is ill and I believe we should call for the doctor promptly."

"I believe he is still in his quarters, miss."

"Might you be so kind as to inform him of his son's illness and have someone dispatched to fetch the doctor."

"Of course, miss. Do you think it is serious?"

"I don't know. But it is best to take precautions. I shall remain with the boy until the doctor arrives."

I returned to the nursery. Charlotte was just arriving with our breakfast trays. The last thing Oliver looked like he wanted was food, but I hoped he might be able to take a bit of the porridge and cream to settle his stomach.

"Might I see ye for a moment, miss?" Charlotte asked, signaling that she wanted to be out of Oliver's hearing. "There's terrible things happenin' in this house," she whispered once we were on the other side of the room. "The kitchen's all aflutter. Seems there's been a murder, an' the constable will be comin' to talk to us all."

"Yes, I know, Charlotte," I replied, surprised that the news should have gotten about so early.

"Oh, poor Miss Smythe. Not that I be knowin' her well, like you. She was an odd one at times, but the good Lord couldn't have meant for her to come to such a terrible end."

"It's terribly distressing for us all, Charlotte. But with Oliver being so ill, I can scarcely keep my mind on her misfortune."

"Who do you think coulda done this thing?"

"I have no idea, Charlotte. Were you aware of anyone who might have wished her harm?"

"I can't say that, miss. She was real tight-lipped, she was. But I do know one thing, there was many a night that her bed weren't slept in. 'Course, I'm no gossip, but seems clear that she was takin' up with someone, if you know what I mean."

"Serena," Oliver called out.

"I better be goin' now anyway, miss, but I was real worried that you should know."

"Thank you, Charlotte. I shall be here at least until the doctor arrives—which I hope won't be too long."

I tried to prop Oliver up a bit on the pillows so that he might better balance a tray, but even the smallest movement seemed to cause him pain. I was able to coax only a few spoonfuls of the porridge into him; I knew he was doing it more for me than for any interest in the food.

I ate my own breakfast automatically, tasting little, conscious only of the need to keep my strength up. I had just finished my tea when I looked up to see Thomas standing in the doorway leading to the schoolroom.

"Thomas, I forgot completely . . ." I said, moving the tray aside.

"I see that. Has your grand weekend at Kelston Manor driven everything else completely from your mind?"

"It is not that. I do apologize, but you see, Oliver is quite ill, and I have just taken steps to call for the doctor. I fear he is in no condition for lessons today. . . . It is nice to see you," I added.

"It couldn't be that you are all simply overtaxed from your journey?"

"No, he is truly feverish," I replied, becoming just a bit annoyed.

Just then the door to the nursery burst open, revealing the Earl, who looked to be in a particularly foul humor.

"Damnation!" he boomed. "What is this nonsense, Miss Miles? Don't we have enough on our minds without your taking it into your head to call for the doctor."

"Begging your pardon, sire, but I must ask that you lower your voice. Your son is very ill, and we should try to disturb him as little as possible."

"Well, Thomas," he said, turning. "It seems I am in the

middle of a dichotomy. On the one hand, my dear wife cares not one ounce for the child, and on the other, his governess is overprotective and jumps at his every whimper."

"Have you called for the doctor, sire?" I asked resolutely.

"Oh, you shall have your doctor, but only because Giles went immediately to my mother, who dispatched a stableboy on horseback before I had a chance to stop her."

"I think you would only have to look at the boy to know that my concern is not foolhardy."

"Fine, I shall look at him and then I shall go downstairs. The constable will be arriving at any moment."

He moved to one side of Oliver's bed, and I moved quickly to the other.

"Look who has come to see you, Oliver," I said, placing my hand lightly on his forehead.

"Hello, Father," Oliver said softly.

"Serena tells me you are feeling unwell," the Earl said gruffly.

"I'm sorry."

"The doctor is on his way, so I am certain you will be up and about in no time. We can't keep Mr. Masters unoccupied, you know."

I was about to vent my anger at the coldheartedness of his attitude when he suddenly reached down and put his hand on Oliver's shoulder, giving it a light affectionate squeeze.

"Take care of him, Miss Miles," he said, looking me straight in the eye.

"I will, sire," I said, meeting his gaze.

As the Earl left, I turned back to Thomas, who had remained at the rear of the room.

"Well, it looks as though you have a reprieve, Thomas, at least until Oliver is back on his feet again."

"So it appears. What did the Earl mean about the constable?"

"I'm surprised that you've not heard. Everyone in the household seems aware of it."

"Well, then tell me, since it is no secret."

I led him out into the small corridor. "It's terribly long and involved, but the essence of it is . . . there has been a murder at Camberleigh," I said, keeping my voice low.

"Well, it's not the first," he said calmly.

"What do you mean?"

"From what I understand, the old Earl was murdered by his own son right here years ago."

"That has nothing to do with this," I snapped.

"Then tell me what happened, Serena."

"You'll know soon enough. There was a Miss Smythe here as a governess before me."

"Hmmm. Margarite. I think the term governess is perhaps a bit flattering."

"Well, you probably know that she disappeared rather suddenly."

"That type usually does, my dear."

"That is harsh, Thomas. The reason for her disappearance was that she was murdered."

"Good Lord," he said, taking my arm. "Do you know what you are saying?"

"That, unfortunately, is what the constable says. I have been apprised of most of the developments. You see . . . I discovered the body."

"You what?" he gasped.

"I really don't want to go into all this now, Thomas. Oliver is ill, and—"

"Can you meet me later? Perhaps for dinner?"

"Thomas, I can't even think of that now. My place is at Oliver's side. Moreover, there is the business of the constable."

"Or is it that after your weekend at Kelston Manor my company seems pale by contrast?"

"Please don't be foolish. You can see the situation here?"

"Of course. But you should be able to escape later this evening. I should very much like to see you—you haven't forgotten that there are some things that I want to discuss with you."

"I haven't forgotten, but please . . . perhaps tomorrow. But I must get back. I want to keep him as quiet as possible."

After Thomas departed I resumed my vigil at Oliver's bedside. He drifted in and out of sleep, mumbling my name whenever he awoke briefly. It wasn't long before there was a knock at the door. I rose quickly, pleased that the doctor had arrived so soon. Instead, there stood my grandmother.

"Good morning. Might I see Oliver?"

"Of course, your ladyship," I replied, standing aside to let her pass. "But I fear that he is not awake for long periods of time."

"You don't mean he is delirious?"

"No, but he does have a very high fever."

"When did this begin?"

"I first noticed it last night. When he wasn't improved this morning I thought that the doctor should be summoned."

"You were right to do so." She walked painfully to Oliver's bedside and sat down in the chair that I had moved close to the bed. "Don't disturb him. It is best that he rest. I should simply like to remain here until the doctor arrives."

"Of course, your ladyship."

I took my seat in a small chair by the window.

"He is such an innocent. And yet he has been through so much for his young years," my grandmother mused quietly.

"Oliver is a very special little boy. It is understandable that you are very proud of him."

"I worry about him. His father is so preoccupied with the running of Camberleigh. His mother, I dread to say, appears to be sinking further and further into that strange world of hers. I only pray that I survive long enough to see him through these difficult years—not that I am able to provide him with very much."

"You give him love, your ladyship," I replied.

"Yes, I do that. But he needs young people around him. You have been good for him, Serena. And of course there is Justin. He treats the boy as his own."

"I suppose," I replied quickly.

"Do I sense some strain between you and Justin Barkham?"

"No, of course not," I replied, perhaps too quickly.

"I have not lived these many years, my dear, not to sense conflict when I see it."

"Lord Barkham and I simply do not agree on certain things, your ladyship."

"I see. That's interesting, for I would say the two of you are quite alike."

"I can't imagine how," I replied, trying to keep any emotion from my voice.

I was not to know her answer, for at that moment there was a knock at the door. I moved to open it, and to my great relief saw Dr. Carruthers. "I am pleased that you could come this quickly, doctor."

"It is Miss Miles, is it not?"

"You have a good memory."

"I'm not so old, Miss Miles, that I cannot recall a lovely face when I see one. Now, how is Master Oliver?"

"He is very feverish and complains of pains in his legs and stomach."

"The symptoms are recurring, then. Well, let me take a look," he said, moving over to the bed. "Your ladyship, I do apologize. I didn't see you."

"Will I be in your way, doctor?"

"Of course not."

"Oliver," I said softly, "Doctor Carruthers is here."

The doctor began to probe around Oliver's throat and midsection; then he lifted and bent his legs. The boy was obviously very uncomfortable.

"Is it serious, doctor?" I asked.

"He has a very high fever, but I must say that I am perplexed at the soreness in his extremities. I wish I could be more definite, but the symptoms do not seem to correlate. I can give him something so that he will rest more comfortably. Other than that, I would advise that he just remain on his regular medication."

"Oh, dear," I said, "I forgot to give it to him this morning." I dug into my pocket and produced the bottle, handing it to the doctor.

"Might I have a spoon, Miss Miles?" I fetched one off the breakfast tray and the doctor poured out some medicine.

"Here, let me lift him a bit," I said, putting my arm behind Oliver and pulling him up gently.

"Miss Miles," he said, turning the bottle over in his hand, "this is not the medicine I prescribed."

"But of course it is. See for yourself."

"I see what I see. I don't know what this is, but this is not what I prescribed."

"But—"

"Please," her ladyship intruded. "Let us discuss this away

from here." Her eyes flicked to Oliver.

"Serena, don't leave me," Oliver cried out, grasping my arm.

"I will be right back," I assured him. "You rest for the moment. We can talk back here, doctor."

Dr. Carruthers helped my grandmother to her feet, and I guided them to the passageway that led to the schoolroom.

They sat on a small blue brocade couch against the wall, but I stood, too tense to relax.

"Now, Serena, I am certain there is an explanation. Come and sit down and let us discuss this," my grandmother said.

I sat.

"How long have you administered this, Miss Miles?" asked the doctor.

"I don't know," I cried out, too distraught to think clearly. "Let me see. Only since just before we went to Kelston Manor . . . three days. . . . Usually Mrs. Scoapes gives it to him, but she had to go away for a few days."

"It is not usually in your possession?"

"No."

"What does this all mean, Dr. Carruthers?" my grandmother asked.

"I apologize, Lady Camberleigh, but I am trying to determine how long Oliver has been receiving this medication."

"But it must be the medication he has always received," I said.

"Without doing some analysis on it I cannot be sure what this is, but I can tell you for certain that it is not the tonic I prescribed originally."

"I've told you everything I know," I said. "Mrs. Scoapes gave it to me—no, wait, it was Molly who gave it to me. Mrs. Scoapes had already departed."

"I should want to talk to this Molly, then," said the doctor. "And also Mrs. Scoapes, if she has returned."

"Can this medication he has been getting be the reason he is so ill?"

"As I said, I will have to run some tests. Even they may not be conclusive. But this fever attack is a pattern that has gone on for well over six months. And I am anxious to get to the bottom of it. Each bout has been more serious than the last."

"You can't believe that anyone would give anything knowingly to Oliver that would harm him? You don't think *I* am responsible for this?"

"I am not making accusations, Miss Miles. I am a doctor, and my duty is to care for my patients."

"Your ladyship, you can't believe that I knew that this was not the correct medicine."

"Serena, at the present moment I am only shocked at this discovery and concerned that no harm has been done to my grandson. Now, please go and find Molly and Mrs. Scoapes and tell them to come to my room. The doctor and I will be there, and we can all discuss this."

"But what of Oliver?" I asked.

"I will give him something to help him rest," said the doctor. "There really is nothing to be done for him for the moment. We just have to wait for the fever to break."

As my grandmother and the doctor made their way back to her quarters, I went in search of Molly. I found her down in the pantry. She seemed terrified by the thought of a command audience with her ladyship, but I chose not to explain the nature of the meeting, knowing that within minutes she would have the kitchen humming with the news.

My grandmother and the doctor fell silent as I entered her quarters. I assumed that they had been discussing me or Oliver or both. Soon Molly and Mrs. Scoapes arrived. The latter was obviously surprised to find the doctor and myself in the room.

Without preamble, my grandmother said, "Mrs. Scoapes, you have been giving Master Oliver his medicine for some time, have you not?"

"Yes, your ladyship," the woman replied. "What with the governesses coming and going, I have taken the responsibility to see that things of that nature are supervised properly."

"I appreciate your concern. I understand, however, that when you went off on holiday you asked Molly to give the medication to Miss Miles to administer."

"That is correct."

"Molly, could you come closer for a moment?"

"Yes, your ladyship," Molly replied, bobbing forward.

"Would you look at this? Is this the bottle that you gave to Miss Miles?"

"It looks like it, but I can't be tellin' ye for sure. Truth is,

295

I didn't be examinin' it all that close-like."

"I see. Would you please pass it to Mrs. Scoapes so she can look at it. Mrs. Scoapes, is that the bottle you gave to Molly?"

The housekeeper turned it slowly in her hands. "No, your ladyship. The bottle looks similar, but I've been giving the boy his medicine for a long time, and I can say for certain that this is not the usual bottle."

"Then this is not the bottle you gave to Molly."

"That is correct."

"Mrs. Scoapes, please look at the bottle again," I pleaded. "You must be mistaken."

"I am not mistaken, miss."

"She is not telling the truth, your ladyship." I tried to hold back the tears. "I don't know why, but she is lying!"

"That is quite enough, Serena."

"I am sorry for having to call you here, Mrs. Scoapes," my grandmother said quietly. "Molly, whatever has been discussed here I know you will keep in strict confidence."

"O' course, your ladyship."

"Then you both may return to your duties."

I looked up in disbelief. I couldn't believe that my grandmother was dismissing them. Did she believe them? Did she think that I switched the medication?

"Your ladyship, I don't understand what is happening here," I said, dabbing at the tears on my cheeks. "I swear to you, I have done nothing wrong."

"Dr. Carruthers, I want to get one thing clear," she said, ignoring my plea. "Is there any chance that you might have prescribed the wrong medication—or that the wrong medication was received by accident?"

"No. This is not even the bottle I use. As the housekeeper said, it's similar but not the right bottle. And I give you my professional oath that I did not prescribe the wrong medicine."

"I see. Well, then there is nothing more to be done until we find out what is in this bottle. You will of course inform me as soon as this has been determined."

"Of course, your ladyship," Dr. Carruthers said, rising to take his leave. "I shall look in on Oliver before I go, and I shall return in the morning. Just keep him warm and as quiet as possible."

"Serena. I would like you to stay here for a moment."

I nodded.

There was silence in the room until the doctor had shut the door behind him.

"Serena, the one thing I warned you about when I allowed you to remain here was that if any harm came to Oliver I would see not only that you were dismissed but that you regretted the consequences."

"Oh, please, your ladyship," I cried. "I don't know how to make you believe me. It appears that you trust nothing I say. I swear to you that I did nothing to harm Oliver—or anyone here at Camberleigh."

"You seem to forget, Serena, that I have not recognized you as my granddaughter."

"I know that only too well."

"That is not pertinent to this discussion, in any case."

"It appears to me that at best these have been difficult times for you, Serena. First your accident, then finding that poor girl's body. Sometimes I wonder if I did you any favors by allowing you to remain at Camberleigh."

"It's true that things have not been easy here from time to time, but I love Oliver, which makes up for a lot."

"The boy worships you, and you have shown him genuine affection. I am not blind to that—which is why I cannot believe that you are responsible for switching the medication."

"You *do* believe me, then," I said with great relief.

"There is something very sinister going on here at Camberleigh. Perhaps everything that has happened is all a series of isolated incidents, but I tend to think not. I believe there is a thread to it all, somehow, although I have no idea what it is, or who is behind it."

"Why would anyone wish Oliver harm?"

"I don't know. He will be a rich and powerful man someday. You, of course, might have a great deal to gain if anything should happen to him, if you are indeed my granddaughter."

"I don't understand."

"Upon my death, Camberleigh of course goes to my son, Richard. But I have made very generous provisions for my grandchildren as well. Were you really of my flesh and blood, you would be entitled to a share. If anything happened to Oliver, you and Clarissa would stand to benefit from his share."

Evelyn Grey

"Then I was wrong—you really don't trust me."

"All I am doing is trying to explore all angles to attempt to get at the bottom of the malicious goings-on in this house."

A knock at the door stopped us from pursuing the matter any further. I rose to answer it, and ushered Giles into the room.

"Excuse me, your ladyship, but the constable is downstairs and has asked that the entire family gather as promptly as possible in the drawing room—oh, and you too, Miss Miles."

"Well," my grandmother said with a sigh, "I can see that I shall have no opportunity for a morning's rest, but I suppose we must get this over with. Would you assist me downstairs, Serena?"

"Of course," I replied, moving to her side and helping her from her chair. "If you are too tired, perhaps I might explain as much to the constable. I'm certain he would understand."

"Nonsense. This is my home, and as long as I am able I shall deal with the good and the bad of it."

As I supported my grandmother's arm as we walked slowly down the corridor, I realized that I had never been so physically close to her. There was a scent of violets about her which recalled to mind the fields beyond Seven Oaks that were always alive in the spring with the deep purple flowers mingled among heather and mountain snowdrops.

Justin Barkham rose immediately and came swiftly to my grandmother's side as we entered the drawing room. "Good Lord, Serena, why didn't you call for me? I should have helped."

"Don't let her fool you, Justin. She's quite strong, and managed very well with a doddering old lady."

"I have no doubt," Lord Barkham replied, catching my eye. "Serena is capable of most everything."

"Does that include murder, Justin dear?" I could scarcely believe my ears at Lady Camberleigh's question.

All eyes turned in her direction. She was still wearing her morning robe, and her hair fell about her shoulders in tangled disarray. Her mouth was heavily rouged, as if she had made that one effort to improve her appearance. It was hard to believe that it was the same woman who only weeks before I had thought to be a fine example of maturing beauty.

"You must forgive my wife, constable. She has been ill,"

298

the Earl said, pressing his finger against his scar as if to quell its betrayal of his anger.

"I have not been ill, constable. I simply haven't behaved properly. Isn't that so, Richard dear."

"Well, there you are," Anne said, addressing me as she swept into the room and over to where I sat on a loveseat. "I was beginning to think *you* had disappeared. But then I heard about Oliver. The poor boy has been through so much."

"What is wrong with Oliver?" Clarissa asked, smoothing a tendril of hair back behind her ear.

"He has a fever," I replied. And then, seeing my grandmother subtly shake her head, I added, "But I am certain he shall be up and about in no time."

"If we might commence," the constable said, clearing his throat impatiently.

"Of course," Lord Barkham replied.

"You are all aware of what has happened here. I do regret having to take up your time like this, but since we now know that Miss Smythe was definitely murdered, it is important that we gather as much information as possible."

"I would suggest that you begin with my husband," Lady Camberleigh said. "He is really the authority on governesses here."

"How long had she been in your employ, sire?"

"Three, perhaps four months. Isn't that about right, Justin?"

"Yes, I would say."

"And when did Miss Smythe disappear?"

"Toward the end of May," the Earl replied.

"And was there any indication whatsoever that she was leaving?"

"None."

"And when did you come to Camberleigh, Miss Miles?"

"In August."

"My husband, you see, has not been able to keep the governesses very long. Would you like to know why?"

"Maura, please."

"I'm only trying to be helpful, dear," she said with a ghostly smile.

The constable cleared his throat again and turned in Lord Barkham's direction. "Are you aware of any friends that Miss

Smythe might have had hereabouts, Lord Barkham?"

A quick look passed between Lord Barkham and the Earl. Was it a warning, I wondered, or was he testing to see if the earl would reveal his threats of the previous evening?

"To my knowledge she had none. She was a strange girl in ways. She kept mostly to herself. But she was not what I would call your typical governess."

"How do you mean that?"

"Well, she used to talk of wishing to travel and see new things. She was quite adventurous—or wanted to be. And I can't say that she had a tremendous understanding of children."

"I see. Might I ask if you have any knowledge of her former employer, sire?" the constable asked the earl.

"I don't see that that is relevant."

"Sire, I would say that anything could be relevant. The more we know, the better."

"She had been employed by Baron Gregory Whittenfield."

"Serena, dear, wouldn't you care for a cup of tea?" blurted Anne in a successful attempt to cover my gasp. "And you, constable?"

"Not for me, thank you, Lady Ormsby."

Anne placed the cup on the table beside me. Had I been forced to handle it, I would have dropped it immediately.

"The Baron Whittenfield, did you say?"

The Earl nodded.

"She was employed by him as a governess?"

"Not exactly. She was more of a . . . housekeeper."

"Which means, my dear constable, that she managed the affairs of the house, and if you know anything about the Baron you will understand," Lady Camberleigh said acidly.

I knew from my grandmother's face that she was shocked, but less from what her daughter-in-law was saying than from learning something of Miss Smythe's background.

"I see," the constable said, scratching a bushy eyebrow that peeked over the rim of his spectacles.

"Did Miss Smythe leave anything behind?"

"No. All her possessions were gone," the Earl replied. "That was why we assumed that she departed of her own volition. I did think it odd that she had not asked for her week's wages, but then, if she was planning to leave with no notice she might have thought it awkward."

"Miss Camberleigh, is there anything that you might add?" the constable asked Clarissa.

"Good gracious, no," she replied. "She was simply a governess here. I barely knew the girl by sight."

"Lady Camberleigh, is there—"

"My wife really had no occasion to be involved with her, constable," the Earl broke in. "Matters that involve the care and education of my son are my domain."

"Well then, I think that should be all for now. I understand that Master Oliver is out of sorts. I'm certain that a day or two won't matter, but I will have to see him at some future point."

"Of course," the Earl replied.

"I have interviewed the staff already, at least most of it, I believe. Are there any who do not reside here but perhaps somewhere close by on the grounds?"

"Only the stable boys and Mr. Masters, the tutor. He has a small cottage down beyond the west wing gardens."

"And would he be about?"

"I saw him this morning," I replied.

"Thank you, Miss Miles," the constable replied. "Don't get up, Lord Barkham, I can see my way out. Needless to say, if anyone sees or hears anything which you think might be important, please let me know."

"I shall have a brandy, Richard dear," Lady Camberleigh said, throwing her hair back in an exaggerated gesture.

"Justin, would you accompany me back to my quarters?" my grandmother asked.

"Of course," he replied.

"Juliette, I shall be leaving later this morning," Anne said, rising.

"You know you are welcome to stay."

"I know. But Justin is off to London, and someone has to be about at Mayfair. We've been gone too long already."

"Knowing my sister, she is longing to get back to be certain that the gardeners are preparing all the flower beds for winter."

Anne laughed. "You had best be careful, Justin, or I will insist on accompanying you to London. That would put a wrinkle in your plans, I am certain."

"Never, sister dear. I would simply drop you at the most fashionable shop in town and be free of you for days."

"The nerve," Anne replied, feigning indignance. "Serena,

would you come up with me for the moment and help me pack? I'm dreadful about these things."

"Of course," I replied, knowing that it was simply a ploy so that we might be able to talk.

We excused ourselves and made our way upstairs.

"I thought I would never have any time alone with you," she said, closing the door.

"I know. Anne I have wanted to thank you for what you did at Kelston Manor. I should never have burdened you with my problems."

"I'm sorry that I had to involve Justin, but I truly had no choice. I think of myself as being resourceful, but I was afraid that Gregory Whittenfield was more than I could handle alone."

"I understand. I would have been devastated if any harm had come to you. But I must tell you that I was totally confused when your brother started talking about a gambling debt."

"And I thought it was a brilliant deception."

"I should never have conceived it myself. It worked, but it cost Justin two hundred pounds."

"What?"

"The Baron had the audacity to claim that is what I owed him."

"That man has no shame—and he is evil. Clever, I admit, but evil."

"Do you think that he could somehow have been involved in the death of Miss Smythe?"

"I don't know. But I can't imagine what possessed Richard to hire that girl. He knows what the Baron is like. Juliette is going to be livid. I'm certain that she had no idea of the girl's background or she would never have permitted her even to get near Oliver."

"Anne, could there by any truth to Lady Camberleigh's insinuations? Might the Earl somehow have been involved with Miss Smythe?"

"No."

"You sound very certain."

"Richard is a strange man and his judgment is often faulty, but I cannot believe that he would be drawn in by someone like our Miss Smythe."

"I shouldn't say this, for it is second-hand information, but

Charlotte told me that Miss Smythe was often not in her room in the evening."

"That is interesting. Obviously she was meeting someone. But who?"

"Perhaps if we knew that we would know who the murderer was," I replied.

"Serena, I must tell you that although I am concerned about Miss Smythe, what preoccupies me *totally* is you—and what you told me at Kelston Manor. I still can scarcely believe it."

"I know it sounds an improbable story, but what I told you is true."

"I didn't mean to imply that I did not trust you."

"Why should you? I have no proof."

"That is true—but you also have no guile."

I smiled at her loyalty.

"What did Juliette say? Lord, it must have been a terrible shock."

"I fear it was. But at that time I knew nothing of my father's past or his father's death. Truthfully, if I had known any of that I would never have come here."

"It must be very painful for you."

"My rightful recognition here means little to me in contrast to my desire to clear my father's name."

"But Serena, how can you hope to do that? It was so long ago, and the findings seem conclusive."

"I'm sorry, Anne. It is simply impossible that my father could have committed murder. You didn't know him as I did. He just was not capable of a violent act."

"But why, during all those years, would he have not come back to try to clear himself?"

"I don't know. Maybe the hurt was too deep. Perhaps he didn't want me and my mother to suffer from the notoriety of it all. Perhaps he intended to, but died before he had the chance."

"I wish there were something I could do to help you, but I wouldn't know where to begin. Perhaps Justin could help, if he were told."

"No," I said emphatically. "No one is to know. If there is an answer somewhere, it is I who must find it. Unless, of course, the solicitor comes up with something, but I don't hold much hope there."

"I must say it is all terribly intriguing. Very romantic."

"I'm afraid I don't see it quite that way."

"How stupid of me, of course you don't. It must have been appalling for you to lose your family, then to come here not knowing what you might find—or who, for that matter. Not to mention everything that has happened to you since."

"I admit that today I feel far different from that young girl whose days were filled only with picking flowers along the cliffs above the harbor and watching the great ships sail in and out."

"Perhaps if you thought back, Serena, there is some clue that you are overlooking."

"I have racked my brain, and can come up with nothing. The only small thing is that there was someone—some friend or acquaintance, perhaps—with whom my mother was in touch who had some connection with Camberleigh."

"You have no name?"

"None. My mother mentions in her last letter to me that there was someone who would give her news of Camberleigh from time to time. That's all I know. There is no reason to believe that he or she even knew of my existence, and no way to know if they are even alive today."

"I loathe leaving you here with all this going on."

"Don't be silly. You have responsibilities too."

"Will you promise me that you will take good care, Serena? This murder has me terribly on edge, and I think it would be wise to take extra precautions."

"Unfortunately, Anne, there is even more disturbing news."

"Dear God, what else. Tell me."

I proceeded to explain as best I could about Oliver's illness, the problem with the medication and the confrontation with Molly and Mrs. Scoapes.

"I can hardly believe this. What does it all mean?"

"I don't know. But I do know that Mrs. Scoapes or Molly or both of them are lying."

"What was in the bottle that you were administering to Oliver?"

"The doctor is going to test it."

"Did he think it might be harmful?"

"He didn't know. I would of course be devastated to think

304

that I had given Oliver something that would cause him to be ill."

"Come now, Serena. Even if the bottle did contain something dangerous, it would not have been your fault."

"If only I had been giving him the medication regularly, then I would have recognized that it was the wrong bottle."

"But you hadn't been, so you cannot be held responsible."

"Speaking of Oliver, I must return to him."

"I shall return to Camberleigh as soon as I can. Most likely, that will not be until Justin gets back from London."

"I shall miss you. I could do with a friend in this house."

We embraced, and I left Anne to return to the nursery.

My heart ached as I looked down at Oliver's small sleeping frame. Whatever wickedness lurked in this house, he did not deserve to have it visited on him. Charlotte crept in with our luncheon trays, but I permitted him to sleep through, feeling it was better for him to rest.

There was only one visitor that afternoon, and I could not have been more surprised to see her. Clarissa.

"I understand my brother is ill, Miss Miles," she said, sailing into the room.

"Yes, he is, Miss Clarissa," I said, jumping up to keep her from intruding on his sleep. "Might I ask that you not disturb him now? He is resting peacefully."

"Miss Miles, I can see for myself that he is asleep."

"Would you like to stay with him for a while?"

"I would not." She looked disgusted at the suggestion. "We don't know what he has, and I cannot afford to be ill with my season approaching."

"Yes, of course," I replied.

"You must be quite concerned, Miss Miles, what with all the to-do with the constable."

"Why do you say that?"

"Well, after all, Miss Smythe was the last governess. What if our murderer has a penchant for women of your station? If he is still about, you might be in danger."

"May I ask why you assume that the murderer was a man?"

"Of course it was."

"I don't remember the constable saying anything to that effect."

"This is ridiculous. Please tell Oliver that I was here to see him."

"I'm certain he will be pleased to hear it."

What had been the motive for this curious visit? I wondered when she had gone. I also had to smile to myself when I pondered what she would think if my grandmother were to recognize my Camberleigh heritage. If the day ever came, I wanted to be there to see Clarissa's face. How she would loathe having to think of me as her cousin. It was a pity, actually, for we were so close in age that we might have had a sisterly relationship; but I was not naïve enough to believe that that day would ever come. Close we were in age, but miles apart in temperament.

Oliver awoke a short time later. He appeared a bit improved, but certainly far from recovered. I called for some tea and biscuits, and they had just arrived when Lord Barkham appeared at the door.

"I'm pleased to have found you here, Serena. I am leaving shortly for London, and—"

"Is that you, Uncle Justin?" Oliver called out.

"It certainly is. Does that mean you are feeling better?"

"He is still feverish," I said. "And his color is not good. But I think he is quite a bit better."

"Oliver, I am off to London for a few days, and I want to see you fully recovered when I return. I have a great number of farms left to visit, and I should like to have you accompany me—after all, someday they shall be your responsibility as well. Do what Miss Miles says and I shall bring you back a surprise from the city."

"Will you bring something for Serena too?"

"Why, that is a splendid idea. Why don't you whisper to me what you think she might like."

"Lord Barkham, there is nothing I want or need," I said curtly.

"I have never known a woman who does not want something, Miss Miles—though what she needs is often more of a problem. Oliver," he continued, "you wouldn't mind if I took Miss Miles away from you for just a few moments, would you? I want to have a few words with her."

Oliver shook his head.

"Can't you say whatever you have to say right here, Lord Barkham?"

"I would prefer not. Besides, by the look of you, a little fresh air would do you good."

"I will be all right, Serena," said Oliver.

"Well, please take some tea and try to eat one of these cakes."

"I will try."

"I think you had best fetch a cloak, Serena. There is a definite chill to the day, and I should not like to see you become ill as well. Meet me in the rose garden, if you will."

I returned to my room for my wrap and met up with Lord Barkham on the footpath leading to the garden.

"I really don't think we have anything to say to each other, Lord Barkham."

"If you won't listen to me about what exists between us, then for God's sake listen to me on matters that relate to what is happening in this house. This latest episode with Oliver's medication is but yet another indication that things are very amiss in this household."

"There is nothing between us, Lord Barkham, and on any other matters I think you have already made yourself clear."

"Good. Then you will heed my warnings."

"How do you know about the medication?"

"Juliette told me."

"I see. I suppose you think that I must be mad. That it was my fault that he received the wrong medication?"

"Don't be absurd. What I want to know is why Molly or Mrs. Scoapes or both are lying. Why would they endanger Oliver's health?"

"Perhaps it is to cast me in a bad light. Perhaps one or both of them do not want me to remain here at Camberleigh."

"Have you had any sort of confrontation with either of them that would anger them so that they would go to these lengths to see that you were dismissed?"

"I have never felt that Mrs. Scoapes had any particular fondness for me, but I don't think she likes anyone all that much."

"Serena, I don't want you to trust anyone while I am gone."

"Lord Barkham, the only person I do not trust is you. Therefore, I shall feel very safe for the next few days. Now, if that is all, I should like to return to the nursery."

"Have I ever told you how very desirable you are when you are angry?"

I raised my hand to strike him, but he grabbed my wrist and pulled me to him. Suddenly he was kissing me hard on the mouth.

"How dare you," I spat as soon as I freed myself enough to speak. "I warned you what I would do if you ever came near me again."

"To expose me, Serena?" He laughed. "To whom? Richard? Do you think he would care? To Maura—or Juliette? No, I think not."

The last thing I wanted to do was cry, but I could not stop the tears that formed in my eyes.

"Oh, Serena," he moaned, holding me tighter. "Why must we be at odds? I know how you feel about what happened that first night, and I have told you that if I could erase it from time I would. But what we shared at Kelston was different. You must see that. It was the act of two people sharing their passion and need in an act of love. You cannot tell me that that was just me. That was us, Serena."

"Please, please let me go," I sobbed.

"I will not hold you against your will. I have vowed never to do that again."

As his arms eased their hold, I wrenched from him and began to run, mindless of the direction I took. I had just reached the arbor when Thomas emerged from under its gnarled awnings.

"Good gracious, Serena, you look dreadful. What has happened?" he asked, coming to my side and taking my hands in his.

"Nothing," I replied, turning to see if Lord Barkham was in pursuit. I realized, that Thomas must have spied, as I did, his towering frame—which even in the distance had a commanding aura—moving back toward the house.

"I see," Thomas said thoughtfully.

"I am sorry. I don't mean to distress you."

"What distresses me, Serena, is your condition. You appear completely undone. This whole thing with Miss Smythe and the constable I fear has been too much for you."

"It's not just that."

"What else, then, my fair princess?"

"I can't tell you that."

"Why don't we sit over here for a moment," he said, leading me to the stone bench.

"I really must get back to Oliver."

"That can wait for just another moment or two."

"Well . . . no longer."

"I don't know quite where to begin, for I am not accustomed to verbalizing what I wish to say."

"You need not be uncomfortable with me, Thomas. After all, we are friends."

"That is just the point. What I feel for you is more than just friendship, Serena. I have grown exceedingly fond of you."

"I am fond of you also."

"Fond enough to marry me?"

"Marry you," I gasped. "But Thomas, we scarcely know each other."

"I know it sounds trite, but I feel as though I have known you all my life."

"Thomas, this is very flattering," I said slowly. "But I am not able to consider marriage to you or anyone at the present."

"Are you telling me that your heart has been given to another?"

"No, it's nothing of the sort," I said firmly.

"Then what is there to prevent it?" he asked, searching my face. "Oh, I realize that I may not have the position or power of Lord Barkham or Lord Kelston, but then, I am certain you realize that any attention they pay you is simply because they want the proximity of a pretty face. No, their interest in a governess could only be prurient. I do not have great wealth, but I am recompensed rather nicely for my position here. And the Earl I believe is quite taken with some suggestions I have made in the financial realm. If that comes to fruition, as I believe it will, I should have quite a tidy sum within the year. Enough to purchase a small home."

"Thomas," I replied, "this is so sudden I can't say that I can give it the kind of thought it deserves."

"I will not rush you, Serena. But I do ask that you think of your own prospects here. I don't imagine that spending your fruitful years as governess to Master Oliver is what you envisioned as your destiny. And at some point, when you are no longer needed in this household, where would you go then? To Kelston or Mayfair, perhaps, where there may be children in need of your care?"

"You make it sound very dreary, Thomas."

"I only paint a realistic picture, Serena. You are too beautiful a woman—and one with too passionate a nature—to be sentenced to such an existence. As my wife you would have the protection of a home and husband—and someday, I trust, a family."

"I don't know, Thomas," I replied, my eyes roving his face, caught by the earnestness of his expression. "There is so much on my mind . . ."

"I don't need an answer today, Serena. But I ask that you not wait too long, for I should scarcely be able to contain my apprehension. Promise me that you will think well on it."

"I do promise," I said gently.

"Splendid," he replied, squeezing my hands. "Might we seal it with a kiss?"

Before I could reply, his lips were on mine, which still felt bruised from the crush of Lord Barkham's mouth.

"There," he said, pulling back. "Now that we are almost engaged, perhaps you can tell me what else is troubling you?"

"I can't."

"I wish you would come to regard me as your confidant, my princess. There should be nothing that we are not able to share. It is likely that if I knew, I would be able to help you."

I truly wished that I could, for it was true that with Anne gone back to Mayfair I had no one to whom I could turn. But what could I tell him? Surely not of the search for my heritage, or the brutalization by Lord Barkham and the scene with the Baron at Kelston Manor. Even the latest incident with Oliver's medication was best left undiscussed.

"Thomas, I appreciate what you are trying to do, but there are certain things that I simply cannot share with you."

"But you can with Lord Barkham," he replied sullenly.

"Why do you say that?"

"I saw the two of you just now there in the rose garden."

"Were you spying on me?"

"Quite the contrary, I only happened upon you as I was coming out of the arbor."

"I see," I replied, wondering how much of the scene he had witnessed.

"I only hope that you are wise enough not to let the likes of him trifle with you. He is a powerful man, and a dangerous one, I fear. You should use care not to provoke him against you."

"Why do you say that, Thomas?" I asked, curious at this statement.

"Well, the constable came to my cottage earlier, and from our discussion, if I am not mistaken, his prime suspect in this horrible murder is Lord Barkham."

"Good Lord, Thomas, you must be mistaken," I said, my heart pounding. "Did he say that?"

"Not exactly. Let's say it was more of an innuendo."

Could it be? Was what I had heard the earl saying to him last night true? Had he been involved with Miss Smythe, and for some reason had she met her demise at his hand? That there was a brutishness about the man I certainly knew all too well. But was he actually capable of murder?

"I'm sorry. I should not have frightened you. But I think it is important that you know."

"Yes, Thomas. Yes, of course," I replied absentmindedly. "You must excuse me now, for I must return to Oliver."

"I guess you must," he said, rising. "But please think on my offer. It would make me a happy man if I knew I would be able to post the banns before the holidays."

I felt badly, for Thomas was so earnest, but my mind could only concentrate on Oliver and on what Thomas had said about Lord Barkham. If he were in fact the guilty party, what would it do to Anne? She was strong, but how strong can you be when your brother is accused of murder? For her sake, I prayed that Thomas's interpretation of whatever the constable had said was very wrong.

Oliver was still feverish that evening, but I managed to coax a few mouthfuls of broth and warm bread into him and he soon settled into a deep slumber. I returned to my room too exhausted to even play with Jaspar, who, sensing my mood, quieted and joined me in sleep at the foot of my bed.

Chapter Twelve

THE NEXT few days passed relatively uneventfully. I was anxious to know about the contents of the medicine bottle, but when Dr. Carruthers returned the afternoon of the second day he reported that he had found his own equipment inadequate for determining the drug and had sent it by coach to a laboratory in London for analysis.

Oliver's fever continued, and he slept a good deal of the time, which the doctor insisted was the best curative and he did not seem to be worried. I took the opportunity to delve into my father's books, and I read each day by Oliver's bedside from morning until evening. Thomas stopped by only once to see how Oliver was progressing, but I sensed that he was really more concerned with how my decision on his proposal was progressing than Oliver's health. In truth, I had given his offer very little thought. I was indeed surprised by that, for it is not every day that one receives such an honor but, I chalked it up to the fact that I had so much else on my mind. Fortunately he did not press me on the matter in front of Oliver, for I had no wish to distress the boy with any thoughts of my marriage or leaving Camberleigh. My grandmother came to visit twice. I saw her so infrequently that I believe her visits pleased me as much Oliver, who was always cheered by her presence.

It was on the evening of the fifth day that I made a discovery that was to change my life forever.

I had returned to my room after having my evening tray

with Oliver, who was showing signs of great improvement and a returning appetite. I was not particularly tired and quite entranced with the book I was reading, and I decided to continue it once in bed by the light of the fire and candles beside my bed. Several hours passed, and as I turned the page—determined that it should be the last of the night—several tissues, which I realized were some sort of letter, fell out of the book.

I opened them carefully and moved the candle on the nightstand closer so that I could better see the contents.

My heart began to pound as my eyes swept over the strong and even flourishes that I knew were made by my father's hand. I was so excited that it was a long moment before I could calm myself long enough to focus on the words themselves.

It was dated June 1, 1810, only two weeks before my father's death.

My dearest mother,

How many times over the past sixteen years I have mentally begun a letter—a letter that was never written. But something tells me that now is the time. Call it instinct, or a sixth sense, but I am compelled to bridge a gap of time and heartache, hoping that there is still time to find the truth and regain the love we lost that night so many years ago.

For some years, my dear Samantha has begged me to write to you to find some way back to Camberleigh and the many unanswered questions. She has sought this not for ourselves—though she knows the torture that this has caused me over the years—but for the sake of our daughter. Yes, Mother, you have a granddaughter. We named her Serena Miles, the last name inspired by the great distances we traveled after we left Camberleigh. In a sense she represented the miles between our old life and the one we sought to build at Seven Oaks.

She is growing into a great beauty, and at times I sense a great deal of you in her—her passions, her spirit, her way with people. Samantha conceived her at Camberleigh. There was no time to tell you before we left— not that it would have changed your decision.

The important thing is that Serena is a Camberleigh.

And she is a Camberleigh in spirit, in stature, and most important in heritage. She should—should she so choose someday—be able to return to Camberleigh. It is my fondest hope that I should be able to travel there with her, but one never knows in this life when fate shall play her final hand. Therefore, if I am not able to accompany her, for whatever reason, I would ask that you receive her with the warmth and love of which I know you are capable.

It is of great importance that I be able to bring your granddaughter to you. Since that fateful day so many years ago, not one has passed without my reliving the nightmare of the discovery of father's body. In truth, I think I was in such a state of shock that I was too numb to decry the evidence pointing to my guilt.

An argument we had earlier that day? My watch fob lying by the side of the pool? Incriminating, perhaps, but all circumstantial. Over the years I realized that Samantha was right. We should have stayed. I should have fought you and your decision and dealt with the constable, for by leaving I cast even greater suspicion on myself. But I was confused, hurt by your condemnation of me, and fearful that what would ensue would prove too great a burden for Samantha and the baby she had only begun to carry.

But I am overlooking the most important reason I should have remained: I was innocent. That you and the others could have thought that I would be capable of murdering my own father was perhaps the most destructive aspect of it all. Nonetheless, innocence must be proven, and I have only myself to blame for not seeing to it that my name and my honor was cleared. If only because of Serena, I know now that I must return to Camberleigh and search for the evidence which, if found, will irrevocably clear me of any misdeed.

However much these feelings have nagged at my soul for these sixteen long years, there is another urgency to this matter that I do not care to dwell upon except to say that you, my dear mother, might be in imminent danger should someone suspect that you have even the vaguest uncertainty about how my father died. It is with that thought that I beg you to share this letter or its contents with no one—servants or family.

I pray that you will see your way clear to welcome us back, not only to see your granddaughter, but to permit me to speak my peace. Samantha joins me in her regards. She has proven an ever valiant wife over these many years.

I hope that I may look for word from you in the near future.

Ever and again your loving
son, William

Tears stung my eyes as I pressed the letter against my breast. Ever my champion in life, it was as though my father had somehow reached out from the grave to give me the thing I most wanted in all the world. I now had the proof that would finally exonerate him and establish me as Serena Miles Camberleigh!

I got out of bed and fetched a handkerchief to help staunch the tears which fell so freely now. It was as though some great unseen presence that had enveloped me, stifled me for these past months, had suddenly been removed. I brought Jaspar up on my bed and held him close to me, feeling a sudden need to share this outpouring that I now felt.

The candles were burning low and I refolded the letter carefully and placed it back in the book and tucked the book under my pillow, not wanting the precious pages to be out of reach even in sleep.

Now that I had the proof I needed, I realized that I would have to think carefully about how to present it to my grandmother. Surely she would know that this was no forgery, but I realized all too well the impact that the letter had on me. Were she to understand that my father not only openly declared his innocence but his willingness to return to prove it, I knew she would be devastated. For that would mean that she had banished him wrongly.

In many ways I was pleased that I had never known Camberleigh or my grandmother before my mother's death, for I was certain that I should have harbored an intense bitterness

for what they had done to my father. But now I knew both this
house and the frail, regal, and sensitive woman who sat as its
matriarch and felt a fervent need to protect them both. If only
Anne were here she might advise me how to best go about
this. The implication that my father had been suspicious of
some member or members of the family or staff was truly
frightening, for I knew that he would never have written such
a thing unless he had been certain of its veracity.

I tried to sleep, knowing that I would have to be up early
with Oliver, but my excitement—or was it apprehension—
overcame my exhaustion. Finally the rhythmic sounds of Jaspar's breathing lulled me off to sleep.

I was just stirring the next morning when Charlotte knocked
at the door. Coming out of my reverie, my hand flew under
the pillow and closed about the leather binding. It had not been
a dream! It was here, I held in my hand the proof of my
patrimony.

"Sorry if I be disturbin' you, miss. Ye be readin' so early
in the mornin'?"

"You didn't, Charlotte, I particularly wanted to be up early."

"Robbie wanted me to tell you that 'e'll only be able to be
tendin' your friend here this mornin'. Seems like there were a
problem down at the stables, an' he's gotta help them get
everything back in order."

"What happened?"

"Coulda been a lot worse than 'twas. A fire broke out right
where the horses are. Luckily me Robbie smelled smoke an'
got everybody up an' out afore any real harm was done. The
rain comin' so hard last night helped, o' course."

"That's terrible, Charlotte. Is Robbie all right?"

"Got his hair singed a bit an' one hand took a knock when
he went in after the Earl's horse. But nobody else coulda got
him out. Saved him, he did."

"Well, tell him not to worry about Jaspar. I shall tell Oliver
of these exploits. He is already most admiring of Robbie's
ability with the horses. I am certain that he will be most impressed by this latest show of skill."

I bathed and dressed quickly. I removed the letter from the
book and placed it deep in my pocket, fearful of having it out
of my sight. I still had not worked out how or when to approach
my grandmother, but my first priority was to see to Oliver,

and I made haste to the nursery.

Oliver was propped up in bed, and from the way he was attacking his meal I could see that he was much improved. "Well, seeing you eat like that is the best news I could have, Oliver. You must be feeling much better."

"I am, Serena. I'm not tired any more and that terrible pain has gone. Could we go out this morning? After you finish your breakfast, of course."

"Oh, not yet. You have been very ill and I don't want to take any chances on a relapse. I think we should let the doctor be the judge of when you might be up and about again."

"But he might not return for days."

"Well, then, we shall just have to find ways to amuse ourselves indoors until the good doctor returns—but that might be sooner than you think."

We spent the rest of the morning reading and playing word games. It was almost noon when my grandmother appeared for a visit. When I saw her now I had the same feeing I had had when I first arrived at Camberleigh: I wanted to run and embrace her, to feel close to this woman who was the one direct link to my father and my true birthright.

"Good morning, Serena. How is our Oliver today?"

"I'm pleased to say, your ladyship, that I can scarcely keep him down. He's truly well on the way to recovery."

"Excellent."

"Good morning, Grandmother," Oliver said.

"How is my favorite grandson?"

"But I am your only grandson, aren't I?"

"Of course you are," she replied. "But you are still my favorite."

"You are my favorite grandmother, too."

"Well, Serena, it looks as though I've been caught at my own game."

"Did you know my other grandmother?" Oliver asked.

"Yes . . . I did, Oliver," she replied slowly.

"I bet she wasn't as nice as you."

"We were very different. But she would have loved you too."

"I don't think so," Oliver replied, toying with the bed-clothes.

"Whatever would make you say a thing like that?" she asked.

"Well, my mother doesn't love me, so why would her mother have loved me?"

My grandmother was completely taken aback.

"You know, Oliver," I put in "some people are just not able to show their love, but that doesn't mean they *don't* love."

"Serena, is right Oliver," said my grandmother recovering. "And now I shall leave you two alone. I have many letters that I must attend to."

"Your ladyship, might I speak with you for a moment?"

"Certainly, Serena. What is it?"

"I think perhaps we had best talk in private."

"I see. Well then come to my quarters after luncheon."

"Thank you."

Charlotte brought our trays, and I joined Oliver in enjoying the roast lamb, small potatoes, and sweet peas. I was surprised by a knock at the door, and rose to answer it.

"Hello, Serena." There stood Lord Barkham, smiling down at me. "Did you miss me?"

"Good afternoon, Lord Barkham. Not that it merits an answer, but quite frankly the last few days have been most pleasant."

"Now, now, little digs like that do not become you, Serena. That's far more Clarissa's style. How is Oliver?"

"Come in and see for yourself."

"Uncle Justin!" Oliver's face was a wreath of smiles.

"Well, this looks more like the Oliver I know. I was worried about you."

"I feel much better, but Serena won't let me get out of bed until the doctor arrives."

"I would say that is a sound decision."

"What is that package?" Oliver asked, spying a long thin box under Lord Barkham's arm.

"Don't you remember that I promised you a present?"

"You really got something?"

"Of course. It's all yours."

Oliver took the package, and I smiled at how carefully he untied the wrappings.

"It's my own crop! Oh, thank you, Uncle Justin," the boy said, throwing his arms about Lord Barkham's neck.

"When you are fully recovered, we shall go riding and I

318

shall teach you how to use it properly. It will help you communicate with your mare."

"It won't hurt her?"

"Not when you use it properly."

"What about Serena?"

"What about her, Oliver?"

"Well, you said you were going to bring her something as well."

"I did? Oh, yes. Well, let me see." He fished into his pocket and pulled out a small box. "How is this?"

"You see, Serena? He didn't forget."

"This is not what I really wanted to buy you, Serena, but when I saw it I thought of you," he said, handing me the box.

"I am sorry, Lord Barkham, but I cannot accept this."

"Why not?" Oliver asked.

"Please take it. If you don't like it, you needn't ever wear it."

My hands shook slightly as I opened the small box. It angered me to be put in this position. I had no intention of accepting this gift—or bribe, or whatever he intended—but I could not create a scene in front of Oliver. I opened it and took out a gold stickpin the top of which was formed in the shape of a rose.

"What is it, Serena?"

"Here, have a look for yourself," I said, handing it to him.

"What is it?"

Lord Barkham laughed. "Well, my gift must be a great success. Serena says nothing and you, my friend, ask what it is."

"It's a pin, Oliver," I said. "And a lovely one."

"Why don't you put it on?"

I replaced the pin against the deep garnet velvet of the box's interior and closed the lid.

"It would be inappropriate with my current attire," I replied.

"It's fortunate that my sister is not here to see you in that dress. I daresay she would be convinced that you are more partial to your old woolens than her new designs."

"I regret that you find my appearance distasteful, Lord Barkham. I also prefer the gowns Anne so generously provided, but given the mood of the household at present, I think it hardly appropriate to aggravate Lady Camberleigh any more than necessary."

Lord Barkham moved over to where I stood and turned my head up to face his. "Someday, Serena, I hope that you will be able to act from your own will and not simply react to the wills of others."

Before I could respond, he had turned and left the room, closing the door behind him.

Oliver had propped himself up in bed and was lost in a fantasy of being atop his mare, his arm bringing the crop down on an imaginary flank.

"You must have traveled miles by now," I said, winking at him. "But I don't want you to overtire yourself; there's time enough." I coaxed him down under the covers, but did not have the heart to remove the crop from his hand. "Oliver, I am going to go visit with your grandmother for a while. If you rest now, perhaps we might read together when I return."

Those large saucer eyes were distinctly sleep-filled and I sensed the boy was almost relieved to acquiesce to my pleas. I kissed his forehead and pulled the coverlet higher up around him. How pleased I was that he was my real cousin. In truth, we had grown so close that I considered him more the brother that I had never had. My hand curled about the letter in my pocket. Perhaps soon I would be able to share my secret with him.

Convinced that he would sleep peacefully for at least an hour or so, I ventured out into the hall and made my way to my grandmother's room. The house was strangely silent, and I was relieved not to encounter anyone. My destiny had been sealed when I first ventured to Camberleigh, and I now was eager to take what I hoped would be the last leg of my journey.

I paused for a moment before knocking at my grandmother's door. I thought I heard voices from within, but I couldn't be certain. I hoped she was alone, for this was not a moment that I could share with anyone save my grandmother.

"Come in," the frail voice called.

I entered slowly. My grandmother was seated by the window. She had an odd, faraway look on her face, her eyes staring at the intricate pattern of the rug.

"Your ladyship," I ventured. "It is Serena. We were to talk this afternoon." I paused. "If it is not convenient I shall return later."

"I think it would be wise if you were to stay, Miss Miles." I turned, startled to see Doctor Carruthers striding from the shadows of the room.

"I'm sorry, I didn't see you, doctor."

"I am paying a rather impromptu but necessary call. Actually, I am delighted that you came, for I was just off to search you out."

"Is there anything wrong, doctor?"

"Why don't you have a seat here by her ladyship."

"I'm sorry, Serena," my grandmother said suddenly. "I seem to have become lost in my own ruminations. Would you care for some tea? Dr. Carruthers tells me that Cook's little cakes are quite good. Try one."

There was a chill in the room and the herb tea was strong and hot.

"Miss Miles, as you are aware I had deep suspicions about the tonic young master Oliver was receiving," the doctor began.

I nodded.

"I sent what remained of the substance to London, where they have the facilities to identify the contents far more thoroughly than I was able to accomplish in my modest lab."

"I assume you have the results, doctor."

"I do, and I fear they are not pleasant. The tonic base is a restorative not unlike that which I had originally prescribed. Unfortunately, integrated into that portion was a mild amount of laudanum and a decidedly heavy dose of arsenic."

"Forgive me, I am not terribly sophisticated about medicinal terms, but laudanum is a sedative, is it not?"

"That is correct, Miss Miles. It is sometimes prescribed for patients who experience a restlessness of mind or have occasional trouble going to sleep."

"But would it have caused Oliver to become so ill?"

"Not by itself. Actually, it was likely the cause of the boy's lassitude at times, though I suspect that that was not the primary reason for its inclusion in this diabolical formula."

"What, then?"

"It's a very clever concoction, actually. I believe the laudanum was used to disguise, if you will, the effect of the arsenic."

"I don't understand. I have heard tell that some women use arsenic to heighten the color of their complexion. It is quite popular in France, I believe."

"An unfortunate habit, Miss Miles, but for those purposes it is used in minuscule amounts. What we have here is a dosage that is lethal."

Once again my mind reeled from yet one more outrageous disclosure. "What you are saying, then, doctor, is that this tonic, had it continued to have been administered to Oliver, would have killed him?" The doctor looked directly into my face and nodded solemnly.

My grandmother, who had remained silent and almost trancelike during this exchange, seemed suddenly to snap from her reverie. My heart ached for her. Instead of being able to relish what I oft heard referred to as the twilight years, she was ever at the center of the pain and evil that seemed to pervade this house.

"I shall see that whoever is responsible for this is incarcerated to the end of their days. If it is the last thing I do, I shall have retribution for this crime against my grandson."

"Do you have any idea who could have done this monstrous thing, Dr. Carruthers?"

"I wish I did, Miss Miles. I must admit that although I cannot conceive of a motive, I have to include you high on my list of suspects, particularly with the confusion about who was actually dispensing the medication."

I started to protest, but my grandmother put her hand on mine. "I may be an old fool, Serena, but I don't think you are capable of such a criminal act."

Dr. Carruthers cleared his throat. "You have quite a defender in her ladyship, Miss Miles. When I suggested your possible involvement, I thought that she would have my head with that cane."

"Do you have any idea from whence the tonic came, doctor?"

"Fortunately I do. The bottle is used by only three or four

pharmacies in London. I have already taken it upon myself to contact these pharmacies on the chance that they will have the name of the individual who requisitioned it."

"Perhaps we should bring the constable into the matter," suggested my grandmother.

"If you will permit me," Dr. Carruthers said, "although I quite agree that this is a criminal matter, I am not certain that it would not be wiser to let me do some investigating without the law and the courts. I should think that one would be far less reticent about providing such details to a country physician."

"I think the doctor may be right, your ladyship," I put in.

"For the moment it would be best, I believe, to keep this matter as quiet as possible," the doctor went on. "Miss Miles, since you have the most contact with Master Oliver, I suggest that—without alarming him unnecessarily, of course—you advise him that he is not to take any medication unless it is administered by you personally. Frankly, unless he has taken a turn for the worse, I would prefer that he not take anything whatsoever."

"I think you will find him much improved, doctor."

"Your ladyship, if you will excuse me, I should like to look in on the boy. I will of course keep you apprised of any news as soon as I receive it."

"Thank you for your concern and your help, doctor."

"I can let myself out," he replied, bowing modestly.

When he had gone, I rose and suggested that I might draw the heavy draperies back farther so as to allow the afternoon sun to fill the darkened parts of the room.

"You are right, Serena, I too often sit in this room veiling myself from the world outside."

"I didn't mean to imply that, your ladyship, it's just that the gardens and landscape of Camberleigh are so lovely, even at this time of year." I returned to sit beside her, slowly withdrawing the letter from my pocket. "I have something that I would like to share with you."

"Don't tell me I am to be given news of something more that is amiss in this house."

I placed the letter in her hands. "I think you will find this far more eloquent than my own words could possibly express."

Her slender bony fingers gently unfolded the tissue, and she brought the letter into focus.

I watched her intently as those violet eyes, faded by time, seemed to drink in every word of my father's letter. Her fingers traced the sweeping swirl of his penmanship as if by doing so she was reaching out to him over the years. I made no move toward her as the tears began to spill onto the lace inset of her gown. Her grief, as mine, had to be spent in privacy. It was a long time before she spoke.

"I wish that I would express to you what I am feeling at this moment, Serena. This letter has taken me back over the years, back to days when my son, your father, was just a little boy. He was such a special child—happy, curious, generous to a fault. I remember one day your grandfather and I were frantic, for he was nowhere to be found. Cook said that he had taken a large hamper of food from the kitchen earlier that morning."

"Where had he gone?" I asked.

"He had gone to one of the local tenant farms. The mother of one of the young stable boys was ill, and William had taken it upon himself to stock their larder with enough food for a week. I was beside myself with worry, but when he finally returned home, as always it was hard to reprimand him."

"He was like that even as an adult," I offered.

"Do you know, Serena, it is one of the saddest ironies of my life. The only time I really ever said a harsh word to William was the last time I saw him."

"Perhaps it would be better not to dwell on that," I replied quietly.

"You are a kind girl, Serena, but we both know that we cannot discuss this without being honest with each other. When you came here and presented yourself as my son's daughter, I must tell you that I immediately wished to welcome you as such. To do so would have given me, shall we say, another chance. For all these years I have been haunted by the possibility that I had committed a terrible injustice against my son. You would have provided a way for an old woman to give herself a bit of vindication. But you must see that, had you been an impostor, it would have only compounded the tragedy further. I could not allow that to happen. You do see that, don't you?" I nodded, wiping at the tears which now flowed uncontrollably. "Serena, come here to me," my grandmother said.

I rose and knelt by her side, our arms encircling each other in a firm embrace. The moment I had dreamed of for so long had finally come.

Her hands cupped my chin and our eyes searched each other as if for recognition. "My granddaughter—my lovely granddaughter. In sending you to me, my son has shown me some small forgiveness. What joy he has brought me."

"Oh, Grandmother," I choked. "I love you so."

"And I you, my dear Serena. Over these months I have watched you, listened to you, prayed that this beautiful young girl who is at once so gentle yet so spirited might indeed share my blood. I should probably not admit this to you, but in all the years that I have spent watching Clarissa grow up, I never once have had the same affinity or feeling of affection that I have developed for you in the short time you have been here."

"You mustn't say that, Grandmother," I cautioned. "We are just different."

"As night is to day, my dear. She is not a terrible child, but you, my dear, are a true Camberleigh—in heart and mind as well as demeanor. I have had hopes that Oliver might too carry on the character and traditions of this family, but he has a long hard fight ahead of him."

"He will recover, Grandmother, we must believe that."

"I am not referring to his present illness. I am talking about the lack of proper nurturing he has received from his father. And as for his mother, she does not even exist for him."

"He has you."

"Caring for the young is not for the old, Serena. But let us not dwell on Oliver. It is you that we must attend to at this moment," she said, stroking my hair gently. "Too much time has already passed. Tonight we shall make it official and add the Camberleigh name to yours."

I rose and moved to the window. The sun had disappeared, and cold gray clouds rolled across the sky. I shivered slightly.

"Grandmother, do you think it is wise to bring this to the surface now?"

"I don't understand, Serena. I thought it was what you wanted."

I moved back to sit beside her. "I do, Grandmother, more than anything. But we must pay heed to my father's warning. He could not possibly have foreseen the unrest that has befallen Camberleigh today, but he obviously felt that from events of the past, that there was an ever-present danger embedded somewhere in this household. My father was not an alarmist. He would not have written what he did unless he felt that his suspicions were well founded."

"As loath as I am to admit it, I must say that this letter has added to my confusion and concern."

"Much as I would like to take my legitimate place in this family, perhaps we should wait, Grandmother, until a few of these matters sort themselves out."

"No. I refuse to be a prisoner to such fears. My time is limited, Serena, and I want to spend my final days—or years, whatever it is to be—with you by my side as my granddaughter. No. Tonight it is to be. I shall inform Richard that I shall want the entire family present at dinner this evening. I shall make the announcement—but I shall not, as your father suggested, discuss the letter or its contents."

"I don't think this news will exactly delight the Earl—not to mention Lady Camberleigh or Clarissa."

"You leave that to me, my dear. Now, we both look like soggy messes and I want us to be at our best this evening. I shall rest for a spell, and I want you to go back to your room and don one of those lovely gowns that Lady Ormsby designed for you."

I laughed. "I must really look dreadful. You are the second person today who has implied that my appearance is less than fashionable. But I did promise Oliver that we might read together. I wouldn't want to disappoint him."

"My dear, I must see Justin briefly, and I will tell him to spend some time with the boy. Oliver does seem to have a special fondness for Lord Barkham."

"I have tired you. I shall go now." I rose and kissed the soft lined cheek of the woman whom I could now call grandmother.

"My dear child, you have breathed new life into this withered frame. We shall all gather in the library a bit before eight. I am quite looking forward to this evening. I shall enjoy it immensely."

I had reached the door when my grandmother called out to me. "Serena."

"Yes, Grandmother."

"Would you mind if I kept this letter?"

I paused. "Let us just say it has finally come home."

Jaspar was poised by the door when I returned, and wriggled with his usual enthusiastic welcome, enticing me to share a playful moment.

"Oh, Jaspar," I cried, embracing him, "we have a grandmother."

He cocked his head as if trying to comprehend.

"Her ladyship is our grandmother, and tonight she is going to tell everyone. Now you have to help me decide what I should wear."

I wished that Anne were here to help me select the proper gown. I wanted to look my best—admittedly in part because I knew that Lord Barkham would be present. Tonight I did not want to be scorned, even if it was only directed to my appearance. No, tonight I wanted to see pride reflected in my grandmother's eyes.

After what seemed an endless debate, I settled on a pale peach silk taffeta with cross-lacing of a deeper peach-colored velvet about the bodice. The neckline I thought perhaps a bit low, but all the gowns Anne had designed—with the exception of my traveling costume—were more daring than the mode of attire to which I was accustomed.

Charlotte arrived with my bathwater, chattering with news that the kitchen was in a turmoil since Cook had been told that there was to be a special menu prepared for tonight's dinner. If Charlotte was surprised that I was dining with the family, she did not express it, and she consented to return to dress my hair, which I had given little thought to since our return from Kelston Manor. I felt less than loyal not sharing my news with her, but as close as we had grown, I knew that it was not my place to preempt my grandmother's announcement of my admission into the folds of the family.

It would be interesting to know what the various reactions

would be. Ironically, I anticipated more adverse reactions amongst my own at Camberleigh. Beyond Charlotte, I also felt slightly guilty at not having apprised Thomas of the upcoming event. I would like to having had the news come from me directly, but I knew the chance of that was slim, since gossip was a way of life amongst many of the servants.

As great as the anticipation of the evening was, I forced myself to keep in mind not only the events of the past weeks, but the caution in my father's letter. I did not take this warning lightly.

Jaspar eyed me suspiciously as I bathed and dressed.

When Charlotte returned to fix my hair, I had all but donned my gown. She undid my hair and deftly combed it into the style that she knew pleased me so.

"You seem a wee bit skittish tonight, Miss Serena," Charlotte said as she placed the final comb in place.

"Do I?" I replied, embarrassed that my nervousness was so apparent.

"Perhaps I am just fatigued," I said without further apology or explanation.

I drew the gown on and allowed Charlotte to lace the bodice, realizing that my hands were best left at my sides.

"'Tis a wonderful color for you, miss."

"You don't think it's too revealing?"

"Miss, if I had to reveal what you've got to reveal, believe me, I'd be showin' it off all around the village."

I laughed. "I can't imagine you doing that, Charlotte."

"It's all in me imagination, miss. But me mum always says it ne'er hurts one to dream."

I paused, realizing that I had been so involved with the events of the household and myself that I had scarcely given a thought to any others. "Do forgive me, Charlotte, for it has been some time since I have inquired about your mother—and also, weeks have passed since I have been able to dedicate any effort whatsoever to Robbie's studies."

"Needn't be apologizin', miss. You're a young girl, and your thoughts should be of livin' and lovin'. But to answer, me mum is fine. I know I have to face losin' her sometime in the future, but for now she is content with her lot. An' as for Robbie, well, the master was so taken with him savin' the horses an' all that he's givin' him extra pence for his labors from now on."

"That is wonderful news, Charlotte. He is well deserving of both the praise and the reward. Once things settle down in the house I shall look forward to schooling him again. He is a bright boy and a joy to teach."

Jaspar sighed as if in agreement.

"Ye looks like a princess, Miss Serena. The only thing that would add to ye would be a beautiful necklace at your throat."

"Perhaps my mother's cameo. I'm certain that it will pale in contrast to Lady Camberleigh's jewels, but somehow it seems particularly right to wear it tonight."

I fingered the cameo as Charlotte clasped it about my neck. There was a solace and a strength which came from it. It seemed absurd that a tangible decorative piece should be such a strong link to my forebears, my past—but there it was. If it were true that one carried within one a portion of the people who had given one life, then tonight I should be in good company. For my mother and father would be with me on this, the most important night of my life. And I was thankful, for I needed strength and support that right now seemed beyond me.

"If you be wantin' miss, I'll have Robbie take the little feller for a run. Seems like it might be a long night."

"Thank you, Charlotte."

The house was quiet as I made my way through the dim hallway to the staircase. As I slowly descended I felt the eyes of my ancestors upon me. My hand reached out and touched the portrait of my grandfather. I knew that my greatest task, that of vindicating my father, still lay ahead of me, and I silently vowed to the kindly face that I should bring honor back to the name of his son.

The library door was open, and I slipped quietly in. My uncle stood at the fireplace, his back to me. I cleared my throat, and he turned slowly to face me.

"Well, Miss Miles, I didn't hear you enter."

"I hope I am not disturbing you, Lord Camberleigh."

"Would it really matter if you were?" he asked, his hand tracing his scar. "I apologize, that was rude. You may as well come in and make yourself comfortable. Since my mother has decided to call a command performance—whatever it may be about—we may as well try to be civil. You cannot be looking forward to it any more than I, though I must say your appearance belies it. If you will permit my saying, you look exquisite this evening."

"Thank you." I replied, moving to take a seat by the fire. "I have Lady Ormsby to thank for that."

"You two are quite compatible, I have observed."

"She has been a great friend to me since I have arrived at Camberleigh. There have been times when I don't know what I would have done without her."

Lord Camberleigh picked up a decanter and poured himself a liberal glass of brandy.

"Will you join me?"

"No, thank you," I demurred.

"Have we been so difficult to live with? You seem so grateful for Lady Ormsby's friendship."

"Everyone needs a friend," I replied noncommittally.

He studied me for a moment, sipping the amber liquid.

"You have made other friends here as well, I am led to understand."

"I hope so, sire."

"I was referring specifically to Mr. Masters."

I could feel a blush spread over my face.

"This should not be an embarrassment, Miss Miles. Although my wife and I are scarcely examples of it, I am not by nature opposed to romance—and I must say that he has impeccable taste."

I was growing flustered by this turn of the conversation. I had always assumed that my friendship with Thomas had been sheltered by some degree of privacy. Obviously, I was mistaken.

"You know, Miss Miles, Thomas—Mr. Masters—has been of exceptional assistance to me in a variety of ways and I fully intend to compensate him for his efforts. That might prove a nice little nest egg for one starting out. It might even be an incentive for a man about to take a wife and start a family."

"I am pleased you hold Mr. Masters in such high regard, but I hardly see how all this relates to me," I said, keeping my eyes fixed on the table before me.

"As you will, Miss Miles. I only offer that in my opinion a young lady of your station could do a great deal worse."

I was about to retort, but bit my lip so as not to betray myself.

"What might a young lady of Miss Miles's station be the worse for, pray tell, Richard?"

I flushed even more deeply at the sound of Lord Barkham's voice. My uncle rose.

"Miss Miles and I were simply conjecturing, were we not? Let me fix you a brandy."

"You look very fetching tonight, Miss Miles," Lord Barkham said, turning to face me as he accepted the drink from my uncle. "Hardly the typical governess. But then I've always said that Oliver was the most fortunate male this side of the Atlantic."

"Justin, what do you suppose this evening is all about?" my uncle asked, seating himself opposite me.

"I haven't any idea, but you know your mother, Richard. She is a woman of purpose. She would scarcely have arranged this dinner without some worthy reason. Wouldn't you say so, Miss Miles?"

I was certain that as I turned to face Lord Barkham I saw him wink at me. Damnation, but that man was impudent.

"I agree that her ladyship is not what one would term a frivolous woman," I replied.

"Well, that may be, Miss Miles, but I cannot say that I am not looking forward to this little gathering. My wife is hardly in a state to endure one of my mother's family dinners. After all these years, mother should know that it is just asking for trouble."

Lord Barkham cleared his throat. "I think, Richard, that we are being perhaps a bit foreboding for Miss Miles. I hate to see a frown drawn on that lovely face—"

This remark was interrupted by the sound of a loud commotion in the hallway.

Clarissa strutted into the room, followed immediately by Lady Camberleigh.

"Father, Mother is being just wretched," Clarissa wailed, rushing to her father's side.

Lord Camberleigh put his arm around her.

"There, there, my pet. It cannot be that serious," he responded, looking over her blond curls at his wife.

"Oh, but it is. I must go to London. If I don't go soon, I

shall be an old hag by the time I am presented."

Lord Barkham burst into laughter. And try as I did to suppress it, I myself could not help but smile.

"Clarissa, the image of you as a craggy-toothed woman is heavenly," chortled Lord Barkham.

"Really, Justin," she moaned.

"My dear daughter, I must agree with Justin. You can scarcely be considered anything but an enchanting young child. I have explained to you that until this disgraceful mess here is over, it would be awkward, to say the least, for you to enter into your season."

"Ah, pearls of wisdom from the Lord of the manor." Lady Camberleigh walked over and fussed at the skirt of Clarissa's dress before dropping into a chair near the fire. Her countenance was ever an enigma to me. She could at times appear a broken old woman. And at others—like this evening—she had the look of a member of royalty. Her gown was of a burgundy velvet with ruffles of ecru lace at the wrists and about the neckline. As always her jewelry was dazzling, a matching necklace and earrings of garnets and tiny diamonds in floral clusters.

"I didn't know that we would have the pleasure of *your* company at this little *soirée*, Miss Miles," she offered, I knew facetiously. "I hope that this is not to be one of Juliette's lectures on cutting back on household expenses."

Just then my grandmother appeared at the doorway on the arm of Giles. "You needn't worry, Maura, I have no intention of discussing finances of that nature this evening, though it troubles me that you have so little concern for the operation of these estates."

I looked up and my eyes met my grandmother's. I felt as though she was willing me a certain strength, that I knew we would both need it for the evening ahead. "You look charming this evening, Serena," she said.

"Thank you, your ladyship."

"Frankly, Grandmother," Clarissa purred, "Miss Miles is scarcely properly attired for her role as governess. Your sister, Justin, seems to be advertising her skills at our expense. Providing these gowns to Miss Miles . . . well, it is certainly not in good taste."

"Your green is showing, Clarissa dear," Lord Barkham replied, winking at me again.

"Justin is right, your envy is most unbecoming," my grandmother responded. I saw my uncle's eyebrows raise, but he remained silent. I was surprised, for he always took Clarissa's side—but this time he seemed to sense that his mother was in no mood to be challenged.

The tension that was mounting quickly in the room was dispersed by Giles's announcement that dinner was served. My uncle escorted my grandmother from the room, and when Lord Barkham moved to take my arm, Maura marched angrily from the room with Clarissa close at hand, still muttering about a trip to London. I wrenched my arm away from Lord Barkham.

"Are you telling me that we cannot even be superficially civil to each other, Serena?"

"As long as you keep your distance, Lord Barkham, we shall have little unpleasantness," I replied as frigidly as I could.

"Ah, but such a waste, my lovely. That we who can share such passion should be denied the benefit of even the slightest touch is a crime. It is an assault on the emotions."

"Assault?" I quelled. "But of course, you are the master of same."

He released my arm and studied me intently.

"Someday, Serena, you shall learn that one of the most important skills in life is the ability to forgive."

I watched him as he left the room. Something disturbed me about his last statement. Perhaps because it was a piece of advice that had also come from my own father.

I drew a deep breath and made my way to the dining room. Clarissa had obviously been making further comments about me, for she suddenly grew quiet as I entered the room.

"Well, champagne and all, Juliette." Maura's tone was sprightly. "This is obviously an occasion, but I can't for the life of me think of what it can be. I haven't forgotten someone's birthday, have I?"

"When, my dear, have you ever remembered one," retorted my uncle.

"Another happy family gathering," Maura replied, lifting her glass and draining it.

"Well, Mother, do you intend to reveal the nature of this

evening at the outset, or are we to be left on tenterhooks?"

"Be patient, Richard, and enjoy your meal."

We were served pheasant in a savory sauce, wild rice and a light squash which smelled divine. I was too nervous to appreciate it fully, however, but only Lord Barkham seemed to notice my preoccupation. I longed for Anne to be with us, as I could have used her confidence and support this evening.

The conversation focused again on the tenant farms, a topic that inevitably created hostility between my uncle and Lord Barkham. I found my uncle to be sorely insensitive to the needs of these people whose labors on the lands were reflected in his pocket.

My grandmother looked over and smiled at me as she said, "I don't mean to interrupt you two, but I sense if I don't I shall never get to the point of this evening. Serena, come and sit by me, would you?"

As I rose and moved down the long table, the sound of the heels of my boots clicking on the floor was the only intrusion on the hush that had spread over the room. I drew a chair over from the side of the serving table and placed it next to my grandmother, my glance darting around the table as I sat. She understood my nervousness, for she reached over and placed a cool hand atop mine. It make me think back to my childhood when I was ill and my mother would place her hand on my forehead. Her touch seemed to draw the fever directly from my being.

My grandmother began slowly, her voice at first almost inaudible, which forced the others into absolute silence.

"The reason for this evening is, in a way, a form of introduction."

"To what, pray tell, Grandmother?" Clarissa challenged.

"Not to what, my dear, but to whom. I know that what I have to say to you is going to come as a shock. Not only the news itself, but the revelation of a deception that I have been forced to enact. This little ruse has not been something that I have been comfortable performing—particularly on my own family. But when I explain, I trust that you all shall comprehend its necessity. The young woman who sits by my side, who over these past months I have come to trust, to respect, and yes, to love, is not Serena Miles, she—"

Sharp laughter interrupted. "Well, well, well," Maura slurred, looking very smug. "I knew she was up to something, Richard. If you didn't look so shocked yourself I would have thought that this was but another of your little games with your dear mama."

My uncle's fist crashed on the table. "Shut up, Maura."

"All of you, be quiet," my grandmother said, rising from her chair. Her voice and her bearing were stronger than I thought possible. "You shall listen to what I have to say and you shall try, as difficult as it may be for you, to be civil. I should like to introduce to you Serena Miles Camberleigh . . . my grand-daughter."

I don't know what reaction I had expected, but certainly not the silence that ensued. I'm certain that it was only seconds, but it felt as though the clock against the far wall was ticking off years of my life.

It was my uncle who spoke first. "I don't wish to be dis-respectful, Mother, but is this some kind of joke, for if it is it is being played in poor taste."

"I am surprised that you think me capable of such an act, Richard. I quite assure you that I am not playing the role of court jester, nor am I a befuddled old woman. I am in total control of my senses."

"Mama, is this true?" cried Clarissa, who looked as if she had been shot.

"Of course not," Maura snapped. "I have thought all along that our Miss Miles was far from the sweet unassuming little governess that she has pretended to be. I can assure you, my dear, that your father and I have only one daughter, and that is you. Of course, this may be some bastard from one of his little trysts, but if it is she has no claim on the name or the estates."

"That will be quite enough, Maura," my grandmother said calmly. "I'm surprised at you. Your tongue has always been twisted, but I always thought your mind was quick and per-ceptive. It seems that you have all forgotten that there are two legitimate heirs to the Camberleigh lineage and inheritance— Richard and William."

Maura gasped and lifted her champagne glass quickly to her mouth. I had never seen my uncle look paler, or his scar pulse more flagrantly. Only Lord Barkham appeared quietly thought-ful, his eyes directed downward so that I could not read any-thing of his reaction.

"When Serena came to us, she did so as a Camberleigh— a fact, I should add, that she had learned only a short time before, upon her mother's death. Need I say that it was a tremendous shock to me, and there was little evidence—other than a letter of introduction from her mother—to support her claim. If you will recall, we needed a governess at the time. You must understand that although I did not have proof, I could not risk turning her away—not after what I had done to Wil-liam. Thus I proposed a scheme. She should remain at Cam-berleigh as Oliver's governess. She knew that I would be watching her closely, and if there were the slightest suspicion that all was not as she purported, she would be expelled im-mediately. Concurrently, I employed a solicitor of sorts to take the small scraps of information that we possessed and inves-tigate fully. That he has done, and totally to my satisfaction. There is no shadow of doubt that Serena is William's legitimate daughter."

My uncle cleared his throat, his hand rubbing the scar. "Have you seen him?"

I heard my own voice saying, "My father is dead. He passed away two years ago after saving a family from a burning home."

"Isn't that touching," spat Maura. "The murderer is re-deemed on his deathbed. Well, Juliette, not that I believe for a moment that this baggage is who she says she is, but even if it were true you certainly cannot mean to keep her under the same roof? Good Lord, with everything that has happened here, maybe it is like father like daughter. Perhaps she is the one who did away with that last chit of a governess. To think, dear Richard, I may have accused you wrongly."

"How dare you," I challenged, getting to my feet. "My father never hurt anyone. He was the most decent man I've ever known. How *dare* you defile his name."

My grandmother reached out and took my hand, entreating me to sit back down. "Let me handle this, Serena," she whis-pered.

Maura laughed. "An excellent performance, my dear. Whoever put you up to this has schooled you well. More cham-

pagne, please, Richard. This is turning out to be quite entertaining after all."

My grandmother pressed my hand, urging my silence.

"You know, Maura, the only reason I am permitting you
to remain in this room is that you are a member of this family,
and as such I want you to hear what I have to say. If only for
your daughter's sake, I once again beseech you to be civil."

"This isn't getting us anyplace," my uncle interrupted. "I
must say that I thought you were too smart to have been duped
by this scheme, Mother. I don't know what this is all about,
but I intend to ferret out the truth."

"Richard, as usual, you are not listening. I have told you
that I have proof."

"Where is it, then?" my uncle asked, throwing his napkin
angrily on the table.

I waited for my grandmother's response. But instead it was
Lord Barkham who spoke.

"I have it, Richard."

"What? What do you know about this, Barkham?"

"I would say that I know just about everything. You see,
it was I whom Juliette entrusted with the responsibility of tracing Serena's story. And I can assure you that Serena is un-
questionably who she purports to be—the legitimate daughter
of William Camberleigh. There are papers, affidavits, records,
all of which I went to a great deal of trouble and expense to
obtain. You are free to examine them if you doubt my word."

I scarcely heard my uncle's response, shocked as I was over
Lord Barkham's revelation. On the one hand I was grateful
that he spoke up on my behalf, and on the other hand I was
angered that he had deceived me for these many weeks.

Clarissa—who had appeared to grow more and more confused during all of this—suddenly burst into tears, blubbering
that she hated me and that I was ruining everything.

"I had hoped, Clarissa," my grandmother said, "that as you
approached womanhood you would develop character traits
befitting a Camberleigh, but I see that that was too much to
hope. Instead of welcoming your cousin, as you should, you
are prattling selfishly. I realize that this comes as a shock to
you, but I ask that you join your mother and try to keep a civil
tongue. From this moment on, Serena shall be recognized as

Serena Miles Camberleigh, and she shall assume all the respect and accommodation that go with the name. I hope that you will welcome her into our home and your hearts, as I have come to do."

"You surprise me, Mother," my uncle said thoughtfully. "Even if Serena is William's daughter, you scarce have had a thought about him—nor should you have—throughout these years. Pardon me for saying this, Serena, but you must understand that we would all have some reservation about your presence here. I find it bothersome at the least to have the daughter of the man who murdered my father living under the same roof. But you, Mother, were the one who banished him."

"It's not true what you say about scarcely having thought about William or about my decision. I have kept it to myself, but I have rued the day ever since, Richard. It was the greatest mistake of my life. Through Serena, I feel as though I am being given a second chance. I am not a young woman, but I shall cherish my remaining days getting to know my other grand-daughter better."

"Well, Serena," my uncle said, "I suppose one of our first tasks is to find another governess. We can scarce have you caring for Oliver given—"

"Excuse me sire—uncle," I interrupted, "but that shall not be necessary. I love Oliver dearly, and frankly he is good company for me. I would be delighted, at least for the time being, to continue to look after him. That is, of course, if that meets with your approval."

"I'm afraid it would hardly be appropriate," he replied, "but all this can be decided in due time."

Maura, who was by now quite drunk, shot a loathsome glance at my uncle. "I think I would think twice, my dear, before I would continue to entrust the care of your precious son to the daughter of a murderer."

I had known that this would not be an easy evening, but I had not anticipated these truly venomous reactions. I fought to stem back the tears that welled in my eyes and dropped my head, determined that they should not see that their comments were cutting me to the quick. I was frustrated by the silence that I had to force upon myself. My instinct was to fight back, to rise to my father's defense, but I knew that to do so might eradicate my only chance to clear his name. I managed to keep the tears in check and finally raised my head, dry-eyed and chin held high.

My grandmother moved forward on her chair as if to rise. "You will excuse me, Justin." Her voice was stronger than ever. "I am compelled to say that my family not only disappoints me but disgusts me. I am ashamed of you all, and I wish to remind you that although you bear the titles, until my death Camberleigh and all its holdings rest with me. I would suggest that to avoid any unpleasantness you accord Serena the respect that she not only deserves but that I insist you afford her. Now I am tired. I have some thoughts about how we shall announce this to our friends and associates, but I shall explore that with you tomorrow. Richard, I would like you to accompany me to my room; there are several matters I want to discuss with you. Clarissa, try to remove that woebegone look from your face and accompany your mother to her quarters. Justin, you are welcome to stay—as a matter of fact, I would quite appreciate your presence here for the next few days."

I helped my grandmother to her feet. I could literally feel the exhaustion in her body, but her gaze was strong and direct as she put her arms out to embrace me. We held each other communicating through our silence. The room emptied quickly, save for Lord Barkham and myself.

"Serena, you are very pale. Come to the library and join me for a brandy."

"Why, so that you can gloat over your role in all this?" I snapped. A darkness spread over his eyes.

"You certainly cannot resent me for my helping to establish your rightful place in this house?"

"If it is thanks you want, it shall not come from me," I replied angrily.

"I didn't ask for gratitude."

I watched him carefully. Was it smugness that I saw in those eyes?

"You are very quiet, Miss Camberleigh." It was the first I had been addressed by my new title, and I regretted it had come from this man.

"I am wondering why you did it—for money, or did you enjoy making a complete fool of me, Lord Barkham."

"My dear, I am rarely pressed for words, but I cannot feign to understand what you are saying."

My voice quavered as I replied. "I think you understand far too well. I'm certain that what you were paid by my grandmother was infinitesimal compared to what you thought you would gain by establishing my true identity. With your stand in the county, you could never have loved, far less married, a governess. But if you could have confirmed my ancestry and convinced me to marry you, you would have assured control of the Mayfair and Camberleigh estates. I must admit it was a clever plan—one that might even have worked, if you had not shown your true nature on a prior occasion."

He rose slowly, his towering frame threatening in itself, and moved not toward me but away, his arms clenched at his sides. His voice was calm and deliberate. "I should not even dignify that statement with a reply, Serena, but I know that you have been under a great strain, and I shall assume that it has affected your mind—though I pray, for your sake, that it is temporary. I am astounded that I could have been so mistaken about you. Don't misunderstand. I know that you have a tempestuous side to you—it's the woman in you struggling to break away from that young girl. But I have never thought you to be irrational. You don't have the sense or the understanding or perhaps even the compassion to understand that what I did was because I love you—perhaps I should say I loved you, for I would have to be irrational myself to care so deeply for one who exhibits such a shallow demeanor."

I watched him walk to the door of the dining room in silence. He paused before leaving, turning back to face me.

"You have made a grave mistake, Serena. I didn't want your money. Only your love."

It was only when Giles and Molly entered to clear the table that I realized that I had sat there for a long time, watching the candles flicker away.

"Is there anything that I can get for you, miss?" Giles asked tentatively.

"No, thank you, Giles. I fear I lost track of time; it must be late. I feel exceedingly tired. Good evening."

"Good night, miss."

As I climbed the stairs, I was surprised by the lack of elation that I had so anticipated experiencing earlier in the evening. It was true that my relatives' reaction, although not unexpected, had been more despicable than I had assumed. But why was I so bereft of all emotion? I paused at the portrait of my grandfather and let my finger trace the lines of color that formed his face. In that moment I knew again that I would never truly be able to call this my home until I had lain to rest the ghosts that still haunted Camberleigh.

Chapter Thirteen

I was awakened the next morning by a knock at the door. It was Charlotte with my morning bathwater.

She entered regarding me oddly, I thought, and set to straightening the room. I was so preoccupied with giving Jaspar his morning affection, of which he was ever insistent, that it was moments before I noticed that her cheerful morning prattle was missing.

"Is there anything the matter, Charlotte?" I asked, rising and moving to where she was reorganizing my toilette.

"No, miss."

"Charlotte, I think we know each other better than that. I don't want to intrude, but you are simply not yourself this morning."

She paused and looked up at me.

"Now, I ain't gossipin', miss, but the kitchen is abuzz with your news."

"You know, then?" I replied, my eyes scanning her face for some reaction.

She nodded.

I reached out and took her hand.

"Forgive me, Charlotte, for not sharing this with you sooner, but for many reasons that are too complicated to go into, I simply could not."

A smile spread across her face, giving light to those dark, flashing eyes. "Oh, miss, I'm so happy for you. I knew all along t'was somethin' special 'bout you. I says to me mum, now there's a real lady."

I laughed, embracing her. "Forever my champion, dear Charlotte."

She flushed and drew away, embarrassed.

"You know, they been sayin' down below that now's you're a Camberleigh, you'll be puttin' on airs like the rest of 'em. But I says no—not my Miss Serena. There's nothin' mean or high an' mighty about her."

"I'm honored to have your faith in me."

I knew that if the servants were talking that they must also be carrying on about my parentage. The tragedy had occurred many years before, but there would inevitably be some who would remember.

As if sensing my train of thought, Charlotte added, "You know, miss, I never knew your father—only to see him from afar. Right handsome, he was. But me mum always said t'was a dark day when Mr. William an' his wife left here. He was a real gentleman, she said, just like his own father afore him."

Tears welled in my eyes.

"I should like to meet your mother someday, Charlotte. She must be a fine woman."

She nodded. "Don't believe none of that 'bout your father, miss. Says he was too gentle to harm a fly."

"It's true, Charlotte. And someday I shall prove it."

"How, miss?"

I pulled my wrap closer. "I don't know. But as God is my witness, I shall."

"Would ye be wantin' your breakfast here this mornin'?"

"I would, but I cannot. I must go to Oliver as quickly as possible, lest he should have heard the news from some other source."

"That boy's gonna be tickled to think you're a relative. He loves you like a sister already."

Charlotte left me to dress, taking along Jaspar, even though I desperately wanted him by my side on this day. I thought that until I had spoken to my grandmother it was presumptuous of me to suddenly give him the run of the house. There was a definite snap to the weather, and I chose my green traveling suit more for its warmth than its appropriateness.

As I crossed to the nursery, I heard loud voices from the floor below. One seemed to be that of my uncle, and I slowed to see if I might discern what was being said. As I did, the voice quieted. I longed to know the cause for this disturbance, but seeing Oliver took precedence this morning, so I moved quickly along.

The boy was up and dressed and had already begun his breakfast when I arrived. I saw that an additional service had been placed, so Charlotte must have communicated my wishes to the staff.

He was all smiles when he saw me.

"Good morning, Serena. I would have waited, had I known that you were to have a tray with me, but no one told me."

I smiled. "Oliver, it's just lovely to see you up and about."

"Oh, I am much better, truly. If I do my lessons well, might we go to the stables with Jaspar today?"

"That just might be arranged," I replied with a wink. I joined him at the small table by the window and relished the hot oatmeal and steaming tea on this chilly morn.

"Has your father or mother been in to see you this morning?"

He shook his head.

"I see. Well then I think the news—as I had hoped it might—can come from me."

"What news?" he asked, looking at me guardedly.

"Oliver, do you remember when I first came here and we met in the library and you asked if I was your new governess and I said no?"

He laughed. "But you really were."

"You see, when I arrived at Camberleigh, I brought with me a letter, written to our . . . to your grandmother by my mother. That letter was a way of introducing me to her ladyship."

"Like a reference?" he asked.

"Well, not quite. You see, the letter stated that I was the daughter of her ladyship's son, which would make me her granddaughter."

I could see from the furrows between his wide pale eyes that he was at a loss.

"Oliver, your grandmother, Cam—as I believe you often call her—had two sons, Richard, your father, and William, my father. Which means that your grandmother is also my grandmother."

All the insult I had endured from the family the prior evening was dissipated by the look of pure joy that spread over Oliver's face.

"Oh, Serena, is it really true?"

I nodded and opened my arms to welcome the delicate frame that had risen and sought my embrace. He buried his small head against my breast and I held him close, but remained silent as I allowed my revelation to sink in.

"What does that make us?" he asked.

"Cousins. First cousins."

"I have never had a cousin before," he mused. "Does Uncle Justin know?"

I nodded.

"Now you shall never leave me. Will you, Serena?"

"I shall try never to be too far away, dear Oliver," I replied, holding him to face me at arm's length. "Now, have you understood all that I have told you?"

"Yes, except why didn't you tell me straightaway that you were my cousin?"

It was a simple question, but one for which there was no simple answer.

"I couldn't, Oliver. And for the moment you shall have to believe that I never meant to deceive you. Someday I hope that I shall be able to share the whole story with you."

"I hope you might with all of us, Serena." I looked up, startled to see my uncle standing in the doorway.

"Father, isn't it wonderful," exclaimed Oliver. "Serena is a cousin! Why, that is almost like a sister."

"In this case, far from it," my uncle retorted. "Serena, I would like to see you in the library. My son, it seems, is heartily improved, and I expect that Master Thomas would like to begin making up for the time he has lost with his studies."

I nodded, angered as always by his abruptness with Oliver.

Confrontation with my uncle was scarcely appealing to me at present, but I knew it was inevitable, and so once Oliver and I had made plans to meet later on, I made my way downstairs.

He was stoking the fire as I entered the library, and appeared not to have heard me enter. I watched him for a moment, looking, I think, for some characteristic in his manner that I might find related to my own father. There was a distant, almost

impenetrable quality about this man, which I found disconcerting. I sensed that there was far more to him than appeared
on the surface, but I knew not how to break through his steely
veneer. Nonetheless, he was my uncle, and I did long to establish some familial response, even if I was always to be kept
at a polite distance.

"Don't just stand there, come over and sit by the fire."

Surprised by his acknowledgment of my presence, I did as
he bade. He took the seat opposite mine, and began to stare
intently at me as if searching for something. His gaze and his
silence caused me to stir awkwardly.

"I am making you nervous."

"A little," I admitted.

"It's simply that I don't know why I didn't see it before."

"See what?" I asked.

"The resemblance. You know, as often as I have looked at
you and thought what a striking figure of a woman you are, I
obviously saw only what I wanted to see. I spent a great deal
of time with my mother and later Barkham last evening trying
to satisfy myself as to whether or not you really could be who
you purport to be."

"And what was your conclusion?"

"Barkham and I do not agree—as you well know—on many
matters, but the man is clever and he is thorough. Not to
mention that he has great affection for Juliette. I have no doubt
that you are William's daughter. But what I started to say was
that the best proof—if one looks for it—is in you yourself.
There are expressions—fleeting ones—that are very like your
father's."

"I take that as a compliment, sire."

"It may prove awkward for us both, Serena, but I think it
would be best if henceforth you addressed me as uncle. It really
wouldn't do to have you call me sire in front of the staff, not
to mention our friends—though I admit the latter to be limited
in number."

I nodded.

"I have made arrangements to have your room changed.
You shall be closer to Clarissa. Since the two of you are almost
equal in age, I thought it might provide additional companionship for you both."

"But I like my present room . . . uncle. Truly. Unless it is an inconvenience, I should be very happy to remain there."

"And have it said that I am mistreating my niece? I'm afraid not. No, you shall be moved within the day."

I clenched my teeth. Obviously my own wishes were not to be respected. I would move, but I vowed not to allow myself to be manipulated any further by this man, who obviously cared more for his own image than for my personal comfort or wants.

"We will, of course, see to it that you have a proper wardrobe, since you shall be expected to dine with us and attend social gatherings on a regular basis. If you have any particular needs, you should address them to me personally. I would suggest that you keep your spaniel out of my wife's way. She is, as you know, easily distraught, and I should like to maintain as much equanimity here as is possible."

"Of course," I replied coolly. "Is there anything else?"

"Just one thing more. I think it best to tell you that I am less than enthusiastic about your presence here. I was very close to my father, Serena. I'm certain you are aware that Juliette is only my stepmother. And although she has treated me in every way like her own son, the fact is that I am not.

"Your father and I were never particularly close, though I suppose he told you that."

"I did not know of your existence—much less that of my grandmother or Camberleigh—until my mother's death," I answered tersely.

"I see. Odd that, since William, far more than I, was enamored with this place. Ah, well, I suppose he was simply trying to protect you. In any case, if you understand how much my father meant to me, you will understand how, after his death, I had only loathing for my stepbrother."

"You too were quick to judge him on what at best seems circumstantial evidence."

"Perhaps, but the facts were there. Even his own mother turned against him, though I must say that surprised me, for I had always thought that she doted on her precious William."

"And she has regretted her decision ever since," I added angrily.

"I fancy that these are more the musings of one who is nearing their end, Serena, than an actual change of heart—

guilt misgivings, shall we call them."

I had controlled myself till now, but the rage welling inside me was too great to contain any longer.

"You may think what you like, uncle," I snapped out my words. "But the only misgivings my grandmother has are borne from the knowledge that she made a drastic mistake eighteen years ago. My father was innocent, and had he lived, I have cause to know that he would have returned here to absolve himself of all guilt. My father knew that there was evil in this house. Moreover, I believe that he sensed or even knew who was really responsible for the murder of your father. If he was right, then none of us is safe here, except of course the person or persons who actually committed the crime."

My uncle rose. I thought for a moment that he was going to strike me, but instead he moved back to the fire.

"Serena, this is madness. Your father fled from this house with nary a trace—obviously the actions of a guilty man who could not face social disgrace and imprisonment. I think it admirable that you defend him, but you do so blindly. Your father was a murderer, and as long as you reside in this house none of us shall forget it."

I rose quickly. "You are a cruel man. And blind to all but your own selfish needs—even those of your own son. I swear to you that someday I shall prove my father's innocence, and when I do the guilt that you will suffer will be greater than any my father endured in his lifetime." I moved quickly to the door, placing my hand on the brass handle. "Oh, and don't worry," I added, "I shall not do anything to embarrass you or upset this *happy* household."

I slammed the door behind me and hurriedly crossed the entry hall to the staircase. It was not until I had started up the stairs that I saw Lord Barkham assisting my grandmother down.

"Serena dear, what is it?" my grandmother asked as I attempted to whisk past them. "You look so distraught."

Lord Barkham reached out to steady my hand, which was shaking.

"I am sorry that I have embarrassed you all by coming here," I blurted, the tears spilling onto my green velvet suit. "But one day I shall make you pay for your injustice."

I wrenched my arm free of Lord Barkham and, picking up

my skirts, dashed up the stairs, turning a deaf ear to the repeated calling of my name.

Wisdom told me to calm myself before returning to the nursery, but I knew that I could not permit myself to wallow in self-pity. Oliver needed me, and to closet myself in my room would be of benefit to no one.

I don't know why I was so startled to find Thomas in the nursery, since my uncle had made it very clear that Oliver was deemed well enough to resume his lessons.

"Well, Serena, what an unexpected pleasure," Thomas said upon my entry.

He looked particularly handsome today. His hair had been cut since I last saw him, and although there had been little sun on these autumn days his color was strong and his eyes bright.

"I didn't mean to interrupt, Thomas. Frankly, I had forgotten that Oliver would be commencing his studies again today."

He smiled. "Yours is never an interruption, Serena."

Oliver came forward with a leather-bound book that I had not seen before.

"Look, Serena. Mr. Masters said that we might commence to study the French language."

"Je suis tres heureuse pour toi," I replied.

"You surprise me, Serena. It appears that there is no end to your talents."

I laughed, pleased at his comment. "My father was a linguist, of sorts. I must admit that my knowledge is limited."

He frowned. "Ah, yes, your father. Also a man of surprises, which you therefore come by naturally . . . Miss Camberleigh."

I looked up quickly. It was difficult to discern what was reflected behind his eyes.

"Isn't it wonderful, Mr. Masters," piped up Oliver. "All this time Serena was really my cousin, and we never knew it."

"I think fascinating would be a more apt word, Oliver," he replied.

"Oliver, would you do me a favor?" I asked, tousling his locks.

He nodded.

"Would you go to the schoolroom and leave Mr. Masters and me alone for a few moments?"

I hated to expel him from the room, but Thomas and I needed

Evelyn Grey

to talk once again without the encumbrance of young ears. When we were left alone, however, I found myself somewhat at a loss of what or how to go about, when I pondered the delicacy of all there was to say and explain.

"You're very quiet, Miss Camberleigh," Thomas said, watching me closely.

"Don't call me that," I snapped.

"Ah, the lady of the manor does not want to be recognized as such?"

"I am not the lady of the manor, and I do not understand why you cannot simply continue to call me Serena."

"All right then, Serena, why did you not tell me?"

"I wanted to, Thomas, many times. I don't like deception, but in this case I had no choice," I replied.

"Ah, that's where you are wrong. You had the choice; you simply chose not to exercise it."

"That is not true, Thomas. But you—like the rest—obviously will believe what you choose to believe."

"I don't like being made a fool of, Serena."

I looked up and was shocked to see the anger in his eyes and the set of his mouth.

"Oh, Thomas, never was that my intent," I replied, distraught by his obvious displeasure.

He laughed. It was not a natural laugh. It was somehow sardonic, almost mocking.

"What did you think when I proposed to you? That I was just another smitten sot who had unknowingly overstepped his bounds? How you must have enjoyed it—'the honorable Earl of Camberleigh takes pleasure in announcing the impending marriage of his niece, Serena Miles Camberleigh, to Mr.—underlined Mr.—Masters'."

"Thomas, you are being unreasonable," I rebuked.

"Why, because I thought it was possible that we might be betrothed?"

"Don't be ridiculous. You know perfectly well why," I replied.

"Do I? Then prove it, Serena."

"How?"

"Marry me."

I looked up at him. The anger still lay in his eyes. But there

350

was a new quality to his expression. Was it hurt? Defiance? No, it was something different. Challenge, perhaps.

"Thomas, you know I can't," I said slowly. "Not now."

There was that mocking laugh again.

"Of course not. You are a Camberleigh. And as such you can only marry one of your own breeding. Well, Barkham seems to have an eye for you, and now that he knows of your potential inheritance, I am certain that he will have your family's blessing to court you right into bed."

Had I been nearer to him, I would have slapped him. I knew that he was hurt and that much of what he was saying was of nothing more than blind retaliation, but I could not abide his inferences.

"Lord Barkham is nothing to me," I said angrily. "Moreover, you insult me by suggesting some sort of merger. I thought we were friends, Thomas, and when I need that most, you apparently have deserted me. I am saying no to your offer of marriage not because I do not care for you but because I need time. Time to adjust, time to discover myself, and time to resolve some things which, shall we say, are part of history here. And now if you will excuse me, I should like to return to my room."

I rose from where I had sat by the window and moved toward the door, only to be blocked by Thomas's arm.

"I have wronged my princess," he said quietly. "Serena, never was that my intent. I have been foolish, but then, in matters of the heart the great writers say that is permissible. I vow not to press you. I only ask that you keep in your mind an awareness of my fondness for you and consider my proposal—perhaps not immediately, but think on it well."

There were many things I wanted to say, but the morning had drained me almost totally. Then Thomas's arms were suddenly about me. My mind was preoccupied, but I acquiesced to the strength of his embrace. I needed a friend, and if he was willing to be that for the time, I was needful of his caring.

Back in my room, I removed my boots and lay down on my bed. I don't think that I have ever experienced such complete exhaustion. I had lain there for perhaps an hour when there was a knock at my door. Whether it was fatigue or the need for privacy, I did not know, but I did not respond. When my name was called out repeatedly, I recognized the voice of Lord Barkham. As disconsolate as I felt, I remained silent. The last thing I wanted was to have my sanctuary invaded by the man whose other intrusions had caused me so much restlessness and so many sleepless nights.

"Serena, open the door. I must speak with you."

"Go away," I pleaded.

"Not until you have heard me out."

I rose and dragged myself wearily to the door, opening it only a crack. "Well?"

He pushed against the door, causing me to stumble back into the room.

"I wonder what my grandmother would think of you if she could see you for what you really are," I seethed.

Instead of exhibiting any embarrassment, he laughed.

"So you think it is amusing," I charged.

"What is amusing, Serena, is you trying to be high-handed in your bare feet."

"I was not expecting company," I snapped back. "Now, what is it you want?"

"Many things," he replied smoothly. "But for now just to speak with you."

"You will do me the kindness of saying what you feel that you must and then leave."

"What went on between you and Richard earlier this morning?" he asked, taking a seat, which I had not offered.

"I don't see that it is any of your business," I replied.

"Ah, but it is. Your grandmother has entrusted your care to me. And when I see you as upset as you were on the stairs, I feel that a lot must have been said to upset you."

"My grandmother has *what?*" I exclaimed.

"She has simply asked that I keep an eye out for you."

"I can't imagine what she was thinking of," I said sharply, "but I shall change that immediately."

A shadow passed across his eyes. "I wouldn't if I were you. That is, if you care at all—and I believe you do—for her. She is not ill, but she is also not strong. I'm certain she has not told you that she suffered several strokes a year or so ago."

I shook my head.

"They were small ones," he continued, "but any further

352

undue strain might prove harmful."

"Are you saying that my presence here has been bad for her health?" I asked querulously.

"To the contrary. I haven't seen so much life in Cam in years," he replied. "No, I was referring to all the awful things going on around here. Oliver's illness—which is confounding us all—the murder of that poor girl, and of course Maura."

"Maura?" I asked, my eyes meeting his.

"Surely you are aware of the seriousness of her condition?"

"I admit that she is odd, but I have supposed that it must be attributable to drink."

"It is far more serious than that. And while it is not the only reason for Richard's behavior, it is certainly a contributing factor. She has not been a wife to him for years, and though I disagree with him strongly on many issues, in this case I give the devil his due. He has stuck by her. Other men would have abandoned her years ago."

"But she is his wife," I reminded him.

"And because of that he must do penance for the rest of his days?"

"It is a matter of principle and duty," I retorted.

"You *are* naïve, my dear."

"I forgot, Lord Barkham, that you would not understand such traits."

He was silent for a moment.

"Is that all?" I asked.

"No. The point of all this is that your grandmother and I are concerned about you. Until we discover who is behind these maniacal deeds, I want you to continue to be very cautious. Stay close to the house, do not leave it unaccompanied, and lock your door when you are here alone."

I wanted to say that he was a fine one to give me warnings about wandering about alone, but I held my tongue.

"Jaspar will watch over me, though I believe that whatever is going on, I am not in real danger, since these misdeeds all began prior to my arrival."

"That may be so, but nevertheless please be careful. If you have any problems, I suggest you come to me—for the reasons I have mentioned."

The last thing I wanted was to have Lord Barkham as my

overseer. However, I agreed that my grandmother should be spared as much further worry as possible.

"There will be no need, but you have made your point," I replied, moving toward the door. He rose and followed me. "You could do me one small favor," I said, watching for his reaction.

"Yes?"

"My uncle seems determined that I should be moved to another room, near Clarissa. I am quite comfortable here, and I should like to remain. Perhaps you could suggest that it would be less disruptive on everyone if I were to stay right here."

"That shouldn't be too difficult."

"Thank you," I offered grudgingly.

"A pleasure to be of service, mademoiselle," he replied, bowing slightly. He laughed again. "You really should put your boots on, Serena. You look quite the gypsy with your hair flowing—and barefoot."

I slammed the door behind him, humiliated by the laughter that continued as he moved down the hall.

If Lord Barkham hoped I would turn to him, I thought as I crawled back into bed, he was sorely mistaken. Yet I could not help but admit that we did share one thing in common— a sincere concern for my grandmother. It confounded me that she placed so much trust in him. Few others seemed to share her opinion.

I was distressed by my conversation with Thomas. I knew that I had hurt him by not sharing my past with him, but I had not expected him to be so spiteful. Perhaps he was right. The simplest way out of this whole affair might be to accept his proposal. We were quite compatible, and it would offer a certain kind of protection. His station as a tutor didn't make any difference to me. I had grown up with so little in terms of material wealth that I would never miss the fineries of life. Strangely, the only disturbing thought about Thomas was a certain assumptiveness in his attitude toward me that had been there from almost the day of my arrival. I thought now that I had probably been so anxious for a friend that I hadn't realized the aggressiveness of his pursuit.

Admittedly, I was also flattered. Thomas was a good-looking man, and I did not doubt that many women my age would be taken by his advances. But it was not the time for me to make a commitment, and despite his vow not to pressure me, the undercurrents of presumptuousness on his part I did not like.

Molly brought me a luncheon tray about noon. I caught her watching me furtively and supposed she was looking for some outward sign of my transition from Serena Miles to Serena Miles Camberleigh. Of course there was none, and she left, I believe, almost disappointed by our encounter.

I had meant only to rest for an hour or so and was dismayed to find that when I awoke it was dark outside. Charlotte returned with Jaspar, informing me that Lord Barkham had taken Oliver for a brief outing and encouraged me to continue to rest until dinnertime.

I longed to change into something more suitable, but realized that other than my green velvet traveling costume and the gray velvet that Maura had insisted be made for me, I had naught else that was warm enough for these chilly evenings. I made a mental note to send a letter to Anne via Lord Barkham asking her, if she had the inclination, to provide some costumes that would see me through the winter.

Charlotte assisted me with my hair, and I set out shortly thereafter for the dining room. At the landing above the stairs, who did I run into but Clarissa.

"How are you this evening, Clarissa?" I asked. While we would never be fast friends, I would at least endeavor to be civil.

"What concern is it of yours?" she lashed back.

"None, really," I retorted calmly. "I was simply trying to be pleasant. I should like to try and be friends."

For a moment I thought that I had reached her, for she looked up at me almost thoughtfully.

"You look very pretty this evening," I continued. That was the truth. She wore a deep-blue taffeta gown, far too frilly and voluminous for my taste, but it suited her perfectly.

"I suppose now that we are cousins, you think I should treat you as my equal," she said, raising her chin. "Well, I shan't. I am appalled that my grandmother would even allow you into this house. After all, your father did murder her husband. But she is old, and father says she must be humored, so I expect you are to remain. However, I want you to know, Serena, that I shall not have your presence here ruin my season. It is already late in commencing, what with this dreary nonsense with the constable, and *you* shall not delay it further or cause a scandal to mar my presentation. Do you understand?"

What I found difficult to understand was how we could share bonds of blood and be so incredibly different.

"Someday, Clarissa, you shall be remorseful, I hope, about what you have just said. Until then, let me assure you that I shall do as little as I possibly can to intrude upon you in any way."

Hearing voices in the dining room, I moved down the stairs ahead of Clarissa. I joined my grandmother and Lord Barkham, who were already seated.

"I apologize if I am late, grandmother," I said, moving to embrace her.

"Not at all, my dear. Justin and I were just having a little chat."

She looked up to see Clarissa enter the room. "And there is my other granddaughter. She looks lovely tonight, doesn't she, Justin?"

"Yes she does, except for that pout," he replied.

"I am not pouting," Clarissa said in what was almost a shout.

"Well, then your mouth has taken on an unbecoming character," he retorted.

My uncle entered with Maura on his arm. I could not help but think back to Lord Barkham's conversation with me earlier. This hardly looked like a woman who was physically unwell or mentally disturbed. She was resplendent in a gown of black faille, her hair piled high, an exquisite diamond pendant at her neck. I again found it uncanny that at one moment she could seem dazed, incoherent, almost without control, and the next appear almost imperial in her containment. Lord Barkham sympathized with my uncle on the plight of my aunt, but I wondered if that were simply not a defense—one man to another.

"Oliver missed you this afternoon, Serena," Lord Barkham commented as Giles seated me opposite him.

I flushed. I did not want my uncle to think that my intention to continue to oversee him was not sincere.

"I do apologize. I fear that I slept far longer than I had intended."

He smiled. "No need for apology. He simply is so taken with the idea of your being his cousin that he is longing to spend more time with you."

"How did you find him, Justin?" my grandmother asked.

"Much improved. I must say, however, that I think Mr. Masters is a bit too demanding of him at times."

"Masters lives up to his name—he is a real taskmaster. Which is what I like about him," my uncle interjected.

"Frankly, I find him an odd chap, Richard. Bright, no doubt, but after all, Oliver is but a child." This from Lord Barkham.

"When you have one of your own, Barkham, you are welcome to raise him as you wish. I find Masters a perfectly suitable tutor," concluded my uncle.

"And you, Serena . . . what do you think?" Lord Barkham asked.

I flushed, for there was a definite suggestiveness to his tone.

"I agree with my uncle," I murmured.

"Well, well. We've progressed quickly into familial references, have we not," my aunt said in a defiant tone. "I suppose next you shall be calling me 'aunt'?"

"Not if it would upset you," I added softly.

"Of course Serena shall call you 'aunt'," my grandmother insisted.

"I rather prefer 'Maura.' That way I do not have to be constantly reminded of this unfortunate relationship."

I sensed my grandmother stifling a comment. Knowing that it would simply serve to encourage further vindictiveness, she let the matter rest.

The first course had been served, and I was pleased to see that it was sole, which had been baked to perfection. Fish was scarce in this part of England, quite in contrast to my home on the coast, where the big boats brought in large catches almost daily.

"You know, Serena, we must start thinking about a ball to introduce you to our friends," my grandmother commented.

"That should not be necessary, grandmother," I quickly said before any of the others could start in on this volatile topic. "I have met many of your acquaintances already."

"Yes, but that was as Serena Miles. You are not going to rob me of the pleasure of introducing you as my new granddaughter."

Maura laughed. "Now that should be truly amazing. How, pray tell, Juliette, do you intend to make the transition? What shall you say? 'Here is my granddaughter, who we originally pawned off as the governess. Clever little joke, wasn't it?' Or better yet, 'Here is my granddaughter. I believe you knew her father. He killed my husband'."

Lord Barkham slammed his napkin down onto the table.

"Richard, if your wife cannot be civil, I suggest you remove her from this table."

This time even my uncle appeared aghast by her outburst.

"Serena," said my uncle, "I apologize for Maura. It is none of Barkham's business, but he is right. The least we can do is maintain *some* level of decorum."

Clarissa, who had been oddly quiet, suddenly burst into tears.

"Good Lord, what now," Lord Barkham asked in an irritated tone and gazing up at the ceiling.

"I think what you are doing is hateful, Grandmother," she sobbed. "This is to be my season, and it shall be ruined if you give her a ball. I shall be the laughingstock of London. You simply cannot be so cruel."

"You, silly girl, are the one who is being cruel," my grandmother replied. "I have half a mind not to permit you to go to London at all. With that heedless tongue, you would likely only attract some dull-witted fop or some clever fortune hunter who would discard you as soon as he had gotten all he could from you."

Clarissa's sobbing increased. "Mama, you are not going to let her do this, are you?"

"Of course not," Maura replied firmly. "You shall have your season."

"I should remind you, Maura," my grandmother pressed on, "that the coffers might be empty, should I intend it."

"Richard, are you going to stand for this?" Maura gasped.

My uncle looked too bored or pained to argue.

I had remained silent during this interchange, but felt I could do so no longer. "Truly, Grandmother, I do not wish to have a ball. I appreciate your thoughtfulness, but it would be far simpler if Clarissa were allowed to have her season without any intrusion on my part."

"But Serena dear, you should meet some nice people your own age. We don't want to deprive all those eligible young men of your beauty."

I flushed as Lord Barkham's eyes met mine.

"Not now, Grandmother," I pleaded. "I should truly prefer to remain here and spend more time with you and learn more of Camberleigh. I know very little of it, really."

"You are so insistent, I can scarce refuse. But I shall do so only if you promise me that in the spring I be permitted my fancy with you."

I nodded. "Of course."

With the threat of my encroachment on her season put to rest, Clarissa ceased to look like an orphaned puppy and began chatting about the upcoming festivities. I had to admit that I longed to travel to London myself one day, but the answers to my many questions lay not on distant shores but right here at Camberleigh.

A delightful venison was served for the main course, and I realized that my sleep and light luncheon had made me hungry. Maura, predictably, was indulging herself with more wine than she should, which would always worrisome, for one never knew at what point she would completely lose control. My uncle and Lord Barkham were having a heated conversation on the issue of taxation. I wished that I understood more of what they were discussing. Again I found my uncle's opinion to be based solely on monetary gain. Lord Barkham, on the other hand, appeared to be compassionate about the farmers, though my own experience with him made me suspect that he might have some hidden ulterior motive.

"You've been very quiet, Serena," Lord Barkham noted.

"I'm afraid I simply have nothing to offer to this conversation."

"This is none of her affair, Barkham," my uncle grumbled.

"I disagree. After all, she is a Camberleigh and she should have some idea of how this place is run."

Maura laughed. "Isn't it wonderful, Richard. Now you can avail yourself of your little niece."

"Keep quiet, Maura," my uncle growled.

"I shall be going on a tour of the estates tomorrow, Serena. Why don't you join me?" Lord Barkham offered.

"I shall be with Oliver."

"We'll take Oliver with us. It would do him good to get out of this house for a while."

"Do go, Serena dear," my grandmother encouraged. "You have been cooped up here far too long, and I believe you will find it quite interesting."

I was about to protest, but my grandmother seemed so anxious for me to go that I agreed.

"You know, if I were able I should like to join you," she continued. "When I was younger, Charles and I used to visit regularly with the tenants. I regret that I did not make more of an effort since his death."

"They've missed you, Juliette," Lord Barkham responded warmly. "Often you are asked about when I am on tour of the farms, even those on the Mayfair line."

"Well, now Serena can go in my stead," she replied.

Maura threw her hands up in an exaggerated gesture.

"That should set tongues wagging. 'Murderer's daughter returns to oversee estates.' I shouldn't take this quite so calmly if I were you, Richard dear."

"Maura—" I interrupted my uncle's reply. "There is hardly anything to be agitated about, Maura. I have no knowledge of farming and certainly not the capability to become involved in the affairs of Camberleigh. On the other hand, I have nothing to be ashamed of. I should be pleased to join you tomorrow, Lord Barkham."

He looked genuinely pleased. I didn't want to give him the satisfaction of thinking that he had won me over. However, I knew that I could not hide from whatever gossip was bound to start once my presence here became public knowledge.

A crash at the other end of the table sent all eyes to focus on Maura. She was struggling to rise from her chair, and had knocked over her wineglass in the process.

"Sit down," my uncle commanded.

"I will not," she shot back. "You are a bigger fool than I thought you were. If you think I'm going to permit this strumpet to ruin everything, you are sorely mistaken. I have put up with your demands and this mausoleum for years. I'm not going to lose it all now."

My uncle rose and grasped her arm, attempting to lead her

from the room. I had never seen him look worse. His face—
which usually reflected an anger that was dangerously close to
the surface—was pale. There was a desolate look to his eyes.
For the second time since I had arrived at Camberleigh, I felt
real sympathy for this man.

Maura struggled to be free of his grasp, and Lord Barkham,
realizing that she had lapsed into one of her rages, leapt to
assist.

Clarissa watched until her mother had been removed, kicking and screaming, from the room.

"This is all your fault, Serena," Clarissa cried out at me.
"You should never have come here. You have ruined everything." She left my grandmother's demands for civility un-
heeded and ran from the room.

I felt genuinely sick to my stomach. Perhaps what Clarissa
had said was true—that I never should have come to Camberleigh.

"Serena dear, please do not take any of this to heart."

"How can I not, Grandmother? I seem to have brought
nothing but grief and bitterness to your home."

"Serena, this is your home as well. Clarissa does not mean
half of what she says. I won't forgive her her selfishness, but
I have learned not to be too critical about her lack of sensitivity. I have always been hopeful that one day she might meet some
man of means who might take her away from here. I have not
been company for her, and goodness knows her mother is more
of a detriment than anything else."

"Maura seemed fine earlier this evening," I recalled, again
puzzled by her rapid swings of behavior.

"I blame myself for that as well," my grandmother replied
wearily. I could not fathom why she would feel any guilt about
Maura's condition. "Those years after Charles's death, I simply
retreated. We used to have gala balls here, there were always
many friends about. But I simply could not face it after I lost
Charles. And then, of course, I also grieved for your father.
Maura was a young woman then, and I did not spend the time
with her that I might. She was always high, strung—a family
trait, I fear—but perhaps if I had shown more interest in her
she might have grown stronger over the years."

It was another perspective, but something in me refused to

have sympathy for a woman who was so distant, almost cruel with her own son.

"You must be tired, Grandmother," I said, noting her hand trembling slightly. "May I help you to your room?"

She agreed, and we left the room. We mounted the stairs slowly, the eyes of the ancestral lords of Camberleigh watching our progress up toward our rooms.

The dinner had proved wearing on me as well. It was difficult to be made to feel unwelcome in one's own home. I had been surrounded by such love as a child that discord of any sort was new to me. Were it not for my grandmother and a responsibility I felt toward Oliver, I think that I would have left Camberleigh weeks before. On the other hand, the viciousness that I was encountering served in a way to spur me on with what had now become a mission—to clear my father's name.

Chapter Fourteen

I WAS still in bed when Charlotte arrived the next morning. "Lord Barkham says I'm to get ye up an' about real quick, 'cause you're going about in the carriage," she said, bustling into the room.

I remembered that I had agreed to go on a tour of the estates, but I resented his sending Charlotte to order me about.

"You know, miss, I think Lord Barkham's sweet on ye. He told me to be sure you had your cloak an' warm gloves an' a bonnet to keep you from the cold."

"He just doesn't want a complaining woman with him on the journey," I replied, moving swiftly to bathe.

"No, miss. I can tell. It's a look he gets when he talks. He's smitten, he is."

"Well, it is of no import to me, Charlotte. That man is not a gentleman. He is conceited and arrogant."

She commenced to fix my hair while I ate a quick breakfast. "Oh, no, miss. He's a fine figure of a man. An' kindly, too. Even me mum says so. An' he's been real nice with me Robbie. You should give him a chance, miss."

"Never," I retorted.

Charlotte winked at me in the mirror. "Still got your eye on our Mr. Masters, eh?"

"Frankly, Charlotte, I don't have my eye on anyone. There are far more important things on my mind."

"I'm sorry, miss. A bit of the romantic, I am. You bein'

young and such a beauty, seems only natural that you should be courted by the likes of Lord Barkham. But I won't be meddlin', so you jest get that frown off that lovely face."

I reached out and took Charlotte's hand.

"You aren't meddling, Charlotte. I just would prefer not to discuss this at present."

She squeezed my hand in response. Jaspar rose and nuzzled her affectionately.

"Oh, Charlotte, will it be all right if Jaspar stays with Robbie all day? I have no idea when we will return."

"I forgot to tell you, miss. Lord Barkham says the little feller's to go along with you. Thought he'd be good company for both ye an' Master Oliver."

I had to admit I was pleased. It had been some time since Jaspar and I had been able to spend a full day together. Oliver, I knew, would delight in it as much as I.

"You're to meet Lord Barkham in the front drive. He was to fetch Master Oliver. An' ye better get goin', or he'll be stormin' up here after you."

Jaspar bounded out into the hall and down the stairs before I could stop him. I went running after him and reached the top of the staircase just as I saw him collide with Maura, who was stepping into the entrance hall and talking to Mrs. Scoapes. I stopped abruptly as I saw Maura swoop down, pick Jaspar up, and literally throw him against the bottom of the staircase. I screamed in horror and flew down the stairs as I heard Jaspar yelp in pain. Maura was advancing toward him, and I threw my body down over him, taking the thrust of her boot on my shoulder. I stiffened against the impending next blow, which never came.

"What in God's name is going on here?" Lord Barkham demanded, yanking Maura away from me.

I struggled to my knees, pulling Jaspar, who whimpered slightly, toward me.

"She threw Jaspar against the stairs," I gasped, my hands examining him to see if I could discover any injury.

"That mongrel attacked me. He charged at me down the stairs," Maura accused, still held by Lord Barkham.

"That's a lie and you know it, Maura," I said angrily.

"Is he hurt, Serena?" Lord Barkham asked.

"His lip is bleeding; his tooth must have cut it. I'm certain he'll be badly bruised, but I don't think anything is broken."

"How dare you take her side, Justin?"

Lord Barkham released Maura and helped me to my feet.

"Are you ready?"

I nodded, relieved that Jaspar was on all fours and, though shaken, none the worse for his experience.

"You know, Lady Camberleigh, I think it might be a bit soon for Oliver to be traipsing about the countryside," Mrs. Scoapes announced.

"If anything, Mrs. Scoapes, the boy needs some fresh air. He'll be in good hands."

"Hardly," Maura muttered. "Let him go, but mark my words, if he has one of his spells again I shall take no responsibility. You can deal with Richard on that."

Oliver, already ensconced in the carriage, beamed when he saw Jaspar. Lord Barkham scooped him up and placed him gently next to the boy.

"Be gentle with him, Oliver," I cautioned. "He has just had a slight accident on the stairs."

I started to climb into the coach myself, but Lord Barkham restrained my arm.

"If you wouldn't be too chilly, Serena, I would like you to ride up front with me. You really will see more of the land that way, and I can answer any questions you might have."

Oliver was obviously well occupied with Jaspar, and it did seem a bit foolish to protest, since the intent of the journey was to acquaint me with the countryside.

The road leading to Camberleigh took on new dimensions at this time of year. The deciduous trees were now barren, their limbs making architectural sweeps against the sky. The landscape was still verdant, however, due to the abundance of formal evergreen planting. The lawns glistened as the morning sun touched the blades of grass still frosted from the night air.

"Are you cold, Serena?"

I shook my head. "No, I was just thinking how beautiful Camberleigh is even at this time of year."

"Do you feel a part of it now?"

"A part of me does, I suppose. But you must understand that until six months ago I knew nothing of Camberleigh, my grandmother, my family—such as it is," I responded truthfully.

"It hasn't been easy, I know."

"Yes. You would," I answered angrily.

"Serena, please let us not argue. Whatever animosity you harbor against me, I beg you to put it aside today, if only for Oliver's sake. The boy has little enough affection in his life. Let us not burden him with our affairs."

"We have no *affairs*, Lord Barkham. But I agree about Oliver. He's been through so much. Have you heard anything further from the constable?"

"Only that he is still working on the case."

"How is Anne? I've missed her."

"I intend to bring her to Camberleigh tomorrow. I'm certain she is longing to see you. Particularly since the announcement of your birthright."

I remained silent, not willing to share with him that Anne had been a confidante for some time. As we moved out into the farming areas, I was struck once again by the expanse of the landscape.

"There is something that I have never quite understood, Lord Barkham," I commented, watching the agility with which he handled the horses.

"What is that, Serena?" he replied softly.

"You and my uncle are obviously at odds on the issue of taxation."

"A polite way of putting it," he replied, "but proceed."

"If you levied just a small tax, let us say, would that not assist both the estate and still not be overly burdensome to the farmers?"

He laughed. "I didn't think that you were a lady of compromise, my dear."

"I am not."

"Good. For in this instance I do not think one can afford to be. The concept of tenancy, Serena, dates back many years. At its best it is a symbiotic relationship between owner and tenant. The land, to be productive, obviously needs to be farmed. The owner receives the profits of that farming, while the farmer receives an opportunity to use his skills and labors for shelter, food, the basic needs of him and his family. To institute taxation would place an excessive burden on most of these people. It would have to come from someplace—food, clothing, or even the meager savings that some who are the most skillful are able to garner."

"Why has Lord Kelston been successful with it?"

"It is too early to tell. I admit he has had a profitable year, but it has not been long enough to judge. Last winter was not a difficult one. I question whether many of the farmers and their families could survive a really rigorous winter if they do not have proper funds."

I was confused, for Robin, although perhaps something of a dilettante, did not seem a heartless sort. Yet, having been raised in a family where every penny counted, I could appreciate the plight of the farmers. We had turned off the main road and were now passing fields which lay fallow during the winter months. Sheep grazed along the hillside, and I called down to Oliver to be certain that he did not miss the view.

"This is the Barnstable tract," Lord Barkham noted, "you will see their home over the rise."

I was surprised by the amount of land that one man was responsible for.

"Does he turn this all himself?"

"Elijah's fortunate. He has three stout sons to help him. Far better off than old Durkin over on the Mayfair side."

"Why?"

He laughed. "Durkin's been aiming for a son for years. And for all his labors he's got eleven daughters. The other farmers feel sorry for him, but personally I think the old boy's just using his aim for a son as a camouflage for his lust."

I blushed.

He laughed again, obviously amused by my embarrassment.

As we approached the farm, a large-boned buxom woman emerged carrying a small baby in her arms. She waved a welcome. Lord Barkham pulled the carriage to a stop and swung down to greet the woman he had called Mary.

"Lord Barkham, what a pleasure it is to be seein' ye round our way," she said loudly in welcome.

Oliver had scrambled out of the carriage, Jaspar leaping and barking behind him.

"An' Master Oliver. My, how ye've grown. An' who's this little fellow?"

"I do apologize," I called out. "He's harmless, but I fear a bit rambunctious."

She bounced the baby a moment. Lord Barkham turned back to the carriage, offering me his hand. The heel of my boot caught on the bottom edge of the door as I was climbing down, which propelled me forward against Lord Barkham. The force of my fall sent him sprawling backward, my body splayed over his. Jaspar bounded over, looking at us both to ensure that we were all right.

Mary rushed over. "Are you all right, miss?"

"I'm fine," I replied, attempting to disentangle myself from my cloak in order to rise.

"Mary, let me present you to Serena Miles Camberleigh, her ladyship's granddaughter," Lord Barkham said as we both struggled to our feet.

Seeing her confusion, I added, "I am the daughter of her son William, and only recently arrived here at Camberleigh." I extended my hand and she drew hers forward, placing it tentatively in mine.

"Well, I'm pleased to be makin' your acquaintance, Miss Camberleigh," she said, smiling broadly.

If she knew of the circumstances surrounding my father's disappearance, she hid it well.

"A beauty she is now, isn't she, Lord Barkham?" she chided, winking at him. "I see you've lost no time in squiring her about."

"Lord Barkham is simply acquainting me with the land and farms of Camberleigh," I put in.

"Well then, come in an' have a spot of tea."

Before I could protest, Lord Barkham had agreed and had fetched a large basket from the back of the carriage.

"I hope you'll join us for some luncheon, Mary," he said as we followed her into the house. "Knowing Cook, she probably has filled this to the brim."

When we entered the small-frame bungalow, I was impressed by both the sparseness and cleanliness of the large room that greeted us. Mary poured from an already brewing pot of tea while Lord Barkham unpacked the basket, which

CAMBERLEIGH

had been stocked with enough capons, fruits, cheeses and scones for twenty people. Mary's eyes widened when she spied the hoard.

"Where are Elijah and the boys?" Lord Barkham asked, handing a bit of meat down to Jaspar, who was mesmerized by the spread.

"They be out tendin' to the cows. We lost a few last week, an' he's a bit troubled about a virus."

"Well, the baby certainly seems much improved since my last visit."

"Thanks to your kind doin's. That was a blessin' your sending the doctor round. I don't think I would have her here today if ye hadn't. I know she be needin' medicine, but the crop didn't yield like we hoped."

We finished our lunch. I was surprised by how much I had eaten, but then, I was very relaxed in this atmosphere. I admit that I was puzzled by the display of genuine friendliness between Lord Barkham and Mary. He not only appeared to be thoroughly knowledgeable about each farm and its particular problems, but he seemed to have an almost intimate relationship with the families. This man was obviously not one man but many men. Unfortunately, prior to today he had chosen to show to me only his dark side. For a fleeting moment I wondered what might have happened if I had never seen it.

We left shortly, Lord Barkham eager to visit as many of the tenants as possible. As we rode through the countryside, I was overwhelmed both by the amount of land and the number of families on the Camberleigh estates. And we had gotten nowhere near the boundary with Mayfair.

I recalled that Charlotte had told me that her mother lived in the area, and I asked Lord Barkham if we might not pay her a brief visit.

The cottage was some distance from our last stop, and we rode along in silence. Oliver and Jaspar, both fatigued by their outing, had drifted off to sleep in the rear of the carriage.

As we topped a small rise, there in a valley below lay a cluster of stone houses, each with a heavily thatched roof.

"Charlotte's mother lives down there," Lord Barkham said. "This area is called Peacable," he continued, gesturing. "It lies directly between Camberleigh and Mayfair."

369

"It's almost like a small village."

"In a way it is. Your grandfather and my father decided that as long as these estates existed under the present auspices, that the people who had worked for them should always have a home here."

"How unusual."

"But very wise. Of course, Richard does not concur."

"Why? After all, he cannot deny these people shelter after they have been in service—some, I would assume, for years."

"Why? Money, of course."

My uncle did seem to have a preoccupation with profits.

"Justin—" I began.

"What have I done to deserve this?" he queried. I looked up at him confusedly. "You called me Justin. And before you tell me that it simply slipped out, I must tell you that as a Camberleigh, it is a bit absurd to have you continually refer to me as Lord Barkham. It is a name, Serena, nothing more. Enough of that. What were you going to ask me?"

I lowered my voice so Oliver could not hear. "Did my uncle stand to benefit in any way from my grandfather's death?"

His eyes met mine. "Do you have cause to suspect him?" His voice was also soft.

I shook my head. "It's nothing tangible, really. But I have gone over and over it in my own mind trying to come up with some clue, attribute some motive."

"I don't think Richard is the place to look, Serena. I grant you, he is an odd sort. And I have no respect for the way he has treated Oliver at times. But a murderer? I think not."

"You haven't answered my question."

"Both Richard and your father would have inherited equally upon your grandfather's death. Of course, the bulk of the estate lies with Cam."

I thought for a moment.

"If my grandfather had simply died, and both my father and my uncle had remained here, which would have inherited the title?"

"Richard, of course, as he was the first born," he replied.

I had thought that power, not money, might have been the issue, but if Richard was the natural successor, there would have been no cause.

CAMBERLEIGH

Barkham led the horses down into the valley. "There was one thing, however," he said.

"What was that?"

"I remember overhearing my father and your grandfather talking one day, perhaps six months before the old Earl's death. Your grandfather said that he had always wished that William, your father, was the elder, as he believed that William cared more deeply about the land than Richard did. My father agreed, and he said that it was a strange thing, because William had always been a strong scholar—more the type to become a man of the courts than of the land. Anyway, my father suggested that this be discussed with both sons. I remember him saying that he actually thought Richard might be happy to be relieved of the responsibility of the estates."

"And did this discussion take place? Was this ever proposed to Richard?" I asked.

He shook his head. "I don't know."

It would help to know if that conversation ever transpired. If it had, perhaps it might have been discovered that Richard was not as amenable to stepping aside as Justin's father had thought. But could he have been so angered that he would have murdered his own father?

As we drew to a stop in front of one of the houses, Justin cautioned, "You'll have to speak up with Mrs. Nexter. She doesn't hear very well."

Oliver and Jaspar had awakened, and Oliver begged to explore the village while we paid our visit.

Age had not diminished the woman's resemblance to Charlotte. The dark curls were gray and the rosy cheeks had been lined by time, but the toothy smile and light in the eyes were one and the same with Charlotte's. She did not rise to greet us, and I realized that time had also seeped the limberness from her bones.

She seemed alarmed by the sight of Lord Barkham, but he went to her and quickly assured her that Charlotte and Robbie were well.

"Thank the good Lord. When I be seein' ye there, I thought for sure that somethin' had happened to them. Now who's the pretty there, don't tell me there's gonna be a mistress at the house."

I stepped forward.

"This is Serena. Serena Miles Camberleigh."

Her face clouded, her mind obviously trying to sort through names and faces that were new since she had tended to the house.

"There's a Serena my girl sees, too. You ain't she, are ye?"

I smiled. "Yes, I am, and she watches over me like a mother hen. Charlotte has been a good friend to me these past months."

"I didn't hear yer full name, dear."

"It's Serena Miles Camberleigh."

She shook her head again.

"You'll be pardonin' me, miss, for not knowin' ye. Me girl just calls ye Miss Serena. I didn't know you was a Camberleigh."

I reached out and took her hand. "Few people did until recently. My father was William Camberleigh."

Her head jerked back almost as if she had been struck.

"Justin, fetch me a glass of water, please. I seem to have frightened her."

He held it as she sipped it slowly, her eyes not leaving my face the entire time. She grasped my hand tightly. "'Tis like watchin' the years melt away afore me very eyes."

"You knew my father, then," I said eagerly.

"An' your mum. Her personal maid I was, after she an' your father was married. T'weren't a finer couple in all the land. Your mother, is she here with ye?"

I shook my head. "She died earlier this year."

"I knew somethin' had happened. Not a word from her I've had in almost a year. But e'en after your poor father died, she always sent me a letter on me birthday an' for Christmas."

"Then you were the one she wrote to for all those years," I said, amazed at my good fortune.

"An' I wrote her back, I did, 'til me health turned. Kept her up on the doin's up at the house." She released my hand and pointed to an old pine jam cupboard. "In there in a box you'll find 'em. Saved every last one, I did. Go fetch 'em for me."

Sure enough, there in the back of the cupboard was a small wooden box and inside was a neat stack of letters. I knew instantly from the writing they were my mother's. I brought the box over to her and laid it on her lap.

"Your mother always wrote about her darlin' little Serena, but all these months me Charlotte's been talkin' about ye I never once thought t'was the same."

I looked up at Lord Barkham. "It's ironic. All the time the proof of my ancestry lay right here."

"She made me promise afore she left that I'd never tell a livin' soul where you was livin'. Sometimes it used to break me heart when I'd see her ladyship 'bout the manor. So sad she was, I was tempted to at least let her know her William was safe. But I couldn't break me word to my Samantha, God rest her soul."

"Mrs. Nexter, do any of these letters refer to why my parents left Camberleigh?"

"Ye don't know?" she gasped, the old eyes wide.

"What I meant was, do they contain any clue that my mother might have had as to who was actually responsible?"

She shook her head. "You're welcome to take 'em and look through 'em. Some go back a lot a years. But I don't remember anythin'."

I couldn't conceal my disappointment.

"But, Miss Serena, mark me words, your father didn't do it."

"Did my mother ever talk of any enemies," I pursued, "anyone who would have wanted to hurt my father?"

"He didn't 'ave any, miss. That was what was so strange. 'Course, I couldn't be knowin' everything, but it was all so sudden like. Your lordship 'ere can probably tell you more than I, seein' the families bein' so close an' all."

We chatted for a few moments longer until Lord Barkham cautioned that it was getting late and that we had best commence our journey back. I promised Mrs. Nexter that I would return soon and took with me the box of letters she pressed into my hands. Oliver and Jaspar were playing about the carriage, and Lord Barkham bundled them into the coach, putting a heavy woolen throw about the seat.

"It's getting quite chilly, Serena," he suggested. "Perhaps you should ride in the back for our return."

"I shall be warm enough," I insisted.

"Far be it from me to stop you, but I will suggest that one

of these days that stubborn streak is going to get you into far more trouble than you have already been in."

"Well, if it does it shall be none of your business, I can assure you," I snapped.

The skies had grown considerably cloudier as the carriage moved out from the valley onto the higher land and back to Camberleigh. It had been a very full day, and I was tired yet exhilarated by all I had seen and, of course, by meeting the woman who had corresponded with my mother for so many years. I had not discovered absolute poverty—at least at the farms we had surveyed—but I had seen and heard enough to convince me that Justin was right on the taxation issue. For a few, those with smaller families or the more prosperous farms, it might prove feasible, but most of the people it would near ruin. I shivered a bit, and Justin drew the robe up over my lap.

"Might I hope to have your support, Serena?" he asked.

"About what?"

"The taxation issue, of course."

"I hardly see that it matters," I replied. "It is really between you and my uncle."

"Precisely. Except for Cam. She has stayed out of it so far, but she has the right to vote, should she choose."

"Well, then, perhaps you should discuss it with her."

"I would rather you do that. She has enormous regard for you. And frankly, if I do it, Richard will accuse me of going behind his back."

"I have never known you to have a conscience before, Lord Barkham," I replied tersely.

He looked down at me, his dark eyes exploring mine.

"That, my dear Serena, is because you do not really know me."

I thought about his suggestion that I intercede for him with my grandmother. Although of no mind to do him any favors, I realized that I would simply be imparting opinions that in this case we shared.

"I will support you," I said resolutely, my eyes fixed straight ahead on the road.

"You mean you will speak to Juliette?"

"Yes."

He shifted the reins and flung one arm about me, pulling me to him. His movements were so swift that I was too startled to protest. Besides, I had to admit that the warmth of his body felt good against my own, which had become decidedly chilled over the past hour.

"That's my Serena," he whispered. "I knew I could rely on you."

I lay against him for a moment, not really knowing why except that it was somehow comforting just to be held. Misunderstanding my relaxation, he kissed my forehead gently and then drew me to him so tightly I could scarcely breathe. I put my hand against his chest and pushed with all the energy I could muster. It caught him off guard and he fell back against the seat. We both gasped. I turned to him. "Justin, there are several things we must settle. First, I am not your dear Serena, nor shall I ever be. I have agreed to support you on this matter, because, in this one instance I think you are right and I do not condone my uncle's point of view. And since we are, it would appear, to encounter each other daily, it is sensible that we both try to be civil toward each other. But do not ever misinterpret this. I have no responsibilities to you—or you to me. Is that clear?"

It was hard to know what lay beyond that stern countenance.

"An unfortunate choice of words, I would say, Serena. You forget that it was I who rescued you from that . . . shall we say, compromising affair with the Baron. I would say that that was an enormous responsibility I undertook. For you specifically, I might add."

I flushed, embarrassed at the reminder.

"I suppose, Justin, that in your twisted way that you think that you bought some right to me when you paid the Baron that night. Well I hate to disappoint you, but you purchased nothing that evening."

He regarded me quizzically.

"You were duped, Justin." I laughed. "The mighty Lord Barkham caught at his own game."

"Serena, don't press," he replied angrily. "I don't think your grandmother would care to hear this story."

"Oh, you may tell her what you like, for it is exactly that, 'a story.' I had never laid eyes on Baron Whittenfield prior to my arrival at Camberleigh. He simply discovered that I was not who I professed to be and threatened to expose me. I would have been banished from the household with no chance of proving my identity. Not to mention the grief it would have caused my grandmother. If you recall, it was not I who pressed you into service, but Anne. I had no gambling debts. In short," I added triumphantly, "you were swindled."

He turned in his seat, flicking the reins firmly. The carriage shot forward, lurching dangerously in the ruts of the road. I grasped the bottom of the seat and buried my head against the harshness of the wind.

"Justin, stop this," I screamed, "you'll kill us all."

"Don't tell me you're frightened, Serena," he shouted. "You braved the Baron, didn't you?"

"Justin, please," I begged. "I don't care what you do with me, but not Oliver."

I grabbed at the reins, but he had already begun to slow the horses.

"You could have killed us," I repeated as we resumed our normal pace.

"In God's name, why didn't you tell me about that deal with Whittenfield? Am I so loathsome to you that you could not have given me the truth?"

"It wasn't that way, Justin," I replied truthfully. "I didn't know what had transpired until it was all over. I was shocked when Anne told me."

"I think the word smug would be more appropriate. It must have given you great satisfaction to know that I had been fair game."

"I'm sorry about the money," I said quietly.

"The money?" He laughed. "Is that what you think is important to me?"

I was silent.

"I'm a bigger fool than I thought. I'm in love with a woman who not only spurns my affections, but challenges my honor. Monique told me to be patient with you, but my God, I doubt at times that there is anything to be patient for."

"So the two of you are discussing me behind my back?" I challenged.

"My dear Serena, Monique is a wise woman. She has been

very much your champion, though at this moment I can scarcely understand why."

I flushed with anger.

"If you find her so attractive, then why don't you return to her bed and leave me alone."

He looked at me and for one brief moment I thought I saw remoteness, or perhaps a sadness behind those angry eyes.

"If I do, Serena," he said slowly, "it will be because you have driven me there."

We rode back the rest of the way in silence. I was not proud of the way I had acted. There was an element of truth in what he said. I had wanted to hurt him, to retaliate for the pain he had caused me. I had not been raised to believe in an eye for an eye, and I was ashamed that I could feel such rage for another human being. It was strange. I had wounded him deeply, which I thought would give me pleasure. But instead all I felt was empty.

It was after six when we arrived back at Camberleigh. Oliver and Jaspar had apparently not noticed the tempestuous moments of our drive, for the two were cuddled together fast asleep when Justin opened the door to the carriage. He lifted the boy out gently and I took Jaspar in tow.

"I shall see that he gets some supper. Serena, you go on ahead."

I nodded and, retrieving my box with the letters, entered the house. I had just reached the top of the stairs when my uncle and Maura rounded the corner. I lunged at Jaspar, fearing a repeat performance of this morning, and in so doing dropped the box, the letters spilling about my feet.

"You are late, Serena," my uncle addressed. "And where in hell is Barkham?"

"He is seeing to Oliver," I replied.

"So much for your overseeing my son," Maura spat. "Don't think I didn't see through your performance the other evening. You may have Juliette fooled, my dear, but no one else."

"That's enough, Maura," my uncle cautioned.

She stooped and picked up one of the letters.

"Well, now, what do we have here," she mused, turning it over, "a love letter, perhaps? Or another of your claims to Camberleigh?"

377

"Maura, I said that is enough," my uncle pressed, taking the letter from her and handing it to me. "Come down as soon as you have changed, Serena."

I nodded, gathered up the rest of the letters and hurried down the corridor, Jaspar at my heels. I would have preferred to have taken a tray in my room this evening, but it was clear that I was expected to join the family.

I bathed quickly and slipped into my peach gown, which was hardly appropriate, but until the dressmakers arrived, I would have to make do. Everyone was in the library when I arrived, and from the look on my grandmother's face, I could see that tension would prevail during this evening's dinner as well.

"Well Serena, come sit by me and tell me all about your day. She looks a bit tired, Justin. I hope you weren't too hard on her."

I saw his eyebrows raise as did mine, but he looked away, realizing that my grandmother was simply referring to the arduousness of the journey.

"It was very enlightening," I replied. "I had no idea of the vastness of the properties."

"I find that hard to believe," Maura muttered.

"Many people asked after you, Grandmother," I continued. "We even went to Peacable, where I met Charlotte McKee's mother, Mrs. Nexter."

"Edwina Nexter," she said, slowly remembering from the past. She laughed. "Your grandfather used to call her Winnie, not only because of her name but because she used to sound a bit like a horse whinnying when she laughed."

"She worked for your mother, did she tell you?"

I nodded.

"She gave Serena some letters her mother had written," Justin added.

I wished he hadn't told her, though in truth he had not revealed how she had them in her possession.

"So that's what those letters were," Maura said. "And what, pray tell, did they say?"

"I've hardly had an opportunity to read them, Maura," I retorted.

"I think you all should know that the constable sent word

that he will return here tomorrow," my uncle said, changing the subject.

"What is he coming back here for?" Maura demanded.

"You know perfectly well that he is investigating the death of that governess."

"She is obviously just someone who suffered some brief indiscretion and was forced to pay for it. As long as the indiscretion was not yours, my pet, I don't think that we need worry about it."

Giles announced dinner at that point, which was timely, for my uncle was becoming extremely agitated. The meal was blessedly uneventful except for one brutal outburst by Maura, which led to a removal of her from the dining room by my uncle. Clarissa, upset by the incident, excused herself shortly thereafter, leaving Justin, my grandmother, and me by ourselves.

"Well, at least I am glad to have this time together with the two of you," my grandmother said quietly. "Do you have any further news, Justin, on that medication that Oliver was given?"

"Nothing more."

"I have been giving it some thought," she continued. "If the faulty medication was administered by Mrs. Scoapes or Molly, we have to determine a motive."

Justin laughed. "You're becoming quite the sleuth, Juliette dear."

"What puzzles me is that neither of them would seem to have anything to gain by Oliver's demise—unless they harbor some strange resentment against the family, but to my knowledge they have always been treated well here."

"You are leading to something, Juliette."

"Perhaps the focus should not be on Mrs. Scoapes or Molly, but on someone who simply used them for their purposes."

"But who, Grandmother?" I asked.

"I don't know. A disgruntled servant, someone who does harbor a resentment. What about one of the tenants? Do you think that there might be some fear or resentment over the possibility of taxation?"

Justin rubbed his brow. "I never considered that."

"I have so lost contact with the people on our land that I would not even know where to begin to think who might be opposed to us. Have you any suspicions?"

"None," he replied quickly. "But I promise that I shall give it some thought, although I do not believe that is where we will find our answer."

"Where, then?" I asked.

"I think that I shall do a little investigating about Mrs. Scoapes," Justin replied thoughtfully. "It is interesting, but very few people seem to know much about her."

"Maura hired her," my grandmother replied. "Of course, with Richard's approval. Perhaps they can tell you something. And now if you would be so kind, Justin, to see me to my room, I shall leave you young people together."

"I am going to bed as well," I added quickly.

I kissed my grandmother and moved back into the entry hall. The door closed to the library as I reached the staircase, and I assumed that my uncle had come back down after putting Maura to bed. It saddened me that I was not able to feel closer to this man who had been my father's only brother. I could not help but be sympathetic to his plight with Maura. As she was no mother to Oliver, I sensed that she shared no intimacy with my uncle. Perhaps if he had experienced more warmth in his own life, he would be more sympathetic to the lives of others. I thought back to my conversation with Lord Barkham earlier that day. Somehow it seemed important to find out whether my uncle had heard that my grandfather perhaps had intended to pass Camberleigh on to my father. And if so, what had been his reaction.

I climbed the stairs angry with myself for where my thoughts had been leading me. Had I become so desperate to clear my father's name that I was willing to suspect my own uncle? The house was very still, and I made my way quickly to my room. I had not truly warmed from our outing and the dress I wore was far too flimsy for winter evenings. As soon as I opened the door to my room, I knew that something was amiss. Jaspar, always at the door in greeting, was nowhere to be seen. I called out to him and he wriggled out from under the bed, hesitant until he was satisfied that it was me.

"Goodness, Jaspar," I said, kneeling down to him, "what is it?"

I lit another candle on the dressing table and looked about

the room. Nothing seemed to have been disturbed, yet I had the definite feeling that someone had been in my room. My eyes were drawn to my father's books. Had they been rearranged, or was it my imagination? The box of letters I had received from Mrs. Nexter lay on top of them where I had left it. I picked it up and opened it. The letters were inside, but someone had neglected—in their haste—to retie them with the ribbon that I had carefully placed about them earlier. I reproached myself for not having counted them, for now I had no idea whether one or more had been removed. I replaced the letters, too tired to read them this evening. As I undressed I mused about who might have been so curious about these letters. Maura? My uncle? Not Clarissa, surely. Of course, there was a possibility that whoever it was had come in here for some other reason, a servant, perhaps, who was simply meddling. Even Charlotte, who might have noticed that the box was new to the room and had been curious when she saw letters addressed to her mother. That must be it, I resolved. I climbed into bed and pulled the covers tightly about me. But, if it had been Charlotte, then why had Jaspar appeared so cowed?

I rose and put the lock on the door. Perhaps Lord Barkham was right that until the mysteries in this house were solved, it was best to be a bit cautious.

A light snow was falling the next morning. When Charlotte arrived, I told her how happy I had been to meet her mother, and I shared with her the excitement of my discovery of the letters. She was thrilled and incredulous as I had been that her mother had secretly corresponded with my mother over the years. Her surprise at the existence of the letters themselves was indication enough that she was not the one who had tampered with them. I would have to look elsewhere for my prowler.

I dressed quickly and made my way to the nursery. Oliver was up and already eating his breakfast when I arrived.

"Well, how are you today?" I asked.

"I am fine, Serena, and I wish that we could go out riding today."

I laughed. "I think once you recover fully, Oliver, that you are going to be difficult to keep indoors."

"Serena, what were you and Uncle Justin arguing about yesterday?"

I was embarrassed that he had, after all, overheard our harsh words. "It was nothing important," I assured him.

"Thomas wanted to know about our trip, but I didn't tell him that you and Uncle Justin were fighting."

"Is Thomas already in the schoolroom?" I asked, annoyed at Thomas's prying.

He nodded. "Constable Morrissey is talking to him. He wants to talk to me too."

"That doesn't worry you, does it?"

"No, but would you stay here with me?"

"Of course," I assured him.

It was not long before the constable and Thomas entered.

"Well, Miss—Miles, isn't it," he said.

"Miss Camberleigh now," Thomas offered.

"Oh, yes, I apologize. Lord Barkham informed me."

"Don't apologize, constable, it is new to everyone, myself included."

"Oliver, I just have a few more questions for you," he said. "You needn't remain, Mr. Masters. I think we have covered everything."

Thomas looked to me as though he wanted me to join him in the schoolroom, but I had promised Oliver to remain.

"Oliver, you remember Miss Smythe, do you not?"

Oliver nodded.

"Did you like Miss Smythe, Oliver?"

I knew from his downcast eyes that he did not want to answer the question.

"It's all right, Oliver, just tell the constable," I said.

He shook his head.

"I see. Was she not kind to you?"

"She didn't stay with me like Serena does. She used to leave me alone a lot."

"Do you know where she went when she left you?"

"No."

"Did Miss Smythe ever introduce you to any of her friends? Or maybe there was one special friend?"

"No."

"Did you ever hear her arguing with anyone, or was there

one person that she did not like in particular?"

Oliver thought for a moment. "She didn't like Mrs. Scoapes."

"Do you know why?"

"No." He paused. "But one day she told Mrs. Scoapes that she knew."

"Knew what?"

"I don't know."

"What did Mrs. Scoapes reply?"

"I didn't hear, but I know she was angry."

"I have just one more question, Oliver. Did Miss Smythe ever talk to you about Lord Barkham?"

"She thought he was handsome."

"Well, I think that is all, Oliver. Thank you for being so helpful."

The constable left us, and we went into the schoolroom where Thomas awaited. I looked out the window and saw that the snow had stopped and a fine blanket of white spread across the lawns and clung to the massive branches of maples and firs.

"Master Oliver tells me that you had quite an outing yesterday," Thomas said.

I turned from the window and nodded.

"Oliver and I shall have to work particularly hard today."

"As long as he does not overdo it, Thomas. He has had a trying morning."

"I suppose that the Earl will be seeking a new governess soon."

Oliver looked at me quickly.

"By no means," I said. "Oliver and I are just discovering each other as cousins. It has been agreed that I shall continue to watch out for him."

Thomas smiled. "Well, that is good fortune for both of us, isn't it, Master Oliver. I was afraid perhaps she would abandon us now that she has changed her name to Camberleigh."

"That is exactly the point, Thomas," I replied. "All that really has been changed is the name. The person is the same."

"I hope so."

I turned to leave, then stopped when Thomas called out to me.

"You are giving thought to what I have asked you, I hope."

I smiled to myself. His persistence was at once annoying and flattering. One of these days I should have to consider his proposal. But the time was certainly not now.

The morning had passed quickly. I paid a brief visit to my grandmother, who was, it seemed, more tired than usual. She suggested that I might like to take a full tour of the house. I realized that there were many parts of it that I had not seen, and my curiosity was great, but today did not seem the day to be adventurous.

Instead, I returned to my room, where I took out the letters my mother had written. In some ways it was unwise, for I could almost hear her speaking the words as I read them. But I knew that I must struggle through them in hopes of finding some clue to past tragedies.

The first letters were filled with memories of my youth. I smiled at descriptions of myself as a baby. "Serena is a joy, but even at this tender age," my mother wrote, "she shows signs of a singular independence." Or a later missive that spoke of the long walks she, my father, and I would take down by the harbor. There was little, if any, reference to their departure from Camberleigh, but then I supposed that my mother preferred to deal with the positive aspects of their present versus the tragedy of their past.

My reading was interrupted by a knock at the door. I asked whoever it was to wait a moment and hurriedly replaced the letters in the box.

I had never been happier to see anyone in my life. "Anne," I exclaimed, embracing her warmly.

"Didn't that brother of mine tell you that I was arriving today?"

"My mind was elsewhere. How wonderful it is to see you."

I pulled away from her, and we stood hand in hand at arms length.

"Serena Miles Camberleigh. I still can't believe it. You must tell me everything. I was furious with Justin when he told me that Juliette had him investigating your past. If I had known, none of that would have happened with Baron Whittenfeld."

"I'm afraid your brother is furious with me about that," I said, drawing her into the room.

"Well, it was hardly your fault. I admit it is unfortunate

384

that it proved so costly, but what was wounded far more than his purse was his pride. He'll recover, don't worry, Justin has extraordinary resilience. Now tell me about you. How does it feel to be a Camberleigh?"

For the second time that day I found myself explaining that the change was principally in name only.

"What was Richard's reaction?" she asked. "It must have come as a great shock to him."

"I think I can say that besides Grandmother, the only one genuinely pleased is Oliver."

"How has Maura been?"

"Not good," I replied quickly. "She had to be removed from the dining room last evening. I find it very puzzling indeed. There are moments when she seems perfectly fine, and then it's as if some dark cloud settles over her and she appears to lose contact with herself."

Anne quietly agreed. "You know, Richard's greatest concern has been that this weakness of hers would be passed on to the children. I used to watch him studying Clarissa when she was younger for some sign of imbalance." She laughed. "As we know, Clarissa's only imbalance, as it turns, out are her petty, selfish ways."

"In some aspects, Anne, I feel that it would have been far better had I never come here. I seem to have brought nothing but unhappiness. I probably shouldn't tell you this, but in a letter that my father had written to my grandmother—which in fact proved my heritage—he warned her that there was real danger in this house. I cannot say for certain, but I believe that my father suspected that he knew who had actually murdered my grandfather."

"Are you implying that whoever it was is still living here?"

"I am certain of it. Of course, I have no proof. And worse yet, I fear that I am no closer to it than when I first arrived."

"Perhaps you should give it up, Serena," she counseled. "With everything else that has happened here, perhaps it would be best to let it rest."

I shook my head. "Never. Not until my father's name has been avenged."

There was a knock at the door, and Anne rose to open it. Charlotte and Molly poured into the room laden with boxes.

Evelyn Grey

"I can't wait to see what's in these, Miss Serena," Charlotte burbled.

"It's my surprise," Anne announced as she commenced to unpack the boxes. "After our success of Kelston Manor, I decided that if it was a shop I wanted, it was a shop I should have. You remember little Fiona, the seamstress?"

I nodded.

"Well, I've taken her from that dreadful woman she worked for and installed her at Mayfair. Initially, all our work will be done right from there—based on measurements she will take, and naturally my designs. I already have a commission from Monique and another from Lady Bellmore for her daughter." She laughed. "The latter should be an enormous challenge."

Molly had begun to unpack the boxes, withdrawing from them the most elegant gowns I had ever seen.

"Well, what do you think?" Anne asked.

"Anne, they are exquisite," I replied, fingering a rich blue velvet with elaborate frog closings across the bodice.

She beamed. "I'm delighted that you like them, my dear, because they were designed specifically for you. And don't tell me you cannot accept them. It really is the only way I can repay you for displaying your prowess in this area. You must humor me with this gift. Besides, Justin says you have nothing to wear in this cold weather."

I bristled. My wardrobe was hardly his business, though I was desperately in need of some warmer things.

"This is my pièce de résistance," she said, holding up a full-length emerald green cape with white ermine trim around the hood and down the sides. "Actually I should credit Monique, for she has always encouraged me to try to do more with furs."

Molly and Charlotte gathered up the boxes and tissue, which was now spread all about the room, and left us alone.

I embraced Anne. "Once again you are my guardian angel."

"Hardly. Now come, sit and tell me more about your plans."

"My plans?"

"Juliette must be planning some parties. After all, this is a rather major announcement for her."

"I have asked that nothing be done right now. With all of Camberleigh in such unrest at present, it would hardly seem appropriate."

"Except, of course, to Clarissa. Justin says all she does is bemoan the lateness of the commencement of her season."

"I can understand her disappointment," I replied.

"I suppose," Anne agreed, "but you must admit that child can be infuriating."

"That *child*," I reminded her, "is my age."

"You know, I forget that at times, but then your upbringing and your recent past has given you a certain maturity that Clarissa shall never achieve."

I thought silently that that was likely to be true.

"Enough of that. I have a very personal question to ask you. I know I shouldn't, but you know reticence is not exactly one of my great strengths, so I shall just come out and ask you. What, if any, feelings do you have for my brother?"

"Did he put you up to asking me that?" I retorted.

"Heavens, no. As a matter of fact, he would never forgive me if he knew."

"Then why do you ask?"

"I suppose because I know my brother very well," she replied.

"I don't understand."

"For one thing, since your arrival he has spent much more time than usual here at Camberleigh."

"He has been trying to resolve this taxation business with my uncle."

"Hardly a need for him to be ever-present."

I did not reply.

"You know what I am getting at, do you not? I quite believe that my brother has fallen in love, and if that is indeed true, that makes me the happiest woman in England, since it is clear to me that you are the object of his affections."

I blushed. "I think your romantic nature is getting the best of you."

"Not at all. I have seen the way he looks at you. Oh, I know there is an arrogance about him, but down deep he is a sensitive, compassionate man—and that is from a sister who he teased unmercifully as a child."

"Well, it is of no import to me."

"You are not still enamored by that tutor of Oliver's, are you?"

"Now, wherever did you get that idea?" I asked, curious at how she knew of my friendship with Thomas.

"Justin mentioned that he appeared to be smitten with you."

"It really is none of his business," I retorted.

She frowned. "I see I am being put in my place."

"It is not you," I assured her. "I just wish that your brother would leave me alone. What I do with my life is truly of no concern to him."

"That may be true, but I think I should tell you that Justin does not like Mr. Masters. He finds him officious and far too presupposing for one of his station."

"Well, the dislike is mutual. Frankly, Thomas has even gone so far as to say that he does not trust Justin," I replied.

Anne was disturbed by what I had said. The last thing I wanted to do was to hurt her, even if through inferences about her brother. She had been a true friend, and one I valued deeply.

"Serena, forgive me, I don't want anything to come between us. I promise that I shall resist all further temptation to play matchmaker."

I relaxed. "Thank you for understanding."

She rose and moved toward the door.

"I must go and settle in before dinner, though I must say that there is nothing particularly settling about this house. I'd hoped they would have discovered who murdered that poor girl by now. It's foolish, perhaps, but I shan't feel really at ease again until her assailant is found."

When Anne had gone, I pored over the vast array of gowns and bonnets she had brought, wondering how I might ever repay her for her generosity. I selected a deep-red dress of a patterned silk brocade to wear that evening. In its simplicity it bespoke a quiet elegance typical of Anne's sense of style.

As I had several hours before dinner, I again withdrew the box of letters and commenced to read those which I had left unread.

Again I was disappointed, for although filled with marvelous reflections of my family and childhood, these too were bereft of any clue as to the demise of my grandfather. Only one passage departed a bit. It was a letter dated two years prior to my father's death. My mother had written: "William seems determined that we should return one day soon to Camberleigh.

I do not share his eagerness, for I fear that it should be too painful an experience for us both. At times he is obsessed by it. Rarely, of course, will he discuss it, but at times I catch him with a faraway look and know that he has left me for a few moments to return to Camberleigh. He has said several times that he feels an urgency about his return—almost as though he senses some sort of danger. It is troublesome, but I pray that somehow he can find peace before life calls him to its end."

I was certain that if my father hadn't known, he had strongly suspected who had been responsible for my grandfather's death. This was simply a reaffirmation of what he said in his letter that I had discovered in the book. I shivered suddenly. As Anne, I found the situation of an unsolved murder to be most unsettling. But the possibility that my grandfather's killer still walked the halls or grounds of Camberleigh was becoming downright terrifying.

There was still a bit of time before dinner, and I lay down on the bed determined not to fall asleep, but simply to rest and think. I had lain there for perhaps twenty minutes when I thought I heard footsteps in the hallway. Undoubtedly, I thought, it was one of the maids, and chastised myself for letting my nerves overtake me. I don't know what caused me to continue to watch the door, but only moments later I saw the doorknob slowly begin to turn. As it was the custom for Charlotte or Molly to knock or call out before they entered, I knew that this was neither of them.

"Anne?" I called out expectantly. The knob spun back. The person on the other side had been startled by my voice. "Who is there?"

I knew that I should rise and open the door, but I felt transfixed.

Within seconds I heard footsteps moving swiftly away down the hall. I was angry with myself for not going to the door and confronting my intruder, but I had to admit that I was fearful. Perhaps it was the person who had searched out the letters my mother had written and now believed that there was more to be discovered here. It was disconcerting, to say the least, for it could very well be that the reason someone was so interested in this correspondence was that they feared the letters might reveal something about them—something they did not want anyone else to know.

I tried to put the intrusion out of my mind, but could not. The events of the past months seemed suddenly to close in on me. I had tried to keep a distance, to play the role of the observer, but I knew that my involvement was far greater. It was like being surrounded by a circle—a circle that was slowly closing. And I seemed destined to be at some pivotal point at the events within, as the circle tightened toward the center.

It was late when I rose to dress, and I changed hurriedly. The new gown fit perfectly. It made me look older, more sophisticated. If a dress could give one a feeling of assurance, then this one did. I uncoiled my hair and was brushing it when Charlotte arrived to assist me.

"Let me do that for you, Miss Serena," she said, taking the brush from my hand and moving it adeptly through my hair. "Miss Ormsby certainly has the eye for what will become ye. Now I would never thought of that color for you, but 'tis just the right thing. 'Tis a pity there won't be more young gents to see you in it."

I smiled into the mirror at her. "Thank goodness for your cheerfulness and flattery Charlotte," I replied. "You always manage to give my spirits a boost."

"Somethin' worrying ye, miss?"

"Not really," I replied, wishing that I could share with her many of my concerns. Trust was not a factor, I simply could not risk involving her in things that had an element of danger in them.

"Charlotte, I know I have asked you this before, but I have forgotten what you said—did you tell me that you had known Mrs. Scoapes for very long?"

She looked at me in the mirror. "Since she come here, miss, but what would be makin' ye ask?"

"Just curious, I suppose," I replied, avoiding her eyes.

"An odd sort, she is," she continued. "Ain't none of us can say we know 'er real private-like. Not that there's sin in that, but 'tis strange, her goin' off like she does an' all."

"Going off?" I asked.

"Yes indeed. Real regular, she is. On her days off she just disappears."

"Perhaps she is visiting friends or family."

Charlotte paused, brush in hand. "But how's she gettin' there? Her ladyship lets ol' Jimmy take us down in the wagon to see our kinfolk, but not her. An' she certainly ain't got no one callin to pick 'er up."

"Well, how do you know she . . . disappears?" I asked, my curiosity piqued.

"Seen her with me own eyes, I have."

"But where could she be going?"

"You tell me, miss. Far as I can see, there ain't no place to go, 'less you got a horse or wagon."

It did seem strange, but then perhaps my imagination was getting the best of me. After all, it was not a crime to go for a walk about the grounds. Perhaps she felt the need of a weekly constitutional after being indoors the rest of the week.

Charlotte finished my hair. She had kept it looser than usual, saying that it seemed to soften the lines of the dress. I suspected she thought the gown was too au courant for me, but was either too polite or too wise to say so. In any event, I had to admit that I was pleased with the effect. I dabbed a spot more color to my cheeks. Charlotte replaced the brush on my dressing table and in doing so inadvertently knocked over the small case that held my mother's cameo and a few other trinkets. She apologized, replacing them except for the last, which she turned over in her hand.

"This must be new, miss, I never have seen you wear it," she said. It was the gold rose pin that Justin had brought back with him from London.

"'Tis a lovely piece, miss. You should wear it on that dress. It's just the spot of brightening it needs."

I started to protest, but quick as a flash she had affixed it to the bodice and looked so pleased with the result that I had not the heart to take it off. It was silly of me anyway. It had been a gift, and whatever I thought of Justin Barkham really had nothing to do with this pin. Besides, it did look perfect against the red damask of the gown.

I heard raised voices coming from the dining room as I made my way down the stairs. I had hoped with Anne present there might be less tension than usual during the meal, but civility seemed to be a scarce commodity in this household.

Evelyn Grey

"Ah, Serena," my grandmother greeted as I entered. "We were just talking about you, my dear."

"From the sound of things, I must have done something wrong," I replied.

"Nonsense, my dear. Actually we were just discussing a ball I plan to give in your honor. I would prefer it to be in six or eight weeks, as it has been some time since all the wings at Camberleigh were opened. But Clarissa is anxious to commence her season, and I do agree that due to unfortunate events, she has had to be patient long enough. So we shall set it for several weeks hence."

I sat down next to my grandmother. Justin Barkham, who sat opposite, eyed me quizzically, and I flushed, realizing that he had noticed the pin. "My sister has obviously been busy over the past weeks, for unless my eyes deceive me that gown is an Ormsby original," he said. "My compliments to you, sister dear. Serena is most alluring in that gown."

"It is lovely, Anne," my grandmother added. "Perhaps I could persuade you to fashion something for me for the ball. It has been so long since we have entertained here that I hardly have much that is appropriate."

"There would be nothing that would please me more, Juliette," Anne responded. "Actually, with the commissions that I now have, I should expect that many of your guests will be attired in my gowns. I had best make very certain that each has a very different look, or I shall never hear the end of it."

I looked down to the end of the table. My uncle's thoughts appeared to be elsewhere. When I saw Maura, I understood why. In contrast to the previous night, when for a while she had seemed almost radiant, tonight she looked drawn and dissipated.

Anne's eyes followed my gaze. "You know, Maura, I would be happy to design something for you for the ball. Not that you do not have beautiful gowns already, but we women can never have too many, can we?"

Maura looked up, and I was shocked at the vacant look to her eyes. Her voice was less shrill and hysterical than usual, but it had a deep ominous quality that I found frightening. "I don't know why you think you should offer your services, Anne. You've never liked me. Could it be that you feel guilty?

655865

Or perhaps I should more appropriately address that question to my dear husband."

I thought for a moment that Richard was going to strike her. I think he might have, had Anne not gasped in protest. I was surprised by Maura's comments. She obviously felt persecuted by people seen and unseen, but her animosity toward Anne was puzzling. Her resentment of me, I could understand, but Anne was another matter.

My grandmother appeared undaunted by Maura's condition and determined to discuss the plans for the ball. I was concerned that such festivities might prove to be too much for her, but she seemed to take such pleasure from the anticipation of seeing Camberleigh filled with people again that I could not dampen her spirits. Selfishly, I knew that the planning for the ball would do me good as well. I had not been relishing the Christmas holidays this year. It would be the first that I would not celebrate with my mother and my usual enthusiasm for the season was simply not there. I had no idea how Christmas was usually celebrated at Camberleigh, but I doubted that the warmth and joy that I had experienced as a child was to be found here. I quietly determined to do some planning of my own for Oliver's sake. The boy had a right to grow up with a true sense of this very special holiday.

The dinner passed without any further controversy. Maura was now oddly subdued. My uncle appeared greatly fatigued and, I knew, had only a half an ear to our planning of the ball. Clarissa, whose departure to London for her season was now definite, was able to put her jealousies aside for the moment and joined in almost enthusiastically at the prospect of a festive weekend at Camberleigh. Anne was filled with ideas for decorations, and by the time the evening was over we had even decided on the menu.

I was concerned about how Maura would react with all those people milling about the house, and I knew that my uncle must be sharing my concern. She spent most of her days hidden off in her suite. I had no idea what she did with her time, but I knew she liked her isolation. There were days when she seemed to be fine, but they never lasted. One would have no way of knowing how she would be during the ball. I suspected that for Clarissa's sake she would make a concerted effort, but whether the pressure of the event would prove too trying, only time would tell.

We finished our dessert, a steamed pudding with a delicate berry sauce, and Richard excused himself—to take Maura up to her room, I knew. Clarissa followed suit, leaving Anne, Justin, my grandmother, and me at the table.

"Good Lord, Justin," Anne exclaimed once Clarissa had departed, "you didn't tell me that Maura had become so much worse. Why, she seems scarcely able to manage a dinner."

Justin shrugged. "She seems worse than usual tonight. Frankly, before our trip to Kelston Manor I had hopes that she was improving."

"I have permitted Richard to have his way in this too long," my grandmother said softly. "Maura should have been under a nurse's care for a long time now. After the ball I am going to insist that he install a companion for her here. It is not healthy for Richard to have to worry about her night and day. It is aging him greatly, and it certainly cannot be helping his relationship with Oliver."

"I think that would be wise, Juliette," Anne agreed.

A look passed from Justin to Anne. Was it my imagination or was it one of warning or reproach?

My grandmother looked tired, and I suggested that I see her back to her room. The next few weeks were bound to be a strain on her and I was going to see to it that she rested as much as possible in advance of the festivities. The hallways were cold, and I was pleased when we reached her room to find that someone had stoked the fire well, taking the chill out of the air.

"Come in for a moment, Serena," she said. "There is something I want to give you."

I took a seat by the fire and watched as she went over to a large chest at the end of the room from which she withdrew a slender black box. She moved back to where I sat and handed it to me.

"I want you to have these, Serena. My father was an importer, and he brought these back from the Orient. They were a wedding gift to my mother, and subsequently to me upon my marriage to Charles. Had I had a daughter, by tradition I would have passed them on to her. I've kept them these many years.

Somehow I did not ever feel that I could give them to Maura, and Clarissa would never understand their significance. Now they have found their rightful recipient."

Pushing back the gold clasp that sealed the box, I opened it to reveal the most beautiful strand of pearls I had ever seen.

"Oh, Grandmother," I gasped, "I hardly know what to say." I turned the length of gray-white spheres over in my hand.

"I had thought one day to give them to your mother, but I never had the chance. I wish I could believe that somehow, somewhere, she knows that her daughter has carried on the tradition."

"Perhaps she does," I said tearfully. "I know that she sent me back here to you and that no matter what had happened, she sensed that this was where I belonged."

I embraced my grandmother and helped her undress and get into bed. When I knew she had drifted off to sleep, I extinguished the candles and made my way back to my room. Jaspar wriggled in delight, and, after placing the pearls on the dressing table, I drew the draperies and sat down by the fire. It was then that I noticed an envelope which lay but a few feet inside the door. I crossed to pick it up, realizing that I must have overlooked it in the flurry of Jaspar's exuberant greeting.

The envelope was sealed, and my hands tore nervously at it. Inside there was but a single sheet of paper on which, in a flourishing script, had been written: "I have important information. Meet me alone in the arbor at midnight." The signature in the same hand was simply a capital "T."

Thomas? But why would he not sign his full name? Moreover, why would he ask to see me at midnight, particularly outside and in this weather? It didn't make any sense, and I could not imagine what information could be so important that it could not wait until morning.

It was troubling. If the events of the past months had not taken place, I would have dismissed it. But I could afford to overlook nothing that might help me solve the mysteries that lay buried here at Camberleigh.

I pulled out my wool cloak and donned a heavy pair of gloves. As I drew the hood about my face, tucking my hair to the back, I shivered with apprehension. Justin Barkham's warnings seemed to whisper all about me. For a moment I considered letting him know of where I was going, but the letter had been specific about my coming alone, and I knew that if I told him he would never permit me it. The nature of any information Thomas could have was also puzzling. As far as I knew, he had no idea that I was determined to seek the identity of my grandfather's slayer. For that matter, I did not even know if he knew the circumstances of his death or my father's supposed involvement. I assumed that a few of the older servants—as Mrs. Nexter—must have suspected or even known, but Thomas had only been at Camberleigh for a few years. The only thing I could think was that he had somehow gained knowledge about the murder of Margarite Smythe. But why would he be so furtive about it unless he was afraid of what might happen if others knew? It was true that he had been eager to spend time with me, but he was hardly the type to dupe me into a meeting under such a pretext.

Jaspar whimpered as I picked up the candle and moved toward the door.

"I will be careful," I assured him, wishing that I felt as calm as I sounded.

The hallway was dark and cold as I made my way to the back stairs. I loathed this end of the house, and yet it was the shortest route to the arbor. I reached the bottom of the stairs and made my way past the kitchen pantry doors to the door leading outside. The snow that had fallen had crystallized in the cold and crunched softly under my boots. The moon was in its quarter phase, which helped illuminate the footpath. I had not gone far when suddenly my foot hit a small patch of ice, causing me to slip; the action extinguished the candle. I chastised myself for not having searched out a lantern before venturing out. I paused briefly to regain my footing and started at what sounded like footsteps behind me. I turned quickly and called Thomas's name in a loud whisper, but no figure appeared or voice responded. As I still had a way to go to reach the arbor, I decided that it must have been an animal of some sort scurrying across the frozen gardens. I wished now that I had brought Jaspar along for company.

I reached the arbor moments later and looked about for Thomas, but not a soul was in sight. Gathering my cloak about me I sat down on the stone bench. I was annoyed that Thomas was not already here, but in truth I had not checked the time before leaving. My instinct was to turn back immediately, but I had ventured this far and had to trust that whatever Thomas had to tell me was important.

Perhaps fifteen or twenty minutes had passed when I decided that Thomas had no intention of appearing. Beyond that, I wondered whether if it had actually even been he who had sent me the note—or simply someone who had wanted me to think that it was he. This last thought was unsettling enough to send a shiver up my spine.

I bent down to tighten the lace of my boot, but straightened quickly at the sound of footsteps behind me. I turned and was shocked to see a cloaked figure bending toward me. The face was totally in shadow.

"Who are you?" I gasped out in a hoarse whisper. "What are you doing here?"

There was no response.

"I'm sorry, but you startled me," I pursued. "Was it you that sent me the note?"

"Clever, wasn't it, Serena?" the figure responded. It was a woman.

"Why do you say clever?" I asked tremulously.

"You thought that I was your lover. I thought that was very clever of me. You see, I've seen you out here in the arbor many times. You didn't know that I saw you, but I did. All the while I watched you. From the tower. You and Thomas. You and Justin. You and Richard. You see, I saw you all those times. You were never alone."

"Who are you?" I pleaded.

She laughed. In the moonlight it looked like a laughing shroud. I longed to reach forward and push the hood back to reveal this mystery woman, but I was transfixed. The voice. There was something about the voice.

"You thought you were different, but of course you weren't. You're just like the rest of them—just like Margarite. You didn't know that, did you? Your precious Thomas used to meet her here at night also. They had their trysts in his cottage just as you have done. They didn't think that I knew, but I have always known. Richard was stupid. He didn't think I knew either. But then, of course, he was more careful. Richard is always more careful. And Justin. Clever of him to use Oliver as his foil. But then Justin has always been cleverer than the rest. I always thought that. Richard thinks that he is so clever, but it is really Justin who is the clever one."

The figure moved closer, and I rose from the bench, turning.

I think I had known from the first who the voice belonged to, but there was no sense to it. As I turned to face the figure head on, I whispered her name. "Maura."

"Yes. Maura," she exclaimed, tossing the hood back. "You've known all along, haven't you?" The moonlight played across her face, creating deep shadows on her cheeks and reflecting eerily in her eyes. It was almost as if the light had searched for this source to touch upon. The eyes that had been so vacant only hours earlier were now alive with reflections of the nocturnal universe.

"What are you doing here?" I asked, rooted to where I stood.

"I want the letter, Serena."

"What letter? I don't have any letter," I replied, placing my hands out to show that they were empty.

"Don't say that," she retorted angrily. "I know you have it. I looked for it in the box, but you'd hidden it. Where did you put it?"

So it was Maura who had gone through the box of letters. But why? I had read them all. Why would she be interested in old correspondence between my mother and Mrs. Nexter . . . unless . . .

"I don't know what letter you are talking about," I repeated.

"You're lying."

I knew that to stand there and try to reason with her was futile. She was not rational, and the best thing that I could do was to get her back to the house before we both caught our death of cold. I held out my hand.

"Come with me, Maura," I urged, "we will go back to the house. We can talk there."

She stepped back, her glowing eyes never leaving mine.

"You can't trick me. You're not going back to the house until you give me that letter. They'll never believe you, you know. Once I have the letter you'll have no proof. They'll think you are quite mad—just like your father."

I stepped forward, my hand reaching for the arm of her cloak.

As I did, she lunged forward and I felt a searing pain on my upper arm. I fell back startled and disbelieving as I saw moonlight glinting off the long blade of a knife she held upraised.

"You shouldn't have done that, Serena. If you had just given me the letter, then everything would have been all right."

I took my hand away from my arm. It was damp, and I realized with horror that it was wet with my own blood.

She thrust the knife toward me once more. I stepped back against the cold stone of the bench.

"Sit down, Serena."

I did as she bade. I was weak, and with the icy snow on the ground I was not sure I could get away from her.

"Maura, I beg you to put that knife away and tell me what this is all about," I pleaded. "I have never meant you any harm, I swear it."

She moved closer. "Then why did you take Richard away from me? That wasn't very nice of you, you know. But you weren't the first you see."

"You don't know what you are saying, Maura," I said dazedly.

"Miss Miles, I know precisely what I am saying."

Why did she refer to me as Miss Miles? Could it be that she had suppressed the events of the last few days? Could it be that her mind was denying acceptance of me as a Camberleigh?

"Maura," I said slowly, "do you know who I am?"

"Of course I do," she snapped back. "You're Serena Miles."

"Serena Miles Camberleigh," I replied.

Even in the darkness I could see the confusion on her face.

"You are trying to trick me again," she said.

"No, no. I am Serena Camberleigh. You knew my father, William. He was Richard's brother."

She rubbed her hand against her forehead as if she was trying to fit the words with memories of the past.

"William. Poor William," she crooned.

"Why do you say poor William?" I urged, suddenly interested despite the pain in my arm.

"He had to go away, you know. I didn't really mean for him to have to go, but there wasn't any other way."

I felt as though I was walking down a long hallway at the end of which there was a large door. I knew that if I opened it that many of the dark secrets of Camberleigh would be revealed. It was a sense that I had had before, and I knew that there were answers there—but there was also grave danger.

"Why did my father have to go, Maura?"

She moved closer to me.

"I planned it very carefully," she whispered. "I told the Earl that I had to talk to him privately. He knew what it was about, and I was certain that he would meet me by the pool. It was very fast. I dropped something into the water and he bent over. I picked up the rock and brought it down on the back of his neck. I knew he was dead right then and there, but I hit him again and again to be certain. Then I put William's watch fob by the body. They never knew. They never even suspected. Juliette even played into my hands and sent William away, so there was no one to ask any more questions. It was very simple."

I was so stunned that for a long moment I could not reply. When I did, my voice trembled with emotion.

"Why, Maura? Why would you kill my grandfather?"

"Because he knew. And I couldn't let him tell Richard, now could I?"

"Tell him what, Maura?" I was almost sobbing.

A frown spread across her brow.

"Tell him what, Maura?" I repeated. "What didn't you want Richard to know?"

"About the child, of course."

"The child?"

"My child—Clarissa. You know her, don't you? She's a very pretty baby and Richard loves her very much."

I sensed that for her time had suddenly fallen away and we were no longer dealing with the present, but some framework of minutes or weeks or months eighteen years ago.

"Richard does love Clarissa very much," I assured her. "But then, fathers always do have a special feeling for their daughters."

"But that's the secret," she said in a childlike voice. "Clarissa isn't Richard's daughter. She's mine. It would have been all right, except that Charles overheard us one day in the stables. He called me a cheap harlot and sent my lover away that very afternoon. He swore to me that he was going to tell Richard. I couldn't let him do that, you see, because Richard could have turned me out and I had no place to go. I told the Earl that I would tell Richard myself and that I would notify him once I had. When he came to the garden, you see, he thought that I had told Richard. He was going to be very generous, actually, and offered to put me in a house in London, but I couldn't let that happen. I only married Richard to become Lady Camberleigh. No, I wasn't about to give that up."

The web was too difficult for me to unweave all at once. The one fact alone that Maura had murdered my grandfather was almost too much to take in, but the reason behind it was beyond thought. My uncle was not truly Clarissa's father! My next question I was almost afraid to ask.

"What of Oliver, Maura?"

"What of him?" she sneered.

"Is Richard his father?"

She laughed a hideous, sardonic laugh. "Of course, dear. Amusing, isn't it? My perfect Clarissa is spawned from a mere stable hand, and that monster is a gift from the earl of Camberleigh."

I cringed at the reference to Oliver as a monster.

"And if it weren't for you, Serena, that misshapen little cripple would be dead by now."

I felt as though I was going to be ill. That this woman was intimating that she had been responsible for the attempt on the life of her own son was more than I could bear.

"Then it was you who gave the poison to Oliver," I exclaimed.

"No, my dear, again I was too clever for that. It was Mrs. Scoapes who gave Oliver the medicine. Of course, I changed the bottles, but it was Mrs. Scoapes who made certain that he took his medicine every day."

I was sickened by the reality that I too had unwittingly given Oliver the poison tonic.

"It was perfect when you became involved. I hadn't planned that, but it played directly into my hands. With the suspicion thrown to you and Mrs. Scoapes, they would never have suspected me."

"You're wrong, Maura," I retorted angrily. "Justin and Dr. Carruthers are investigating the source. It will only be a matter of time before you are discovered."

401

She held the knife before me menacingly. "You're lying again. It doesn't matter now anyway, for I shall have to be rid of you too. Don't you see, if you had just given me the letter then I wouldn't have had to kill you."

"I swear to you, Maura," I cried, "I don't even know what letter you are talking about."

I knew that I could no longer just stand there. I had to make a move. That Maura was totally deranged was now clear to me. She had already killed. And there was no doubt in my mind that she could kill again. My eyes looked beyond her, searching for the best path to attempt an escape. My arm had been too badly injured to attempt to overpower her. My only hope was that my bolting suddenly would startle her enough that I could put enough distance between the two of us to reach the house before she did. I braced my boot, ready to take flight.

"Don't move, Serena," a man's voice called out.

Maura spun about, the knife glistening in the air poised against the intruder. Her back was to me and almost instinctively I kicked out my leg, attempting to push her forward. After that, everything happened so quickly that I don't know if I will ever realize how close I came to death in those next moments. Instead of causing her to fall forward, the thrust of my leg spun her about and she came directly at me. The look on her face was grotesque, resembling an ancient gargoyle ready to devour its victim. The point of the knife was against my throat when Justin reached her. The sight of the two struggling was like a ghastly ballet. Justin, who was a good head taller and possibly twice her weight, was fighting as if with an equal.

I thought the battle would never end, as first she would have the upper hand, then he. Finally a moan escaped her lips as his grip tightened on her wrist and the knife slipped to the ground near my feet.

"Get the knife, Serena," he shouted. "Can you make it back to the house?"

I picked it up and stood away from Justin, who had now managed to fully subdue Maura. I was weak, but I nodded in response.

"Get Richard up, but try not to alarm anyone else in the house. I will meet you in the library. Be careful, it is very slippery underfoot."

I don't know how long it took me to return to the house. My mind was so filled by the events of the past hour that I scarcely paid attention to the treacherous footpath or the chill of the winter wind. As I climbed the back stairs I wondered what I would say to my uncle. He was going to be devastated. There was no way, of course, of keeping any of this from him. I was less concerned about Oliver than of Clarissa. Maura had never really been a mother to him, though I supposed he was still the only mother he had ever known. But for Clarissa, this was going to be an enormous shock.

I moved down along the hallway to my uncle's quarters. I knocked on the door. There was no answer. I knocked again and pressed my ear to the door. No sound came from within. I turned the knob slowly and entered the room. One small candle burned on a nightstand. I called out his name in a hushed whisper. The bed had obviously not been slept in. I turned and left the room, convinced that he must be up and about somewhere in the house. I dared not let myself think that some harm had come to him. It was me Maura had been after, I told myself as my panic grew. As I passed Anne's room I thought I heard a sound from within. Justin had cautioned me not to alarm anyone else, but I needed her support and aid in finding my uncle.

I knocked and called out her name.

It was several minutes before she came to the door.

"Serena, is that you?"

"Yes. Oh, please, let me in."

She unlocked the door, opening it only slightly.

"Anne, you must help me," I pleaded. "Something dreadful has happened, and I must find my uncle."

The sound of my voice must have frightened her, for she did not pause to ask me any questions, but simply replied, "I will get dressed immediately."

"Meet me in the library, but tell no one about this," I bade. "If you see my uncle, send him to the library as well. I shall search downstairs."

I hurried back to my room to discard my cloak. The sight of my arm was shocking. The knife had cut right through the heavy material and had left a deep gash above my elbow. The bleeding has been profuse, and my arm was thoroughly matted with my own blood. I washed it as best I could and wrapped a towel about it, but it still oozed. It would need treatment later, but Justin would have returned by now and be worried at finding no one downstairs.

Anne was on the stairs when I got there and, much to my relief, my uncle was a few steps ahead of her. I quickly caught up to her.

"Anne, do you have any sedatives or do you know where Maura might keep hers?"

"Serena, what is this all about?" she whispered, turning to face me. "Good Lord! What has happened to you? Your dress—your arm. Serena, you are covered with blood!" she exclaimed, reaching out and putting her arm about my waist and helping me down the remaining stairs.

"It's Maura," I said as my uncle turned to investigate. He stopped the minute he saw me, his gaze frozen on my arm. "The library," I said softly.

He stormed across the entrance hall and burst into the library.

Anne supported me, and we followed swiftly behind.

None of us was prepared for what lay beyond those doors.

Maura was seated on a chair by the fire. She gave no sign of recognition that we had entered the room. Her fingers picked senselessly at a spot on her dress. She hummed a tune so softly that it was barely audible. Richard started to move toward her, but Justin reached out and restrained him.

"There is nothing you can do for her now, Richard," he advised.

Anne looked at Maura in disbelief. "What happened, Justin?" she asked.

Justin poured a brandy for Richard. The second I assumed was for himself, but instead he brought it over to me.

"Drink this," he urged, pressing the glass to my lips.

I did not protest; whether I was too weak or too numb, I knew not which. Anne guided me over to the fire and seated herself next to me.

"Do you think Maura needs a sedative, Justin?" I asked, calming a bit as my system responded to the brandy.

He shook his head. "She has been like this since you left to go back to the house. I don't even think she hears what we are saying."

"For God's sake, Barkham. You owe me an explanation," my uncle's voice boomed angrily. "I'm told it's urgent that I come to the library, and when I get here I find my wife, who doesn't even seem to know who I am. She's never been a specimen of mental or emotional balance, I grant you, but she's never before not known me."

I was so thankful that Justin was there. I truly do not think I could have remembered enough about the events of this night to tell anyone about it. It seemed too bizarre, too incredible for any of it to have happened. But it had indeed all happened, and as I listened to Justin I knew that none of our lives would ever be quite the same again.

Justin recounted that he had been at the bottom of the stairs when he had seen a cloaked figure scuttle past down the hallway. He had not known it to be me, but was suspicious of someone lurking about at that time of night. He had followed me, but at some distance, lest he arouse suspicion. He had waited in the bushes by the entrance to the arbor and had just been about to confront me when he saw another figure move out from the other side. Unlike me, he had known instantly that it was Maura. At first he was confused—as I was—by her ramblings. Moreover, why, he wondered, had I chosen to meet her here? The meeting certainly seemed, to him, planned. But then the ramblings began to take form, and he realized that I was in grave danger. He chastised himself for waiting a moment too long, but I was simply grateful that he had been there at all—he saved my life.

I do not know how one can weigh one pain against another. I only know that this tragedy was not of a single dimension for my uncle. Not only did he have to accept that his father had been murdered by his wife, but that his daughter—who had been the pride of his existence—had been fathered by another man.

I knew that there was no way he could be spared this anguish, and it cut me deeply to watch a man who had been strong to the point of impenetrability crumble before my very eyes. All strength seemed to drain from him, his eyes taking on a vacancy not unlike his wife's.

I looked quickly to Justin, who simply shook his head. There was nothing that any of us could say or do.

Anne was the first to break the silence.

"What are we going to do, Justin?" she beseeched.

He paused in thought.

"I don't know. There is obviously no need for an investigation, but the incident must be reported. We know that she has committed at least one murder."

"You mean you think there were others?" I asked in disbelief.

"We can't be certain," Justin replied, "but I think it is more than likely that it was Maura who killed Margarite Smythe. She is obviously obsessed with the thought that Richard has been carrying on with every young woman who was ever brought into this house. Perhaps it was some bizarre way of quelling her own guilt about her adulterous affair with the stable hand. It is sad to think that such an obsession led to Margarite Smythe's demise, but I fear it may be true."

"There is another thing," I added. "I'm certain that it will only be a matter of time before Dr. Carruthers discovers who was responsible for the poison administered to Oliver."

My uncle rose and knelt before Maura, stroking her hair back from her face. She continued to pull at her dress, seemingly oblivious of his presence. I was mesmerized by the sight, for I never would have thought my uncle capable of such gentleness.

It was some time before he spoke.

"I cannot go to the constable with this, Justin," he said, his voice breaking. "You know as well as I that they would take her away to one of those ghastly prisons. She would never survive it, and I do not think that I could endure the thought of her being there."

"You cannot be thinking of keeping her here, Richard," Justin implored.

"I can," he said emphatically. "There are parts of this house that are not in use. I can employ however many people it will take to keep her comfortable. If what she is at this moment is her fate for the rest of her life, there should be no need to restrain her."

"But what of Clarissa and Oliver?" Anne asked.

"It shall be difficult on them, but far less so than if she were to be hauled off to some dungeon filled with every sordid type of lowlife that stalks this land."

Justin walked over and poured another brandy. He turned to face me.

"As I see it, it is really up to Serena."

"Up to me?" I gasped in disbelief.

"If we do as Richard wants, then you will have no opportunity to once and for all clear your father's good name, for this secret would have to remain with us for at least the rest of Maura's life."

How ironic life was, I thought, with its twists and turns. My obsession was to restore honor to my father's name and memory by revealing the identity of the true murderer. Yet through the obsession of another, I was being forced to decide on whether to protect the very person responsible.

It seemed unjust, but I knew there was really only one decision for me. I would always wonder if Oliver had not been a factor, would I have chosen the other path, but then, that is something I shall never know.

"Maura should remain here," I said resolutely. "But there is one condition. My grandmother is to be told the truth. All of it."

My uncle nodded. "Thank you, Serena. I know that this was a difficult decision for you. And by all rights you should not have been asked to make it, but as violent as the acts have been, I cannot let the blame rest solely with my wife. I must ask myself what role I have played—if even unwillingly—in all this. I knew our marriage was a mistake from the start. Maura was young and beautiful, and I rejected her. Strange, really, she was obsessed with Camberleigh at that time and I was obsessed with getting away from here."

He fingered his scar. "It seemed so unfair to me that just because I was the eldest I would assume the management of Camberleigh. I longed to be in London, and eventually to set forth to America. My father, I know, sensed this, and had it not been for his untimely death, I believe he would have permitted me to go, leaving your father, Serena, the title of earl of Camberleigh. William loved this place and he, far more than I, should have been its caretaker."

"Did Maura know that you wanted to leave?" I asked.

He nodded his head. "But she wanted none of that. This

house meant power to her, and she was not about to abandon it for my need for change or adventure. With my father's death and with Clarissa's birth it became impossible, of course, for me to leave. Perhaps I visited my resentment on her. Perhaps had I not always been so absorbed with my own needs I would have seen what she had truly become."

Anne rose and moved over to him. She placed her hand on his arm and coaxed him to move away from Maura.

"You are too harsh with yourself," Anne said. "You don't know if it would have been any different had you and Maura been closer."

"Anne is right," Justin added. He looked over to me. "Right now I want to get Serena to bed. That arm must be looked after, and there is no sense belaboring this any further tonight. I suggest that you take Maura up and give her a sleeping draught, if you feel she needs it. We all need to get some rest. The next few days will not be easy—on any of us."

My uncle agreed and moved over and scooped Maura up in his arms. She looked like a wounded bird, her head drooping against my uncle's waistcoat. Anne and Justin both moved to help me, but I assured them that I could maneuver on my own. I did until I reached the stairs, when a wave of nausea overtook me and I fell dizzied against the balustrade. This time I made no protest, only a wince of pain as Justin gathered me up and carried me up the stairs to my room, Anne close behind.

Jaspar barked at our approach and was most solicitous as Justin placed me on the bed. Instructing Anne to help me undress, he left, saying he would return shortly. Anne managed to get me into my nightdress without disturbing the wound to my arm, which by now had stopped bleeding. Justin returned moments later with a pile of pads and bandages, which he applied after drenching my forearm in something that smelled strongly of alcohol.

I studied him as he did so, his dark eyes intent and filled with what appeared to be genuine concern. I was too exhausted to talk, and yet there must be something I could say to him for saving my life. It would wait, I thought. There was tomorrow, time enough for me to express my gratitude.

Chapter Fifteen

It was raining when I awoke the next morning. I lay in bed listening to the pelting on the roofs outside my window. My head throbbed and there was the dull ache in my arm. I realized that I had slept very little. It must have been almost dawn by the time we had retired from the library. Jaspar nuzzled my arm, and I welcomed the friendly warmth he exuded. I thought of my mother suddenly. When I was about ten there was to be a party for one of the girls in the village. I longed to have a new dress for the occasion, but money was particularly scarce that year and my mother had refused me, saying that it would have to go toward my school books instead. I had been heart-broken. My mother had found me on the path overlooking the harbor. I remember her saying "You know, Serena, sometimes what we appear to want the most is often not what we want at all once we receive it." I had thought it was nonsense, for at that moment nothing could have dissuaded me from believing that that dress was the most important thing in all the world.

But as I lay there in the darkness of my room, I knew now what she had been trying to tell me. Clearing my father's name had been the most important thing to me in the world. But it had not brought me the elation that I had anticipated. How could I take joy from the pain of others? I knew that the decision that I had made the night before was the correct one. My uncle and my grandmother would suffer for the rest of their lives because of the events of last night. To ruin other lives as well would only be vindictive, and I knew that there was no satisfaction in that.

There was a knock at the door. I drew back into the bedcovers instinctively.

"'Tis Charlotte, Miss Serena."

I opened the door, and Charlotte bustled in with my bath water and some tea and scones. She placed them nervously on the bureau, knocking several combs to the floor.

"Are you all right, Charlotte?" I asked anxiously.

"Yes, miss, but Lord Barkham says if you're feelin' up to it ye should get dressed an' go to the library straightaway."

I wished that all this did not have to be faced so early in the morning, but supposed that we had to address the issues as quickly as possible.

I nodded.

"If that be all, miss, I'll be goin'. Robbie will see to the little feller," she said, scurrying from the room before I had a chance to reply. Her behavior bothered me. Curtness was not a trait of Charlotte's, unless she was worried about something. I did not see how the events of last night could have reached her ears so soon, but it drove me to bathe and dress as quickly as my throbbing arm permitted.

Save for the echo of the rain, the house was still as I made my way downstairs and crossed to the library. Therefore, I was startled when I opened the door and found that I had been far from the first to rise. My uncle was seated on the couch by the fire, which was only smoldering embers from the night before. His elbows were on his knees and he cradled his head in his hands. Anne was beside him. I was shocked at her pallor. My grandmother sat nearby. Justin stood behind her with his hands on her shoulders. I don't know why, but I had the impression that if he let go she would slump over in a dead faint.

I felt it too. Last night there had been a certain energy which had been born from shock. Today there was only a sickening numbness that seemed to drain one of all self-protective resources.

I moved over to my grandmother and knelt before her.

"You know, don't you," I said softly, my fingers stroking the furrowed softness of her cheek, still damp from tears that had been shed.

She nodded.

"Serena," Justin said, "there is something that you do not know."

A knot clenched in my stomach. "Nothing more, please, Justin," I begged.

"Maura is dead."

I don't know what I had thought I was going to hear, but it was not that. The words hung in the air, and I repeated them to myself almost as if by doing so I could give them some dimension, some reality.

"How?" I asked.

"Richard had put her to bed," Justin replied. "She fell asleep almost instantly. He went to his room, which adjoins hers, and locked her in. We cannot be certain what happened next, but can only assume that she awoke some time later. There was an empty vial of tonic next to her bed. It is impossible to know whether she thought she was taking one of her medicines or whether she somehow had a moment of lucidity during which she became aware of the severity of her crimes and decided to take her own life. The irony is that once the vial is examined I think we will find it akin to the medicine that Oliver was taking."

"Have Clarissa and Oliver been told?"

He shook his head. "Actually, I was just trying to broach the subject when you arrived."

My grandmother took a breath so deeply that I became alarmed, although I need not have been, for at the same time she lifted her head and squared her shoulders. She looked over at my uncle.

"I am somewhat chary of saying this," she said resolutely, "for it will sound callous and vengeful. For myself I am glad that Maura is gone. I shall always prefer to believe that she did this purposefully to protect Clarissa and Oliver—and even you, Richard. In death she has found redemption that in life she could not."

"How can you of all people say that, Juliette?" my uncle said indignantly.

"Because I am older and perhaps therefore wiser in these matters. You would do well to share my opinion, Richard," she counseled. "The weeks ahead are going to prove most trying, and you have a son and a daughter to protect. They will need your strength through all of this."

"You seem to forget," he retorted angrily. "I have only a son."

Anne looked up, startled. "Richard, you can't mean that."

"In God's name I do," he cried out. "Every time I look at her I shall see Maura. Maura carrying on her sordid cheap affairs. Maura murdering my father. Maura torturing her own son. And finally Maura who did not even know me—or perhaps cared not enough to know me."

"But that has nothing to do with Clarissa," I heard myself saying. "Surely you would not punish an innocent victim of all this? Don't you realize that to do that would mean you were no better. than Maura herself?"

"Serena is right," my grandmother admonished.

"But what am I going to say to the girl?" my uncle continued. "'Clarissa dear, I have something to tell you. Your mother is dead and you are not my daughter.'"

"That is cruel," Justin said angrily.

"You can never tell Clarissa that you are not her natural father," I beseeched. "It would destroy her."

"And what, pray tell, do you suggest that I do?"

"To continue to raise Clarissa as your own daughter," I replied evenly.

"Again, I agree with Serena," my grandmother said. "Though she scarcely seems it at times, Clarissa is a grown woman. She will be meeting some young man one day soon and she will marry and possibly live a distance from here. Ruining her chances for a successful marriage would hardly be wise, and the less scandal there is about all this the better."

"They are right, you know, Richard," Anne said quietly. "Promise me you will try—for my sake."

My uncle acquiesced, but I sensed that it was Anne who was somehow the most convincing. I thought that "for my sake" was an odd thing for her to say, but then, he held Anne in high regard, as we all did.

It was agreed that Anne and Richard should tell Clarissa of Maura's death. The task of informing Oliver rested with me. Justin was to fetch the constable and make plans for a funeral, which it was agreed should be limited to the family.

It was almost eleven when I made my way to the nursery. Hearing voices in the schoolroom, I crossed over quietly and stood unseen in the doorway for a few moments. Oliver was progressing nicely with his French.

"Well, Serena, I didn't see you standing there," he hailed. "Come join the class."

I shook my head. Oliver turned and beamed at the sight of me, and I struggled a smile in return.

"Might I see you for a moment, Thomas?"

"Your call is my command, fair princess," he jibed, sweeping his arm down in a mock bow.

When we reached the nursery, his hand took my arm. I grimaced in pain.

"I would wish that my touch was not so repellent," he said, studying me intently.

"It is not that," I insisted. "I had a slight accident last night and cut my arm. I fear it is still tender."

He smiled. "I am sorry about your arm, but I am relieved to know that it was not me that you were retreating from. Could I dare hope that you have considered my proposal?"

"Please, Thomas, not now," I answered impatiently. "There are far more pressing things to be discussed at this moment."

"You do seem serious," he replied, taking stock of my mood.

"I am, Thomas, Oliver's mother has died."

He stepped away from me and moved toward the window.

"So it finally killed her," he said matter-of-factly.

"What?" I replied, confused.

"You don't mean to tell me you didn't know?"

"Obviously, Thomas, I wouldn't ask if I knew."

"She'd lived on powders and opiates for years."

"But they were medicinal," I retorted, shocked by what he was suggesting.

He laughed. "You are naïve, princess, but then, that is one of the endearing things about you."

I was angered. "I do not find this a laughing matter, Thomas. Oliver has lost his mother, and you act as though I have just told you something amusing."

He turned to face me, his eyes meeting mine. "I'm sorry,

413

Serena, but we both know she was hardly a mother to that child."

What Thomas said of course was true, but the news would be a shock to the boy nonetheless. I felt that Thomas was being very unfeeling. I wondered how many others knew about her addictions. It was no secret that she was often not well and her frequent outbursts could not have gone unnoticed by the servants over the years. Ironically, this would serve us well now, for no one need know how she died. They would simply assume that she had succumbed to her years of indulgences and abuses.

"Needless to say, Thomas, I must ask that you cease the lessons for a few days," I said. "I am going to try and spend as much time with Oliver as I can. Then, of course, there will be the funeral."

His eyes darkened. "I don't take orders from you, Serena. If that is what the Earl wishes, I will abide by it, but frankly I think it would be better to have the boy's mind occupied elsewhere."

I was startled by his tone. I had not meant to be officious, yet he had clearly taken umbrage at my request.

"Then speak with the Earl, if you must," I said, shrugging my shoulders.

"I am certain that he will confirm what I have said," Thomas said flatly.

I turned on my heel and left the nursery, moving back toward the schoolroom. It was petty of me not to have waited for Thomas to respond, but my nerves were on edge and I did not want a confrontation.

Telling Oliver about his mother's death went far differently than I had anticipated. I suppose because of the closeness I had had with my own parents, I had transposed my own feelings on to him. There were no tearful outbursts, no prolonged questions. He simply studied me with those translucent blue eyes that I always felt saw far beyond their years. I opened my arms to him and he came to me, satisfied, it seemed, to be in silent thought. My mind was racing with things I should be saying or doing, and yet I understood that sometimes the greatest solace comes through the ministrations of one's own mind.

It was locked in our unspoken embrace that my uncle found

us. I relaxed my hold on Oliver, but he made no move toward his father. I wished in a way that he had waited awhile to see the boy, for his appearance was alarming even to me.

"How is Clarissa?" I asked.

"Devastated. Anne is with her," he replied as he approached and stood close to us.

He reached out and stroked Oliver's hair. "Would you leave my son and me alone for a spell, Serena?"

I nodded and, kissing Oliver's forehead, pulled him to his feet. His eyes beseeched me not to leave, but I knew that I must. It had been difficult for my uncle to come here, but I sensed that he did so with good intent. Surely the bridge that existed between the two was not going to be crossed in a day— more likely it would take years. But because of this tragedy my uncle would, for his and Oliver's sake, try to take a first step.

My arm was bothering me as I left the schoolroom. I knew that I should lie down for a while, but I truly did not want to be alone. I returned to the library in hopes of finding my grandmother. Instead I found Justin. He looked exhausted. I realized that he had not even changed his clothes from the night before. Spots of my blood still remained on the ruffle of his shirt.

"How is Oliver?" he asked.

I shrugged. "I don't really know. He was so quiet. I longed to say something that would help, but nothing seemed appropriate."

"Is he alone now?"

"No," I replied, crossing to sit by the fire. "Richard is with him."

His eyebrows raised. "Do you feel that is wise?"

"I don't know, but they have to start someplace. My uncle is hardly the warmest person in the world, but I have to believe that he will not punish Oliver for any of this. They could really help each other, you know."

Justin seemed to be deep in thought.

"I've been thinking that after the funeral I would take Oliver with me to Mayfair for a bit. Anne is fond of him, and I can rearrange my affairs in order to spend some time with him."

"He adores you," I acknowledged.

"Cam is determined that right after the funeral Richard take Clarissa to London."

"So soon?"

"I think it is precipitous myself, but she may be right. Clarissa has been obsessed with this season of hers. And there really is nothing for her here except a loss that will be fresh in her mind. Richard, of course, doesn't agree, but I think that after the funeral he will see the sense to it."

"What of the estates?" I asked, knowing that the management of Camberleigh could scarcely be handled from afar.

"I shall simply have to assume Richard's role for a while. As you know, Camberleigh and Mayfair work largely in tandem, though I must admit that since he is the one who maintains the ledgers, that area will necessarily suffer while he is gone."

"It needn't," I found myself saying. "Certainly I would be no replacement for Richard, but I am quite facile with figures. My father believed that women should have certain skills in life, and I often helped him with his books."

Justin smiled. "It is kind of you to offer, but you have no background in these matters. I don't question your intelligence, only your experience."

"I wish you would let me help," I urged. "Particularly if you take Oliver with you, it shall be ever so lonely for me. Besides, it would be some small way that I might be able to repay you for saving my life."

Justin's eyes met mine. "You should know it is not payment that I want from you."

"Please let us not go into this now," I begged. "I am tired and I truly don't wish to argue with you anymore Justin. I do owe you my life, and for that I thank you. If you should change your mind and desire my assistance, you need only call on me."

He rose and moved to the door. "Get some rest, Serena. The constable will be here this afternoon and will want to speak to you, I am certain."

His abruptness startled me. I could hardly expect him to be solicitous, but I had hoped that he would take more kindly to my statement of gratitude. I was confused by my own feelings. Justin was a riddle. He had infuriated me, humiliated me, even betrayed me. And yet he had shown great strength and sensitivity during these nightmarish hours. Perhaps one day we might be able to put our hostilities aside and be friends, but the hurt that we had inflicted—purposefully or not—on each other was still too fresh for that now.

I returned to my room to find that Charlotte had left a luncheon tray. I was too tired to eat anything, and lay down on the bed to rest. It was still raining, and the sound was somehow soothing. I was startled back to consciousness by Charlotte, shaking me.

"Ye had me worried, miss. I knocked, but you didn't answer. You was sleepin' so soundly I wouldn'ta bothered you, but Lord Barkham says you got to see the constable. He's down in the library right now."

"Thank you, Charlotte."

"I know I shouldn't be sayin' nothing, miss, but everyone's talking about poor Lady Camberleigh. She weren't much of a favorite here, but none woulda wished this on her. That poor little boy. Robbie feels real bad for him. I was so put out this mornin' I couldn't e'en talk to ye an' Lord Barkham tells me not to tell you."

I rose and straightened my skirt.

"Have you seen my grandmother?" I asked.

"Her ladyship is with the constable in her rooms. So much trouble there is. 'Tis a cryin' shame that she has to suffer so."

So the constable was here already. I did not relish having to go through a session with him, particularly since I would have to conceal the truth of what had really happened here last evening.

Charlotte left me, and I went to my grandmother's room. The constable was still there and, to my relief, so was Justin. His questions were easier than I had anticipated. He was obviously satisfied by the web of half-truths my grandmother and Justin had woven prior to my arrival. That Maura had been responsible for Margarite Smythe's death of course could never be proven. But the evidence was there. With no one to prosecute, it was easy to convince the constable that revelation of his suspicions would only serve as a source of pain for those who remained. And so when we buried Maura we would bury almost two decades of secrets that had haunted Camberleigh.

I had never known time to pass so slowly as it did over the

next few days. The routine of our lives was unchanged, and yet each of our lives had been changed drastically by Maura's death. In some way we all seemed to be besieged by guilt. My uncle was convinced that had he been more attentive Maura might have never been driven to the dark sinister world that claimed her. Oliver was troubled, I knew, by the lack of emotion he was experiencing over the loss of his mother. My grandmother was tormented by the knowledge that she had lost her son by the error of her own judgment. Even Clarissa seemed to have some remorse for not having spent more time with her mother. And for me, there was the haunting fear that my obsession with clearing my father's name had driven Maura to take her own life.

I don't know what I would have done for the next few days without Anne. Justin was away most of the time making arrangements for the funeral and overseeing the running of the estates. It was Anne who provided the solace and strength. Just her presence somehow assured me that these troubled days would pass and would someday be only a painful memory.

I awoke the day of the funeral to find that the rain that had begun days before had still not stopped. The nearly constant precipitation had not helped to lighten spirits already fraught with gloom.

The cemetery was on the crest of a hill not far from the roadway that led to the house. Had things been different, the graves of my father and mother would have rested nearby. Instead, my grandfather was to be joined in death by the very person who had robbed him of life.

There was no clergyman present. Justin read the psalm that had always been my favorite, for it spoke not of fear but of hope, not of aloneness but of guidance to another dimension. Oliver huddled close to me under the protection of my cloak. As Clarissa placed a simple spray of holly on the grave, I looked over toward my uncle. To my surprise, just then Anne reached out and took my uncle's hand. A look passed between them. It was fleeting but unmistakable; it was not the look that one friend bestows upon another. I don't know why I hadn't realized it before. Perhaps because I had never thought of Anne as a woman for whom love would play an important role in her life. And yet that seemed so foolish, for she was one of the most loving and giving beings that I had ever known.

I looked over at Justin and knew that he had seen it too. Was it a surprise to him as well, I wondered, or had he known? I suddenly recalled an argument that I had overheard between Justin and my uncle when he had so angrily threatened him to "stay away from her." It had been puzzling to me at the time. Could it be that he had been warning my uncle to keep away from his sister? If my suspicions were correct, then Maura had not been entirely mistaken, which would explain the overwhelming guilt that Richard seemed to be experiencing. Margarite Smythe, then, might have been an innocent victim. I shuddered to think what might have happened had she known or even suspected that he was seeing Anne.

My grandmother had not joined us to bury Maura. She had not the strength to attend, particularly in this weather. And in any case it would have been cruel to have asked her to be a part of this day. She was not a vindictive woman, but I knew that forgiveness would be something that she could never extend to Maura, even in death.

The following week was spent quietly. Justin left almost immediately for London to tend to some business and arrange for the house on Crowley Square to be opened for Clarissa and my uncle.

Christmas was but weeks away, and I pressed him into purchasing some small trinkets for Oliver and my grandmother and Charlotte and Robbie. I was embroidering some handkerchiefs for Anne. Hardly a repayment for her generosity, but I knew that she appreciated fine needlework. I selected one of my father's books for Thomas. It was only Justin for whom a gift seemed difficult. The holidays would be far from joyous this year, I knew, but I was determined that it should not be a time that would be associated with unhappiness for Oliver in years to come.

My grandmother was adamant that the plans for Clarissa's season not be altered. It turned out to be a wise decision, for my cousin was forced to plan and pack, and it served to occupy her mind. The festivities that had been planned for the ball for me at Camberleigh were, of course, abruptly halted. My grandmother tried to convince me that I should join them on the trip to London, but I had no desire to spark the resentment that

Clarissa still harbored against me. Besides, my place was here with Grandmother and Oliver, here at Camberleigh.

The day before Clarissa and my uncle were to leave, Anne came to my room.

"Am I intruding?" she asked.

"As always, I can't think of anyone I'd rather see," I assured her.

"I've come to tell you that I've made a decision—or shall I say that Juliette and I made a decision."

"And what is that?" I asked, pouring us both a cup of tea.

"I am going to London with Clarissa and Richard. Actually, it was Cam's idea. She feels that Clarissa should be chaperoned, and I certainly can be of assistance with her gowns and schedule of balls and parties. I am here to try to convince you to join me. It is not healthful to have you cooped up in this house. We would have such a gay time. Robin, of course, will be there, and Monique and scores of eligible young men who would be undyingly grateful to me for bringing you along."

I was devastated by the thought that Anne would be leaving as well, but resolute about my decision to remain. It crossed my mind that if my grandmother shared my hunch about Anne and Richard's relationship, I doubted that she would have been so quick to push them together, but it did seem a sensible decision for Clarissa.

"You seem troubled, Serena, what is it?"

"Nothing, really," I tried to assure her.

"I don't believe you. Something is wrong."

I decided I might as well say it. "I was just wondering whether it is wise for you to go to London at this time with Richard—after all, we did just bury Maura. There is bound to be talk, and I just wouldn't want you to be compromised in some fashion."

Anne studied me for a moment. "You know, don't you?"

"I don't truly *know* anything, Anne. Let us just say that I have sensed certain things."

"Between Richard and me?" I nodded. "Serena, I have wanted to share this with you for so long," she replied slowly.

"That night at Kelston Manor, I wanted to tell you then, but with things as they were, there was no possibility."

"We do not need to discuss this, Anne," I reassured her.

"Yes, we do," she insisted, "because I will not have you

420

thinking badly of me. If you know the facts, I think you will understand. After Anthony died, I was not myself. On the one hand I was almost relieved; on the other I suffered terribly from feelings of guilt. Richard was spending a great deal of time at Mayfair in those days, and he was a good friend to me. It was not long before he also began telling me things—thoughts and emotions that he had kept secret for years. I suppose it was inevitable that our friendship should have grown into intimacy. I know that it seemed perfectly natural."

"But what about Maura?" I asked.

"We were always careful—or tried to be. Obviously less so than we had thought."

"Justin knows, doesn't he?"

She nodded. "Cam as well."

"My grandmother knows?" I asked unbelievingly.

"Juliette is a very perceptive woman, Serena—and a compassionate one. She was aware of the relationship between Richard and Maura—or I should say the lack of one. Maura did not share a bed with Richard after Oliver was born."

"But that is no reason to have had affairs with everyone," I argued. "Perhaps if he had shown her some affection . . ."

"It wasn't like that," Anne insisted. "No one really knew how ill Maura was. She fantasized that he pleasured himself with all these women, but I can promise you that was not true. He needed someone as I did—and do."

"But why did he not leave Maura years ago?" I asked.

She shrugged her shoulders. "Loyalty. And the children, of course."

"And now that is no longer the problem," I replied.

It was some time before Anne responded.

"I am disappointed, Serena. Perhaps it's to much to expect you to understand completely, but I had hoped that you would not react so harshly. I love Richard, and someday I hope we can build a life together. I want you to be happy about that. I feel as close to you as a sister, and your approval is terribly important to me."

I rose and put my arms about her. "I do apologize, Anne. I wouldn't hurt you for anything," I assured her. "It's just that so much has happened—you must understand that it is all a bit overwhelming."

"I do, and one day you shall experience for someone the

same passion I feel for Richard, and my actions will not seem quite so distasteful. I had secretly hoped that Justin might have proved to be that someone, but you both seem to have a way of antagonizing each other. Of course, if Juliette is right, the two of you are simply so blinded by your stubborn streaks that you are not able to see how deeply in love you both are."

Astounded by what Anne had said, I moved abruptly away from her.

"Are you telling me that my grandmother truly believes Justin Barkham and I love each other?"

She nodded.

"Well, in this instance she is *sorely* mistaken," I insisted.

"Methinks the lady doth protest . . ." she said softly, her voice trailing off.

"I'm sorry, Anne, what is it?"

She stood up. "Nothing. I do believe I have said quite enough already."

"Must you go?"

"I really must. I have to return to Mayfair to prepare for our trip. I do wish you would change your mind and come with us."

"Not now, Anne. I couldn't in good conscience leave Grandmother and Oliver. I fear I am not feeling terribly festive these days anyway. But promise me you shall return immediately after Clarissa's season ends. I shall be desolate here without you."

She assured me that she would. We embraced, and too soon she was gone.

Chapter Sixteen

THE NEXT weeks passed routinely. Justin returned from setting up the London house and Clarissa and Richard departed soon after. In the days before they left I often caught my uncle studying his daughter. It was as though he was searching for some look, some characteristic that would disprove the true paternity of his beloved daughter. He made daily efforts—prompted, I knew, by Anne—to reach out to Oliver, but it was going to take a long time to bridge the distance between them. It was to me that Oliver turned. The death of my own mother was still fresh in my mind and I think it assisted me in relating to Oliver's loss. While I said nothing about it, I sensed that he suspected the true nature of her death. As always, his silence was as expressive as his words.

My grandmother had aged drastically since Maura's death. It was as though she had summoned a last bastion of strength to help us through those dark days and then had fallen, exhausted by her own labors. We spent many hours together during those weeks. She was desperate to know as much as I could recall of my childhood and of course of my memory of my father. I tried to focus on the happy times, of which, fortunately, there were many.

The weather was particularly bleak. The rain and intermittent snows made it difficult to venture out of doors. I saw Thomas only briefly each day and was grateful that he understood that this was not the time to press me about our association. In truth I think it was during that time that I realized that I had been avoiding coming to terms with my feelings toward Thomas. In the beginning I had welcomed—and been flattered by—Thomas's advances. But now the fervor of his interest had proved to be mostly confusing. He was offering me safety and a life not terribly different from the one with which I had been raised. And while a promise of solace and protection was certainly not an unwelcome thought—particularly now after all that had happened—I seemed to be incapable of reaching a decision. I longed to discuss it with my grandmother, but it did not seem appropriate, given her condition—not to mention given her fancies about Justin and me.

As for Justin, our relationship changed as the weeks passed. He had said nothing further about my offer to work on the books of the estate, and we actually saw very little of each other. During the day he would venture forth at the break of day and return in the late afternoon. Most evenings he spent poring over ledgers in the library. We were civil, almost cordial. It was odd, almost as though the antagonism that had existed between us had disappeared. I suppose that when one goes through as much as we had together, the angers and hostilities simply fade into the background. I cannot say that I missed his barbs. I did not. But I found myself dissatisfied by the estrangement. There was little enough to keep me occupied, and I was miffed at Justin's rebuffs of my offer of assistance. There was no doubt that there was a truce between us, but he obviously preferred it to be a silent one.

My loneliness led me occasionally to wish that I had taken Anne's offer and gone to London. Robin had a charming, exuberant nature, which, though I recognized to be frivolous, had a way of taking one out of oneself. Laughter had always been a part of my life before I had come to Camberleigh, and I missed a certain carefree abandon that I had experienced as a child.

But then, the truth was that I was no longer a child. I don't know how a girl realizes that she has taken that step into womanhood. I had always imagined it as some momentous happening, like curtains being drawn back revealing a whole new scene. But I think in fact that the actual transformation is a series of tiny changes, each so infinitesimal that one does not even recognize the experience.

One afternoon a few weeks after everyone's departure, I went to the nursery to visit Oliver and found Thomas still with the boy. "Thomas, I am surprised to find you here."

"I was just telling Master Oliver that it is time you got out of this house and got some fresh air. You have been looking terribly piqued lately, Serena."

"I suppose I do," I replied, touching my face self-consciously.

"Now you see she agrees with me, Oliver. That settles it. I am going to take you out for a long walk this afternoon. The rain has stopped, and a brief stroll will do you a world of good."

"That is not necessary, truly, Thomas," I protested.

He looked at me with that boyish grin that I always found so disarming.

"We won't take no for an answer, will we, Oliver?"

Oliver looked at me expectantly. "Please, Serena?" he begged.

I was truly surprised, for it was the first display of enthusiasm he had shown since his mother's death.

"You are both quite convincing. I suppose I cannot refuse."

"Might we take Jaspar?"

"He is down at the stables with Robbie, but if Thomas doesn't mind we might wend our way down there."

I smiled to myself as I returned to my room to fetch my cloak. Thomas was right, I did need a change, and Oliver's eagerness was infectious.

It was not as cold as I had thought. The air was crisp, but there was little wind. The footpath was amazingly dry, given the amount of rain we had had, and walking was not difficult. I never ceased to marvel at the landscape. Each season it took on a new dimension. The trees without their leafy ornaments were gargantuan in form, their limbs lifelike tentacles stretching under distant skies.

I paused briefly at the fork leading to the stables. I had not returned to the pond since the day I had discovered Margarite Smythe's body. It was such a beautiful oasis, but one that had been the site of such tragedy. I was furious with myself for feeling as I did about it. Intellectually I knew that the garden itself was not evil, that it had simply been the arena of evil deeds; nevertheless, I knew I would never again be able to think of it with pleasure. It would always harbor an aura, even a fearfulness, for me.

"Are you coming, Serena?" Thomas called back.

I shook myself free of my thoughts and followed him. Robbie waved as he saw us approach and Oliver scurried down to greet him. It pleased me to see Oliver move with such agility. In time I sensed his handicap would almost completely correct itself.

"How are you, Robbie?" I said as I shook his hand, Jaspar barking at my heels.

"I be doin' fine, miss," he responded, grinning ear to ear. "'Tis a far time since I be seein' you."

"Too long," I responded. "I haven't forgotten my promise about your studies, but I am certain you know that that has been impossible of late."

He nodded. "I was real sorry to hear 'bout your mum, Oliver."

I turned quickly to Oliver, who looked gratefully at Robbie. It occurred to me that Robbie, in his natural simplicity, might reach Oliver in that special way only young friends can, and I suggested to Thomas that we take a stroll while Robbie showed Oliver the new foals.

"I am surprised that you are encouraging our being alone together, Serena," Thomas said as he took my arm.

"I didn't," I replied. "I'm simply hopeful that Oliver can forget, if only for a time, the strain that has been placed on him these past months."

We had retraced our steps back up the footpath and had turned at the fork before I realized that Thomas was intending to go down toward the secret garden—and the pond.

"Must we go that way?" I asked, holding back.

Thomas turned me toward him and brushed a lock of hair back under the hood of my cloak.

"You sound almost as though you are afraid of going there, Serena," he said.

"It's probably silly of me, but so much unhappiness is represented there."

"But that is over now," he insisted.

426

I played with a stone with the toe of my boot. "Is it?" I asked.

His eyes darkened, a frown played above.

"Why do you say that?"

"I don't know," I replied. "It is as if there is some evil force there that lies in wait for its victims."

He laughed. "You do sound sinister, fair princess. The only evil, Serena, is in your imagination."

"Perhaps," I admitted.

"Which is even more reason for you to return there. I can't have you going on being haunted by ghosts that do not exist. It is simply a place like any other place."

Thomas pulled me forward. Rationally, of course, what he said could not be denied. But I doubted—despite his reassurance—that I would alter my views. Perhaps it was only a symbol, but for me it was a symbol of hatred, jealousy, and death.

"You know, Serena, I have been very patient these last weeks," Thomas said as he guided me along the path.

"And I have been grateful for that, Thomas," I responded sincerely.

"But I am not a saint, you know, my dear. It has been weeks since I have spoken to you of my intentions. I find it more and more difficult to address you from afar."

We reached the entrance to the garden. The gate was open, and I noticed that someone had cleaned away some of the undergrowth beneath the iron pickets and had replaced the latch. The weeds and brush were not as rampant as when I had last seen it, but then, that was but nature's hibernation during the winter months. Thomas guided me to the bench beside the pool.

"Now, you see, it is simply a pond. I don't see any monstrous creature rising from the depths, do you?"

I shook my head.

He took my gloved hands in his. "Are you cold?"

I smiled, appreciative of his concern. "No, I am quite comfortable, thank you."

"Excellent, for I would not want you to be so numb that you cannot respond to my endearments or earnest plea for your hand in marriage."

I don't know why I had been so naïve to think that Thomas would not grasp the opportunity of our being alone again to bring up the subject. The truth was that I simply hadn't thought beyond Oliver's enthusiasm about our outing.

"Thomas, must we discuss this now?" I begged, withdrawing my hands. "It is simply not the time or the place."

"What *is* the time and place, then?"

The question unnerved me, for I suddenly realized that to answer specifically would be in a way a form of encouragement.

"You haven't answered me, Serena."

"I know," I replied.

"You know that I love you, don't you?"

I brushed the hood back from my face. "Thomas, I don't know. I know that you have been kind to me, that you were a friend when I desperately needed one. But there is very little that we truly know of each other."

"You always seemed to enjoy our dinners and our talks," he pursued.

"I did."

"But that was as Serena Miles," he countered, a bit irritably.

"What has that to do with it?" I asked.

"You cannot deny that you have changed since assuming the name of Camberleigh," he responded bitterly.

"If I have changed, it has nothing to do with that," I insisted.

"Does it not? I think differently. You were always quite responsive to me before that time."

"If you haven't noticed, Thomas, my life has been in chaos since then."

His fingers brushed lightly against my cheek. "Of course it has, which is precisely why you need someone to care for you. I beseech you to let me be the one. We could stay on at Camberleigh. I would even be willing to continue tutoring Oliver. I would prove quite useful to Richard, you know, in managing these estates."

Nothing seemed to be making any sense. Where was the talk of the little house we were to have—and the children?

"I would say that it is you, Thomas, who has changed, not I. Am I now even more attractive as a Camberleigh? Does the prospect of my inheritance hold a new fascination for you?"

He stood up, took a few steps, then turned back to me.

"And if it does, Serena, would that be so wrong? It is not as though it is criminal to want that money. It will be yours, after all. And why should we live in poverty when we can live well. Your grandmother cannot live forever. We can travel if you want, spend some time in London each year. You wouldn't truly want to live on a tutor's wages, not when you could have all this."

I couldn't believe what I was hearing. This was not the Thomas I knew. Though, perhaps the truth was that I did not really know Thomas at all. I resented his comments, was appalled by his assumptions, and furious with myself for ever having encouraged him at all.

"I think we should go back now," I said, gathering my cloak about me.

"No!" Thomas shouted angrily. "I want an answer from you. I am not inviting you to tea. My God, I am asking you to be my wife.'

"The word *inheritance* seems more important than *wife*," I snapped.

"Of course it is not, Serena," he said, returning to where I sat. "If you recall, I spoke of my feelings for you before your grandmother recognized you as a Camberleigh."

That was true. But I had to wonder whether he would have been pressing me quite as hard had I simply remained Serena Miles. Thomas was right in one instance—he did deserve an answer from me. He had been too much of a friend for me to play with his emotions.

"Thomas, this is very difficult for me," I said, taking his hand and encouraging him to sit beside me.

"It needn't be." He smiled reassuringly.

"You know that I am terribly fond of you, but I do not feel about you the way one should of a husband or wife. I have not had experience in these matters except the knowledge of my own parents. Theirs was a very deep and passionate love. There was an unbreakable bond between them. Had there not been, I don't believe that they could have endured what they did over the years. You will find someone, Thomas, who is truly deserving of you one day, but it is not I. To marry you simply to escape from my own problems is not an answer for either of us."

"It is Barkham, isn't it?"

"Of course not."

"I've seen the way he looks at you. He devours you with his eyes. And that would be a handsome catch for you, the marriage of two of the largest estates in the county."

"Well, he is of no interest to me," I answered angrily.

"Then kiss me and tell me you do not want Barkham to seduce you."

With that, he grabbed me so suddenly that I gasped for breath.

"Thomas, you are hurting me," I said, twisting my arm from his grasp.

His lips came down hard on mine. I choked as air escaped me.

"Please," I moaned as his lips pressed insistently against my cheeks and mouth.

"You love it, don't you," he murmured, drawing me closer.

"Please don't, Thomas," I begged. "Not this, please."

"Don't say that," he shouted.

"But you're hurting me. My arm—please."

"I told you not to say that," he snarled at me. "That is what she said. She was in love with Barkham too, you know. Can you imagine that trollop fancying that he might even marry her? Marry her—that was a laugh. He didn't even know she existed."

None of this was making any sense. I was beginning to feel sick from the pain in my arm. It had not completely healed, and as Thomas continued to twist the flesh about my wound, I cried out.

"Screaming won't help you, Serena. She tried the same thing. I told her no one would hear her."

"Who is 'she'? I don't know who you are talking about."

His fingers tightened their hold. "Why . . . Margarite, of course."

"Margarite?" I gasped. "What has she to do with this?"

His face darkened, his eyes troubled. "She said she loved me, but she didn't really. When I asked her to marry me, she laughed. She was going to marry Barkham. Can you imagine? That whore thought she could ensnare him? He's no fool. He knew quality when he saw it. Barkham will only marry his equal. That is why he is so desperately in love with you, my fair princess."

I was frightened. There was more going on here than I understood. Thomas, I knew, was hurt by my rejection, but I had never known him to display any brutality. If Margarite had been involved with Thomas, then why had he not mentioned it before? And what did Justin have to do with all this?

"You should not have done this, Serena," he whispered, pressing his face close to mine. "We could still marry and go away from here. We will forget about Camberleigh and Margarite and Barkham. We will go where they will never find us and start a new life. Mother will help us."

"I do not want to marry you, Thomas, I just want to fetch Oliver and return to the house," I pleaded.

"I cannot permit you to do that, Serena . . . not now."

"Why, because you told me of your affair with Margarite?"

"I can no longer trust you, you see. I did not mean to hurt Margarite. Truly I did not. But she laughed at me. That little slut laughed at me. She wouldn't stop. I begged her, but she would not stop, and so I hit her. And then she wouldn't die. I hit her again and again, and finally she did not laugh anymore."

"Oh, God. No, oh no, Thomas," I moaned. "Not you, oh please God, not you."

I looked up and through the tears that spilled from my eyes I saw not the friend I had come to cherish, but a man who was a total stranger to me. How could I have been so wrong? Was Justin right, was I so naïve, so blind that I could not truly see things as they were?"

"I don't want to hurt you, Serena, but I have no other choice. I cannot have you telling anyone, you see."

I struggled to free my arms. "Oh, please, Thomas, you needn't do this. We can do something. We will tell Justin. He will help, I am certain."

"Barkham's never going to know, fair princess. You will simply have vanished. I will say that you disappeared after we went to the stables, that I searched for you back at the house and saw you get into a coach."

"They will know, Thomas," I cried out, trying to think quickly. "My grandmother knows I would not leave so abruptly and that I would never leave Jaspar behind. There will be all my clothes."

"My mother will see to that," he replied.

"Your mother?"

"Ah, yes. My mother the actress." He laughed. "A great actress, but the only role she ever played was right here at Camberleigh as the housekeeper."

I couldn't believe what I was hearing. "Mrs. Scoapes is your mother?" I cried out in astonishment.

"Ah, you see, you did not really know. Mother was certain that you suspected. She warned me about you—and she was right all along."

"No, she was not, Thomas," I sobbed. "I am your friend, and I will help you in any way I can, but please release me now."

The sting of his hand across my face startled me into the monstrous awareness that Thomas had no intention of letting me go. And what he'd said was true. No one would hear my screams, and though I doubted that anyone would truly believe his story, I knew that he would be long gone by the time the discovery was made. It would be much too late.

"Serena. Serena, where are you?"

"Oliver," I gasped.

"Serena," the call came closer.

Thomas turned for a second to hear where the voice was coming from. I wrenched free, startling him as I did. I was up and running, through the hedge that bordered the bottom of the garden and led to the fields.

Weeks later I would wonder what had carried me as swiftly as it did. It was Oliver's voice that had given me the chance to escape, and it was also a fear for Oliver that drove me on. I was almost relieved when I heard Thomas calling my name in pursuit, for I knew that although he was close on my heels I was leading him away from Oliver.

I dared not turn for fear of losing even seconds in my flight. My lungs burned. With the grasses long before harvested, the field was but a rough washboard of rutted earth and stone. There was no shelter, no place that I could escape to, and yet I kept running blindly on.

There was another sound now, a rapid beating which was resounding louder and louder as I ran on. The horse and rider appeared suddenly, growing larger as they approached at breakneck speed. I shouted for help, but no sound escaped my lips. There was a sudden pull at my back, and my cloak was pulled back.

"Serena, get down," the rider yelled.

I did not heed the warning. I was obsessed with my escape; my feet and legs had a mind of their own.

"Get down!"

I remember falling to the ground or being pushed, my cheek striking a stubble of dead wheat. I spun about in time to see King's Ransom loom into the air like some prehistoric mammal. The sound was deafening as the hoofs fell in wild fury, trying to drive Thomas to the bowels of the earth. Justin pulled on the reigns, but he could not budge the horse off Thomas's broken body. It was as though he was the victor lording over his prey.

I turned away, sickened by the sight, and sobbed blindly into the earth. Arms reached down and scooped me up, stroking my head ever so gently.

"Justin, I . . ."

"Hush, Serena," he whispered.

"Thomas?"

"He's dead. Let us not talk about this now."

"No, we must," I insisted weakly. "Margarite . . . it was not Maura who killed her. It was Thomas. All along, Justin, it was Thomas."

He brushed some pieces of earth from my face, his eyes burying into mine.

"Good God, why?"

"He wanted to marry her, but she refused him. He said she wanted you."

"But I scarcely knew the girl," he said incredulously.

"I only know what he told me. He was obsessed. He was going to kill me too."

"Does that mean that you too refused him?"

I nodded. "He had been a friend to me, Justin—when I had sorely needed one. I suppose I was flattered by his attentions, but I do not think I ever intended to marry him. It was he who talked of marriage, never I."

"You and I once talked of marriage, Serena."

"That seems long ago."

"Well then, let me freshen your memory."

His lips brushed mine, softly at first and then enveloping me in warm, moist response.

"I have loved you from the first moment I saw you, that day on the steps—so defiant, so proud, and yet so young."

"I am no longer that girl, Justin."

"I beg to differ. There will always be that willful magnificence about you, but you have something now that you did not have when you arrived here."

"What is that?"

"An ability to forgive. I have watched you grow into womanhood as you have laid to rest the sins visited upon your father. I have hoped and prayed that some day you might also open your heart and forgive my own indiscretions."

"And if I cannot, Justin?"

"Then you and I should both be lost. For what we have, most search a lifetime to find and never truly do."

I studied those solemn eyes that I had beheld that first day at Camberleigh.

"Take me back, Justin."

The hurt that played across the strong planes of his face were evident. He helped me silently to my feet, his arm shielding my sight of Thomas's broken body. King's Ransom, who had stood by at close attention, seemed strangely calm as Justin helped me into the saddle and then climbed up himself.

Dusk was gathering as we rode back, and a new moon had risen in the southern sky. My mind was filled with words that were not my own but seemed somehow important for me to remember. They were written someplace. The letter, that was it. The letter my mother had left. I could see them as if I were holding the tissue on which they had been written.

"May you find the strength to endure, the insight to forgive and the love to protect."

I licked at a tear which had fallen to my lips.

"Justin?" I asked, watching a star that had just twinkled on.

"Yes, Serena."

"Do you think that even in marriage I shall be your damselle in distress?"

His silence was my answer.

Postscript

IT SEEMS hardly possible that ten years have passed since I first
arrived at Camberleigh. Although we now reside at Mayfair,
I find myself compelled to return often. To visit with Anne,
who became the new Lady Camberleigh just short of a year
after Maura's death. I am embarrassed today for thinking that
I could have judged her about her relationship with my uncle,
for she has brought both joy and tranquility to his life over
these past years. He, of course, rails against her modern ways,
but I think he is secretly proud of the success her designs have
had both here and in France.

My grandmother died shortly after our wedding. I was heart-
broken and, had it not been for Justin, I don't know if I could
have so quickly gone on with my life. She had never truly
recovered after Maura's death, though I know that the union
between Justin and myself had been her fondest wish. As it
was, it was also her last.

Our first child, Daphne, was born a year after our marriage.
Justin carried on that it was but yet another female for him to
have to rescue from herself, but I know that he is secretly
enchanted by her. Our son, Alexander, is the image of his
father and I am certain he will cause me many a sleepless night
in the years to come.

Oliver has grown into a fine healthy young man. As he
matured a thirst for adventrue, which circumstance had not
permitted his father to develop, became strongly apparent in

435

his nature. I worry that one day soon he may announce to us that he is leaving to discover new continents, but then he too must try his wings. The children will miss him dreadfully when he goes for he is like an older brother to both.

Clarissa, much to everyone's relief, met a young financier during her season in London, who fell instantly in love with her and courted her steadfastly until she accepted him. They reside in London and are scarcely seen except on holidays. I do not think my uncle has ever truly recovered from the shock of discovering that she was not his natural daughter but he has kept his vow of silence over the years. Clarissa's child looks much like her, and, if I am to believe Justin will grow to be as thoughtless and as insensitive as her mother.

Mayfair is the site of many balls and parties these days and although I revel in having friends about, I would not be able to manage without Charlotte, who is with us now as our housekeeper. Mrs. Scoapes was of course dismissed but not until the whole sordid truth had been revealed. It appears that she had for years been blackmailing Maura over the knowledge that she was regularly ingesting massive doses of drugs and finally even poisoning her own son.

I almost felt sorry for her when she left. She was devastated over her son's death and departed a broken, old woman. Justin had little compassion, for, in some strange way, he blamed her for turning her son into the monster he had become before his death. None of us could forget that she had contributed to Maura's demise.

One of our frequent guests to Mayfair is Robin Kelston and his wife. I had been dumbfounded when I had learned that he was betrothed to Mrs. Lilliane Robertson, though Monique and Justin laughed conspiratorily as though they knew it was meant to be all along. As I grew older, I understood it better, for Robin, always slightly naughty and playful, needed someone who was perhaps as nicely misbehaved as he.

Robbie is now the stable master at Mayfair, though Justin relies on him greatly on his decisions about the tenants and their farms. Richard is less involved these days the running of the Camberleigh/Mayfair estates. He finally conceded on the issue of taxation and even agreed to invest in new equipment. Though Justin and I never discuss finances, I have overheard him speaking to Robbie on occasion and know that the lands have never been more prosperous. Robbie has been seen of late with one of the daughters of the most successful of these farmers, and I know that Charlotte is hopeful that there should be a wedding by spring.

The Baron Whittenfeld has never proved a threat socially since he simply vanished from England many years back. He had been disgraced by some affair in London. I had pressed Justin for more information but he teased that the last time he had been involved with the Baron it had cost him 200 pounds.

Justin often still teases me, I think because he knows it rankles me. I still do seem to be prone to mishaps, though thankfully they are confined to far more trivial matters these days. Sometimes when we are in bed and Justin is sleeping, I find myself watching him for hours on end. I am thankful that I crossed from girlhood to womanhood at Camberleigh, else I should never have known the depths of our passion and love all these years.

Justin has often said that we should travel more, but I have no desire to do so. It seems as though it has been such a long journey getting to where I am today, that I am loath to move away from it, even briefly.

Jaspar is still my ever-constant companion. He is very old now, of course, but age seems not to have deterred his zest for life. I often think back to our journey over a decade ago. We knew then that Camberleigh was our destination. It appears that it was as well our destiny.

Turn back the pages of history...
and discover

Romance

as it once was!

Sweeping Stories of Captivating Romance

☐ 16663-6 **DRAGON STAR** Olivia O'Neill $2.95

☐ 20548-8 **THE EMPEROR'S LADY** Diana Summers $3.50

☐ 69659-7 **QUEEN OF PARIS** Christina Nicholson $3.95

☐ 86072-9 **THE VELVET HART** Felicia Andrews $3.95
(Available in April '85)

☐ 05321-1 **BELOVED CAPTIVE** Iris Gower $2.95

Prices may be slightly higher in Canada.

Available wherever paperbacks are sold or use this coupon.

 CHARTER BOOKS
Book Mailing Service
P.O. Box 690, Rockville Centre, NY 11571

Please send me the titles checked above. I enclose _____ Include 75¢ for postage and handling if one book is ordered; 25¢ per book for two or more not to exceed $1.75. California, Illinois, New York and Tennessee residents please add sales tax.

NAME _____

ADDRESS _____

CITY _____ STATE/ZIP _____

(allow six weeks for delivery)

A5